Bake Until Golden

The Potluck Catering Club #3

# Bake Until Golden

*A Novel*

## Linda Evans Shepherd
## Eva Marie Everson

Revell

*a division of Baker Publishing Group*
Grand Rapids, Michigan

Published by Revell
a division of Baker Publishing Group
P.O. Box 6287, Grand Rapids, MI 49516-6287
www.revellbooks.com

Printed in the United States of America

Library of Congress Cataloging-in-Publication Data
Shepherd Linda E., 1957–
    Bake until golden : a novel / Linda Evans Shepherd, Eva Marie Everson.
        p.   cm. — (Potluck catering club ; #3)
    ISBN 978-0-8007-3210-3 (pbk.)
    1. Women cooks—Fiction. 2. Prayer groups—Fiction. 3. Female friendship—Fiction. 4. Colorado—Fiction. I. Everson, Eva Marie. II. Title.
PS3619.H456B35  2011
813'.6—dc22                                                              2010038936

This book is a work of fiction. Names, characters, places, and incidents are the product of the author's imagination or are used fictitiously. Any resemblance to actual events, locales, or persons, living or dead, is coincidental.

11  12  13  14  15  16  17      7  6  5  4  3  2  1

To "Miss Colorado," who called one day and said, "Hey, Eva! I've got an idea for a book . . ." Thank you, friend, for bringing me along for this incredible ride!

What made us friends in the long ago when first we met?
I think I know.
The best in me and
The best in you hailed each other
Because they knew that always and always
Since time began, our being friends was
Part of God's plan.
—Unknown

Eva Marie Everson

To "Miss Florida," who answered my call with an enthusiastic, "Let's write it!" Thank you for traveling this journey with me as it took us from Colorado to New York City. Girlfriend, we've had the adventure of a lifetime.

Linda Evans Shepherd

And to all our fans . . . We love you!
Eva & Linda

# Contents

1. *Lizzie*—High Altitude Cooking  9

2. *Goldie*—Glazed Shock  16

3. *Evangeline*—Flaming Tempers  24

4. *Lisa Leann*—Frosted Love  33

5. *Donna*—Crushing Circumstances  38

6. *Vonnie*—Preserving Secrets  47

7. *Lizzie*—Crusty Encounters  54

8. *Evangeline*—Dicey Run-In  64

9. *Lisa Leann*—Scalding News  72

10. *Goldie*—Bittersweet Sorrow  80

11. *Evangeline*—Rehashing the Past  88

12. *Vonnie*—Family Dinner  96

13. *Donna*—Stirring Disaster  104

14. *Lizzie*—Bite to Eat  111

15. *Goldie*—Simmering Suspicions  120

16. *Lisa Leann*—Baby Food  127

17. *Donna*—Spicy Agent  135

18. *Vonnie*—Biting Betrayal  144

19. *Evangeline*—Grilled Over a Hot Flame  153

20. *Lizzie*—Chilling Spy  162

21. *Goldie*—Tasting the Truth  171

22. *Vonnie*—Hot Dog  181

23. *Lisa Leann*—Poached  190

24. *Donna*—Scorched Heart  200

25. *Evangeline*—Jail Dressing  210

26. *Goldie*—Sweet Tea  220

27. *Lizzie*—Research Relish  228

28. *Lisa Leann*—Fishy Business  236

29. *Vonnie*—Bubbling Memories  246

30. *Donna*—Gnawing Doubt  256

31. *Goldie*—Condensed Meeting  267

32. *Lizzie*—Dishing Drama  275

33. *Vonnie*—Deep-Fried Danger  282

34. *Donna*—Chewing Over a Clue  286

35. *Lisa Leann*—Half-Baked Romance  291

36. *Donna*—Case Crackers  297

The Potluck Catering Club Recipes  309

Acknowledgments  347

# 1

# High Altitude Cooking

We were famous. The women of the Potluck Catering Club were nationally and even internationally recognizable. Six ordinary women from Summit View, Colorado—a small town near Breckenridge—had been catapulted from stirring up homemade soup on cold winter days and putting in our hours at our typical jobs to signing autographs, being featured on magazine covers and interviewed on talk radio and television shows, and presenting awards at glittery, star-studded galas. And how it came to be was a story in itself.

Of course, we have to give Lisa Leann Lambert, newest member of the potluck prayer group—or, the Potluck Club, as we've always called ourselves—her "props," as students at the high school where I'm the media specialist like to say. Because of our collective culinary skills, Lisa Leann came up with the idea to form a catering business and then, by some stroke of either genius or madness, her son Nelson entered us as contestants for the reality show *The*

*Great Party Showdown*, where we came in first place. The grand prize was a million dollars (a million dollars!), which we intend to use for a variety of things for the catering business but mainly to aid in our church's building renovation and—shall we call it—"salvation" program.

"Renovation" in that the old building was in dire need of some restoration—things like new boarding, new insulation, and some additions to the youth wing. "Salvation" in that, according to our beloved pastor Kevin Moore and my husband Samuel, Grace Church was going under financially.

"It's heading directly for bankruptcy," Samuel confided to me several months earlier. Samuel was on the finance committee and would know. "A real sign of our times, I'm afraid."

Our winnings would keep this from happening and would allow for the expansion. I was especially pleased knowing the youth building would be a recipient of our hard work and wild escapades while in New York City filming the show. It had been quite the journey.

How were we to know that weeks later, we'd see it as only the beginning of an exhausting road that would lead to murder.

———

Upon our return to Summit View—after filming in New York City for weeks on end, being interviewed across the country by a variety of radio and TV talk shows, newspapers, and magazines, being photographed ad nauseam, and being the belles of the ball at other miscellaneous events—we were honored with a parade and a dinner at the church, where we were the guests of honor. And we were going to be guests on Daystar's *Denver Celebration* television program—the final three within one short week.

It was nearing the end of September, and the weather was still a little warm. Lisa Leann insisted that we always wear our signature pink bib aprons when on television and for most photo layouts, but what we chose to put on under them was up to us. Wanting to stay cool—as I seem to run hot in this blessed stage of life I find myself in—I chose a Max and Cleo V-neck shift dress in pale yellow with three-quarter cuffed sleeves I'd purchased at Macy's on 34th during some of our downtime in New York. I'd not had a chance to wear it yet, and I hoped it looked as sharp and sassy on me as it did on the department store mannequin.

My husband seemed to think it did. "Wow," he said, eyeing me. "Wow," he said again.

Standing in the center of our bedroom, I twirled before him, feeling the soft material of the dress slink around my slender form. "You like?" I asked with a wink.

"Wow."

I dramatically allowed my shoulders to droop. "You have a wider vocabulary than that, Samuel Prattle, and don't tell me you don't." I pointed at him as I squared my shoulders. "I've been married to you for far too long to think any differently."

In his sixties, Samuel is still good-looking by every measure of the word. His hair has silvered and thinned, and the skin around his eyes has drooped a little, but the sparkle of those baby blues can still melt me even on the coldest of Summit View days. "How about wowzer?" He moved toward me like a cat on the prowl.

"Back away," I said, laughing. "I'll be late if you try to start anything I can't finish."

He was hearing nothing of it, instead pressing me toward the edge of the dresser. "Where'd you say you were going?" He wrapped his arms around my waist and nuzzled my neck. "You smell too good to be around other males, I'm thinking," he added with a laugh. "I don't want anyone getting the wrong idea."

I pushed him away with the palms of my hands against his broad chest. "You know good and well where I'm going. To the Daystar studios in Denver. They're doing an interview." I feigned snobbery as I said, "We're such *stars*, you know. That's why we're on Day*star*."

"Har-har." Samuel walked over to the bed and sat, then pulled his dress shoes from where he'd left them the night before. He was nearly dressed for work—crisp white shirt tucked into dark belted pants and finished with a complementary tie. All he had left to do was slip his feet into the leather loafers, grab his suit coat, and head out the door. "What I want to know is what in the world can you say in this interview that you haven't said in all the others?"

I reached for a pair of gold small hoop earrings lying on the dresser and slipped the post of one into the tiny pin-sized hole in my left ear. "Well, for one, this is a Christian station. Which means we can talk about God a little more openly. No worries that we're going to be censored."

"Sounds fair. I hate the way that network anchor made you look after the win, as though it seemed so odd that your catering business began as a prayer group."

I finished with my jewelry then stepped over to the closet for my dress sandals. "She was just doing her job."

"Still . . . she's too liberal for me."

I laughed lightly as I slid my feet into my shoes. I moved to where my husband looked up at me from his perch on our bed, kissed him on his forehead, and said, "Me too, but I'm sure she's a good person. See you when you get home this afternoon." I pointed up with my right index finger. "Oh. Corned beef and cabbage for dinner tonight, your favorite."

"I'll come straight home then," he said with a wink, then his face sobered. "I'll be praying for you today, Liz. Call me when you're done."

"Will do," I said from the door. I blew him another kiss and then was on my way.

————

The girls and I decided to meet at our catering shop and then drive in to Denver together. "No need to waste gas by taking six cars," Evangeline had said. "Lizzie, your car should be big enough for all of us."

I've known Evangeline Benson Vesey nearly my whole life, and

I can lovingly but honestly say she's always been bossy. She also carries with her a sense of pride about coming from Summit View, and is rich in knowledge concerning its landmarks and its history, including its gold mining legends and myths.

"There's no way you're stuffing me into one SUV with the five of you," Donna Vesey, Evie's stepdaughter and our youngest member, said. "It's two vehicles or I'm not going. Besides, four in the back means we'll break seat belt laws." Donna was the deputy sheriff to her father, sheriff Vernon Vesey.

"Donna's right," Vonnie Westbrook said. She smiled at Donna, who'd been like a daughter to her ever since Donna's mother, Doreen, abandoned her and Vernon to run off to California with Grace Church's choir director. Donna had been only about four at the time. "It's a good thing David and Wade are both stuck at work or we might need three cars."

I watched Donna pink at the names of the young men who had been part of our team in New York. Feeling her discomfort at the mere mention of their names, I quickly added, "I agree with Vonnie."

Evie pouted, but in the end we took two cars: Evie's and mine. We arrived in Denver with just enough time to be welcomed by the receptionist, escorted into the green room by the producer, and briefed as to what to expect. A half hour and a cup of coffee later we were arranged on the chairs and sofa of the rich, elegant studio set. We'd gotten to be old pros at hearing the banter of the cameramen with the producers and hosts, understanding the cues. Settled in, we waited for the "In three, two, one . . ." and waited as the hostess said, "Welcome to *Denver Celebration*! Today we are so excited to have six women I'm sure you all know—the ladies of the Potluck Catering Club, our very own Team Potluck from Summit View."

I watched the host's eyes dance in the stage lighting. Her hair, long and dark, gleamed under the lights' illumination, casting a sheen about her pretty face. I listened intently to the questions she posed for each of us and was then captivated when, unexpectedly, she said, "My research tells me that you, Evangeline, are a bit of a Summit View historian."

Evie squared her shoulders as she smiled broadly. "My father," she began matter-of-factly, "was the mayor for many years until he and my mother were tragically killed in a car accident."

We all cast Evie a sorrowful glance.

"Daddy always said that knowing the history of one's town was the first step in having hometown pride."

"That certainly makes sense to me," the hostess said. "So, what kind of things can you tell our audience about Summit View? What makes it so special, other than being home to the six of you?"

"Oh, well, my goodness! Where do I begin?" Evie beamed. Then she pointed her finger. "First let me tell you that even though we have a population of about 25,000, we are still small-town friendly." She turned her face toward the camera. "And like all of Colorado, our Summit View is as pretty as any place you'll ever come to visit or call home."

"Hear, hear," Vonnie chimed in.

We all laughed lightly before Evangeline continued. "Now, Summit View was established in 1856 during the Colorado Gold Rush, which for all of you who know your American history was about ten years after the California Gold Rush. I believe I'm right on that, aren't I, Lizzie?" She turned to me, as did everyone else on the set.

"Uh—yeah, that is correct," I said.

"Lizzie is our high school's media specialist," Lisa Leann said.

"Marvelous!" said our host.

"I'm on a temporary leave," I pointed out, as if it were important to note. "Until we're done with our post-win interviews . . . things like that."

Evie discreetly sighed. "Back to what I was saying," she told our host. "Summit View has a small museum where anyone who comes by and pays a dollar entry fee can see old photos from those days and read about lost gold mines and the stagecoach robberies and even the famous mother lode of gold that was supposed to rival all others, stolen and never recovered, though legend has it that it's still buried somewhere right there in Summit View."

Donna shifted in her seat. "Every few months or so I get a call—I'm a deputy in the sheriff's department—from some mother who can't find her kids and I end up finding them out in the hills, looking for that treasure chest of gold." Donna chuckled. "If that gold is really buried in Summit View, I'm sure it would have been discovered by now."

The host crossed one leg over the other as she looked at Goldie Dippel. "What can you tell us about the prize money and how you plan to use it?"

Goldie cleared her throat before answering. "Well, we do plan to use a little of the money to pay off our business debts that accumulated while we were away from our jobs and to purchase some things we need. But the majority of the money will go to Grace Church, which is where we all attend."

"For renovation of an old part of the structure," Lisa Leann interjected, "and to add on to the youth wing."

By this time, Pastor Kevin had made us all privy to the church's dire financial straits, which we all agreed to leave private.

"Your church was established by the famous Father Dyer, the circuit preacher who visited his churches by cross-country skiing through the mountains."

"In the mid-1800s," I supplied.

"And is your church *that* old?" she asked.

We all nodded. "It is," Evangeline said. "And just loaded with amazing stories."

The host looked at the camera. "And I would have to add that, thanks to the ladies of the Potluck Catering Club—Team Potluck—the amazing stories continue."

*Goldie*

# 2

## Glazed Shock

After we'd eaten lunch at Applebee's, we piled back into our respective automobiles and headed southwest, back to Summit View. I was pretty tired and—in spite of a couple cups of coffee—could have easily napped the entire trip, but the two new best friends Evie and Lisa Leann jabbered away nonstop about one thing and then another.

The relationship between the two former foes—if they could be called that—had come to some sort of healing while they were in New York. Before the rest of Team Potluck had arrived, these two headed off to get the lay of the land, so to speak. None of us except Lizzie, if memory serves me, had been there before, and she said it had been several decades.

Until about a year ago, when Lisa Leann moved to Summit View, Evangeline had "ruled the roost," as my mama always says. Evangeline was the original Potluck Girl. She decided who became a part of the group and who was kept at arm's length. She wasn't trying to make us an exclusive group, I suppose. More than anything, she was trying to keep it small and intimate.

Yes, I'm sure that's it.

Then Lisa Leann moved to town with her recipe for yummy gooey cinnamon buns and marched right into our club. Nothing or nobody, not even Evangeline, was going to stop her either. Not that Evie didn't try. Goodness knows she tried. But she failed, Lisa Leann became a part of our group, and all the while those two went after each other like two cats.

Until New York.

I'm not sure what happened before we all arrived to compete on the show; I only know that the two of them have been humming like songbirds ever since. Typically, it's wonderful to be around. But on the way back from Denver, when I wanted a nap, their chatter kept me from fully dropping into la-la land.

"Can I ask you a question?" I heard Lisa Leann say from the front seat. I was sitting in the backseat, head against the window, eyes closed. "Hello back there?"

I opened my eyes to see the petite redhead staring at me with her big eyes. Lashes batted before I croaked out, "Um . . . what did you say?"

"A question, Goldie. Can I ask you a question?" She shifted in her seat so she'd have a better view of me.

Or me of her, I'm not sure which.

I cleared my throat and said, "Sure, Lisa Leann. What is it?"

"How long did it take you to forgive Jack for his indiscretions? Completely, I mean."

I blinked several times as Evangeline jerked her head to the right and said, "Lisa Leann! That's not a question you ask! It's too personal."

Lisa Leann turned more toward the driver's side of the car. "And why not? I have a question and Goldie should have the answer. After all, we're friends, aren't we? Can't friends ask personal questions? I mean, if not friends, then who?"

I took a deep breath and exhaled. "It's okay, Evangeline. I

17

suppose given Lisa Leann's own indiscretions, she'd want to know."

"Bite me," Lisa Leann said.

"Bite you?" Evie said. "What kind of a thing is that to say?"

Lisa Leann turned a pleasant shade of pink before answering. "I honestly don't know. I've heard Nelson say it a few times when he's insulted by something someone has said to him."

"Imagine that," Evie muttered.

I wouldn't have minded if their tête-à-tête kept going without me. After all, it *was* a personal question, one I wasn't too sure I could answer.

Lisa Leann had recently admitted to having had an affair, and we all knew she and Henry were struggling to keep their marriage afloat as it healed. On the other hand, my husband Jack had been unfaithful more times and with more women than I cared to count. Then, a year ago, when I'd had enough and moved out, he sought counseling. Since then we'd worked hard to put the broken pieces of our lives back together. Jack was loving and attentive, but more than that, I'd seen him seeking the Lord's face daily to be the man of God he had always claimed to be.

"It takes a long time," I said, my voice quiet, "to rebuild trust. Forgiveness is another matter, I think. I can *say* I forgive, I *can* forgive, but forgetting and trust are related, and it's an awfully difficult thing to forget."

Lisa Leann's shoulders slumped. "So, you still don't trust Jack? After all this time?" Lisa Leann is typically a little spitfire, but right about then she looked distressed and sad.

"Well, Lisa Leann, it hasn't really been that long, you know. It hasn't even been a year. But . . ." I looked down at my hands clasped together, then back up. "I have to admit, since Jack's heart attack, I've hardly had anything to worry about. Jack doesn't have enough energy to even think about having an affair these days."

Evie turned her head ever so slightly toward the back. "How is Jack, Goldie? Really."

"We take it one day at a time," I answered.

Team Potluck had been nearing the finals of the competition in New York when I'd gotten the call that Jack had suffered a heart attack during a flight from New York to Chicago, on the way back to Summit View. Instead of finishing out the show, I flew to the Windy City, where Jack underwent several tests and procedures. After being given a "pass" to fly to Denver, he eventually had bypass surgery. Since then his progress had been slow but steady—difficult for a man who was used to being physically active.

Jack had been Summit View's high school coach since we'd married more than twenty-five years ago. Though it was now still summertime, the long break was coming to an end; Jack had been forced to stay home while the school's football team held preseason practices. I filled Evangeline and Lisa Leann in further by saying, "He's gone out to the football field a couple of times since practices have been underway, but for the most part he leaves everything up to the assistant coaches."

"Is he exercising like he should?"

"Not really," I said. "He says he's just so tired, which I think is because of the beta-blockers." I sighed. "But he's faithful with his meds, so I guess that's something to be grateful for."

Lisa Leann gave me a wink as she said, "Of course it is." She swung around to face the front again. Thinking our conversation had come to an end, I closed my eyes. Evie and Lisa Leann were quiet as the car rocked gently, lulling me to sleep. But before I could slip away I heard Lisa Leann's familiar voice again. "Goldie?"

Once again I opened my eyes. "Yes, Lisa Leann."

She faced me. "Do you remember that guy you were sort of dating last year?"

I heard Evangeline sigh. "Honestly," she said.

"I wasn't dating him, Lisa Leann. He was just a friend. And of course I remember him."

"What was his name?"

"Van. Van Lauer."

"Did you ever think that maybe if you *had* dated him, you might have exacted some sort of revenge on Jack?"

I didn't answer right away. I had to process what this little powder keg was asking.

Goodness, I hadn't thought of Van Lauer in months. How could I? When he'd come into my life—the friend and fellow attorney of my boss, Chris Lowe—he'd been like a healing balm on a gaping wound slashed across my heart. There'd been little doubt that if I'd not been married to Jack, I would have dated Van. The feelings we'd felt were undeniable and strong. But strong and undeniable or not, they were wrong—as my married daughter Olivia had pointed out to me every chance she had—and so I brought our friendship to a swift end and began working on salvaging my marriage.

"Lisa Leann, my relationship—my friendship—with Van wasn't about revenge. He was a nice guy who was there to help me process where I was in my life. In my marriage. In my . . . well . . . everything."

"But it wasn't about revenge."

"No."

"What are you getting at, Lisa Leann?" Evie asked.

Lisa Leann turned to face Evangeline again. "I've been wondering . . . worrying, I guess . . . that Henry might try to have some sort of relationship with a woman to get back at me for . . . you know."

"Has he said or done anything to make you think that?" I asked.

"Oh heavens, no."

"Then I wouldn't worry," I said.

"I agree with Goldie," Evie added.

But I could see a flicker of worry in Lisa Leann's eyes. God bless her, I could feel a little of her pain. Maybe mine was, in some ways, different. But in many ways it was the same.

———

We arrived back at the shop in the late afternoon. The sky was clear, and though the sun had begun its descent toward the western horizon, the weather was still quite warm. I'd worn a couple of gold bangle bracelets and pulled them off immediately upon exiting Evangeline's car. Somehow it just seemed to help ease the heat.

"Is it me, or is it unusually hot?" I asked.

Lizzie had pulled her SUV into the parking place next to ours and was stepping out of it. "It's you," she said with a smile. "In that glorious time of our lives."

"Wipe that evil grin off your face, Lizzie Prattle," I teased. "Just because it's almost done for you . . ."

"If ever there were joys in being so close to sixty, this is it. At least I think it's almost over."

I'd worn a summer's pants set made complete with a short-at-the-hip jacket. I shook the jacket off as I walked toward the front door of the wedding boutique Lisa Leann owned. It also housed our catering office and kitchen.

"Are we needed inside?" I heard Donna ask. "Because I have to scoot. Dad assigned me to the night shift tonight to make up for being in Denver all day."

"I told him not to do that," Evie threw in.

"Well, apparently, he's not taking orders from you today."

I turned in Donna's direction and was relieved when I saw her wink at her new stepmother.

That relationship was another one that could be unsettling at times.

"I think we can all go home," Lisa Leann said. "Unless one of you has something you want to go over?"

We all said the only thing we wanted to do was go home. Minutes later I was in my car with the air conditioner blasting. I used the time to call my daughter, Olivia, to see how her day had gone and to ask if she'd watched the show. When she answered I could hear her toddler, Brook, playing boisterously in the background as her newborn squalled, apparently while being held close to the phone's mouthpiece.

"Sounds like you've got your hands full," I said after she greeted me.

"All this and the spaghetti sauce is spilling over onto the stove top. Mom, I really have to call you back."

*Spaghetti sauce . . . dinner!* I thought as I disconnected the call. An idea for what Jack and I might call supper hadn't even crossed my mind. And, whatever it was, it had to be easy, delicious, and low in fat and sodium. I snapped my fingers. Vonnie had made two chicken potpies and had brought one over a week or so ago. I'd placed it in the freezer for an occasion like this.

I pulled into the driveway of our ranch-style home, shut off the car, grabbed my purse and the discarded jacket, and headed inside. "Jack?" I called out. "Jack?"

He didn't answer.

I could hear the muted sound of a television from the back of the house, probably the one in our bedroom. Knowing Jack, he'd gone there to take a nap and had then turned on the television upon waking. I sighed. I just *had* to get him exercising again.

But when I stepped into our bedroom, I found that Jack hadn't *been* napping. He was *still* napping, oblivious to the television's blaring volume. I put my purse on the dresser, laid my jacket across the end of the bed, and turned off the TV. I looked to see if the lack of sound might wake him, but it didn't.

I crossed my arms as I leaned against the dresser to stare at my husband. Even with his mouth open and his eyes at half-mast, he was still the most handsome man I'd ever known. I was a young girl in high school when we'd met. Totally infatuated *with* him and completely "gone" over him. While I'd grown less infatuated over the years, I was still in love—that much was for sure. Maybe now more than ever after seeing him work so hard to regain my affection and trust.

I shook my head lightly as I smiled, then blew him a kiss from across the room as I turned toward the door. Once there, though,

I looked back over my shoulder. Something was wrong. I felt my brows knit together as I inched toward the bed to get a closer look. What was it?

Then it hit me, as if in one moment I had no comprehension of the truth and then, in the next moment, I did. *Jack isn't breathing.*

I bolted to his side and grabbed his shoulders. Even through his clothing I could feel the icy cold of his skin. "Jack!" I screamed. "Jack!" I shook him. Tears pooled in my eyes and spilled down my cheeks. "Jack! Oh God, oh God, oh God!" I threw my head back, my face toward the ceiling. "Jack!" I shouted once more. "Don't you die on me, don't you die on me!"

But he wasn't listening. His head lopped over, and when it did I sprang from the bed, tripped over bedroom slippers I'd not noticed before, and fell onto my backside. Wailing, I crawled to the bedside table and picked up the phone to dial 911.

"Police or medical," the voice on the other end said.

But I gave neither answer. "Donna Vesey," I cried out. "I need Donna Vesey and I need her now!"

*Evangeline*

# 3

## Flaming Tempers

I called Vernon from my parking space in front of the Gold Rush Grocery Store. I had in mind to speak with him about two things.

The first was that I was picking up some pork chops for our dinner and wondered if there was anything else he might know of that I needed to buy while I was there. "No need to waste trips," I said.

"Get some of that rocky road frozen yogurt you brought home last time," he said.

"Why? Don't we still have some in the freezer?"

He chuckled. "Not anymore."

"Vernon Vesey. You'll get fat as a pig if you keep this up."

"I can't help it," he said. "It's just so good! Besides, it's yogurt, not ice cream. I can afford to splurge."

I pulled the keys from the ignition and dropped them into my open purse, which sat on the front passenger's seat. "First of all, your waistline says differently, and second, just because it's yogurt doesn't mean it's fat free."

"Don't toy with me, woman," he said, his voice low and appealing. "Just bring the rocky road yogurt home and no one gets hurt."

"Funny." I opened the door of the car but didn't budge from my seat. "Before I go inside, there's one other thing I wanted to talk to you about."

"And that is?"

"Why did you schedule Donna for tonight? I thought I asked you not to do that."

"Evie-girl," he said, using the term of endearment he's called me by since we were kids. "I don't tell you how to run your tax business and you don't tell me how to run the sheriff's office." There was a firmness in his voice that just ticked me right off. At times I find that vocal bravado quite sexy, but right now wasn't one of those times.

"But Vernon . . . you don't know how difficult these interviews can be. How tiring."

"I do too know. You manage to tell me after every one of them. But Donna's a deputy first and a reality celebrity second. She's got a job to do, she's got citizens to protect, and my job as the sheriff is to make sure she does it well and when we need her."

"Well, you may be her boss but you're also her daddy and—"

"And she's a grown woman, Evangeline. Now quit arguing with me, get your chops and my yogurt, and come on home so we can eat one and snuggle up with the other. I'll even let you have the bowl with the most marshmallows."

My arguments weren't going to get Donna out of her shift; there was no doubting that. I might as well get what I needed from inside the store and go on home. "All right, Vernon," I said with a sigh. "I'll see you in about half an hour."

I got four thick center-cut pork loin chops from the meat department, a box of onion and mushroom soup mix from the soup aisle, and the yogurt from frozen foods, placed each in my handheld basket, then headed up to the checkout lanes at the front of the store. And, wouldn't you know it, there was Doreen Roberts standing last in the shortest line.

When we were children, Doreen was one of my best friends. That is, until the day she stole Vernon Vesey's love with her twelve-year-old lips, which were free and available for full-on-the-mouth kisses. She and Vernon began a love story that was on again/off again until we'd all graduated from school. Then, one sweet and sunny (and I say that with all the sincerity I can muster) Saturday afternoon, they met the preacher at the front of Grace Church, where they said their "I do's," sealing their lives, one to the other. Sometime later they welcomed Donna into the world, and four years after that, Doreen, who sang a lovely alto in the Grace Church choir, took off with the choir director, leaving Donna and Vernon to pick up the pieces of their lives.

None of us—not Donna, not Vernon, and certainly not me—had heard a word from Doreen until late last year when she returned as Dee Dee McGurk, a worn-out, washed-up, pathetic waitress over at the Gold Rush Tavern. We might not have ever realized it was her if it hadn't been for the fact that her daughter Velvet James, whose father is *not* Vernon, looks so much like our Donna.

Dee Dee (aka Doreen) and I have had our squabbles since her return, but we've also had a couple of moments when we (mostly me) made efforts toward putting the past behind us and getting on with our lives. After all, Doreen's return to Summit View was a chance for Donna to get to know her mother. Not that Donna has always been warm to the notion. Still . . .

"Hello, Doreen," I said as I stepped behind her. She was wearing the tavern's golf shirt and a pair of too-tight black jeans. I wondered how she could even sit down in them, not that I said it. In fact, all I did was stare at the back of Doreen's head; she didn't acknowledge me in the least. "Hello, Doreen," I said again, refusing to be ignored.

She turned then, eyes red-rimmed, the blue of them looking more like water than sky. Her face was splotchy, her lips swollen.

"You look awful," I said. My words didn't sound at all the way I meant them. I felt sorry for Doreen, I really did. But my words came out catty.

"I guess if I had makeup artists doting on me 24/7, I'd be lucky enough to look like you." Her voice was loud enough and snide enough to draw some attention.

I felt myself grow warm. "I didn't mean—"

"You didn't mean . . . you didn't mean . . ."

The smell of stale alcohol assaulted me as she spoke. When my eyes lowered, I noticed that her basket was filled with a bag of chips, a bottle of Cold Duck, and a six-pack of beer. Seemed to me she had enough opportunity to drink at the Gold Rush Tavern, and I couldn't imagine why she'd need to come all the way to the grocery store to purchase what she had plenty of at work.

"Shhh," I said. "There's no need to draw a crowd."

"What?" she stormed, turning her head to the left and then the right as she turned to face me head-on. "What is it you don't want people to hear?"

Well, for pity's sake. She was speaking loud enough now to alert people in distant counties. "Doreen, maybe you shouldn't be buying that beer and—"

"Maybe you should mind your own business!"

I felt the sting of tears. Why did she have to be like this? Hadn't I gone to her not too long ago and asked her if we could let bygones be bygones? Hadn't we agreed to work through our differences for Donna's sake? Hadn't we grown, even a little?

"Okay," I whispered, holding up my free hand. "You go ahead and do whatever you want to do. Just . . . please, keep it down. I have a reputation in this town."

She barked in laughter. "Hey, everyone! This little lady's got a reputation in this town! Well, my gosh! Everyone knows who *you* are, Evangeline. You're the star of *The Great Party Showdown*. And you're the sheriff's wife." She stumbled back, banging against the display of wrapped candy bars and packs of gum. I moved to try to help her, but she waved me away. "Well, I was his wife first and I'm the *staaaaar* of the Gold Rush Tavern." She righted herself as the customer in front of her—who had turned for a better look—took a step backward and then gripped the arms of a toddler sitting in the buggy seat, as though to protect the child.

Everyone was now staring. Cash registers had ceased ringing up purchases. Children had stopped begging for sweets. Shoppers had quit shuffling through their coupons and scanning their bank cards.

And I'd had enough.

"Doreen, so help me, if you don't stop this nonsense—"

"What? You'll what? Call Vernon and have him arrest me?"

I saw the manager then—a short fellow wearing a white oxford shirt, black slacks, and a thin tie—walking around the front side of the checkout lines, cordless phone to his ear. "Sheriff," I saw him mouth.

"Doreen . . ."

"Dee Dee! My name is Dee Dee!"

"Shhh . . . you're making more problems than you realize." The manager was now looking out the large glass panes along the front wall, no doubt waiting for someone from my husband's office to show up.

She leaned over. Her eyes converted to slits as words hissed through her teeth. "I know things you *wish* you knew," she said. "You have no idea how much grief your little win on national television has caused." She took another unsteady step. "Why couldn't you just leave well enough alone?"

"What are you talking about?"

From over her shoulder I saw Donna's Bronco rolling into a parking spot. My shoulders drooped. No daughter should ever have to arrest her own mother. *Oh Vernon, why didn't you listen to me and give this child the night off?*

"You don't know, but you will soon enough," she said.

I reached out my hand. "Doreen, please. Let me help you."

"Stay away from me!" she said, slapping my hand away just as Donna, dressed in her starched deputy's uniform, stepped through the front door.

"Please, Doreen." I reached out again. As I did, Doreen fell backward against the display rack, falling to her backside. As packets of candy and gum jostled from their places, the chips, beer, and wine bottle tumbled out of Doreen's basket, onto her abdomen, and then the floor.

I dropped my basket then, tried to retrieve some of the falling merchandise, stumbled over the bottle of wine, and then promptly fell on top of the crumpled barmaid.

"She's killing me!" Doreen screamed in my ear.

"If you don't shut up!" I yelled back.

"All right, all right, all right!" Donna's hand wrapped around my bicep and then jerked me off her mother as though I weighed no more than a flea. "Ladies!"

"I fell!" I pointed to the guilty bottle of Cold Duck. "Because of that thing!"

I heard people laughing then. Well, I was certainly glad they thought it was funny, because I surely didn't. All I'd wanted was some pork chops and frozen yogurt. Why did I have to run into the likes of Doreen Roberts?

"She pushed me down!" Doreen was saying as Donna helped her mother up. "You all saw her! I've got witnesses!"

"You're drunk," Donna said. Her face was etched with sadness and anger, and I'm not sure which emotion was taking front billing. "Come on. I'll get you home."

"I've got my car."

"You can pick it up tomorrow."

Doreen wrapped her arms around Donna like a limp rag doll. "Oh, my baby. My baby girl. You've come to your mama's rescue."

"Stop it." Donna righted her mother, turned her toward the door, and escorted her forward. "Show's over, folks. Go back to your shopping."

I kept my eyes on the two of them until they reached Donna's Bronco, then started picking up the items from the floor. The manager was by my side, asking if I was all right. I assured him I was, though my whole body was quivering and my voice gave it away. "I just want to get my pork chops and get home," I said. "Vernon's waiting for supper."

———

I decided against driving straight to the house. I was too shaken by the whole incident with Doreen. Instead, I stopped at Lake Dillon, got out of the car, and walked to a little bench overlooking the water and the mountains behind it. I took a seat, a deep breath, and then exhaled. My hands rested on my knees for a moment before I closed my eyes and allowed the late afternoon's sunshine to warm my bones, which were now growing stiff from the fall.

I opened my eyes and studied the mountains. They were so majestic, one giving way to another, one rising higher than the last. Some peaked. Some rolled. Each was filled with stories and history, myth and legend.

One I remember well. One my father used to tell me when we'd sit on this very bench as he regaled me with story after story.

"There was an old miner," Daddy had said, "named Zeke Hannah. 'Old Zeke,' they called him. 'Crazy Old Zeke,' said some. Now, Father Dyer—who established Grace Church—was always kind to Zeke. Every Friday after a week of mining for gold and finding none, Old Zeke would come to town—not Summit View, another town on Father Dyer's circuit—go to the saloon, and get liquored up. He'd always tell folks he was just this shy of finding the mother lode." Daddy pinched his thumb and index finger together. "But when Zeke was asked where the gold was, he'd always say he couldn't tell. If he told, then they'd all want a piece of it. Not that anyone paid attention to Zeke. No one even believed he'd found a glimmer of gold, much less a lode. But Father Dyer would always listen to him like he had sense. Treated him with respect, like Jesus did the lepers.

"Now, one Friday night came, but Old Zeke didn't. Didn't show up Friday or Saturday. Then, on Sunday morning, just as Father Dyer was finishing up his sermon, Old Zeke stumbled into the church, shouting at the padre that he needed to see him *bad*. The two men had a meeting behind the church building, and then Father Dyer went one way while Old Zeke went another. Someone said later on that afternoon that they'd seen Zeke give the Methodist preacher a satchel full of something. Someone else said that was all just malarkey.

"Legend says that a group of men determined that Zeke had finally done it. He'd finally found the mother lode, had given Father Dyer some gold for safekeeping, and had gone off to mine the rest. The men saddled up, split into two groups, one to find Old Zeke, the other to find Father Dyer."

"But they never did find Old Zeke," I said to my daddy.

"Nope. Old Zeke was never heard from again, though the story goes that if you sit right here, late at night, you can see his old miner's lamp swinging back and forth up there in those mountains. Some say he died in an accident. Others say he was killed by those men when he wouldn't own up to where the gold was."

"And Father Dyer claimed to not know anything," I supplied, having heard the story twenty times or more. "That he had loaned the old miner a Bible and that the miner had given the Bible back."

"But to this day," Daddy said, pointing, "folks say that somewhere—maybe buried in one of the churches Father Dyer established—is a mother lode of gold."

"Maybe right here in Summit View," I whispered.

"Maybe."

———

I laughed now at the memory, then stood to go. If I sat there much longer, dark would overtake me, and I'd be able to search

31

the mountains myself for the light of a swinging lantern. Not to mention there was frozen yogurt growing soft in the car.

I turned and walked up the slight incline toward the road and my car, then stopped short. A man—old and thin, wearing a ragged ball cap, a khaki-colored safari jacket over a plaid shirt, and a pair of dark slacks, stood near my car. He was unshaven. He wore dark glasses, but even still, I could feel his stare slicing right through me.

"Who are you?" I asked, keeping my shoulders straight. "What are you doing at my car?"

The man jerked, turned, and ambled away. "Sorry," he mumbled over his shoulder. "Didn't mean to bother you."

# 4

## Frosted Love

One thing I'll tell you in confidence is that I'd never have cheated on my husband if he'd even noticed we were a couple. Honestly, the two of us have spent our thirty years of marriage as two singles who coincidently lived in the same house with the same children. I don't know if my Henry is merely passive-aggressive, or if he's a Vulcan like *Star Trek's* Mr. Spock, who doesn't have the words or the capacity to communicate his feelings. Then again, maybe Henry is so into his own little galaxy that he forgets I exist. Even after all these years, I still don't know what to think about his conduct or lack thereof.

Of course, his recent discovery of my indiscretion, which happened a few years back, hasn't helped our relationship. Though, it at least got him to talk to me about our issues in the privacy of our pastor's office. Plus, our time together in New York helped us decide to stay together, though our marriage isn't out of the woods, not by a long shot.

I know my husband's lack of interest doesn't make up for or

even excuse my affair with that despicable Clark Wilkes. I mean, what was I thinking? Clark may have given me enough attention to make me lose all sense of propriety, but he turned out to be—as Evie is fond of saying—a snake, snake, snake.

But what does that make me for rolling in the hay with him? I can tell you, it makes me pitiful, not to mention ashamed. It's a good thing I've developed my own interests and talents as a businesswoman or I'd have nowhere to escape my past, not to mention my present. Of course, knowing God forgives me has been a great comfort—not an excuse, mind you, but a comfort. Though, I've noticed that being forgiven by the Almighty hasn't stopped the pain created by my mistake.

Still, I'd like to try to improve my relationship with Henry, if I can. But how can I break through his resentment much less his passive demeanor? The whole sorry situation would be hopeless if I weren't such a good cook. As my mama always told me, if you can set a tasty table, you can always call them home.

There's a lot of truth to her wisdom, which is why I was just pulling out the fudge pie, hot from my oven. The pie was a recipe I'd engineered to taste like the fudge pie they serve in the Bluebonnet Café in Marble Falls, Texas, a place Henry and I used to roam during bluebonnet season back when we still lived in the Woodlands.

I sliced my pie and placed two warm slabs of the chocolate treat on my rosy dessert plates before topping the slices with scoops of vanilla ice cream. I placed the plates on my kitchen table's beautiful rose chintz placemats complete with matching cloth napkins. I poured two steaming mugs of coffee, which I splashed with vanilla-flavored cream, and served the mugs as if they were a garnish to the pie.

I handed Henry a shiny dessert fork over his newspaper and sat down in my chair across the table from his. He stared at the pie in front of him, then up at me.

"Looks good," he said.

I had already slipped a bite into my mouth. If this didn't taste like love, nothing did.

"Anything happen while I was in Denver?"

Henry shrugged. "No," he said as he cut his fork through the rich fudge.

I pressed on, hoping for a snatch of meaningful conversation. "So what did you do with yourself while I was gone?"

"Not much."

"Any calls?" I asked.

"Hmmm," he said as he thoughtfully chewed. "Seems like the phone rang when I was in the garage earlier this afternoon."

*Hurray! A multiword response!*

I took another bite of pie and a sip of coffee, then stood and walked over to the answering machine, which was perched on our kitchen desk, and pressed the message button.

To my delight, our daughter's voice filled the room. "Mom, where are youuuuuu?" I could hear my grandson cooing in the background, probably balanced on his mother's hip.

I had to smile at that picture: my baby with her baby. How I missed them.

I listened as Mandy waited for me to pick up. When I didn't, she continued her message. "Listen, I'm on my way to the airport. I'm giving Ray a quick send-off as his company called him to Cairo to resolve some sort of emergency, a problem they're having with the latest software update they installed in the subway system, the Metro, they call it."

I looked over at Henry, who was still enjoying his afternoon snack. Our daughter continued, "With Ray's mom on her Hawaiian cruise, I thought I'd check the fares to Denver for the weekend so I wouldn't be here alone with Kyle. So, believe it or not, I found a wonderful deal and . . ."

Kyle laughed, followed by what sounded like Mandy readjusting him on her hip. "So, Kyle and I, we're on the way to Denver, today. Surprise!"

I clapped my hands and squealed in delight.

Mandy added, "I'll be in Denver about 7:30 tonight. I hope you get this message and you'll be there to pick me up." She hesitated. "I'm on the Southwest flight 335 from Houston, okay?" She continued, "I hope to see you in the pickup lane at DIA."

I grinned and glanced back at Henry. "That's what I get for forgetting to turn my cell phone back on after the TV interview." Henry simply nodded, then stood to take his empty dessert plate to the sink.

Though I felt like twirling around the kitchen, I suppressed my delight for Henry's sake. "If we leave now we'll have just enough time to run by Walmart before we head out to Denver," I said.

"Let me grab my wallet and keys," was his no-nonsense response.

I spent the two-and-a-half-hour drive to the airport with an all-but-silent Henry, who played Kenny Rogers's classics on the CD player, including his favorite song, "Ruby, Don't Take Your Love to Town." Unfortunately, those lyrics stood as a musical wall between us every twenty or so minutes of our trip. I was relieved when he pulled our Lincoln into the underground pickup lane at the Denver International Airport. It was there, just under the Southwest sign, where I spied my babies. Mandy—a redheaded beauty like her mama—was standing next to her luggage, a collapsed stroller, and a car seat that was shrouded by blue fabric. All I could see of the baby were two chubby hands reaching for his own kicking feet. Mandy, who was already back in her prepregnancy jeans, was looking good while fumbling in her large red-leather purse for her cell phone, to call me, no doubt. I pointed and exclaimed, "Look, Henry, there!"

"I see them," he said as he pulled up to the curb into a space a car was just exiting. Before Henry came to a complete stop, I'd shoved my door open and bounded toward my daughter, my arms outstretched. "My darlin'," I cried as I wrapped her in my arms. I hadn't seen her since she and Kyle had vanished some eight months earlier from the departure lane one level above me in this very airport. It wasn't that I hadn't tried to get down for a visit; according to Mandy, it was never "the right time." But what I really think is that she was just trying to show her independence after having to live with us through so much of her pregnancy.

"You got my message," she breathed with relief as she hugged me back. "Where were you all day?"

"Didn't I tell you? I had a TV interview in Denver. I forgot to turn on my cell phone after the show," I admitted as I turned to my grandson. There he was, my beautiful, precious grandchild in his car seat. I leaned over and spoke in a soft singsong, "How's Mimi's little Kyle?"

Behind me, Mandy hugged her dad, just before he scooped her luggage into the trunk of our car.

Kyle gave me a cute little baby grin and raised his arms to me. I quickly unstrapped the child and lifted him into my arms, and he snuggled onto my shoulder while I patted his bottom.

I turned with my prize and said to my daughter, "He's beautiful."

Her smile faded. "I had him all settled in his car seat, Mom."

"Never mind that," I said. I lowered him so I could gaze into his startling blue eyes. "I'll get him resettled into that contraption when I'm done squeezing him." I turned back to Kyle. "Now you're with your Mimi. Don't you worry about your ol' mommy."

I grinned at my daughter, who seemed as dumbstruck as her father.

Well, she is his daughter, after all.

"This is going to be the best visit ever," I said, ignoring their rude behavior.

I put my grandson back into his car seat while his mother watched. "Now Mimi is gonna take you home, little darling, right where you belong."

*Donna*

# 5

## Crushing Circumstances

My mother leaned on me as we walked out of the Gold Rush Grocery Store. Her frail body was shaking, probably from the alcohol in her system as well as the confrontation she'd just had with Evie. And, as far as I'm concerned, regardless of my mother's blood alcohol level, Evie had no call to create or add to such hysterics. I sniffed. Why, if I could charge Evie for either her immaturity or lack of good judgment, she'd be in handcuffs right now, stepmother or not.

Why couldn't she see Dee Dee for who she is, a woman who'd lost so much? I mean, if Evie was the good Christian she claimed to be, where was her compassion and grace? As far as I could tell, Evie was still stuck in junior high, brawling with some girl over a guy. I shook my head. *Poor Dad, what has he gotten himself into with this new bride of his?*

When Doreen stumbled on a small stone in the parking lot, I pulled her close in an effort to help her catch her balance. Being in this near embrace ignited a thirty-year-old memory of her as my mom, snuggling with me in a rocking chair, reading a bedtime story, singing a lullaby as I drifted off to sleep in her arms. Her voice had been so beautiful. It was as if, even now, I could hear her sing, "Twinkle, twinkle, little star, how I wonder . . ."

When Doreen looked up at me, I was surprised to see her tears. "I've gone and embarrassed my baby," her voice cracked. She patted my shoulder, as she'd swung her arm around me for support. "Donna, can you ever forgive me?"

"Sure, Mom."

My use of the word *Mom* brought another gush of tears. "You know I love you," she said. "No matter what happens or what anybody says, you know I came back to Summit View to tell you I love you."

I could only nod as I opened the passenger door of my Bronco, glad I'd called in a 10-7 when I arrived at the market, letting dispatch know I was offline. I'd turn my radio back on when I got Doreen settled. For now, I pushed aside my brown bag lunch of cold pasta chicken salad to clear off the seat before finally facing my mother. "I do know you love me, Mom," I said with a slight crack to my voice.

Calmed, she climbed into the passenger side of my truck, then looked down at me. "Are you taking me to jail for embarrassing you and your stepmother?"

"No, I . . ."

She held the door open. "You should. I mean for my safety. That woman threatened me, didn't you hear?"

I shook my head and looked up at Doreen. The lines in her forehead had hardened into such desperation I had to pause. "No, Mom, I'm not taking you to jail. I'm taking you home."

Her shoulders slumped, and she flopped her graying head back in her seat and looked straight out the cab window. "Oh."

I seat-belted her in then scurried around the truck to the driver's side. When I climbed inside, she picked up where she'd left off. "How will you protect me at my home?"

"Protect you from what? Evie's rudeness?" I snorted a laugh.

"Evie wouldn't hurt a fly, you know that. Just steer clear of her and you'll be all right."

"If only it were that simple," Dee Dee said through soft sniffles. I brought the engine to life and pulled onto the street. As I drove the few blocks to her trailer park, she asked again, "Donna, will you ever forgive me?"

"For what?" I asked, knowing there were a thousand answers I'd never speak aloud, at least not today. I pulled into the trailer park and drove down the asphalt road toward her ancient aluminum home. The trailer reminded me of a beached whale wearing a skirt of turquoise siding. Its cloudy eyes were outlined in aging black shutters. Beer bottles, cigarette butts, and crumpled malt liquor cans littered the front porch, which also hosted a couple of rough cedar chairs that had darkened with age.

Out of habit, I turned my radio on, then stepped out of my truck, my feet crunching on the gravel of her short driveway. I hurried to open Doreen's side of my Bronco so I could help her walk to her front steps. But before I got more than a couple of feet, my half sister Velvet came charging out of the trailer, her blonde ponytail swinging behind her. With her angry scowl and her red-rimmed blue eyes, she looked like she had tipped back a few longnecks herself.

I'll admit that seeing Velvet up close always gives me a bit of a start. She looks a lot like me, except for the longer hair, the false eyelashes, short cutoffs, and of course the lime green tube top. Her cheeks burned with indignation. "What have you gone and done to my mother?"

I stepped past Velvet and walked over to the passenger side of the truck, where I helped Doreen step out and onto her remnant of a lawn, which consisted mainly of yellow-flowering noxious weeds known around here as Alpine Parsley.

"Now, hush, Velvet," Doreen said. "Donna ain't gone and done nothing to me. She was just giving me a lift after I had the misfortune of running into that witch of a stepmother of hers in the checkout line."

Velvet pushed past me and pulled Mom out of my grasp. She turned to me and glared. "You Veseys are nothing but trouble," she hissed through her teeth.

"It ain't her fault," Doreen slurred, trying to defend me as she leaned on Velvet.

As Velvet guided our mother to the front steps, I looked up to see Wade skipping down the steps of his trailer a few doors down.

"Everything okay over there?" he asked.

His sudden appearance during this ugly family scene caught my breath. Wade and I had a past, a past that had almost made us a family when I became pregnant at eighteen. And if the truth be told, our past almost tempted me to reconsider his quest to look past our old issues and pick up again. And maybe I would have, if I hadn't met David Harris, the new man in my life. I mean, I cared about David, but our relationship was too new to ease all of my regrets, especially when it came to Wade.

Velvet turned and fluttered her fringe of lashes at him, "Oh, Wade, you're just the man I hoped to see. Could you help me get Mom inside the house?"

"What happened?" Wade asked as he sprinted over. He took Doreen's elbow and helped Velvet walk our wobbly mother up the porch steps.

"Why don't you ask her?" Velvet said, pointing at me over her shoulder with her chin.

"I already told you," Doreen said. "It weren't her fault."

Before I could join the conversation, the radio in my cab crackled to life. Was that Dad's voice? He wasn't supposed to be at work. What had happened to his night off? I hurried back to my cab, worried that Evie was still on her rampage.

As I opened the door of my Bronco, Dad's voice blared, "DB at 250 Mountain Meadow Lane, 10-55d."

So help me if I didn't gasp. Dad was calling for a coroner? At Goldie's address? I called back to Wade, "Take care of my mom, okay? Got a real emergency here."

I didn't wait for his answer. I hopped inside my truck, slammed my door, and hit my siren switch in one swift move. I did pause long enough to catch Wade's nod and rather worried expression just before he disappeared into the trailer with the women.

I drove my Bronco hard through town, a total of seven blocks, to discover my dad's truck as well as the paramedic's van in front of the Dippel residence. With the motor still running, and against all protocol, I jumped out of my truck and ran into the house, following the trail of people leading to Goldie's bedroom.

I stopped in the doorway and stared as David Harris, who was working the scene as the on-call paramedic, rolled a gurney next to the bed. He looked up at me and shook his head. My lips parted, but I couldn't speak as I gazed back at the body sprawled across the bed.

It was Jack. He must have had a heart attack.

Clay Whitefield, one of our local reporters, materialized from a corner of the room, where I assumed he'd been scribbling notes on his pad to go with a story he was writing for the paper. I grabbed his shoulders. "Where's Goldie?"

"She's in the kitchen with your dad," he said in a voice that warned me I needed to calm down. He was right. Even though I'd been thoroughly trained not to lose my cool, I was almost in a panic.

I blew out a breath. "Thanks," I said. I turned, acknowledging David with a glance as I left the room. David looked up at me with those wistful, puppy dog brown eyes of his. He was at least as handsome as Wade, though in a more Julio Iglesias kind of way. Too, I loved the fact that David was a paramedic; he of all people knew what I experienced on the job because we often worked the same calls. If only we could take a moment to confer about his impressions of what had happened, or if I could at least get one of his comforting hugs, but that was impossible, at least for now.

Maybe we'd meet for a midnight lunch behind the Gold Mine Bank. Besides, I was anxious to talk to Goldie.

Just as Clay had promised, I found Goldie sitting in one of her oak captain chairs at her kitchen table, with my dad sitting across from her. Dad, dressed in his full sheriff's garb, was handing Goldie a tissue as he used his gentlest voice to say, "The coroner should be here soon, Goldie. His visit is just a formality, of course. We all know Jack was having trouble with his heart, so it's pretty obvious he had a heart attack."

Goldie sucked in her breath. "If only I'd been here and not off doing TV interviews . . ."

Dad patted her hand. "The good Lord was here with Jack when he passed. He wasn't alone now, you know that."

Goldie nodded, and Dad slipped her one of the many business cards we in law enforcement carry in our wallets for such occasions. I looked over his shoulder and saw the black-and-gold foil card that belonged to Hugh Mitchell, the local funeral home director.

Dad said, "Just call Hugh and he'll help you make your arrangements."

Goldie nodded and looked up at me. She said in a little-girl voice, just above a whisper, "Donna, you came."

"Oh, sweet friend," I said and leaned down to hug her neck. She half stood and hugged me hard, her arms tightening in a grasp around my neck that almost toppled me onto her lap. I would have fallen if I hadn't pressed a palm onto her oak tabletop to steady myself. Somehow, I managed to detach myself from her grip and pull up the captain's chair my dad had just vacated, though he still hovered above us. I looked up at him as he said, "You sit with her for a while, okay, Donna? I have some things to check on."

I nodded. "Will do."

I took Goldie's hands. They were small and cold, despite the rainbow of sparkles from so many diamond rings. Gracious, Jack had managed to turn this woman into a walking jewelry store.

"You're cold as ice, girlfriend." I stood. "Let me start a pot of coffee." She started to rise, but I protested, "You hold on. I know my way around your kitchen."

She nodded while I put together a quick pot to brew.

While the coffee percolated, I sat with Goldie as she told me her horror of finding Jack dead when she returned from our trip to Denver.

"When did you call dispatch?"

Goldie looked up at me, her blue eyes hazy with grief. "Less than an hour ago, I guess."

"Ah, I was offline on another call," I explained. I felt my brows knit. "Wish I could have come immediately to be with you."

She squeezed my hand. "Don't you worry about it," she said before drifting into silence. After a few moments she looked up at me with starling clarity, as though she were about to make a confession. "Donna, it's no secret that Jack and I had issues but . . ."

I waited while she collected herself.

Her voice was low and shaky. "Still, I loved him and forgave him for cheating on me with all those women."

I looked around nervously, hoping no one overheard what could be construed as a motive, just in case there turned out to be any question about the cause of Jack's death.

I lowered my voice. "But he hasn't, I mean, he hadn't cheated on you lately, had he?"

She looked startled. "Why do you ask?"

"I have no cause to think he was seeing anyone," I said gently. "I'm just wondering if you suspected him of being with anyone else."

She shook her head absently. "No, no. Not now that he was losing his health."

She stared at the white knuckles of her balled fists on her lap. "But at least I got a chance to sit with him before your dad arrived," she said as she spread her fingers, smoothing the fabric of her beige pants. "I got my chance to tell my Jack that despite it all, I loved him, and that I was sooo sorry."

Jerry, one of the other deputies who often partnered with me, interrupted us.

"Sorry for what, Mrs. Dippel?"

I narrowed my eyes. Now, I liked Jerry. He was a big roly-poly teddy bear sort of a man. But the problem with Jerry was that he wanted nothing more than to sink his teeth into "real police work," as he was fond of saying. I held my breath, waiting for Goldie's answer, hoping it wouldn't set my partner into detective mode.

Goldie responded, "I was sorry that the two of us had so many regrets."

I stopped her before she could say more. "Meaning she's sorry that she wasn't here when Jack had his heart attack. Right, Goldie?"

She nodded. "Among other things."

Jerry nodded too but didn't look convinced. "Donna, may I have a word with you outside?" he asked.

I looked at Goldie, who said, "I'll be okay. Really." She stood up and walked over to the coffeepot. Her grief made her a bit unsteady on her feet.

I went out on the back porch and into the evening chill with Jerry, who shifted his weight from foot to foot. "Jerry, what's wrong?" I asked.

Jerry pulled out my Bronco keys from his pocket and dangled them in front of me. "This is what's wrong." He tossed my keys to me, and I slid them into a pocket.

"Where'd you find them?"

"In your Bronco. You left them in the ignition with the motor running."

"Oh! Yeah. Well, it looks like I owe you one."

Jerry chuckled. "The way I figure it, the next time we have lunch at Higher Grounds, you're buying."

I nodded. "That's fair."

"Now for my question: is it your opinion that Jack died of natural causes?"

I shrugged. "He had a heart condition, what else could it have been?"

"Do you know if Goldie had any big insurance policies out on him?"

"Even if she does, it's not a concern here."

Jerry looked over his shoulder and through the door. "How can you be so sure?"

"Because we're talking about Goldie. She wouldn't hurt a fly."

Jerry shrugged. "Only if you say so," he said as he pushed open the door to go back into the house. "But I'll let you know if I find any evidence to suggest otherwise."

I almost laughed. "You do that, Jerry, and if you find anything, which you won't, I'll handcuff Goldie myself. But trust me, that's not going to happen."

"Well, something is going to happen."

"What do you mean?"

"Just a gut feeling," Jerry said.

"For that they make antacid," I teased. "Besides, this is Summit View, what could possibly happen here?"

# 6

## Preserving Secrets

I was absolutely tuckered when the girls and I got back from Denver. The first thing I did upon entering my little high country home was kick off my heels and plant my bare toes into my new chutney-colored carpet I'd ordered in extra soft deluxe.

Since the Potluck Club's big win, I'd taken my share of the proceeds, after contributing big-time to the church's new youth wing, and splurged on wall-to-wall carpeting, not to mention the lovely granite countertops in the kitchen.

"It'll really add value to your home," Helen, the decorator at the local carpet store, had explained to me a few weeks back, and by George, I believe she was right. I loved the new look, and I must say it certainly cheered up my ever-expanding doll collection. "A sea of eyeballs," Fred often called the never-blinking faces peeking out from every flat surface of our house.

My appreciation for collectable dolls developed sometime after I'd lost my baby.

I'd found out that my husband, Joseph Ray Jewel, had been killed in Nam the morning my labor stated. As I was rather hysterical, there's no telling what the doctors used to medicate me through my baby's birth. But whatever it was, I was too groggy to understand I was signing away my parental rights when my mom handed me the paperwork. I thought I was signing the baby's death certificate. If you can imagine how that broke my heart, losing both my husband and my baby the same day.

Well, as it turns out, my son David didn't die but was lost to Hollywood. You see, his adoptive mother was Miss Harmony Harris. And yes, I do mean the recently deceased actress known mostly for her musicals some decades back.

Frankly, I'm still appalled that my baby was stolen away from me because my mother didn't think it would be proper for me to raise a child with a skin tone a few shades darker than my own, seeing as David's daddy was of Hispanic descent. How could she have been so . . . okay, *stupid*?

But it was David who suffered the most. He'd lost not only his dad but also his mom. It seems Harmony had little time for him, and it was the hired help who raised him, not to become a spoiled Hollywood heartthrob but, believe it or not, a paramedic who happens to be a millionaire, seeing as he inherited most of Harmony's wealth. It warms my heart to know David went into the medical profession, just like his biological mom and dad.

Still, David loved Harmony and saw her through her death from cancer, though he won't talk about it much. Her passing was the main reason David came looking for me.

You can't imagine my surprise to discover my son was alive after all this time. I must say, it was a wonderful reunion, though not so much for my husband Fred. The news that I'd been married before and had a child came as a shock. I'm really proud of the way Fred has warmed up to David, though. In fact, the two of them have been getting along rather well, like real family, which of course is what we are.

I leaned over the antique wicker cradle nestled on my hearth to fold back a soft, miniature blanket covering Joey, a porcelain-faced baby doll with pouty lips and wide, brown eyes. "There you go," I said before slowly straightening, with one hand on the small of my back as if that would stop its complaining. I turned and headed toward the kitchen, walking past the guest bedroom, which had until recently been my mother's home while she convalesced from a broken ankle.

Nursing my grumpy mother back to health had been anything but nice, but the experience had helped me work out a few of my issues with her, plus it gave Mother a chance to get to know David. But even after seeing their affection for one another grow, it was hard to let go of my grudge. The fact that I'd made progress was nothing short of a miracle. Still, I can't say I'm not glad she's back home with my dad in the nearby mountain town of Frisco.

I padded across the carpet and yawned, then climbed into my new, velvety-blue recliner for a nap. I snored while my large bichon frise, Chucky, slept on my lap until Fred pulled his truck into the driveway.

As soon as Fred slammed his door, Chucky yapped and I was on my feet running for the kitchen. I don't think I really woke up until I was standing at the sink, heart pounding as I rinsed out my big, greasy skillet. I don't know why the thought of Fred finding me napping caused such a panic. But since I'm a retired nurse, I merely entertain dust bunnies when not entertaining America on reality TV shows. So, there seems to be no harm in my afternoon snoozes. Of course, I manage to stay awake whenever one of the Potluck gals calls me over for coffee, a beverage I seem to drink by the gallon.

I quickly retrieved my refrigerated chili from my big sealed Tupperware tub, scraping every drop into my skillet before turning up the gas. By the time Fred walked into the front door, the chili was heating up on the stove and I was peeling carrots for the salad, the very picture of a woman who'd been cooking for hours.

"How was your TV interview in Denver?" Fred asked as he kissed me on the top of my head.

With my vegetable peeler in hand, I turned to give him a hug. "Good!" I said. "Though, Evie wanted to talk about Colorado's gold rush history more than our big win in New York, if you can believe it."

Fred laughed. "I bet the librarian in Lizzie had a lot to offer on that topic."

I giggled as he brushed my cheek with his five o'clock whiskers. "When she managed to interrupt Evie, she did."

I turned back to my work while Fred scratched his balding head, as if he were hesitating. "Do you know why an ambulance is in front of the Dippel house?"

I whirled back around. "This is the first I've heard of it," I said. "But Donna's on duty tonight. I'll text her to see what she can tell me."

"You do that," Fred said as he looked in the refrigerator for my pitcher of iced tea and began to pour the tea in glasses of popping ice.

I could tell he was glad I was checking in with Donna. Truth be known, she truly was like a daughter to us. When her mom had abandoned her dad when she was only a tiny thing, I'd stepped into her life to become the mom she'd lost. I'd started out as her Sunday school teacher in fifth grade, but we grew close as I took her shopping and talked with her about stuff like boys and why she needed to take algebra. Even now we were close friends. That's one reason why I'm so tickled that she's dating my David. If those two got married, she'd become my real daughter. How perfect would that be?

I walked over to my purse, which was still next to my recliner, and pulled out my recently purchased cell phone. "A must-have," Donna had explained to me when she drove me over to the cellular phone store in Breckenridge. I flipped open the phone, which was sort of a raspberry pink, and selected Donna's name in my contact list, then the "text" option. I carefully typed out my message: "Y ambulance @ dippels?"

I hit send and waited for Donna to text back. I was surprised when she actually called. I picked up. "Donna? What's going on?"

"It's Jack."

I felt my breath catch. I swallowed hard and repeated the name for Fred's benefit. "Jack? Is he going to be okay?"

"There was nothing they could do. Goldie found him when she got home from Denver."

Luckily I was standing next to one of my kitchen chairs, and I sat down hard.

"Oh dear. Are any of the Potluckers with Goldie now?"

"Lizzie's on her way."

"Maybe I better have Fred drive me over too," I suggested.

"You hang tight. Goldie's place is starting to look like a zoo with so many of her and Jack's friends pouring in. I have a feeling Goldie is going to need you more tomorrow when things start to quiet down," Donna advised.

Fred looked at me with quizzical eyes, and I blinked hard as I shook my head to indicate Jack was . . . well . . . gone. I stood on wobbly legs and walked toward the end of my counter, where I snatched a tissue to dab at my eyes. "What a horrible thing," I stammered just before I blew my nose.

"Are you going to be okay?" Donna asked. Her voice was filled with concern.

"Yes, of course," I said. "Fred's here with me. But will you drop by later? I have your favorite—chili."

"I think David and I are going to brown-bag it tonight for our dinner break. That is, if we can find the time."

"Swing by here first," I insisted. "I've got a couple of scoops of pecan cobbler for the two of you, for dessert."

"Yes, ma'am," Donna said. "If you don't mind waiting up."

———

When Donna finally arrived about 10:00 p.m., I'd already gone through half a box of tissues just thinking about poor Goldie without Jack. I mean, first Goldie's daddy's dying and now Jack. It didn't seem fair.

I hated to answer Donna's knock with such a puffy face, but my looks weren't so much an issue, not compared to the news about Jack.

"Aw, Vonnie," Donna said as she wrapped me in her arms. When we pulled back, Donna flicked away a rare tear, and I realized she was grieving as hard as me. I shook my head, marveling at her professional fortitude, knowing instinctively this was the first tear she'd let escape over Jack's death.

Donna flopped down in one of my kitchen chairs. "It really stinks," she said as I hurried to scoop pecan cobbler into empty whipped topping containers. I dabbed the cobblers with homemade whipped cream, which resembled fluffy clouds of goo.

I resealed the plastic containers and handed them to her, along with two plastic spoons wrapped in paper napkins.

"How're you holding up?" I asked.

"Just feeling sad," Donna said. "Sad for Goldie and how she'll miss Jack."

I nodded silently, thinking how much I'd miss Fred if he were to suddenly depart without me. The very thought prompted me to grab another tissue and blow my nose again.

Donna continued, "And I guess, if the truth be told, I feel kind of sad for me."

"How's that?" I asked as Fred joined us in the kitchen. We sat down at the table with Donna.

"Well, just look at the two of you," she said as Fred cupped his hand over mine. "You have each other. But me, I've never settled down."

Fred chuckled. "It's not that the boys around here haven't tried to win your heart," he said.

Donna's cheeks pinked, but she didn't respond.

"So what are you going to do about it? About settling down?" I asked. "I mean, you're dating David, right? He's already proposed to you once. Seems to me you could settle down whenever you want."

"I care about David, I do," Donna said. "It's just, we're still getting to know one another, you know? I mean, if he's really half the man he seems to be, then, well, I'm certain I *could* give him my whole heart." She shrugged. "But as for that proposal of his, he sprung that on me when we'd only just met. There's no way I could have accepted."

"But what about now?"

So help me if Donna didn't blush. She said, "We've only been going out a few weeks, though I definitely have feelings, it's still too soon to tell."

I could see I was getting too personal, so I switched topics. "Are you excited to meet David's friend Bobby?"

"Bobby?"

"You know, his friend flying in from LA."

"David never told me he had a friend flying in."

Fred and I looked at each other, then back at Donna. "Really?"

Donna shook her head and shrugged. "I'll have to ask him about that when we meet for dinner in a few minutes."

I nodded as she stood to go. After we said our good-byes and she'd bounded out the front door, Fred leaned in and whispered in my ear, "I'm not so sure it was a good idea to mention Bobby."

I continued to wave but raised a brow. "Why not?"

Fred leaned his head closer to my ear and said, "That's the 'Bobby,' as in 'Bobbie Ann,' you know, David's fiancée."

My jaw dropped. "What?"

He patted my arm. "I mean his ex-fiancée. You know, the one he broke up with just before he moved out to Colorado."

I watched as Donna's Bronco pulled out of our driveway and into the night before I turned and stared at Fred. I felt a bit weak and reached for his hand. "Oh dear."

*Lizzie*

# 7

## Crusty Encounters

It had been nearly a week since the girls and I had been on television and Jack had died.

Sunday morning I made a pot of coffee, prepared two cups, and joined my husband in the family room of our home, where he sat nestled near the corner windows. The day had dawned overcast; though the sun had surely risen from its sleeping place, one could not prove it by looking at the sky. Gray clouds obscured the mountain peaks, and even they, in all their glory, seemed less majestic underneath. Shoulders slumped, I handed Samuel's cup to him then took a sip and swallowed hard.

"You know, it wouldn't take much to talk me out of going to church this morning," I said. I slipped into one of the nearby chairs then crossed my legs, right over left. I jiggled my foot to adjust my bedroom slipper then leaned my head back and closed my eyes. "I'm just so tired after this last week."

"Now, Liz . . ."

"This last month. These last few months. Gracious, I know sixteen-year-olds who couldn't keep up with my schedule."

Samuel reached over from his chair, cupped his hand around mine, and said, "Tell you what. Today I'll take you out to lunch at Higher Grounds, then we can come home, have a slice of that peach cobbler you brought from Goldie's, and take a nap."

I smiled, opened my eyes, and turned my head toward him. "Nice try on the nap. You know Michelle and Adam are coming over this afternoon. Michelle promised to go with me to check on Mom." I sighed deeply. "I haven't been to see her since before the funeral. Between that and work and everything in between, I've just not had time."

"I know. That's why I went by to see her on Thursday. She was doing fine."

I shifted in my seat. "You did? Why didn't you tell me?"

Samuel took a sip of coffee, then said, "There was nothing really to tell. She didn't know who I was, though she told me I was quite good looking and she wouldn't mind one bit if I took her out to dinner." He winked. "I think your mother had quite the devilish side to her in her early days."

I frowned as I looked forward again. My mother, who'd always been the epitome of dignity and decorum as she raised her family, had—since being diagnosed with Alzheimer's—done things hardly considered appropriate. Including convincing a young college student named Kimberly who volunteered at the nursing home to buy a black teddy so Mom could "spice up her love life."

As far I knew, my mother's love life had ceased the day my father died.

"I'd rather not talk about that," I finally said to Samuel. I cupped the warm coffee mug between the palms of my hands and took in the splendor of the world around me. Nothing but nothing, even on a gray day like today, could touch the beauty of Summit View, Colorado. Whenever I took in the sights—from her lush valleys to her lofty mountains—I couldn't help but wonder what our Native Americans must have thought as they came across her. My mind wandered to our earliest settlers and how they carved out the roads here as they came to mine for gold. They built the town while they built their families, never fully conscious of the generations who would follow. How could they have known the impact they would have on my grandparents' world, my parents', or my own?

My husband interrupted my musing. "A penny for your thoughts."

I smiled at him. "I was just thinking how blessed I am to live here. Not just this house. Here, in Summit View." I took a breath as I pondered my own thoughts. "You know, Samuel, New York City is a vibrant place. I'd daresay the city itself is alive. It pulsates. Do you know what I'm saying?"

"I do indeed."

"But nothing mankind has ever built can compare with what God has done here. No amount of riches ever obtained can compare with the most simple life right here at home."

"Kind of like that song we sing at church."

"What song?"

"You know, the one that says God is more precious than silver and nothing can compare with him."

"Ah yes." I leaned my head against the back of the chair. "Yes. And you're right. I shouldn't pass up an opportunity to be in church this morning." I rose from my chair. "I'm first in the shower," I announced.

"You always are."

———

As we stepped across the lawn of Grace Church, I asked Samuel if he thought Goldie would be in church this morning.

"Don't know," he answered. "What would you do?"

"I don't think I could come so soon," I said. We walked up the few steps to the front door, where we were met by Vernon and Evangeline, who served as greeters.

"Good morning," we all said to each other.

"Have you seen Goldie?" I asked Evie as the men shook hands.

She shook her head. "No. I was just saying that I wondered if she'd come."

I looked to Samuel and then back to her. "I just said the same thing not one minute ago."

"Great minds," Vernon commented, then added, "but quite frankly, I don't understand why she wouldn't come to church. I mean, it's *church*. It's not like she's coming to a party."

Evie bristled. "We cannot expect you men to understand the ways of women."

"Thank the good Lord for that," Samuel said with a chuckle.

I looked at Evie again. "But have you talked to her? I tried to call her yesterday, but she wasn't answering."

"I did too. Got the same response. So I drove over."

"And?"

"She wasn't there. Nor were any of her family members."

"Hmm. Well, she needs time to grieve, but she also doesn't need to shut herself off from her friends. I admit, Evie, I'm concerned about her. That relationship was nothing short of tumultuous, and then to have it right itself only to end so abruptly." I shook my head as I crossed my arms, holding the Bible I carried close to me. "I don't know."

Evie patted my hand. "Don't worry, Lizzie. We won't let her fall into a depression. She's got good friends here for her once her family and Jack's are all gone."

I felt Samuel's hand touch the small of my back. "Come on, woman. Let's get inside."

We said our good-byes, then went inside. I saw Michelle and Adam sitting in our usual pew, so we joined them. Several minutes later the service began. As part of the announcements, Pastor Kevin gave a report on the financial status since our winning *The Great Party Showdown* and where things stood with the renovation of the church.

"As many of you know," he said, "this part of the church dates back over 150 years. Part of what we'd like to do is to pull up this carpet—which has seen better days—and restore the old flooring beneath us. Needless to say, some of that flooring will need to be replaced. We're going to do our best not to remove any of the planking unless we absolutely have to. In other words, we'll restore what can be restored and replace what cannot be." He chuckled. "Restored, that is."

A ripple of laughter floated from the congregation.

"All that to say," Pastor Kevin continued, "we'll have to meet in the fellowship hall for a few weeks, starting next week. And, with that, we'll need some help with setup early Sunday mornings and breakdown after Sunday evening services."

Heads nodded around me. The church's fellowship hall was used for so much during the week, it would be impossible to keep it set up for church services, Sunday to Sunday.

"If you would like to be a part of our chair moving team," Kevin added, "drop a volunteer card into the offering plate during the offertory." He smiled. "Now, stand with me as you turn to page 249 in your hymnbook . . ."

———

Samuel told me he needed to speak with the pastor before we left the church, so I waited out by the car. The day was still overcast, but the weather was warm enough that I didn't need a sweater. I leaned against our SUV and peered up at the sky, trying to gauge the position of the obscured sun. I breathed in the pungent aroma of the evergreens that dotted the church grounds, then thought how—soon enough—they would be laden with snow, their branches heavy and drooping. The town of Summit View would deck the halls as the air turned from cold to frigid. It was absolutely my favorite time of the year, and it was just around the corner.

I closed my eyes at the thought, then opened them in time to see a strange man walking from the far side of the church. He wore a coat, oversized pants, and a cap with its rim pulled low over dark sunglasses. Though he looked toward me, he didn't acknowledge me. I found myself almost calling out to him, as though I knew him, and then—realizing I did not—said nothing. He walked to the sidewalk, turned right, and ambled toward a cluster of buildings on Main Street where Higher Grounds is located.

My stomach growled at the thought of the restaurant. I glanced at my watch—it was now 12:30—then looked back to the front door of the church just in time to see Samuel and Pastor Kevin coming out of the door. When they reached me, I said, "Kevin, will you join us for lunch?"

"Nah," he said with a smile. "I'm pretty tired today. Think I'll go home, eat a peanut butter and jelly sandwich, and take a nap."

Samuel nodded. "Are you sure?"

"You two go have yourselves a nice lunch," Kevin said. "Hopefully you'll not have to wait too long for service."

I glanced down the street, shifted, and said, "Hey, guys. Do you two see that man walking there? Just in front of the Wild Wild West Sports Shop?"

"Yeah?" Samuel said. "What about him?"

"He just came from around the church."

"Okay . . ."

I shook my head. "I know, it sounds silly. But it was like he was walking so close to the building. In a shady kind of way."

"What does that mean?" Samuel asked.

I couldn't explain what I meant; I could only express what I felt. There was something odd about that man. "Never mind. He just seemed a little out of place," I said. I gave the ambling stranger another hard look just in time to see him cross the street and then dart into the lobby of the Snow Capped Motel. I looked back at my husband. "Let's go. I'm hungry."

———

After lunch, the men took Adam and Michelle's car and went to our house to watch some television and, possibly, nap. Michelle and I took my SUV and headed toward the care center where my mother was now living.

"Thank you for coming with me," I said to her, signing as best I could with one hand while the other clutched the steering wheel.

"No problem," she signed back. Our daughter—our beautiful youngest of the brood—had been born deaf. Not that her disability seemed to stop her from doing anything and everything she ever wanted to do. While she went to a school for the deaf in Denver during the school year, her childhood summers were filled with activities and friends from Summit View. She was active in sports, enjoyed dancing, Girl Scouts, and—most of all—reading books and discussing them with her mother as if we had our very own book club for two. She went to college, earned a degree, and then took a job at a Breckenridge resort.

She's not only remarkable, she has always been her grandmother's pet grandchild. Because I had not been to see Mom in over a week, I thought having Michelle with me might be a good way to ease into the room, so to speak.

I parked the car and the two of us quickly went into Summit Center, a new home I'd recently moved Mother into. Though the staff works hard to keep the place deodorized, there is still the faint odor of urine that assaults the senses upon entry. Michelle signed, "I hate this smell," and I wondered about that old adage about how losing one sense causes others to be more alert, making Michelle's nose more sensitive to the scent. But with no way to know for sure, I simply nodded.

We reached the main nurses' station, where I stopped to talk with the head nurse, who was talking to Mrs. Hirvela—a woman I've known all my life and who had to be the oldest resident in the facility. Mrs. Hirvela sat somewhat slumped over in a wheelchair. Her face, however, registered complete control of her faculties.

"Why, Lizzie Trawick," she said, referring to my maiden name. "However are you?"

"I'm fine, Mrs. Hirvela," I said. "And you?"

She gave us a lopsided grin. "I'd be better if I were out of this chair." She slapped the armrests with the palms of her hands.

The head nurse motioned for one of the nursing assistants as she said, "Can you get Mrs. Hirvela back to her room, please?"

"I guess that's my cue to go," the old woman said. I had to admit, she seemed a little saddened by it.

I waved good-bye, then turned to the head nurse, who rested her right hip against the counter and said, "Should I live to be that old, I hope I'm still that sharp." She frowned. "God love her. Not a soul comes by to see her. No family here, at least not anymore, and she's outlived all her friends."

"How sad," I said, then turned the conversation to ask how Mom had been getting along.

"Well, on *that* one," she said, "all I can say is that I'm glad you're here. She's been quite a pill to swallow lately."

"Wonderful," I muttered, then signed to Michelle what the nurse had said.

Michelle made a face and signed, "Aren't you glad you brought me?" which I translated for the nurse.

The nurse pressed her painted rose lips together and said, "Mmm-hmm. You better believe we are."

We found Mom in her room, watching the little television Samuel and I had provided for her. The sound was completely off, but Mom seemed captivated by whatever show was featured.

"Hi, Mom," I said from the door. "Look who came to see you." I forced a smile as I waited for Mom's reaction.

Michelle stepped around me, signed, "Hi, Grandma," to which Mom, face scowling, said, "Who in the world are you?"

"It's Lizzie, Mom. Lizzie and Michelle." Mom was sitting in one of the two chairs the room provided. I took a seat on the twin-sized bed and indicated to Michelle that she should sit next to her grandmother. "You remember Michelle, don't you, Mom? She's your granddaughter."

"Never heard of her," Mom barked. "And what in the world is going on with the television? I can't hear a word these people are saying!"

As Mom rambled on, I signed for Michelle, whose eyes expertly shifted from my hands to her grandmother's face and back. When I'd finished, Michelle used her voice to say, "I know how you feel, Grandma."

Michelle rarely spoke aloud, though she does well with pronunciation. She has always insisted that she simply prefers to sign when she can.

Mom furrowed her brow at Michelle. "Why are you talking so funny?" she asked. "What's wrong with you?" She jerked her head from Michelle to me. "And what are you doing there with your hands?"

"Mom," I said. "You remember that Michelle is deaf." I didn't say the words as if they were questions but more as a matter of fact. Mom's doctor insisted we try to keep control over all conversations and, rather than sounding as if we were begging her to remember, state our words factually.

Mom's hands gripped the arms of her chair. "I tell you what I remember. I remember that nurse who came in here this morning with that awful stuff they call breakfast."

"It wasn't good?" I asked.

"It was poison!"

My shoulders sank. "Mom," I said. I felt tears sting my eyes. But before I could say another word, Michelle whipped a photo album from her purse. It was one I recognized—a small version of her wedding album, covered in white satin and graced with a cross appliqué.

"Look, Grandma," she said, opening the book to the first page, which displayed Michelle dressed like a princess in her wedding gown. "Isn't this pretty?"

Mom's anger was diverted as she peered down at the photograph.

"Oh my," she said. Her gnarled fingers reached forward and lightly grazed the cellophane over the picture. "How'd you get this?" She looked from Michelle to me and then back to the photograph. "A picture of me on my wedding day . . . Oh, what a day that was . . ."

# 8

## Dicey Run-In

I suppose I was a little surprised that Goldie didn't come to services on Sunday, but, in thinking about it from all sides, I couldn't say I blamed her. She'd probably had enough of hearing people tell her how sorry they were for her misfortune. And, I suspect, she had heard all she wanted to hear of those lines people say when you've lost a loved one, words meant to sound encouraging but falling short. Things like, "Well, you're still young, you know . . ."

Meaning, Goldie is young enough to find some nice man, date him for a while, then get married and sail off into the sunset years with New Mr. Right.

During the week following Jack's death, Goldie's house had looked like Old Home Week. I'd never seen so many people in one place in my whole life. Certainly not so many Southerners. Summit View's inns, hotels, and our one motel could hardly hold them all. Some had to stay in Breckenridge, and a few went to Frisco.

And I'll tell you something else I've never seen so much of: food! Every kind of pie you can imagine. All sorts of cakes and breads,

casseroles, and vegetables. Of course, Lisa Leann was in her element (even with her daughter home) but was nearly upstaged by
Goldie's sister Diane, who made peanut brittle I'd sell Vernon for.

As anyone who knows me will confirm, I have never been much
of a cook, and these times of bringing food to the home of the family
have always left me feeling a bit insecure. That is, until a few years
ago when I got wise. Instead of bringing a plate of prepared food,
I would swing by Walmart, where I'd purchase things like toilet
paper, paper napkins, and disposable utensils and plates. I quickly
became the hit at any funeral.

If one can be a hit at a funeral.

———

So, while Goldie wasn't at church and I didn't blame her, neither
were her daughter nor her son-in-law, which surprised me. Olivia
has always been a stickler for how things look and going to church
and all that. Naturally, after church I called Goldie to see if she was
okay. When she didn't answer, I called Olivia's house, but she didn't
answer either. I figured they were having some quiet family time
or maybe even returning family members back home. It was, after
all, Sunday. Time for all God's children to go home.

Monday morning, after Vernon had left for work, I dressed,
got in the car, and headed toward Goldie's. She didn't answer the
door. Not when I knocked and not when I rang the doorbell. I got
back in the car and drove to Olivia's. A quick look at my dashboard
clock told me it was already after 9:00. I figured by now that Tony
would have left for work and the kids would be up, fed, and doing
whatever it is little ones do at 9:00 in the morning.

Not ever having children of my own, I really can't say *what* that is.

But Olivia didn't answer either.

I returned to my car, retrieved my cell phone from my purse,
and called Lisa Leann, whose daughter and grandchild had made
an unexpected visit. Lisa Leann was so beside herself with glee
over this, she'd hardly mentioned any of us coming to the shop to

65

work on our catering business. Just as well, in my humble opinion. I was worn out from it all anyway.

But Lisa Leann answered with a sigh.

"What's going on with you?" I asked.

"Nothing," she said. "Well, nothing I can talk about right now."

I heard the cooing of a baby obviously being held close to the phone.

"Have you talked with Goldie today?" I asked.

"No, why?"

"How about yesterday?"

"She wasn't in church."

I rolled my eyes heavenward. "I know that, Lisa Leann. I was in church, remember?"

"Of course I remember. Why are you being so snippy with me?"

I leaned back against the car seat. "I'm sorry. I'm just worried about Goldie, and she's not answering the door."

"Maybe she's out."

"Well, of course she's out, Lisa Leann. I didn't think she was deliberately *not* answering the door. Do you know when all her family was leaving?"

"Yesterday, I was told."

"Hmm . . . so then, where do you think . . . surely she hasn't gone back to work!"

"Oh no. She told me Chris told her to take two weeks off and not to worry about the law practice one bit. He's brought in some temp secretary. Oh! I bet I know where she is."

"Where?"

"She's probably meeting *with* Chris."

Chris Lowe, attorney at law, was Goldie's boss. If he'd told her to take time off, why would she be meeting with him? Unless . . . "Oh, of course. She's probably meeting with him to go over paperwork, the will, and all that."

"I bet if you drive past the law office you'll see her car."

"Well, that's okay. She's a grown woman, after all. I was just a little worried."

I hung up the phone, started the car, and then drove to Main Street and past the law office in search of Goldie's car. Sure enough, there it was.

Chris Lowe's law office is directly above a Hallmark card store. I parked nearby and went into the store, where I perused the "Thinking of You" kind of cards I thought would bring Goldie comfort as the weeks went on. I remembered how, when my parents died—both tragically killed in a car accident—once the funeral was over and the last of the out-of-town guests had left and friends had ceased to come over to check on me and I was left alone with my heartache and emptiness, it was my friend Ruth Ann's cards that helped me keep one foot in front of the other. I knew they'd help Goldie too.

I purchased four then returned to my car. But before I could get in, I heard a voice behind me. "Hey, lady!"

I turned to see Donna's half-sister Velvet James. She stood on the sidewalk, hands planted on her hips and her jaw set.

Velvet and Donna look remarkably alike, but their similarities end there. Donna is practical. She's conservative. She's law-abiding. Donna is tough and vulnerable, all at the same time. Velvet is . . . well, she's the opposite of all those things.

"Hello, Velvet. Nice to see you today." I peered upward. "Isn't it nice the sun came out for us this morning?" I opened the car door and swung my bag of cards over to the passenger's side, where it dropped with a *swish*.

Velvet took several steps toward me. "Don't even start the nice chitchat. I wanna know what you did to my mother last week."

I noticed those who were passing by on the sidewalk, craning their necks to see what might be about to go down. Goodness knows I didn't want to start a fight and certainly not in the middle of town. "Look, Velvet. I have no problem with your mother. But your mother obviously has a problem—"

"Don't talk about her like that!" Velvet's voice rose an octave as she took another step toward me. Her face flashed fury, and for a second I felt fearful.

But only for a second. "Now look here!" I pointed a finger toward her as I gained momentum. "I've had just about enough of you and your mother to last me a lifetime. I've been nice to you. I've been nice to your mother. She and I have laid all our cards out on the table and . . ." My voice was becoming louder than I wanted it to be. I dropped it by taking in a deep breath and then releasing it. "It's really none of your business."

"She's my mother and it *is* my business!"

I leaned closer to her. As angry as I was, though, I couldn't help but notice how vibrant her blue eyes were. Donna and Velvet were two peas in a pod when it came to their eyes. Every emotion held inside could be read right there. "Well, I will tell you this, Velvet James. If you are so worried about your mother, I'd suggest you get her into some kind of rehab program."

"And I suggest *you* get into some kind of rehab program."

"Me? Why would I need to . . ." I took another deep breath and exhaled. "Don't be ridiculous."

"You know, JA, maybe? Jealous Anonymous."

"Make jokes, Velvet. But I'm not kidding."

"I'm not kidding either. Leave my mother alone!" With that, she turned on her heel and started walking away.

I felt a million pinpricks along the skin of my body, head to toe. Heat rose in my cheeks as my eyes made contact with several of the passersby on the sidewalk and those going into and coming out of the card shop and other nearby establishments. I couldn't let her have the last word like this. I just couldn't. Besides, she needed to listen to what I was saying. Or at least to what I was trying to convey. "Mark my words, Velvet James!" I hollered like a child reared in a barn. "If your mother keeps this up, she won't live long!"

Velvet spun around. "Is that a threat?" she bellowed, arms crossed.

"It's a promise!" I hollered back. I cut my eyes to everyone else. "Oh, go home and mind your own business!" I shouted.

I then got in my car and went home myself.

Within an hour, Donna arrived in her Bronco. I invited her in. I'd just put a kettle of water on the stove for a cup of tea and asked her if she'd like to join me.

"No," she said. Her voice was soft.

I turned to go back to the kitchen, and she followed me. I heard the gentle squeaking of her leather belt against her holster and all that other stuff law enforcement officers wear around their waists. "So what brings you by?"

"Evie, listen," she said. The tone in her voice made me turn around.

"What's going on? Is it Vernon?"

Donna's face registered surprise. "Dad? No, no." She paused. "I'm here on official business. But to be honest with you, Dad doesn't even know."

I crossed my arms. "What kind of official business?"

Donna pressed the palm of her right hand against the kitchen countertop and rested her hip against it. "I got a call from Velvet a little while ago."

My arms dropped. "Oh. Her."

The whistle of the teakettle shrilled from the stove. I turned to prepare my tea.

"Evie, did you threaten my mother?"

I spun around. "Did I . . . ? Are you serious?"

She raised her left hand to stop me. "I've interviewed two witnesses, Evie. They said they heard you tell Velvet that you were going to kill my mother."

I coughed out a laugh. "Oh, Donna. Don't be absurd." I went back to preparing my tea. "Look. I told Velvet that if her mother—your

69

mother—didn't stop drinking she was going to kill *herself.*" I paused to think as I bobbed the tea bag in and out of the hot water. "Actually, what I said was that she wouldn't be alive much longer." I took a sip of the tea. "I think those were my exact words. Maybe not, but something close to it. To be honest with you, I was so upset I sort of don't remember my exact words." I took another sip. "But I think that was what I said. Oh well, at least that's what I meant. Are you sure you don't want a cup of tea? It's peppermint and it's very good."

Donna shook her head. "Evie, I don't think you understand how serious this is. Velvet wants me to arrest you. For that matter, so does Doreen."

"Arrest me?" I had to put the cup of tea down now. "Are you kidding me?" I felt myself flush. "You aren't actually going to arrest me, are you?"

Donna gave me a half smile. "No. I'm not. But you've got to be careful, Evie. I know my mother drinks too much, and I know my sister is a hothead, but you can't just go around knocking them over and screaming at them in the middle of the street."

"Now wait a minute." I pointed my finger at my stepdaughter. It was the second time today I'd raised a finger.

But Donna shook her head. "No, Evie. Let's leave it at this."

"But you haven't heard my side of this!"

"I've heard enough." She took a step backward, gave a half turn, then looked back over her shoulder. Her eyes were filled with sorrow, and for a moment I saw the little girl who'd been abandoned by her mother so many years ago, left alone with her father to pick up the pieces when she hardly knew where the pieces were.

As Goldie often said, bless her heart.

"Donna . . ."

I didn't say anything else. I was afraid if I did, Donna would begin to cry. Then I'd be crying right along with her.

"Enjoy your tea," she said, then walked out of the kitchen.

I stood motionless, listening to her footsteps as she made her way to the front door. It opened, then rattled shut. A minute later the Bronco roared to life. Even from the kitchen I could hear its tires backing out of my driveway, turning, and heading toward town.

I looked down at my teacup, a blurred vision of respite in the vale of tears that now refused to be stopped.

*That Doreen*, I thought. It was time for the two of us to talk. Again.

# 9

## Scalding News

I was amazed at all the high-tech baby gadgets Mandy had brought to Colorado in her red diaper bag backpack. The gadgets included such items as a baby monitor with a video camera—if you can imagine—a baby iPod that played Mozart, for goodness sakes, a bottle warmer, not to mention an electronic breast pump. Amazingly, there was also a diaper-wipe warmer so that a baby wouldn't have to shiver through a diaper change, and an actual sling for carrying the baby—a piece of cloth worn wound around the neck and waist, like African mothers I'd seen in *National Geographic* magazine photos. Only, according to Mandy, this sling was made out of peanut shells so as to be environmentally friendly.

Hello? Hasn't anyone heard of peanut allergies? I mean, maybe I'm not as "green" as this younger generation, but how are peanut shells environmentally friendly?

Then there was also a fancy-shmancy stroller that was so smart it was impossible, much to my chagrin, for this grandmother to open without help from her daughter. But Mandy's all-time favorite gadget was a large, C-shaped pillow called a Boppy. "It's for positioning the baby ergonomically," Mandy informed me, as if it made all the sense in the world.

I didn't get it until I saw how she balanced Kyle on it as she fed him, using the pillow to fill the gap beneath her cradling arm and her lap.

"That's cozy," I said.

Mandy nodded. "Babies are more high tech today," she explained. "It's *better.*"

"Well, excuse me for being from the dark ages," I teased. "An era you yourself survived, you know."

We shared a laugh, and a few minutes later, as if to prove her generational superiority, Mandy repositioned Kyle inside the Boppy on the bed. He looked so cute with his little head supported as he snuggled inside pillow arms. He kicked his legs through the semicircle's opening, safe from rolling off the bed.

I looked up at Mandy. "I hate to admit it, but this thing is pretty slick."

I sat down on the edge of the neatly spread rose-colored bedclothes and reached for my grandson. He grinned a toothless smile as I pulled him onto my lap. I held his tiny hands as he pushed his bare baby feet against my thighs until he stood in a jiggly stance. "My, he's strong," I commented as Kyle and I gazed into one another's eyes.

"Mom, put Kyle back in his Boppy and help me with this packing. Kyle doesn't have to be held every minute, you know."

I tried to hide my frustration with a good-natured observation. "With all your high-tech gadgets, you don't really have to play with Kyle, do you? With his sound-activated mobile, not to mention his baby swing and a bouncer, all you have to do is push a button and the gadgets do the rest, right?"

Mandy raised one eyebrow and gave me that look I'd so often given her when she'd been in pigtails. "But still," I pressed on. "How do you know if the baby's getting enough of *your* attention?"

"Oh, Mom! Kyle is not hurting for my attention," Mandy said as she lifted my grandbaby from my arms and plopped him back into his pillow. She turned back to me, a hand on one hip. "We've got to get moving if we're gonna leave for the Denver airport. That is, if Kyle and I are going to make our flight."

I reached over and rubbed the back of Kyle's little hand with my index finger. I was rewarded when he entwined his fingers around mine. "I love you, little boy," I said.

He smiled and my heart soared.

Mandy's voice was firm enough for me to look up. "Mom, really."

As I stood to help my daughter pack, Mandy's cell phone rang with Mozart's "Twinkle, Twinkle, Little Star."

"Cute," I said, meaning it. I wasn't against technology, unless of course it got in the way of real relationships.

Mandy gave me a sort of half smile and shook her head before walking to the dresser to pick up her cell phone. "Hello?"

I opened the guest bedroom closet door and stood on tiptoe to retrieve the missing bag from the top shelf. I'd stowed it there shortly after Mandy arrived last week, mainly to get it out of the way. Before I could pull down the bag, Mandy gasped. I could hear the squeak of the bedsprings as she sat down on the bed, hard. "No!"

I whirled, slinging the suitcase around me so fast I almost knocked the baby monitor off the dresser.

"What's wrong?" I demanded. But Mandy ignored me as her hand covered her mouth and her eyes glistened. "How bad is he?"

"Who?" I demanded, my alarm growing.

She shook her head and held up one hand, as if she were trying to shush me so she could hear. I whispered, "Something's happened to Ray?"

Mandy looked at me out of the corner of her eyes and nodded while I instinctively reached for Kyle. I stood next to the bed and rocked him in my arms as I shifted my weight from hip to hip.

Mandy looked up. "Do you have a pen and paper?"

I nodded and scurried to the bedroom desk, shifting Kyle in my arms before retrieving a notepad and a pen from a construction-paper-covered orange juice can, made by Mandy when she was only eight.

I handed Mandy the pen and pad, and she scribbled with fury. "Yes, I'll catch the next plane out. Yes, tonight."

The baby and I sat down beside her as she hung up the phone. Her shoulder blades sagged as she absently ran a hand through her hair.

I fingered Kyle's soft strawberry curls with my free hand while I rocked to and fro as if the baby needed comforting. "So what happened?"

"That was Ray's office. He's in the hospital." Before I could ask more, Mandy stood abruptly and looked down at me. "I'm supposed to drive to the Denver airport, where I'll find a ticket waiting for me, to Cairo, tonight. When I get to Cairo sometime tomorrow, someone from the company . . ." She looked at her notes. "A car will be there to pick me up. He'll take me to see Ray at the . . . Kasr El Aini Hospital."

"But what happened?" I asked again.

Mandy stared back at me. Her mouth opened, then closed, then opened again. "Ray's in a coma, from a fall. He fell off a train plat-form, I guess. It's not too clear, really."

"Fell or was pushed?" I asked.

Mandy's brows knit together. "I . . . I . . . ah . . . don't know."

"But you can't go. You don't have your passport with you, right?"

Mandy nodded. "I do. We've started carrying them when we travel."

I stood up and faced her, holding Kyle close. "But, you're not taking the baby to Egypt, are you?"

"I wish I could, but . . ."

I finished her sentence, "But it might not be practical or even safe?"

Mandy nodded and opened the suitcase before walking to the dresser, where she opened a drawer to retrieve a stack of folded jeans and tees. She spoke without making eye contact. "I do think it would be best if I left him here with you and Dad." She looked at me then, her cheeks splotchy. "Would you mind? It probably won't be for long . . ."

My heart lurched to see my baby in pain. I rushed to her, wrapping her in an embrace that included the baby. "Darling, Kyle will be okay here till you and Ray return. You hear me?" I pulled back and looked into Mandy's eyes. "Okay?" I asked again.

She nodded. "But are you up for a baby, Mom?"

I nodded as I placed Kyle back in his Boppy. "Well, yes. I did manage with you and your brother, you know."

She brushed her eyes with the back of her hand. "Okay," she said so softly I almost didn't hear.

"I'll help you pack."

Hours later, after tears, hugs, and a curbside huddle of prayer, Mandy walked toward the entrance of Denver International Airport, leaving her baby behind. She turned, one last time, and blew us a kiss, then pushed through the door, where she was quickly absorbed into the sunset's reflection on the glass.

I had every intention of following her in with the baby in my arms, but Henry stopped me. "You know we can't leave the car," he reminded me as he glanced at the policeman observing us.

I sighed. "Wishful thinking, I guess," I admitted as I waved baby Kyle's hand in the direction his mother had disappeared. I stopped waving and turned to Henry. "I'd actually be excited about keeping Kyle, if Ray was okay," I said, sniffing.

Henry nodded the way he always nodded. A technique he sometimes used to make it look like he was actually listening whether he was or not. I tested to see. "Don't you agree?"

"Very sad," he said in a tone that showed he meant it.

I patted Kyle's little bottom. "It will be nice to give the baby some hands-on attention."

"Do you think you can handle him?"

I felt shocked. "Well, of course. It will be like the old days, Papa. Or don't you remember?"

Henry nodded again, and I would have thought he was zoning out of our discussion if it weren't for the look of concern in his eyes.

I placed Kyle in his car seat in the center of the backseat and strapped him in.

"That's the safest place for a baby in a car crash," Mandy had explained in one of her many baby tips she'd shared on our way down the mountain. All the while she explained, she scribbled instructions on baby care in a notebook that she'd finally passed to me from the backseat.

We were soon on the road and driving up I-70 toward the mountains. I was thankful Henry hadn't turned on his songs of betrayal as we rode in silence, munching on the cashew chicken wraps I had packed for the trip. They were still crisp, and I hoped the two I'd given to Mandy would be this good when she got ready to eat them.

An hour later, darkness drifted down the mountain road, covering us in a heavy cloak that seemed to absorb most all of the moonlight that occasionally winked between the tall peaks. Kyle slept and I stared at the shadows, lost in my worries until Sandi Patty began to sing "Majesty." Glad to have her voice set as my ringtone, I reached for my cell phone.

"Hello?"

"Lisa Leann, it's Wade."

Wade and I had gotten close after our time with Team Potluck on the reality TV show *The Great Party Showdown*. Still, we made an odd pair, me a . . . ah . . . fiftyish married woman, and he, a thirtysomething "friend" of Donna's.

I knew she was still the love of his life, despite the fact she had recently been dating David, a little detail that I knew simply broke Wade's heart. I secretly sympathized. I'd always thought it was a shame that he and Donna had never married and had a family. To tell the truth, those two had seemed to play the part when Wade had taken in his twelve-year-old cousin for a time a while back. If Pete hadn't gone back to his mom, I think Wade and Donna might have been engaged by now.

I sat a little straighter in my seat. "Well, Wade, nice to hear from you. Is everything all right?"

"Fine," he said. "How's your visit going with that grandson of yours?"

"You have the right to ask," I teased, "as you and Donna helped deliver him. I mean, I call you over to my condo to fix a squeaky door, and you end up delivering my grandchild. That's what I call service."

"Just doing my job, ma'am," Wade teased.

I backed up to his question. "I just dropped Mandy off at DIA," I admitted.

"I know you're going to miss those two."

I glanced over my shoulder to the backseat. I watched Kyle rub his sleeping face with the back of his hand. The act startled him, but not enough to wake him up.

"Kyle's still here with me," I said, realizing my words sounded like a boast. I softened my tone with genuine concern. "My son-in-law was in an accident in Egypt, and Mandy's taken the first flight out to be with him."

"Thank goodness she could leave Kyle with you. Is Ray okay?"

"I won't know until Mandy checks in, though word is he's in a coma."

"Lisa Leann, I'm so sorry."

I sniffed. "Me too."

"Well, maybe this isn't a good time to talk," Wade said.

I glanced over at Henry through my watery eyes. "Well, Kyle's asleep and Henry and I are just sitting here, driving up 70. Go ahead and tell me what's on your mind."

"Well, ah, Donna, I guess."

I propped my elbow on the passenger's window and held my phone closer to my ear. "What about her?"

"Well, I need some advice."

"How can I help?"

"I know I made a mess of things. I know she's dating David, though I don't think things are so serious between them, do you?"

I shrugged. "She hasn't said anything to me," I said as the eighteen-wheeler ahead of us slowed down. Henry slowed too.

I looked at my watch, hoping this mountain traffic jam would be short-lived. I had a baby who was going to wake up hungry, probably sooner rather than later. I was glad I wouldn't be empty-handed tonight, as Mandy had prepared for her trip back home to Houston by pumping several bottles of breast milk, bottles I had inherited.

Wade took a deep breath. "I miss her, Lisa Leann. I know I've blown it, but do you think there's anything I can do to win her back?"

"You mean other than hog-tying that mom of yours?"

Wade almost laughed. "Well, yeah."

"Well, then, you've come to the right place for advice. I've helped many a lad in your situation. But you'll have to do exactly as I say. Okay?"

"Yes, ma'am. I'm listening."

*Goldie*

# 10

## Bittersweet Sorrow

Absolutely nothing in this world can prepare a wife for the death of her husband. I believe that even if the husband has been ill for a good long time, even that does not prepare her.

Jack had been healthy his whole life until this past summer, when he admitted a few cardiac issues. Then, of course, the bypass surgery. And for what? For what?

Jack, barely into his fifties. Gone. His life cut short entirely too soon.

*Why, God? Can you tell me why? Can you give me even the slightest hint? I'm not asking to understand all the complexities of the world. Just this one thing. Just tell me why you've left me here all alone. And why now . . . after Jack and I were finally making our marriage work. After it had begun to sing such a sweet song. A melody of love . . .*

———

I now have only vague memories of those first few minutes. Hours. I called Olivia, our daughter, but I didn't speak to her. Her husband answered, and I told him about his father-in-law. Told him to tell Olivia. Told him to tell her gently.

The two of them came as soon as they could get the children settled at Tony's parents' home. Immediately, Olivia took over placing calls to family members, friends, and my boss, Chris Lowe. She called the Department of Education office and the high school principal. I'd not have thought to do that.

She called our family physician, who came right over as though we were living in the sixties and making house calls was the norm again. He gave me something to calm my nerves and help me sleep. I told him—told them all—that it wouldn't work, that nothing could, but in the end, it did. I slept as though nothing out of the ordinary had happened. It had been a run-of-the-mill day in my less-than-ordinary life. When I woke the next morning, the sun was slicing through the half-opened blinds. I was wearing my favorite French terry pants and matching hoodie as though I were about to go for a leisurely walk. In spite of their warmth, I shivered in the early morning chill and rubbed my arms with my hands.

Shifting on my bed, I realized another body was beside me. Initially I assumed it was Jack. Why, of course it was Jack. But, opening my eyes, I saw that it was Olivia, whose green eyes were focused on me. "Olivia . . ."

"Hey, Mom," she said. Her short red hair spiked against the crisp white linen pillowcase.

It took a moment for reality to set in, to remember that Jack had died the day before. The realization must have registered on my face. My daughter smiled weakly and then whispered my name again.

And I began to cry.

———

The initial business of dying keeps those left behind from spending too much time grieving their loss. Before we'd had a chance to even make coffee—as soon as the blinds opened across the house—the doorbell rang. And rang. And rang.

At some point Olivia ushered me out of the house and into my car, which she then drove to the local funeral home. We were greeted by Wendy Morrow Mitchell, a woman I've known since Jack had brought me to Summit View and whose family has owned this funeral home for at least three generations. She met us in the front parlor of what had once been a part of an old miner's mill, took my hands in hers, and spoke her condolences. "Goldie, we're so sorry . . . the whole family . . ."

*The whole family.*

It was all I could do to speak. Wendy's sister Amy had, many years ago, had an affair with my husband. One of his many affairs over the years. She'd been no more special than the last or the next.

I slipped my hands from hers as I cast a glance at Olivia, who nodded ever so slightly as she said, "Tell your family thank you from all of ours."

If Olivia knew about her father and Amy Morrow Jenkins, she certainly wasn't letting on. She was, as she always is, the epitome of grace, charm, and control.

We were escorted down a long and narrow hallway whose walls were lined with old black and whites of the way things had been at the turn of the last century. Old miners with weathered faces and tattered clothing stared after us as their big floppy hats worn low provided shade from the sun or snow. Many carried battered pans in their gnarled hands. Others were wrapped in frayed blankets, standing just outside makeshift lean-tos, their dark boots laden with mud and slush.

I thought of how—just twenty-four hours earlier—I'd been sitting in a television studio, listening to Evie speak of the old miner legacies and myths. It was an odd thought, but there it was.

At the end of the hall was a white-paneled room dominated by two cluttered desks, no less than a half-dozen chairs, and several filing cabinets. Wendy turned, indicated with a sweep of her hand that we should sit in one of the vacant chairs in front of one of the desks. "Hugh will be with you shortly," she said.

Hugh was her son. His nameplate sat straight at the front of the desk we were being led to.

Hugh managed the funeral home along with his cousin Andrew. Olivia and I sat. We took deep breaths. We released them.

A few minutes later Hugh Mitchell—a rather gangly man who was a few years older than Olivia—entered the room, then closed the door ever so quietly. "Mrs. Dippel," he said, extending a hand.

I slipped mine into his. It was cold. Wax-like. As though he were dead too.

"Allow me to express our sorrow at the loss of your loved one." His words sounded rehearsed.

Olivia squared her shoulders. "Thank you." I appreciated that she was speaking for the two of us.

"What we need to do first is look at caskets." He pulled a binder from a shelf behind him, laid it on the desk between us, then flipped open the cover to reveal several glossy pages of orderable caskets. "I'd be happy to show you some of my personal favorites. Of course, feel free to take your time looking at the selection." He cleared his throat. "Mrs. Dippel . . . Mr. Dippel was my Phys-Ed teacher for two years and . . ."

I listened as the young man's voice cracked. "Thank you, Hugh," I said. I laid my hand against the slick pages between us. "Do you mind if my daughter and I take some time to look at these?"

"Not at all," he said, then stood. "Why don't I give you two a few minutes alone. Can I offer you a cup of coffee, some water . . ."

We both declined.

Hugh left, then returned about fifteen minutes later. By this time Olivia had picked out Jack's casket, something I allowed her to do. It felt to me as though she needed this last gift to her father. Hugh declared the choice to be "fine" and then walked us through the remaining items necessary for death and burial.

He asked about Jack's life insurance. To my surprise, Olivia whipped a large manila envelope from her hobo purse.

"What's that?" I asked.

"Dad's papers," she said.

"How'd you . . ."

"He showed me a few weeks ago."

It struck me then that Jack had prepared himself and his daughter for his possible death but had left me out of the mix. How could he have?

I sat in stony silence as Olivia went over the details of her father's insurance policies, all of them. Three total. Listened as she talked about the money in his savings account and how I would write a check from it to cover the expenses. Automatically I dipped my hand into my purse, pulled out the joint savings account checkbook, and handed it to Olivia. She scooted up in her chair, laid the checkbook open against the dark grain of the desk, then wrote the date, the name of the funeral home, the exorbitant amount Hugh had just quoted, and then slipped the book toward me as she extended the pen. "Here, Mom. You'll need to sign it."

I wrote my name like an obedient child.

Olivia tore out the check, handed it to Hugh, then folded the checkbook closed and handed it back to me. When she stood, I followed her lead. When she shook Hugh's hand, I did the same.

Hugh—who had stood, put the check in the new file with Jack's name printed neatly on it, and placed the file atop other files—escorted us toward the door. I moved behind my daughter, feeling more like a zombie than a widow, more like a widow than a wife. I stopped as Hugh opened the door, pausing before the second desk in the tiny office. I glanced down at it, noted the nameplate sitting askew near the front left corner. I reached out and straightened it, then took a deep breath as I slowly read the name.

Andrew J. Morrow, it read.

The following days were a blur. Vonnie told me—in a precious private moment—that eventually it would all come back. At first I questioned how she knew, then remembered she had lost her first husband. I wondered about the details—probably for the first time since I'd learned about Joseph Jewel—of his death, his funeral, and all those two things entail. I knew she'd given birth to David shortly after hearing that her husband had died. I felt so sad to think I'd never asked for enough details to put together a complete picture.

Widows, I decided, need to share details of their sorrow.

When they could, that is.

———

Monday evening marked a week since Jack had died. Seven days toward an endless list of days my life would be spent without him. But not without Olivia. She and Tony had somehow managed to arrange for Tony's parents to keep the kids while Olivia kept *me*. She had taken to running my house and my life as though she'd been born to do it. She made certain all my family members got to the airport in plenty of time. She'd made an appointment with Chris— my boss and the attorney who would probate Jack's estate—and then drove me to it. She then brought me back home and, while I took a much-needed nap, straightened the house and then made a supper of leftovers and fresh-made baked corn.

We ate around 6:00. Spoke little. We cleared the table and did the dishes in silence. Then Olivia said, "Mom, I'm going to run home for a little while and then I'll be back." She hung the limp drying cloth over the handle of the refrigerator. "Will you be okay alone or would you rather ride with me?"

I leaned against the counter, where I stood rubbing hand lotion into the palms of my hands and around the backs. "Olivia. Seriously, honey. You need to go home to your family."

"But Mom—"

"No buts, Olivia. You can't take care of me forever. I'm a grown woman and I will have to be left alone eventually."

I watched her slump her shoulders and cross her arms. If she cocked her hip, we were in for a fight.

She cocked her hip.

"Mom . . ."

I held up a finger. "One more night," I said, too tired to argue. Besides, one more night wouldn't hurt one way or the other.

"Are you sure?"

"I'm positive."

She sighed. "Okay, then. One more night. I'll be back in about an hour."

She left. While she was gone I decided to soak in a hot tub of water filled with bath salts. When I'd languished long enough to turn my skin to wrinkles, I drew myself out, dried off, and slipped into a favorite thick robe and matching slippers. As I ran a large-toothed comb through my hair, I heard a knock at the front door.

I gave myself a quick glance in the mirror before walking the long hallway to the living room. Expecting to see one of the girls, I swung the door open and then gasped.

"Hello, Mrs. Dippel."

I blinked several times. "Andrew," I said. "What in the world brings you here?"

The handsome young man shoved his hands into the front pockets of his jeans. Unlike his cousin, Andrew Morrow was muscular. His hair was thick, blond, and sometimes unruly. His eyes were an amazing deep shade of blue. He was still unmarried, though I often wondered how any red-blooded woman in Summit View could have possibly allowed him to stay that way this long.

"I was just wanting to come by. To check on you. It's been a week . . ."

I stepped back. "How kind of you. Would you like to come in?

86

We've got plenty of food here. Have you had your supper? Maybe some ham?"

He blushed. "No. Thank you."

"Well, would you like to come in?"

"I'd like that," he answered, then stepped over the threshold.

# 11

## Rehashing the Past

I decided to go to Doreen's that afternoon, after lunch. I served sandwiches with a tasty apple salad Vonnie had given me the recipe for. As Vernon and I ate, I avoided the topic of Doreen or Velvet or even Donna, keeping our conversation light and upbeat. Vernon, bless him, was none the wiser.

Then, after lunch, Vernon returned to work. Quick as I saw his car disappear down the road, I got in my car and drove toward the trailer park where Doreen and Velvet shared a home. I half-prayed and half-hoped Doreen would be there when I arrived and not at the nearby Gold Rush Tavern, where she worked most afternoons and evenings. Sure enough, when I pulled into the short drive, I saw Doreen's car parked alongside the trailer. Velvet's car, however, was nowhere in sight, and for that I breathed a sigh of relief. The last thing I wanted or needed was another confrontation with *her*.

Before leaving my car, I offered up a prayer to God, asking for his mercy and guidance. "Give me the right words to say, Lord," I whispered into the stillness of the car. Then I grabbed my purse on the seat beside me and slipped out of my automobile and into the chill. It seemed to me that since I'd left home not fifteen minutes earlier, the wind had picked up and the temperature had dropped about ten degrees, give or take. I shoved my arms across my middle, ducked my head, and marched toward the front deck.

When I reached the door, I raised my hand to knock, then paused. Sounds from the interior of the old 1960s trailer indicated another person was inside. I listened intently, but I couldn't make out the voices. One was definitely male, one female. But the tones were whispered and hurried, not spoken in a normal rhythm.

I figured it was the television, took a breath, sighed, and knocked. Then knocked again for good measure.

The whispering inside ceased before footsteps inched toward the door from the other side.

I took a step back, knowing that the door opened from the inside, out. Just as I did, an automobile pulled into a nearby driveway. Another whip of the wind cut around the corner of the house, and I crossed my arms again as I looked over my shoulder. Wade Gage's truck rumbled to a stop before he slid out, nodded toward me, then ran into his trailer.

When Doreen's door creaked open, I jumped, startled. "Oh!" I said.

Only Doreen's head was shoved between the door and the frame. The rest of her remained safely inside. "Evangeline," her voice croaked. "What do you want?"

"I need to talk to you."

She sighed. "Now is not a good time."

I crossed my arms again. "Why not?" I remembered the voices from inside. What if the voices weren't the television? "Who's in there with you?" An old angst welled up inside me. Doreen—who'd been my childhood best friend, who'd known my feelings for Vernon all the way back then when we'd all been no more than twelve years old and foolish with our emotions—had deliberately stolen him from me with her loose ways. She'd allowed him to kiss her on the mouth—something my mother would have whipped me for, had she found out—and with that action came what then seemed like a lifetime of his devotion to her. Now, with his marriage to me, I wondered if once again she was stealing him from me. Was it my husband who was inside this broken-down mobile home? When Doreen didn't answer right away, I said, "Well?"

"It's just not a good time, Evangeline."

My mind searched the surroundings. Vernon's car wasn't anywhere to be seen; that much was for sure. Still . . . "Who's in there with you, Doreen?"

She sighed again. I smelled stale coffee and cigarettes on her breath. Well, at least it wasn't whiskey and cigarettes. "No one is in here with me, Evangeline. Now, shoo on home."

"I heard voices."

"When?"

"Before I knocked. I heard voices."

Doreen slipped out the door then but not without me trying my best to peek inside. She shut the door behind her, leaving me without any further clue as to what might be going on. I watched as she ran tobacco-stained fingers through her short, damaged hair. She leaned her backside against the door, pulled one foot up as though to brace it shut, then crossed her arms. "You heard the television, is all."

I raised my chin and tried to think everything through in as brief a time as possible. Then, realizing this wasn't why I'd come, I said, "Doreen, I want to come inside. I want to talk to you about something."

"Whatever it is, say it right here."

I dropped my arms. "Oh, *why* must we always be at odds? Every time I think things are going to be okay with us, something goes wrong."

Doreen set her jaw even as she spoke. "And I suppose that 'something' is me."

I swallowed. "I'm not saying that. However, you and I wouldn't have had any altercation the other night had it not been for your drinking."

"Leave my drinking out of this. If *you* had my life . . . if *you* were living in a tin can working day and night as a barmaid . . . without a husband to help with the finances and with your kids strewed willy-nilly . . . and if *you* had a daughter who hardly recognized you as her mother . . . *you* might drink too." By now Doreen had one fist at her side and the index finger of the other hand pointed toward my face.

"Maybe," I admitted. "And maybe not." I pressed my lips together, then said, "I'm here because I care for you, Doreen. I care *about* you. I want to encourage you to get help for your problems in other ways besides alcohol. Like I told Velvet—"

Doreen's foot slid from the door to the pine boards of the deck. "You talked to Velvet? You talked to my baby?" She crossed her arms again. "Who do you think you are?" she asked, her words clipped and precise.

"Doreen, I—"

"No! I don't want you talking to my baby!"

"She's not a baby," I shot back. "And she's the one who accosted me on the sidewalk in front of God and everybody else in Summit View. It was embarrassing. Humiliating! Who did she think *she* was?"

I realized too late how loud I had become. A quick look toward Wade's trailer showed the blinds at the window facing Doreen and me being pulled up, Wade looking toward us, then dropping the blinds when he spied me spying him. I dropped my voice. I looked back at the fragile, pitiful woman standing near me. "Doreen," I said, my voice whisper soft, "I just want to say that *if* you want to get help, I'm here for you. I know we've had our problems in the past, but they are in the past. I genuinely mean this."

Doreen's eyes narrowed then relaxed before she leaned against the door again. This time both her feet stayed planted on the floor-boards, but her arms crossed over the washed-out T-shirt that seemed to hang on her frail frame. "I'll think about it."

"Think about . . . what will you think about?" I was now a little lost. "Think about what I said? Think about my sincerity? Think about going into some kind of rehab program?"

The rise of her voice startled me. "Rehab? Are you completely out of your mind, Evangeline Vesey?"

Doreen's shouting ceased as we both heard a door open and close. We turned to look toward Wade's trailer, saw him bound down his front steps and then make a beeline to and into his truck. He appeared to ignore us as he started the engine and then drove out of his driveway. When his truck had disappeared down the road and around the bend, I turned back to Doreen, who said, "Wonder what that boy is thinking about the two of us out here?"

"He's probably wondering why you haven't asked me inside. He's probably wondering why two grown women are fighting outside a trailer on a front porch deck. I know that's what I'm wondering."

Doreen shifted. "I don't want to talk about this anymore, Evangeline. I just want to go inside and get ready for my workday." She looked at her wristwatch. "I didn't realize how late it was getting, and I haven't had a shower or nothing."

I nodded. "Okay, then. I'll leave. I understand you don't want to talk about this. I was just hoping . . ."

"Look, Evangeline," Doreen said. Her voice was now gentle, laced with sadness. "I want to tell you something. I want to tell you that I'm sorry about what happened all those years ago."

I blinked. "You mean between you and Vernon?"

She blinked back, then shook her head. "Goodness, no. I'm talking about after Vernon and I got married. I'm talking about leaving here with . . ." She swallowed, then lowered her voice. "Horace Shelly." She took a deep breath, sighed, then continued. "I'm wishing I'd never gotten involved with that man." Tears pooled in her eyes.

"You don't know . . . you don't know what I know about a man like that. A man who sees your vulnerable side as a woman and then uses it. Preys on it. Convinces you to leave your husband—and Vernon was a good husband—and your little girl. An innocent little girl who didn't deserve the mess I'd become as a person but surely didn't deserve what I left her with. Not that I would have taken her with me. Horace wouldn't have allowed it."

The air went still around me. For a moment it seemed that time was suspended, that I'd been dropped into the middle of an intense scene within a movie or a book. It was as if I was supposed to know the words to say next, and yet they wouldn't come to mind. Finally I whispered, "What *did* happen, Doreen? You've told me before about everything that happened after you left, but you've never talked about what went wrong between you and Vernon."

"Hasn't Vernon told you?" She raised her brow.

"No," I said. "He has never spoken ill of you, Doreen. That much I can say for sure. You are and always will be Donna's mother, and no matter what, he won't say an ill word against you."

The tears that had lingered in the wells of her eyes now spilled down her cheeks. She pointed toward my car and said, "Let's go down here."

I noticed chill bumps popping out up and down her arms. "Doreen, you're cold. Let's go inside and talk," I coaxed.

But she shook her head as she walked past me, down the steps, and toward the car. I followed like a puppy, though it was Doreen who looked more like the lost dog. "Doreen," I said. "Doreen."

She kept walking. "Just come on," she said. When she reached my car, she opened the driver's door as though to encourage me to get inside, but I resisted, instead shutting the door and leaning against it as she'd done to her trailer door earlier. Doreen might not want me in her house, but she was not going to force me into my car.

"Talk to me," I said.

93

She shook her head but spoke anyway. "I'd never really dated anyone other than Vernon when we were in school, you know that."

"I do."

"I mean, when Vernon and me were on the outs, I might go out with this one or that one, but I was true to him all the way." She swallowed. "Vernon and I did things we should not have done, you know, before we married, but I swear to you I was never with another man until . . ." I watched her eyes glance toward the trailer and then back to me. "Until Horace." She laughed sardonically. "I was never so scared in my life as when he started coming on to me. Scared and excited all at the same time. Vernon was . . . Vernon was always gone, you know? Always off on patrol. Trying to earn his way to being the sheriff around here. I've never seen anyone in my life work so hard to get somewhere in life. He was driven."

"Well, he's good at what he does."

"Yes. Yes." She crossed her arms again but this time without the anger. This time as though she were trying to keep herself from falling down. Or falling apart; I couldn't tell which.

"So what happened?" I prodded.

"Donna was four. Ever been around a four-year-old 24/7?"

"No."

"Well, it's not always so much fun for the adult. Suddenly you find yourself at home all the time with a little one, watching *Bozo* and *Sesame Street* and reading books with simple words and never having time for your own kind of reading or your own kind of television. Every day it's the same old thing. And Donna . . . Donna was a whiner back then. That girl managed to find something to cry about every single day. If she couldn't find her toys, she cried. If she wanted to watch something on television and it wasn't on, she cried. If she wanted SpaghettiOs and all I had was canned ravioli, you would have thought the world had come to an end."

I couldn't help it, I chuckled.

"And so it just seemed to happen, Evangeline. I was lonely. I was bored. And Horace Shelly offered an adventure I thought I was entitled to. Lord knows what it got me, that adventure."

"I'm sorry, Doreen."

"Me too. Like I said, meeting that man was the worst thing that ever happened to me, even with all the other bad things that happened after he and I parted ways."

"Have you told Donna how you feel about those days?"

"No."

"You should."

"Maybe I will. One day." She stepped back. "Go home, Evangeline, and I promise I'll think about what you're saying. I do know I drink too much. I know I've got to get a handle on things." She glanced back at the trailer again. "Sometimes, though, life has a way . . ." I saw the tears pool again in her eyes, then spill down her cheeks once more. "Life has a way of coming around to bite you in the rear end, you know?"

I didn't know. But I nodded all the same. "Yes, I know."

Doreen reached for my arm, wrapped her bony fingers around my wrist, and squeezed. "Be careful, Evie."

*Evie.* Not a name Doreen called me by. "Be careful of what?" I asked.

She squeezed again. "Just be careful." She stepped away from me then. Stepped away, turned her back, and then walked toward the trailer. Her head hung low between her shoulders, and her steps seemed numbered.

How numbered I wouldn't find out until the next day.

# 12

## Family Dinner

I glanced out my kitchen window as I poured tea into five of my tall, blue tumblers. The sun had just settled behind the peaks that stood guard over our valley. The surrounding mountains glowed pale yellow while a darkening sky winked the first stars of evening. I was glad the wind had died down, though it left a cold shiver in its wake. "David, are you going to be able to stay warm on your shift later tonight? I hear it's going to hit twenty degrees before sunrise."

David, who stood next to me, plopped ice into the tumblers. "Donna's on duty too, so if I can get her to take her coffee breaks with me, I'll be warm enough," he said.

I laughed as I helped David whisk the tumblers to the table, where my mother and dad already sat, waiting for me to pull my onion and cheese meatloaf from the oven.

Soon enough, the meatloaf sat cooling on a ceramic trivet, surrounded by CorningWare bowls filled with mashed potatoes, green beans, and, of course, warm dinner rolls. Fred, who had been tending the fire in the fireplace a few feet from our kitchen table, hurried over to join us. As he sat beside me, David cleared his throat. "May I have the honor of saying grace?" he asked as if he were a shy schoolboy.

Pleased, I nodded and closed my eyes. David reached for my hand and gave it a squeeze. "Lord, I'm still new at talking to you, but I want to say I so appreciate all you've done for me. Thank you for my family and my new life in Summit View. Amen."

I squeezed David's hand in return, then used my dinner napkin to blot the moisture gathering in the corners of my eyes. It was so sweet to have found my boy after all these years. I looked across the table at my mother, the very woman who had kept him from me. I was glad when I saw that she too was moved by David's prayer.

It was getting harder to hold a grudge against her, especially now that she regretted her role in secretly giving David up for adoption after telling me my child had died at birth.

But tonight, I told myself, none of that mattered. We were a family that was healing from the wounds we'd inflicted on ourselves. I reached for the rolls and took one before passing the platter on.

As my dad put a roll on his plate, he looked up at Fred. "How's that church remodeling going?"

Fred ran his forefinger over his upper lip and narrowed his eyes, as if picturing the progress. "Not bad. We've laid the foundation for the youth wing, and so things are starting to take shape."

Mother, who was already buttering her roll, asked, "But aren't you going to remodel the sanctuary too?"

I fielded the question as I reached for my dish of green beans. "We wouldn't dare touch its charm, at least not the front of the sanctuary. A lot of that old stone and all is original. We want to stay true to our colorful history."

"What kind of history are we talking about?" David asked as he helped himself to the mashed potatoes before smothering them in thick gravy.

I sliced into the butter and spread it over my steaming roll. "Our church was founded by Father John Dyer, a circuit preacher who made his rounds here in the high country when our little town of Summit View was nothing but a mining camp. He walked his rounds in the summer, but in the winter, he snowshoed from camp to camp."

Mother stopped heaping green beans onto her plate and broke into the telling. "Those snowshoes, as Father Dyer called them, were really eleven-foot-long split pines."

"Sounds like cross-country skiing to me," David said.

"That's about right." Fred chuckled. "Our church was started by a fire-and-brimstone cross-country-skiing evangelist."

David laughed outright. "That *is* colorful." He took a bite of my meatloaf. "This is good," he said, glancing up at me. "It's my newest favorite Mom meal."

"Glad you like it."

"Just trying to make my own history with all of you," David said as he blotted the gravy off his lips with his napkin. "But the history I'd really like to know is Donna's. You were her Sunday school teacher back in the day, right, Mom?"

I gave my mashed potatoes a fresh coat of pepper. "I was. She was in my fifth grade class."

"What was she like as a little girl?"

"My heart went out to her. She was kind of shy and awkward." I stood, walked to the hearth, and pulled out the picture Donna had recently framed for my birthday, then showed it to David. I watched him study a younger me with my class of grade-schoolers, my hand on the shoulder of then ten-year-old Donna with her tangled blonde hair and mismatched clothes.

Mother, who sat on the other side of David, leaned in for a look. "Donna looks like an orphan."

"Why is that?" David asked, leaning his elbows on the table, concern in his voice.

Mother was happy to explain. "She was motherless after Doreen

98

took off with that old choir director. How that woman could have left her husband and precious daughter, I'll never know."

I shot Mother a look, then glanced back at David. "Mother's right. Donna certainly missed her mom," I said gently. "Which is why I took her under my wing."

"That you did," Mother replied, pointing at me with her empty fork. "You dragged that girl all over town. Still do."

"It was my pleasure," I said, glancing back at David. "But my favorite memories of her are the ones of her here in my kitchen. I taught her how to cook and even make brownies. Plus, we spent many afternoons discussing our Sunday school lesson. It was here, right here at this table, where she found the Lord."

David grinned. "Same as me."

"Finding the Lord didn't keep Donna out of trouble," Mother interrupted. "She still fooled around with that Wade boy, home alone after school. I'd see his truck in front of her house while her dad was at work. It's a wonder she didn't end up pregnant."

Fred and I stared at our plates for a second, knowing but not wanting to tell Mother that Donna had indeed gotten pregnant by Wade at seventeen, though it was a pregnancy that sadly had not come to fruition.

David broke the awkward silence. "Mom, why did Dee Dee leave Vernon? Do you know?"

"Doreen? She was another one who spent hours around my kitchen table. I did my best to help her, but . . ."

"I knew you two were friends," Mother said as if she were reprimanding me, "but I've never heard a thing about you trying to help her."

"It was me she'd call when she was lonely for Vernon. His job took him away from her too many evenings to count. She thought having a child would ease her loneliness, but—"

Mother interrupted, "So then why didn't you get her more involved in the church?"

"I did, Mother. I got her to join the choir. She had such a lovely voice."

"That she did," Mother agreed as she looked around the table. "And does to this day, as I remember from our Christmas Tea."

"So what went wrong?" David asked, reaching for his tumbler of tea. "What caused Dee Dee to leave her family?"

"She had an incurable case of the blues. When she started to get a little attention from Horace . . ."

"Horace?" David asked.

"I'm surprised no one's discussed this with you before; Horace was the church choir director," Mother answered for me as she dabbed what was left of her roll into her gravy. "Never liked that little weasel, myself."

I pushed a green bean with my fork before looking up. "She was desperate for approval, and he flattered her," I continued. "He was around when Vernon was busy. He told her she should be singing professionally, on the country music stage, with him."

Mother snorted. "We know how that worked out."

I patted the back of Fred's chair. "I sat right here in this chair and tried to tell her. I held hands with her, cried with her, prayed with her. I tried to warn her . . . but she wouldn't listen. She said that, as a fallen woman, she was such a pitiful mother, Donna would be better off without her." I sighed. "I just couldn't get through, and the next thing I knew she and Horace were planning their getaway. That next Sunday, they stood up in front of the church and sang one last duet in front of Donna and Vernon and . . . well . . . everyone. Little did we know that was to be their farewell performance. After that service, Doreen and Horace ran off together. They never looked back."

"Doreen finally came home," Mother said, pulling her brows into a scowl. "So, she did look back. And she gave us all a chance to see the mess she'd made of her life."

"Mother," I said sternly. "Try to be kind."

Mother looked up at me as if she were stunned. "My dear, it's just an observation. I can't help but notice these things, you know."

David sliced his fork into his meatloaf and stared back at me. "Poor Donna," he finally said. "How glad I am she found you, Mom."

Dad, who was not one to gossip, was ready to change the subject. He leaned back in his chair and rubbed his full belly. "So, what's for dessert?"

"My apple pie's still in the oven, Dad," I said, pushing my chair back from the table, "but maybe I should check it."

I walked over to the oven and peeked inside. The lattice crust was still a bit underbaked. I shut the oven door and walked back to the table, where I slid into my seat, noticing that David had somehow finished his entire plate of food.

"Help yourself to seconds," I said. He smiled and reached for the meatloaf.

"Now that I've shared a bit of history with you, I'm wondering about your history, David."

David looked up from heaping a large second helping of mashed potatoes onto his plate.

His brows rose quizzically. "What would you like to know?"

"About this Bobbie who's coming in a few days to visit you. You two were engaged?"

David shot a look at Fred, who said, "Sorry, son. That sorta slipped out."

David looked back at me. "Yes, we were. She left me for Derek, my former best friend."

I leaned back in my chair and turned to study my son. "Ah, so she's married now."

He looked up at me, a bit sheepish. "Well, not exactly. It seems they broke up."

Mother pushed her plate back and piped up. "Is that why she's coming to see you?"

"No, no. She's just a friend now. She's coming to town to look at properties for her boss."

Mother snorted. "So she says."

David shrugged his shoulders. "It's true. She was my mother's personal assistant and now she's working for Wayne Scott."

Fred, who was still leaning back in his chair, asked, "The big Hollywood producer?"

David looked up from his mashed potatoes. "Yeah, and I guess he's thinking about buying a house in Aspen."

"This isn't Aspen," Mother said as she stared over the top of her new bifocals. "So, what's she doing coming around here?"

"Summit View is on the way to Aspen from the Denver airport."

"But why didn't she take a direct flight from LA to Aspen? They have those, you know," Mother said as she folded her hands together where her plate had until recently resided.

David shrugged. "She says she wants to talk to me."

Fred and I exchanged glances. "Son, do you know why?" he asked.

David shook his head. "It's nothing personal; it's just one friend visiting with another. That's all."

"That's all, my eye," Mother said before turning to me. "Is something burning?"

I scooted my chair back so fast I almost tipped it over. As I scurried to the oven, I called to David over my shoulder. "Does Donna know about Bobbie?"

"Yeah, I told her."

I opened the oven door and saw my pie was a tad dark. I reached for my pot holders and pulled it out and set it on top of the stove to cool.

"Did you burn it?" Mother called out.

"Not too bad," I said, hoping a little vanilla ice cream might hide the damage. I turned and looked back at my son as I opened the freezer door and pulled out my carton of ice cream. "Did you tell her Bobbie was your ex?"

David looked worried, and he studied the last bit of green beans on his plate before looking back at me. "Ah, no. Somehow that just hasn't come up."

Before I could find my words, Mother filled in the silence. "Well, then, this is going to get interesting."

# 13

## Stirring Disaster

David and I sat in my Bronco over our respective mugs of hot coffee, watching the Gold Mine Bank's digital sign blink a message that it was a cozy twenty-eight degrees at 2:00 in the morning.

David, in his paramedics uniform, snuggled next to me as much for warmth as for affection. It had been a slow night for both of us. I was glad that no one had been injured on any of our roadways, but slow nights were dull. In between my patrol routes and a couple of games of solitaire on my onboard computer, I'd sent a few text messages back and forth to David on my cell. That's how we'd finally decided to take our break at the bank's drive-thru. Higher Grounds Café was closed until dawn. That meant the cab of my Bronco was one of the warmest places we could meet. I opened my lunch sack and pulled out a Tupperware container of brownies.

"What's this?" David asked.

"Oh, I whipped up a batch of Gold Rush brownies for our break."

So help me if David didn't look touched. "My mom taught you how to make these, didn't she?"

I nodded, impressed. "How did you know?"

Before he could answer, my cell rang. I stared down at the caller ID. "Who is it?" David asked.

I felt my eyebrows arch as I pressed my lips together. "Hmm—it's Wade."

"You aren't going to take it, are you?"

"Well, it's a bit unusual for him to call so late. Maybe something's wrong." I clicked into the call. "Hello, Wade?"

Wade sounded pleased to hear my voice. "Hey, Donna. I was having trouble sleeping so I thought why not make some hot cocoa and invite you over. You must be just about frozen out there tonight."

"Thanks for the offer, but . . ."

"You gotta take a break sometime, right? Why not with me?"

"Well, ah, as a matter of fact, David and I are on break now."

"Oh, oh. Sure. Yeah, I forgot about David." His voice sounded cheery but forced. "Well, bring him along then."

I smiled at David and shook my head. "Maybe another time, okay?"

"Sure," Wade said, the hurt in his voice sending me a twinge of regret. "Sure, another time." He continued trying to pretend as if feeling rejected was easy for him.

We said our good-byes, and David asked, "What was that about?"

I shrugged. "He wanted us to drop by for some cocoa."

David gave me a knowing grin. "He wanted *you* to drop by, not so much me, that's what I'm thinking."

I had to laugh. "Maybe, but let's not talk about Wade."

"Why not?" David said. "You're not still seeing him? Are you?"

I was glad the darkness hid my blush. I shook my head. "No, but back to your friend from LA who's coming to visit. So, when does Bobby arrive and when do I meet him?"

David frowned. "Bobbie will be in a rush to get to Aspen, but I'll check into it."

"Oh, come on, David. You know all my friends, but I've never met a single one of your friends. So, let me in on this little visit."

"Well, I guess there are some things I should explain—"

My phone rang again, and I checked the caller ID.

"Wade?" David asked.

I nodded. "I'll get rid of him."

"Don't pick up."

I shook my head. "What if—"

David laughed. "What if . . . something's wrong. I know, it's the cop in you. Tell your *boyfriend* good night, okay?"

"He's not my boyfriend," I mouthed as I clicked into the call. "Hello, Wade? Long time no hear."

A terrible wail came from the phone. I pulled it back and stared at it for a second before replacing it to my ear, in time to hear Wade say, "Donna, you and David—you gotta—come—now. *Now!*"

"Wade? Is everything all right?"

The shrieking grew louder. "No. It's Velvet. She just came over here, pounding on my door, screaming something about her mother."

"Is Mom okay?"

"I . . . I'm not sure."

I began to make out Velvet's voice as she continued to scream, "I tried to tell Donna. I tried to tell her. That Evie woman is a witch."

I ran my hand through my hair and looked at David. "What's this about? Did Evie have another fight with my mother?"

"Well, yeah, I think so, but I'll tell you about that later. I think Velvet needs help, maybe a sedative or something, and you . . . you need to check on your mother."

I hung up a bit rattled and told David what I'd heard. We decided to drive our emergency vehicles over without our sirens blaring in case this was some sort of family theatrics authored by Velvet. Or even my mother. As I pulled into the trailer park, I could see Velvet in a halo of light standing on Wade's porch. She was wrapped in a blanket, shivering in Wade's arms. But what disturbed me was the way she was sobbing, in deep gulps, barely able to breathe.

"What's going on?" I asked as I hopped out of the cab of my truck and ran toward them.

Wade shook his head, meaning he didn't have a clue. I turned back to see David's white and red ambulance as it crunched the gravel before it pulled to a stop in front of Mom's trailer. I turned back and approached Velvet. "What is it? Velvet, what's happened?"

"I told you," Velvet practically growled. "I warned you."

I stood in front of her, nose to nose, my hands on my hips. "You warned me of what?"

"That woman, that stepmother of yours. You wouldn't listen, and now she's dead!"

I froze, my hand instinctively resting on the handle of my gun. "What did you say?"

Velvet dropped her blanket. Her pale, bare arms flailed around her, almost knocking Wade in the chin as he dodged the blow. She said, "It's that Evie woman. She, she . . ."

"Is Evie in there? Did someone hurt Evie?"

Velvet offered a high-pitched laugh, and I visually checked her to see if she showed evidence of an injury or a struggle. I mean, I barely knew my sister or what she was capable of. Had she lured Evie over to the trailer in the middle of the night and attacked her?

"Is Evie hurt?" I demanded.

Velvet shook her head no, unable to express herself through her hysterics. I took a step back and pointed at her dark trailer illuminated by a nearby streetlight. Even in the dim light, it looked unkempt, even forlorn. "Where? Where is she then? Can you show me?"

Velvet was crying so hard she could only shake her head.

I kept my voice steady. "Is she in the trailer?"

Velvet nodded, her face now pressed into Wade's chest.

My heart pounded. I pulled my gun from my holster. I held it in one hand, with the barrel pointing skyward. I held my flashlight in the other hand as I turned and stared at Mom's trailer.

David, who was now standing a few paces away, took a step toward me. "You might need backup. You're going to call this in before you go in there, right?"

"Yeah. Though I'm not sure what's happened."

"All the more reason to call," David coaxed. I holstered my gun and pulled my radio off my shoulder strap. "Officer needs backup at the Higher Grounds Trailer Park. Possible injury or . . ." I swallowed hard. "Homicide."

Thelma, who had been my dispatch friend this evening, responded, "Ten-four. Will dispatch backup to the trailer park."

I turned back to Velvet. "What exactly did you see?"

Velvet was shivering harder now, perhaps from the cold or even from shock. Wade redraped the blanket around her bare shoulders, and she held the wrap together with a hand at the nape of her neck. From the look of things, Velvet was just coming in from a night of partying as she was wearing her fitted black jeans and, beneath the blanket, a shimmering halter top. I could smell alcohol on her breath. Was that what this was all about—Velvet's drunken rage?

"Mom" was all she would say before her sobbing began again.

"Mom?" I asked. "Is anyone in there with her?"

Velvet shook her head no but said, "Evie."

"Evie's in there, at this hour? Are you sure?"

Wade interrupted. "I saw her, for what that's worth."

I turned and looked at the cowboy. He had on his camel-colored fringe jacket and cowboy hat, his company-best clothes. Why was he dressed like that at this hour? Feeling more confused by the moment, I said, "Let me get this straight, Wade. You saw Evie at the trailer?"

"Yeah, earlier this afternoon. She and, ah, Dee Dee, were exchanging words."

It was then my backup, Jerry, arrived. With his sheriff's Bronco in full emergency mode with lights twirling and siren blasting, I could see through the windshield that he'd been pulled out of bed by the call. As he pulled beside the trailer, his siren blipped into silence while his rotating lights caused the trailer park to explode into alternating bursts of red and blue.

I rushed to greet him as he climbed out of his truck. He was a heavyset man who wore his once-blond hair shaved to hide a receding hairline. "What's the trouble here?" he asked as he studied Velvet and Wade.

"Something is wrong inside," I said, pointing to Mom's trailer. "I'm thinking there was some sort of struggle. Since this is my mom's house, I didn't think I should go in there, alone, in case . . . well. Glad you're here."

"Do you suspect foul play?"

I nodded slowly. "Maybe."

Jerry took charge. He whipped out his gun and held it with the barrel up. "Follow me," he demanded.

I drew my gun too as I followed Jerry up the front steps. I braced myself flat against the wall beside the door while Jerry leaned over from the other side to knock. "Sheriff's department," he barked. "Open up."

No answer.

Velvet called from Wade's front porch only a few feet away. "She won't answer, I told you that. I told you."

I ignored her babble and tentatively cracked the door open. "Mom?" I called into the darkness. "Evie?" I pulled out my flashlight and shone it inside.

The place was a wreck—with chairs toppled and . . . wait, what was *that*?

The beam of my flashlight illuminated a shoe on the floor.

Jerry pushed past me, and his voice remained calm. "Donna, step back."

"Why?" I demanded, looking at his softly illuminated face. Even in this dim light I could see beads of sweat pop across his face and down his neck.

He hesitated before he answered. "It's a body."

"What?" I steadied the beam of my light on the tennis shoe before realizing it was attached to an ankle.

I stepped through the threshold and allowed my beam to travel up jeaned legs, a T-shirted torso, then a gray, horrified face with unblinking, cloudy blue eyes.

"Mom?"

Jerry pulled me back. "I don't think she can hear you."

I sucked in my breath. "Maybe she's just fainted."

"Get David," Jerry said.

I stumbled back to the door and signaled. "You're needed," was all I could say.

David rushed in, illuminating his footsteps with his flashlight. He didn't hit the lights because Jerry and I hadn't. We couldn't, that is, until we determined if this was a crime scene.

As David checked on my mother, I flicked the beam of my flashlight around the scene. Yes, there had been some sort of struggle here from the looks of this room. Not only were chairs on their sides, but the coffee table next to Mom was covered in a puddle of beer. At least that's what I made from the fact that there was an empty beer bottle on the floor.

I watched the back of David as he leaned over my mom, taking her pulse. He looked up and shook his head. "I'm sorry, Donna—but Dee Dee is gone."

I stepped backward, reeling. I turned and looked out the front door, noticing a crowd of neighbors was gathering in front of the trailer as Velvet continued to scream on Wade's front porch, "It was that Evie woman. She's gone and killed my mother! I tried to warn you! You wouldn't listen! Why wouldn't you listen?"

# 14

## Bite to Eat

I had called Evangeline Monday afternoon after work to ask if she'd like to go by Goldie's with me on Tuesday. "I thought I'd take her a breakfast casserole," I said. "I'm sure she has plenty of casseroles, meats, and desserts to last her a lifetime, and I don't want her to stop eating breakfast."

"That would be the first thing I'd do," Evie said from the other end of the line. "If anything happened to Vernon, I'd just quit eating and I'd begin with breakfast."

"I was thinking the same thing," I told her.

"I went by to see her, but she wasn't home."

"I wonder where she was." I walked from the kitchen, where I'd retrieved the cordless phone from its perch, to the family room to sit in my favorite corner of the sofa. "I do hope she wasn't home and just not answering the door."

"No. I saw her car at Chris's office. Lisa Leann said she was there to take care of some, you know . . . business."

I heard clanging and clattering from the other end. "What in the world are you doing?" I asked.

Evie sighed. "Well, if you must know, I'm working like a maniac now to get supper ready."

I shook my head. I knew that Evie stayed busy with her home-based business, but I never understood how a woman who worked from home would have to rush to get supper ready. With that thought, I looked at my watch. It was 4:30 and Samuel would be home within the hour. I, too, had best get dinner prepared, I thought, though I'd surely had less time than Evangeline. "Why do you wait so late to start?" I asked. "If I were at home all day—even if I were working—I'd start dinner before noon."

"Wouldn't it be cold by the time Samuel got home?" she came back. "Besides, I've had a very hectic day."

I stood to walk to the kitchen. "Oh? What have you been up to?"

"I had to go talk to Doreen."

"Doreen?"

"Long story. I'll fill you in tomorrow. What time do you want to go to Goldie's?"

"I'm off tomorrow, actually. I have some things I need to do concerning my mother. So, how about I meet you there at 9:00?"

"I'll be there at 9:00, then," she said. "Vernon should be out of the door by that time."

"Good."

"Do you want me to call Goldie to let her know we'll be stopping by?"

"Would you?"

"Sure."

———

The next morning I pulled into Goldie's driveway immediately behind Evie. I slipped the egg casserole off the passenger's seat before exiting the car and meeting Evie at hers.

112

"How are you this morning?" I asked her. We walked toward the front door of Goldie's home.

"Sleepy. Vernon got a call at about 3:00 this morning."

"Goodness. What in the world?"

"I have no idea. He's been gone ever since, and I haven't heard a word from him."

I stopped at the front porch steps. With one hand on the wrought iron railing and my left foot on the bottom step, I stopped and said, "Well, you don't look sleepy. You look absolutely marvelous this morning. Is that a new sweater?"

Evie nodded. "It is. I'm beginning to think that pink really is my color." Then she frowned.

"Why the frown? Are you worried about Vernon?"

Evie shook her head. "Oh no. But whatever has happened must be a doozy."

The front door opened, and we both looked up to see Goldie, well-dressed in a skirt and matching sweater and ready for company. "Good morning, my friends," she said.

Minutes later the three of us sat around Goldie's kitchen table, eating the egg casserole and sipping on orange juice from tall glasses that winked at us in the morning sunlight spilling from eastern windows.

"How are you doing, Goldie?" I asked her. "You look good but . . . really. How are you doing?"

Goldie's eyes misted over, but she shook her head as though willing herself not to cry. "I'm doing okay." She forced a smile. "You have no idea how much there is to do when someone dies. I suppose it's all to keep one grounded."

"Oh, I do," Evie said. "I won't pretend that losing a parent or even both parents is the same as losing a spouse, but I handled everything when mine died."

Evie's parents had been killed in a car accident years ago.

113

Although her sister had come from the East Coast to help, eventually the bulk of it all fell on Evangeline.

I reached over and patted her hand. "Those were tough days," I said to her so as not to diminish what she'd gone through. I turned back to Goldie. "What's next for you?"

Goldie took a bite of food, then swallowed. "I'm going through Jack's files today." She jerked her head backward. "The ones in his desk in the back. There's a small filing cabinet in one of the bedroom closets." She sort of laughed. "I have to find the key first."

"Find the key?" I asked.

"Mmm. I'm sure it's in his desk somewhere. Andrew says that usually things like that are in plain sight and not hidden like most people think."

"Andrew?" Evie asked.

Goldie nodded. "Andrew Morrow."

"From the funeral home?"

"Yes. He's been very helpful with everything."

"Andrew Morrow from the funeral home," Evie pressed.

I thought I saw Goldie blush. "Yes, Evangeline. Andrew Morrow from the funeral home."

I could see Evie's suspicion tentacles rising. "Goldie," I spoke softly. "Why is Andrew Morrow helping you . . . with everything?"

Goldie shrugged. "I suppose that's part of his job. He came by about a week after Jack's . . . passing."

Evie opened her mouth to say something, but I stopped her by continuing, "What did he say when he came by?"

Goldie's hands dropped to her lap, and she sighed. "Oh, I don't know, really. He said he was coming by to check on me. We had cake and coffee together and talked about what I should expect over the next few weeks and months—you know, the kind of things he sees in his business. He's a sweet kid."

Evie bristled. "Anyone besides me ever wonder why Dutch

Jenkins never adopted that child? I mean, Amy married Dutch when Andrew was—what—six or seven?"

"He was five. And I can't say I ever really thought about it," Goldie answered.

"What was the deal with his biological father?" Evie continued.

Goldie took a sip of juice then nodded. "I think he died."

"He died? Now, how in the world did you hear that, Goldie Dippel?"

"Gossip," Goldie said. "Years ago I heard . . . when Amy was pregnant . . . I heard that she'd met the young man one summer when she was working at the recreation department in Fort Collins and that they were planning to get married but that he was killed somehow. I don't know how. Car accident? I don't know."

"Have you asked him about it?"

"Evangeline!" I exclaimed. "What a thing for Goldie to ask a man young enough to be her son."

Evangeline widened her eyes at me as she said, "Well, how in the world am I supposed to know what people talk about in situations like this?" She looked again at Goldie. "What about Olivia? How is she doing?"

I was grateful the conversation was turning from Andrew and his mother to something else. For a moment there I thought Evangeline had lost her mind. Or maybe she just didn't know what I knew, that years ago Jack and Amy had had an affair. The last thing Goldie needed right now was to be reminded of Jack's past indiscretions.

"Olivia clucks over me like a hen," Goldie answered. "You'd think she was the mother and I was the child." She smiled. "Enough about all this. What about you two? What's going on?"

I finished the last of my breakfast with a quick swallow before I answered. "I have to go see about my mother today. The issues of Alzheimer's are so vast, I hardly get used to what's happening when something new comes along." I looked at my watch. "But before I go there, I'm supposed to meet Michelle for an early lunch at Higher Grounds." I laughed. "All I'm doing this morning is eating, I guess."

Evangeline shook her head. "I'm going home and going back to bed." Evie explained the events of the early morning to Goldie before raising the index finger of her right hand. "Oh, that reminds me. I went to see Doreen yesterday . . . to talk with her about getting some help for her drinking."

"Really?" I asked. "How'd that go over?"

"I actually think it went over pretty well. She brought up Horace Shelly. About all that happened years ago when she ran off with him. How she was sorry she'd left Vernon and, most especially, Donna." Evie sighed. "It really was a strange conversation."

"Where were you?" Goldie asked. "When you talked to her, I mean?"

"At her trailer. I'd gone over there to talk to her . . . to ask her to get some help for her drinking, if for no other reason than for Donna, I suppose."

"She was receptive?" I asked.

Evie shook her head. "Yes and no. No in that she wouldn't let me inside her house and yes in that she truly seemed willing to at least *think* about what I'd said to her."

I smiled. "Well, we can only hope she'll take your words to heart."

———

By the time we'd eaten and cleaned up the kitchen, it was nearly time for me to meet Michelle. I dropped by the house to brush my teeth and then drove to Higher Grounds Café, where Michelle stood waiting outside for me.

"What took you so long?" she signed as I approached her on the sidewalk, which stretched the full length of Main Street.

I gave my watch a quick look. "It's not quite 11:00," I signed back.

"I guess I'm just anxious," she said. "I really need to talk to you."

116

I looped her arm in mine and with one hand indicated we should head inside.

I'd wondered why my daughter wanted to meet with me for lunch, and with her nervous demeanor, my curiosity was piqued. We couldn't be seated fast enough or order soon enough for me.

"You took off from work today," I said when the server was done placing water with lemon on our table and taking our orders.

Michelle nodded, then added, "I had a doctor's appointment."

I froze. "Why? What's wrong?"

Michelle shook her head. "Nothing. I just had some questions."

"About?"

Michelle's shoulders dropped as she continued. "Mom, Adam and I have been talking about a family."

"A family?" I shot back. "So soon?"

Her hands flew over the next few words. "You don't understand, Mom. I'm worried about whether or not my baby could be deaf. It's hard enough to live and work within the hearing world, but what about me as a mother and . . . what if I was a deaf mother with a deaf child? I have so much to consider here, and I don't know what to do."

I leaned back in my seat. "Michelle," I began slowly. "Michelle, I've honestly not thought of this. What does Adam say about it?"

"He says that if we have a deaf child he would be the hearing parent and that I would be the parent who gives so much love it wouldn't matter that I am deaf. But . . ." She shrugged her shoulders as if to say there was little else to say.

"What did the doctor say?"

She took a sip of water before answering. "That our child has a 90 percent chance of being a hearing child."

"Well, then, what are you concerned about . . ." I stopped. "Your child? Michelle are you—"

Michelle popped her thumb against her index and middle fingers several times. "No, no, no."

117

I sighed. "Oh, good grief. You scared me."

She laughed out loud. "Would it be so horrible? If I were pregnant, I mean?"

I shook my head. "No, it wouldn't be horrible. I only mean to say that you should have plenty of time—just you and Adam—before you start thinking about a family."

"Maybe in a year," she said.

"Think of waiting at least two," I encouraged.

"Two?"

"Trust me," I said. "Life happens so quickly. Don't lose this time with your husband. Just the two of you." I thought of Goldie then. Of her being alone at this prime time in life. "It's precious," I said.

Just then the cell phone chirped from my purse. I held up a finger to Michelle, indicated I had a call, and then looked at the caller ID. It was Lisa Leann. "Hello, Lisa Leann," I said.

"Oh, good. You answered," she said. "I was afraid you'd be busy at work."

"I'm off today," I said. "I have to do some things to help with Mom."

"Oh. Well, then. What are the chances you can come by later this afternoon? By the boutique, I mean."

"The chances are good," I answered. "Why? What's going on?"

"I just got a call from Pastor Kevin. He wants us to cater a city-wide party for the Founders Day celebration coming up."

"Sounds like fun."

"We need to start planning right away," she said.

*Of course we do,* I thought. "What time should I be there?" From behind me I heard the front door bells of the café jingle their welcome. From the look on Michelle's face, it was someone she knew. But, just as quickly, the pleasant expression gave way to concern. I looked over my shoulder. Donna and Vernon—looking haggard—shuffled toward the front counter before looking our way.

"Can you be here at 4:00?" I heard Lisa Leann ask.

"Um . . . yes, 4:00. I'll see you then. I, um . . . I need to go now, Lisa Leann."

I hung up without saying good-bye.

Vernon and Donna were now walking toward the table I shared with my daughter. Vernon gave his forehead a quick rub. Donna's eyes looked bloodshot and swollen. My breath caught in my throat as I whispered, "What in the world . . ."

I didn't bother to sign, not even for Michelle's sake. From the looks of things, there was no need.

*Goldie*

# 15

## Simmering Suspicions

*They think I don't know, Lord. My friends. My precious friends who I love and appreciate. They think I don't know the truth.*

*The truth about Andrew.*

*Andrew and his mother, Amy.*

*Amy and Jack.*

*God, please help me as I try to say this. Holy Spirit, help my heart form the words . . .*

I watched as Lizzie backed out of the driveway, followed by Evangeline. I stood at the window and peered through the lacy sheers and counted the beats of my heart as I watched the wheels turn. And when their cars had disappeared from sight, I stared ahead for a good ten minutes. Maybe fifteen. Counting. Counting. Wondering how many breaths I had left before I, too, joined Jack in heaven. And wondering how many times I would inhale and exhale before I just simply broke down and screamed until there was no air left inside of me.

One or the other. Death or screaming.

*Help me to say it, Lord. Help me come to grips with it.*

When I was too tired to continue staring, I walked into the kitchen, rinsed the dishes, and then slipped them into the dishwasher. When the kitchen was clean—when the casserole dish was sealed and placed in the refrigerator—I ate a handful of the prissy pecans my sister Diane had left for me and then turned off the light and walked down the hall toward the spare bedroom.

The spare bedroom and the desk.

Inside I flipped on the overhead light, then moved purposefully toward the wall where the oversized clunky desk was pressed. I sat in the chair then pulled open the middle drawer. In it were the usual suspects. Paper clips. Rubber bands. Pens and pencils. A few Post-it notepads, one in the shape of a football. I picked it up. I fanned through it. I pretended to hold it as though it were real pigskin. I imitated a long pass. I chuckled.

I threw it back in the drawer.

In the back of the drawer I found a small bottle of aftershave. I pulled it out. Stetson. I started to put it back, but then I twisted the cap—it had been screwed on tight—and when it slipped into the cupped palm of my hand I drew the bottle up to my nose. I waved it back and forth, back and forth, and when I had gathered up my nerve, I inhaled.

*Jack.*

The tears formed like pools in my eyes, spilled over like streams down the sides of my face. I replaced the cap and laid the bottle near the football Post-it notepad.

I took a deep breath and shut the drawer.

I then moved to the right top drawer. More odds and ends. Envelopes. Stamps. Bank deposit books and old checkbooks.

I looked at the date of the last check. One month previous, written to Simmons Jewelry & Gift.

"Seven hundred and twenty-five dollars," I whispered. *For what?* Surely not jewelry. Since Jack and I had reunited, his giving me jewelry was taboo. Before, in the years when Jack had strayed, his restitution had always been an extravagant piece of jewelry. My jewelry armoire was packed with oodles of it.

"I want no more jewelry," I'd told Jack when we'd worked through our issues, when he'd gone to counseling for his—what do they call it?—sexual addiction.

Jack had agreed. So then what was this?

I shut the top drawer and opened the bottom. There, nestled between a row of manila files, was an oblong box wrapped in pretty paper, tied off by a light pink bow. I picked it up. It was heavy, so I rested its bottom in the palm of my left hand, then turned it over carefully. On the bottom, where the bow's ribbons came together, was the oval sticker with "Simmons Jewelry & Gift" embossed in gold.

I stared at it for several moments before I slit the first piece of tape with my fingernail. Then another. And another. And another until the paper fell away, exposing a Lladró box and a tiny card. Across it, my name. *Goldie.*

Jack's handwriting.

I breathed out a sigh of relief then opened the box. Inside was the unmistakable porcelain craftsmanship worthy of the Lladró name. Pastel paints. Fine workmanship. "A Little Romance" this statuette was titled. A pretty little maid, a handsome gentleman, hands clasped on a linen-draped table between them, a tiny bud vase filled with flowers on the table. The maiden sat demure. The lad sat intent.

*Jack and me . . . like when we met.*

"We were so in love, weren't we, Jack? Back then? And then again?"

I put the figurine on the desk then started going through the files. Most were labeled with the names of creditors. Bills to be paid, one read. Another, bills paid.

But no key.

*Help me, Lord. With your help I can do anything. I can even say out loud what my heart knows is true.*

I moved to the top left drawer, and there I found what I'd been looking for. A ring of keys. I held them in my hand, my palm flat out. I fingered each one. Could it be this one? Or this one? That one?

Then I threw the keys on the desk, stood, and walked away. Out of the room. Down the hall to the kitchen for a glass of water and then to the sofa for a nap.

*I just need to lie down and take a nap.*

---

I woke over two hours later and only because Olivia was knocking at the front door.

"Oh, Mom! Were you sleeping?" she asked, making her way into the living room.

"Is that a crime?" I asked, standing before her.

She wrapped me in her arms. "No, of course not, Mom. You're bound to be tired."

"Just playing catch-up with my sleep," I said. "I thought I'd get it while I can. Do you want some coffee? I can make some . . ."

"Let me," she said then brushed past me as she walked toward the kitchen.

I nodded. My daughter. Always taking charge.

"Where are my babies?" I asked, taking steps behind her.

"With Tony's mother."

"Ah."

Olivia pulled the carafe from the coffeemaker, walked over to the sink, and began to rinse leftovers from the pot. "By the way, you should see Evangeline Vesey's house right now."

I felt my brow rise. "Why?"

"Donna's car is there. Vernon's. A couple of the other deputies. It looks like the sheriff's department is having a picnic or something."

I ran my hands up and down my arms for both comfort and

warmth. Lately, it seemed, I was always cold. So empty and so cold. "I hope everything is okay."

By now Olivia was pouring fresh water into the coffeemaker. She looked over her shoulder and smiled. "I'm sure it is. They may be having lunch there or something. Anyway," she said, returning her attention to the task at hand, "what are your plans for the rest of the day?"

"I'm going through some of Dad's things in his desk."

She replaced the pot before turning fully to face me. "Mom, I thought you were going to wait for me to do that."

I sighed as I walked to the table and sat. "Olivia, it may come as a shock to you, but I am perfectly capable of taking care of these things on my own."

My daughter stared at me for long seconds before continuing to prepare the coffee. "I know that, Mom. I just don't want this to be too hard for you."

"I'm a big girl."

She smiled sadly then said, "I know. It's just that . . ."

I clapped my hands together in a light pat. "Why don't I come to your house for dinner tonight? I would love to get out of here for the evening, and I'm fairly tired of the food folks have been bringing over." I paused. "I wonder when all that stops. Two weeks, someone told me. After two weeks, friends and family figure you're over it."

"Oh, Mom."

I stood. "Let's have our coffee in the living room and let's talk about something other than your father or my being a widow. Deal?"

This time her smile was sincere. "Deal."

———

After Olivia left—after I was done playing the brave mother and the valiant widow—I went in search of the funeral home guest-book I'd been given after Jack's burial. I found it where I'd left it nearly a week ago, in a blue, zippered, vinyl pouch filled with blank thank-you cards, the cards from the floral arrangements, and the financial paperwork from the funeral home.

Pouch in hand, I returned to the living room, where I sat on the sofa and began pulling cards and paperwork and the book from its soft interior. There were only a few floral cards because we'd asked that in lieu of flowers, donations be made to the American Heart Association. Since last week, the contribution cards had been piling up in a shoe box in the dining room.

I picked up the thank-you cards and examined them.

*I should start these soon, Lord. I should have started them days ago, maybe.*

I opened the guestbook. Read each name. Each address, as though I didn't already know them by heart. The names I'd expected to see were all there. The girls. The men in their lives.

*Vonnie's parents came. How sweet. Funny, I don't remember seeing them . . .*

From the names scribbled across the lines, it looked as though every student and every graduate of Summit View High had come by to pay their respects. Their parents, too, of course.

My index finger ran the length of each page as my mind repeated the names, each one a treasure in my heart. Then it stopped, resting on a name I'd not expected to see. Just under Chris Lowe's name was the name of my sweet friend Van Lauer, a man I might have developed feelings for had my marriage not meant so much to me.

How was it I had not seen him at the funeral? How could I have missed his being there?

*Jack . . .*

I stood from the sofa and returned to the spare bedroom, where I went back to the ring of keys I'd left on the desktop. When I had them in my hand I went to the two-drawer filing cabinet Jack had kept on the floor on the right-hand side. Kneeling before it I tried each key until I found the right one. When the lock popped open I dropped the keys to the floor and opened the top drawer.

More files. Mostly taxes. One manila folder held this year's paperwork.

*Having this stuff will come in handy, Lord. Thank you for showing it to me.*

The second drawer slid open easily, revealing packets of photographs, mostly of football games. There were score pads from years gone by as well as recent. But tossed in the midst of it all was the one thing I'd been looking for all along.

An envelope—yellowed with age—with a Fort Collins return address.

I opened it gingerly, slipped out the tri-folded paper inside, and then began to read.

It was a birth certificate.

*Help me say it, Lord. Help me say . . .*

"Jack had a son."

# 16

## Baby Food

I rubbed at my eyelids. It had been an anxious night since Mandy had left the evening before. So I was relieved when Mandy had called about 3:00 a.m. Tuesday morning, finding me dozing on the sofa after surviving one more round of rocking a crying baby. I'd grabbed the phone on the first ring. "Mandy? Where are you?" I'd whispered.

Her voice sounded weary. "Mom, I'm safe in London. My plane boards for Cairo in about six hours."

"Thank the good Lord. Any more word on Ray's condition?"

"I'm afraid I won't know any more until I get there," she said. "How's Kyle?"

"Good as gold," I lied.

I heard her sigh in relief. "Then he's sleeping okay?"

"Sure is," I said, even though I could hear the baby fussing from the crib in the guest bedroom. Apparently the phone's ring had awakened him. I shook my head. I'd worked so hard to get him

127

back to sleep, but from the sound of things, Kyle was about to play war on my eardrums.

Once again.

I tried to rush Mandy along before she heard Kyle's nighttime hysterics for herself. "Glad you called, honey. Call me the minute you get to the hospital, okay?"

"Sure will, Mom. I love you."

"I love you too." I hung up as Kyle let out a bellow.

———

After a sleepless night and a busy morning, I glanced at the clock in the kitchen and saw that it was nearly noon, which meant it was about 8:00 p.m. in Egypt. Hard to imagine, what with the sun shining outside my kitchen window. I paused and stared at the shimmering Gold Lake across from my condo. *Oh Lord*, I breathed a prayer as I took the dishes out of the dishwasher. *Please, please let Ray be okay. Please.*

As I finished the dishes, I could hear Kyle stirring from his mid-morning nap. The poor little thing was all tuckered out from the previous night's tears. I'd swear that little guy knew something was wrong. Well, at least he knew I wasn't Mandy.

Even though I'd been able to give him Mandy's bottled breast milk up till now, I'd had a time getting it down him. It seemed he wanted his mother more than a bottle or even the baby food I'd tried to feed him. Nothing would do until I joined in with his cries as I rocked him in the same old rocking chair I used to rock his mother in when she was but a baby. So help me, I just couldn't help it. The lack of sleep, the thought of my Mandy out there all alone trying to get to Ray, and the thought of how this precious baby's daddy was possibly dying in some strange hospital finally got to me. It seemed natural to join Kyle for a good wail. My cries somehow quieted him, probably out of shock that his granny could make such a fuss. But the truth was, when Henry had checked on us at sunrise he'd found us still in the rocker where we'd wept ourselves to sleep.

———

I could hear the garage door open. I looked out the kitchen window as Henry pulled into our driveway in his red Bronco. He was just in time, I'd say. With the breast milk gone, I was going to have to start Kyle on formula.

I ran to the door that led to the garage and opened it just as Henry carried in a bag of groceries. He bussed my cheek as he swept passed me, plopping his bag on the kitchen counter.

"Have you heard any more from Mandy?" he asked.

I shook my head. "She should have landed in Cairo a few hours ago."

Henry pulled a loaf of bread from the bag. "I just can't believe that something like this could happen to Ray."

I walked over and peeked in the bag, glad to see the can of powdered formula and a couple of extra baby bottles. "I made you a sandwich and cut a piece of smash cake," I said as I pointed. "It's there on the counter."

"Looks good," Henry said as he scooped up his plate. He stopped and looked around the kitchen. "Kyle's asleep? Where'd you put Mandy's baby monitor?" he asked.

"It's in our bedroom, I guess."

Henry cocked one of his gray eyebrows. "Don't you think you should bring it into the kitchen?"

"Goodness, why?" I asked. "The two of us have ears. We'll hear Kyle as soon as he wakes up. Didn't we raise two babies without such a gizmo?"

Henry chuckled as he walked his plate of food to the kitchen table. "That we did."

I opened the refrigerator, pulled out my pitcher of sweet tea, poured it over a glass of crackling ice, and rushed it to Henry's side.

"Thanks," he said as a sudden cry filled our home. Our eyes met and Henry chuckled again. "I was going to invite you to join me for lunch," he said. "But . . ."

"But it seems I have a date with a younger fellow," I teased as I began to make a bottle of formula, following the directions on the back of the can.

Kyle's wailing grew louder, and I hurried about my task so I wouldn't have to greet the child empty-handed. Henry pushed his chair back. "I'll go get him."

"Thanks," I said, measuring the powder into the bottle with the plastic scoop I found under the foil lid.

A few moments later, Henry reappeared holding a wide-eyed Kyle, whose face just peeked over Henry's shoulder. Henry turned so Kyle could see me.

I smiled and spoke in my best baby talk. "How are you, little one?"

"I know he's missing his mama," Henry said. "Poor little guy."

I put a hand on one hip. "But he seems happy to have found his grandpa, I see. Henry, you always did have a way with the babies."

I tested the milk on my wrist then turned to take the baby. "Kyle is bound to have worked up an appetite by now."

———

After I fed Kyle his lunch and got him into his swing, I set my sandwich on a rosy plate and pulled up a chair next to Henry, who was just finishing his smash cake. He gave me an approving nod. "This is good stuff," he said before shoveling down his last bite.

I turned to look back at the clock and announced, "We should be hearing from Mandy soon."

"I hope so. The sooner she's back home to Houston with Ray, the better. I'm not too sure the two of us are up for this babysitting job. Not after last night."

I chuckled under my breath. "You don't know the half of it," I said as I turned to answer the ringing phone. "Hello?"

Thank God I heard Mandy's tired voice. "Mom, I made it. I'm in Cairo."

I felt my heart leap at the news, and I turned to Henry and gave him a thumbs-up. "Have you been by the hospital yet?"

"Arrived a few minutes ago," she said. "I'm with Ray now."

I sucked in my breath. "How is he?"

"He's asleep, I think. I mean, he's not conscious anyway. It's late here and so the doctor won't be in to talk to me till the morning. How's Kyle?"

"Fine, fine. I just gave him his first bottle of formula."

Mandy sounded concerned. "How did *that* go?"

"Relatively well, though he knows I'm not his mama. He's missing you."

"Is he being difficult?"

"Oh no, not at all," I lied again. "So, Mandy, what do the nurses have to say about Ray's condition?"

I could hear my daughter sniff. "All they'll tell me is that Ray's had a bad fall. But *that* I already know."

"How does he look?" I dared to ask.

"He's black and blue with casts on both legs and a bandage around his head. His face is, well, pretty swollen. To tell you the truth, I barely recognized him."

I closed my eyes and tried to rub the wrinkles of concern out of my forehead. "Oh no."

Henry was standing beside me now. "What is it? What's wrong?" he asked.

I held up a finger at him as I diverted my eyes. "Do you have any idea when the two of you can head for home?"

"I'm not going to know anything until I can talk to the doctor in the morning."

"You'll keep me posted then?"

"Of course, Mom."

"Your dad wants to say a word," I said as I handed Henry the phone.

"Baby, you okay?" he asked.

I noticed Kyle's swing had stopped rocking. I walked over to the baby, who was holding out his arms to me. I picked him up and hugged him for comfort. He smelled faintly of diaper wipes; I breathed in the scent as I nuzzled the top of his silky red hair.

I listened to Henry as he spoke with our daughter. "If you need anything, baby, you call, okay? Any time day or night. Your mom and I love you."

When Henry hung up, I asked, "Did she say if she was heading for the hotel?"

"Not tonight. She said she's going to sit with Ray so she doesn't miss the doctor when he makes his rounds in the a.m."

I hated the thought of her sitting there with her unconscious husband, so alone and anxious. She must be exhausted. "Poor dear."

Henry turned and opened up his arms, and I, still holding Kyle, nestled inside. We stood that way for a full minute, our hearts breaking as one.

I snuggled in deeper. "Could we pray? For Mandy and Ray?"

Henry nodded, and together we prayed and wept while little Kyle cooed between us.

---

Sometime later, while Henry bounced the baby on his knee, I busied myself cleaning up the kitchen. Henry called from the couch in the living room, "Lisa Leann, have you called any of your Potluck friends to let them know what's going on?"

"We've been playing phone tag," I admitted. "Why?"

"There was some talk in the grocery store, something about a murder last night."

I stopped what I was doing and turned around. I could see the top of Henry's gray head jutting above my mauve couch as he jostled our laughing grandchild.

"A murder? Are you serious? Here in Summit View?"

"Someone over at the trailer park."

"Lord have mercy," I said. "I'll have to call Donna later and catch up on the news." I walked around the couch and looked down at Henry. "In the meantime, I'd like to run over to the library and get a couple of books about Summit View's history."

"Why the sudden interest?" Henry asked.

"Pastor Kevin has asked the Potluck Catering Club to cater the Founders Day celebration in a few weeks."

"No kidding."

"Yep, it's been 150 years since Father Dyer founded the church, and though the new building won't be ready in time for the anniversary, the pastor wants the club to help make the dessert for the Friday concert, then cater a sit-down dinner in the fellowship hall for about four hundred on Saturday."

Henry whistled under his breath. "Let's hope Mandy and Ray will be back by then. But how are you going to juggle all those catering preparations and take care of Kyle?"

"Well, surely Mandy will be back to claim him at some point, plus I've got my friends to help me, and . . ." I gave him a wink. "Then there's you. So, how would you feel about watching Kyle while I hit the stacks for about an hour?"

Kyle let out another peal of giggles and Henry looked up at me, concerned. "Well, what if this little guy gets hungry while you're gone?"

"He just ate, and besides I'll be back in a jiff."

"But what if he dirties his diaper?"

"Henry, don't tell me you've forgotten what to do!" I teased.

He gave me one of his classic smirks. "It never hurts to play ignorant."

"Come with me," I said as Kyle's coloring suddenly changed to bright pink. "I think Kyle just made a little present for his grand-daddy." Henry stood, holding Kyle at arm's length while I chuckled. "Time for a diaper-changing class."

"Fine," Henry said. "I'll supervise."

"Oh no you won't. I'd say it's time you got your hands dirty."

———

Ten minutes later, after helping Henry change Kyle's diaper, I was on my way to the library. I turned the corner near the Higher Grounds Café, passing the entrance to the Higher Grounds Trailer Park. I cut my eyes down the driveway to see if I could discern the trouble Henry had mentioned earlier. Sure enough, I could still see yellow crime tape somewhere in the vicinity of Wade's trailer. For heaven's sake, I hoped everything was okay with Wade. Surely my plan to have Wade invite Donna over for hot chocolate in the middle of the night hadn't ended in the death of one of the two.

I shook my head. No, no, of course not. That was a ridiculous thought.

I drove toward the town library and pondered the possibilities. Someone had lost their life last night. But who?

And why?

I felt my brows knit together. Someone I probably knew. This was a small town, after all. I'd have to call someone as soon as I got home. But as I only dared to leave Henry alone with the baby for an hour, I couldn't get sidetracked from my mission with a phone call. First, I'd explore the history of Summit View and our beloved Grace Church, then I'd call Wade on my way home. I needed to be sure his dream date with Donna hadn't ended in someone's death.

I shuddered. "That would be impossible. Right, Lord?"

# 17

## Spicy Agent

I don't remember much about my childhood with my mom, but I do recall she'd let me help her with her baking. It seems like yesterday, me standing on a chair next to my mother by the kitchen counter. I'd put my little hand beneath hers and we'd stir the batter with her silver whisk. "A secret wand," she'd call it as we'd assemble the ingredients for her favorite recipe, sunshine cake, in her blue mixing bowl. I smiled at the memory: me coated with cake batter and whipped cream while Mom, wearing her blue plaid apron, sang round after round of "Your Cheating Heart," a Hank Williams classic. We'd giggle while she'd exaggerate the song's pathos as she'd topped her mandarin-orange-filled cake with frosting just before sprinkling it with blueberries.

The ringing of the cell phone pulled me back to the present, and I found myself once again sitting at my desk in the office I shared with Jerry. I was by myself, as Jerry had abandoned me for a few hours of sleep. I flipped open my phone. "Hello?

Vonnie's voice was breathy. "David just left. He dropped in and told me the news before he left for the airport to pick up his friend. How are you doing?"

I triple-clicked the top of the ink pen in my hand and swiveled my chair so I could see out the only window in our little office. "I'm okay, though still in a state of shock, I guess."

Vonnie's voice was soothing. "You poor dear, you sound exhausted. When did you sleep last?"

I glanced at my watch and saw it was 4:00. "The night before last, I think."

"Goodness, your father needs to send you home."

"He would, but we're a little shorthanded here."

"It's all so horrible. I'm so upset for you, for Doreen. I can't imagine who would want to harm your mother." I could hear Vonnie sniffle. "Do you have a suspect in mind?"

My heart sank. She didn't know. Why did I have to be the one to say it? I must have hesitated because Vonnie sounded alarmed. "Donna, then you *do* know who did this?"

I stood up and shut the door to the office before confiding, "There is a person of interest but—"

"Just tell me it's not Evangeline!" Vonnie blurted.

My voice sounded flat as I sat back at my desk. "I find it interesting you should ask me that, Vonnie. Do you know something?"

"Well, no! I just, well, I don't want you to suspect her, I mean."

I shook my head and looked down. "Me either. She is my stepmother, after all."

Vonnie sounded eager to agree. "That's right, Donna, she's family."

"But for that matter, though we may not have been close, my mom was family too."

Vonnie sighed. "I know, dear. This must be so terrible for you."

I nodded as if she could see me through the phone. "You can say that again."

There was a pause as Vonnie mustered her courage to ask, "So, you're not going to arrest Evie?"

"Oh no. Well, at least not yet. For now, the department is examining evidence and putting together a time line of all her movements yesterday."

The phone line crackled a bit as Vonnie asked, "Can't you put a stop to it? Make this all go away, for Evie's sake?"

I contemplated her question as I watched an aspen just outside my office window quake its yellow leaves.

"I wish I could, but it's out of my hands."

"Can't Vernon do something?"

"You'd think," I said sarcastically, "but he's only making matters worse. He's gone and called in the Colorado Bureau of Investigation, from the Denver office." I imitated my dad: "'To take suspicion off of the *innocent*.'"

Vonnie was silent for a moment. "Surely, you don't think Evie's capable of murder?"

I picked up my pen and tapped it on the edge of the desk, feeling jittery from the gallons of coffee I'd consumed. "You tell me."

"What are you saying?"

Leaning forward, I put my elbows on the desktop. "I'm saying we're talking about a woman who has screaming fits on public sidewalks, or don't you remember the Bob Burnett incident last year. If you recall, Evangeline flipped out just before her wedding, yo-yoing between two fiancés. Or, how can we forget all the times Evie has hunted down my mother just to give her a piece of her mind? Apparently, that's exactly what, at least according to one witness, she did yesterday."

I could hear Vonnie suck in her breath. "Oh my! Well, that makes it all sound . . ."

"Bad. It sounds bad, Vonnie. What can I say?" Someone tapped on my door. "Listen, I gotta run."

"Okay, but drop by here on your way home. I have something for you, something of Doreen's. Something I think she'd want you to have."

I froze as time seemed to melt. Once again, I could see my mom, the way she looked when we'd baked together in our kitchen. She was young, tanned, and beautiful. I imagined her wearing her favorite coral tee with her bell-bottom jeans, and I could almost smell her lilac talcum powder. My voice softened. "What do you have, Vonnie?"

"Recipes. I have Doreen's favorite recipes, written in her own hand. You know, I spent many a morning at your house, having cake and coffee with your mom, when you were just a little thing. Do you remember?"

"Not really, I . . ."

The knock was louder this time.

I stood up. "You wouldn't happen to have Mom's sunshine cake recipe in your collection, would you?"

Vonnie sounded pleased. "I do! In fact, I'll run to the store and get the ingredients. I'll bake one for you today, okay? For later when you stop by."

I blinked. "That would be nice, Vonnie," I said as I clicked out of the call.

"Donna?" It was my dad's voice at the door.

I walked over and opened it to find my dad looking as haggard as I'd ever seen him. I put a hand on my hip. "So, Dad, shall I arrest her or will you?"

"Donna, no one is being arrested today, not until we have more information. I for one just can't believe . . ."

I crossed my arms and leaned a hip on the doorway frame. "We've got our sworn duty to protect the public, you know."

"The evidence against Evie, well, it's all circumstantial. But once we've done the interviews and rechecked the evidence, I'm sure we'll come to a different conclusion."

"Dad, I hate to say it, but we need to put your wife behind bars so we can conduct our investigation before she sways her friends with all her blabbing. They're a pretty tight group, you know?"

Dad closed his eyes and took a deep breath. "This is exactly why I've called in the Colorado Bureau of Investigation. You and I, we can't be objective here."

I shrugged. "Well, yes, I'm starting to see that."

"Excuse me?" A tall man in a dark suit rounded the corner of the hallway and headed toward us, staring at my dad. "Are you Sheriff Vernon Vesey?"

Dad turned and extended his hand. "Yes, and you are?"

"Agent Nate Sawyer. The Colorado Bureau of Investigation's Denver office sent me over. I understand you have a situation, a murder victim to whom you're related?"

Dad looked sad as he nodded. "Yeah. My ex-wife."

Nate shook his head. "That *is* sticky. Any suspects?"

"Only those we're related to," I said.

Nate turned and seemed to notice me for the first time. His green eyes flashed concern under his dark brows. "And who are you?"

I didn't extend my hand.

Dad spoke for me. "This is Deputy Donna Vesey, my and the victim's daughter."

Nate looked from Dad to myself, then addressed me. "You say you have a suspect? In custody?"

I felt my eyes narrow. "No, and that's the problem."

Dad turned to me, slowly shaking his head. "She's not guilty, Donna. You know that."

"Who's not guilty?" Nate asked.

Dad cleared his throat. "My wife."

Nate took a breath. "Okay, I'm going to need a strong cup of coffee and a desk, then I'd like to interview you two separately, all right?"

Dad nodded. "Let me show you the way to our coffeepot," he said. "Then we'll head to my office, okay?" Dad turned to me. "Donna, you look beat, why don't you head for home? I'll have Nate call you later."

I shook my head. "Nothing doing. I'm staying till Nate's ready to talk to me."

I went back inside my office and sat down at my desk and tried to refocus on the reports in front of me. But I was too tired. Every time I blinked, a memory would flash before me: Mom and me having words in the grocery store. Over Evie. Velvet's screams on Wade's porch. Mom's lifeless eyes staring up at the daughter who'd failed to protect her.

A cough startled me. I opened my eyes and jumped at the sight of Nate standing in front of my desk.

His amused expression only served to annoy me. "Pardon me, deputy, I didn't mean to disturb you."

I found my voice as I glanced at my watch and saw it was 5:30 p.m. "I'm well into my third shift in a row, as if that's any of your business."

Nate sat down in the chair across from me with his clipboard. "Didn't mean to upset you."

I folded my arms and leaned back in my chair. "The fact that you were called in is upsetting enough. I mean, it's not like I can't speculate as to what happened."

"Then would you care to share your thoughts?"

I frowned. "Well, it appears my stepmother had another one of her little spats with my mother. Considering I have a witness that puts Evie at the scene about the time Mom died."

"That's unfortunate for Evie if she's innocent," Nate said, interrupting me.

I frowned again, then continued. "I think my mother somehow hit her head during her *discussion* with Evie. But that would mean Evie left my mother to die, alone." I shuddered at the thought. "That's the part that makes me wonder. Is Evangeline really capable of such a thing?"

Nate shrugged. "You know her better than I do, but like your dad says, the current evidence is only circumstantial."

140

"You know people have been put on death row with less than that," I said, feeling my scowl deepening.

Nate shrugged. "Who knows, maybe your mother stumbled. The tox report isn't back yet, right? But I understand the deceased was an alcoholic."

"Don't refer to her as 'the deceased.' She was my mother, and you weren't there. I was on the scene and I'm telling you there was a struggle. You'll find it all in my report along with Clay Whitefield's photos."

Nate pulled his pen off the clipboard and began to make notations. "So, what you're saying is . . ."

"What I'm saying is, you shouldn't be here. You're impeding my investigation. We should be calling for a grand jury."

"It may come to that." Nate reached over and picked up my report and thumbed through it. He looked up, impressed. "Looks like you're being thorough."

"Well, yeah, I'm trying to put together a time line of Evangeline's whereabouts. But there's a ton of interviews to do. That's why Evangeline needs to be in custody before she gets into cahoots with her friends."

Nate raised an eyebrow. "Do you really hate your stepmother so much?"

I felt heat flush my cheeks. "Of course not. We've actually been getting along for a change. It's just the evidence points to her."

"Then you're really worried her friends will give her a fake alibi?"

"Maybe."

"Then maybe you'd better fill me in on these so-called friends of hers. From what your father said, they're pretty notorious, right?"

I leaned back in my chair, unsure of how to answer. "Well, ah . . ."

Nate looked at the notes on his clipboard. "They're all potheads. Correct?"

I felt the blood rush to my cheeks again, and I slowly stood up.

I leaned over, pushing the palms of my hands onto the desk. Nate looked up at me from his chair, a hint of fear in his eyes.

He might be cute, but this man was an idiot.

I tried to steady my voice. "This is exactly why we don't need outsiders on this." I spoke slowly. "No, they are not *potheads*. Those friends, of whom I am one, are in a cooking club of sorts. They call us the *Potluck* Catering Club."

To my annoyance, Nate actually laughed. "The Potluck Catering Club? You mean as seen on TV? What are you, some sort of TV reality show wannabees?"

I stood my full five-foot-two inches and folded my arms. "We are not wannabees. We won a million dollars on *The Great Party Showdown*."

"That was you? Well, then." Nate made a few more notations. "So money was definitely a motive."

I reached for my leather jacket, which was slung around the back of my chair, and slipped my arms into the sleeves. "Money was not a motive. Maybe Evie was full of spite, but this murder was not about money. Be assured."

I zipped up my coat.

Nate looked up, surprised. "Where are you going?"

"Home." I pushed the rest of my papers toward the man I'd forever refer to as "the idiot." "I've been on duty almost twenty-four hours and I've had enough. Here are my notes. I've already interviewed Evie, and here's the time line of where she says she was before, during, and after the murder. I'll leave it to you to follow up with the interviews of her other potential victims."

"You mean witnesses?"

I was too tired for his banter so I turned and walked toward the door. "Whatever. I probably shouldn't even be on this case anyway."

I paused as Nate studied my notes before glancing back at me. "Technically true, but as I'm the lead investigator and a bit short-handed, I'm not letting you off the hook that easy."

I caught a flash of a grin that seemed to fade under my glare. He cleared his throat. "On another topic, I know you've got tons of boyfriends from watching you on TV and all. But even so, can I take you to dinner and discuss this? I mean, I really do need your help."

I hesitated. "Nope, as far as I'm concerned, I've done my duty. If you need help with finding addresses and phone numbers, ask Carla, the department's secretary. I'm out of here."

I scurried from the building and into the cool afternoon air. I climbed into my Bronco and buckled my seat belt. As much as I wanted to go home and lay my head on my pillow, I was going to swing by Vonnie's first. If it was true that she'd made me Doreen's sunshine cake, I wouldn't rest until I tasted one of my only childhood memories of my mother.

May her soul rest in peace.

*Vonnie*

# 18

## Biting Betrayal

I heard Donna's tires crunch across the gravel in my driveway, and I hurried outside, motioning for her to pull her Bronco to the side of the house. That way she wouldn't block Fred from pulling into the garage later.

When I met her on my front porch, I gave her a hug. "How are you holding up?" I asked, taking note of the dark circles under her eyes.

"I'm pretty tired; I can only stay a moment."

I patted her shoulder. "Come inside then. I've saved you a plate of Fred's barbecue chicken."

Donna followed me up my front steps, through the front door, and to my kitchen table. I'd already had a place setting ready for her and hurried to retrieve her foil-covered plate of barbecue chicken from my warm oven.

Donna studied the chicken before looking back at me. "This looks wonderful, though I'm not sure I'm all that hungry."

"Then let me show you the sunshine cake," I said, hurrying

over to my countertop. I tilted the white-frosted cake just a bit so Donna could see it before I caused the blueberries to roll to the floor.

"Wow, it looks just like I remember."

I carefully set the cake down and retrieved my cake server from a drawer and set it on the counter. "I'll join you for a slice after you eat your dinner."

Donna looked surprised. "Aren't we going to wait for Fred?"

I walked to the table with a glass filled with ice and a pitcher of water from the fridge.

"We've already eaten, so help yourself."

Donna looked around. "Where *is* Fred?"

I sat down next to my friend. "He's on the building committee at the church; they're having some sort of meeting tonight. I'm hoping it won't take too long. He's worried about you, dear. I know he wants to see you after all you've been through."

Donna nodded. "I'd like to see him too." She bowed her head in prayer before biting into the chicken. "This is good."

I nodded, watching her eat, and worked up the courage to ask, "Have you talked to Evie about Doreen's death?"

Donna nodded as she pushed her green beans around her plate. "Yeah, I was over at the house earlier today. I got her statement and created a time line of all her activities yesterday."

"What did she have to say for herself?"

Donna shook her head. "As you're on the list to be interviewed in that regard, I can't say much, but according to Evie, she's only guilty of 'caring too much,' whatever that means."

I slowly nodded, imagining Evie saying just that to offer proof of her innocence.

"But Donna, what I really want to know is how *you* are doing. You've just lost your mother and . . ."

Donna stopped chewing and stared at me. She swallowed then said, "That's why I'm here. I wanted to find someone in town who saw Doreen through the eyes of love and compassion. You're the only one I could think of who would."

I stood and walked over to an old scrapbook I had on the kitchen counter. "I loved your mother. We were friends." My voice dropped to a whisper. "Good friends."

Donna pushed her plate back and I placed the aging scrapbook in front of her. "Look what I found." I flipped through the cellophane-covered pages till I came to a faded photograph of a tiny child with blonde pigtails; her face was lit by the glow of four candles on top of a white birthday cake topped with blueberries. In the photo, the child clapped her hands as a proud and younger Doreen smiled down at her.

Awe filled Donna's voice as she said, "Is that me and my mother?"

I nodded. "Sure is. Your mom invited me over for birthday cake on your fourth birthday."

Donna gently touched the photograph face of her former self. "We looked so happy."

Her finger slid up the photograph to Doreen's face, and she touched her smile. "She looks like she loved me," she finally said.

"Honey, your mother did love you. The trouble was she wasn't so fond of herself."

"But why?"

I shrugged. "I think there were a lot of factors. She had a difficult childhood, you know. Her mother died when she was only five, and she buried her father when she was just nineteen. I think being left an orphan made her feel she didn't really belong anywhere. That's probably the motivation that led her to breach her marriage and to slip into . . ."

Donna looked at me and blinked. "You can say it, Vonnie. The arms of another man. Yes, I know she ran off with the church choir director. Evie mentioned that to me a time or two when I was a kid."

So help me if I didn't gasp. "She didn't."

"She always couched it in one of her famous backhanded

146

compliments. 'I'd never run off with that choir director and leave such a precious child behind. What was your mother thinking?'"

I shook my head. "Evie was hurt, and people who hurt—"

Donna finished one of my favorite sayings for me, "Hurt others."

I nodded. "Evie had hoped to marry your father herself, you know, before your mother captured his heart."

Donna gave me one of her looks. "Evie's mentioned that a time or two also."

I rested my elbows on the table and placed my chin on my folded hands. "Do you think you can prove her innocence?"

Donna lowered her eyes and shook her head. "If I can . . ."

Instead of prying, I stood and walked to the counter to retrieve the recipes. "Here are those recipe cards I promised you."

Donna gently took them from my hand and spread the yellowed cards on the table. A look of wonder crossed her face as she touched the handwritten words with a fingertip: best chocolate cake, lemon bars, onion soup, pot roast.

She found the sunshine cake card and turned it over, seeing her mother's handwritten note: "Donna's favorite."

To my surprise, Donna's head slumped and her shoulders began to quiver. I jumped up and grabbed the box of tissues from the phone desk and placed it on the kitchen table. I handed Donna a tissue, and she buried her face in it before she finally whispered, "My mother's life was such a waste. And here I am following in her footsteps."

"Now, wait. Doreen was a woman I called my friend. Her life was not a waste, neither is yours."

"How can you say that? I've never settled down, I've never gotten on with my life, and if I'm not careful, I'll end up with no one to come to my funeral, just like my mother."

I leaned over and gave Donna a hug. "There are a lot of us who love and remember Doreen. But you're not your mother. You make great choices."

147

Donna wept harder, something I hadn't seen her do since the day I'd seen her weep in the cemetery over her baby's grave. She was as inconsolable then as she was today. "How can you say that?" she said with a sniff.

I patted her hand. "Well, I know my son loves you."

Donna nodded. "I know . . ."

"But?"

"I'm starting to care about the man, but he's still a bit of a mystery to me. It's like he showed up here in Summit View, all the way from California, raised by Hollywood royalty. I just don't know what to make of that, plus he doesn't seem to want me to meet his friend Bobby. He picked him up from DIA this afternoon and they're going to dinner before driving to Aspen. You'd think he would have invited me."

I rubbed my upper lip with my index finger. "Is that *so*."

"Yeah. I mean, I have feelings for the guy. But maybe our timing is, well . . . off."

"Meaning?"

"When he was ready to marry me . . . I was . . . well, not even interested. And now, now that I would almost be willing to reconsider, he seems distracted."

"Are you saying you're ready to settle down with David?"

Donna looked miserable. "I'm not about to settle. David will have to prove to me that he's the one by being the man I hope he is." She sighed. "But I've said too much. Do me a favor and don't mention this conversation to him, okay?"

"You know I've never broken your confidences," I said as I watched as she pulled out another tissue before dabbing her eyes. "Donna, let me cut you a slice of that sunshine cake, then let's talk some serious girl talk."

"All right."

"I'll meet you at the recliners with plates of cake and tall glasses of cold milk. You relax for a while, okay?"

She nodded and I busied myself in my kitchen, but not before I watched her slump into Fred's blue recliner, recently updated from worn-out corduroy to shiny leather. Donna pushed back in the chair, kicking up the leg rest.

"Don't get too comfortable," I called as I turned back to my work and sliced two thick pieces of cake, trying my best to keep the blueberries in place. I laid the cake on my blue dessert plates then grabbed a couple of napkins and forks. I opened the refrigerator and pulled out my gallon of ice cold milk and filled two glasses to the brim. I put everything on one of my blue polka-dotted TV trays and carried the treats to my recliners. I carefully set the tray down on the little coffee table between the two chairs. "There," I said to Donna, "what do you think?"

When she didn't answer, I turned to discover that the poor dear had fallen asleep.

I watched her steady breathing, then tiptoed away. I didn't have the heart to wake her. But what could I do? I couldn't leave her here till morning. Maybe Fred would drive her home when he got in.

———

For the next hour, I crept around my house and fretted. I fretted about poor Evie being accused of a crime she surely didn't commit. Evie had her faults, but murder? That *couldn't* be possible. I also fretted about poor Donna and the heartbreak of losing her mother, not to mention her growing feelings for my son, the one bright spot of the day.

And to top it off, I fretted about David. He'd left for the airport hours ago to pick up that Bobbie woman and apparently, he still hadn't explained this Bobbie-gender-confusion thing to Donna.

When the gravel in the driveway crunched, I hurried to the front window and peered out, expecting to see Fred.

But when David dimmed the lights of his Mazda, so help me but my mouth fell open. Judging from the silhouette in the passenger seat, he'd brought Bobbie home to meet his mother.

I glanced over my shoulder and saw Donna was still sleeping in the recliner, so I grabbed the sweater I kept on the wall hook and slipped outside.

David was opening Bobbie's side of the car. He looked up. "Hey, Mom, I'd like you to meet Bobbie."

I gently shut the front door behind me and hurried out to the car as I pulled on my wrap.

"No need to get out," I said as if I was just being friendly.

Bobbie stepped out anyway.

Once again, my jaw dropped.

Bobbie was all glam. She had pouty lips—in an extra large—and a low-draping blouse that shimmered silver in the moonlight just beneath what had to be artificial cleavage. Her silky red hair fell artfully around her shoulders and glided almost to her waist. Her blue eyes looked knowing, haughty even. She extended her hand as if she were a queen meeting the peasants. "You must be David's mother." She laughed. "Your Colorado mother is a bit different from Miss Harmony Harris, wouldn't you say, David?"

David nodded. "Thank goodness, though I mean no disrespect to Harmony." He stepped around the car and gave me a hug. "We thought we'd drop by on our way to Aspen."

"I see that," I whispered.

"Where's Fred?" David asked, looking expectantly at the front door.

"He's at the church; maybe you should drop by the church, with your, ah . . ."

"Friend," David said.

Bobbie walked over to him and kissed his cheek. "Now, come on, David. You and I both know we've been more than friends." She flashed her eyes at me. "We were engaged once, you know."

I nodded. "I've heard."

The couple walked forward, as if they wanted to maneuver around me and head into the house. I blocked their steps by positioning my portly body on the front step of the porch. I stammered, "Well, it was nice to meet you, Bobbie, but you must be going, I'm sure. It's hours to Aspen from here."

David laughed. "Not so fast. I thought I'd treat Bobbie to a slice of whatever you've got baking."

"Oh, that's not such a good idea, not tonight."

David put his foot on the first step, and I moved backward and up one step.

"Why not?" he asked.

Bobbie laughed. "Oh, please, Mrs. Westbrook. I'd love to taste your baking. It must be good if it had the power to take my David away from me."

I stood immovable as I looked down on the couple. "I thought you two broke up."

Bobbie laughed loudly. "We did. But that didn't work for me. So, I decided to mix business with pleasure. I'm here to take David home."

I clenched the rail. "What do you mean?"

"Since I had to come out to Colorado anyway, I thought I'd try to reclaim what's already mine."

Before I could gauge David's reaction to those words, I heard the door creak open behind me. I turned to see Donna step out onto the porch. Even in the moonlight, I could see her face blanch.

"What's going on out here?" she asked.

I turned back and looked at David, who had frozen in place. "Donna!" was all he said.

"So, who's this?" Bobbie said with a frozen smile. Then her eyes lit with recognition. "Well, if it isn't that law enforcement officer from that party reality show you were on, David."

Donna folded her arms. "Okay, it's clear you know who I am. But what I want to know is, who are you?"

Bobbie laughed and looked around at the faces that glowed in the moonlight. "Well, I'm Bobbie. Bobbie Ann, you know . . . David's ex."

Donna narrowed her eyes. "Ex what?"

Bobbie narrowed her eyes too. "Honey, this man and I were almost husband and wife." Bobbie turned to David. "Babe, didn't you tell her about us?"

David stared at Donna. "I started to but then we got interrupted by the call to the trailer park and . . . "

Bobbie Ann stared from David to Donna. "Is there something going on between the two of you?"

Donna put her hands on her hips. "Not anymore, there's not." With that, she stomped down the steps, pushing past David and Bobbie, reclaimed her Bronco from the side of the house, and swerved around the Mazda still parked in the driveway as she roared into the night.

Oh dear.

# 19

## Grilled Over a Hot Flame

I sat in the family room of my old home, the home I'd been reared in by my mother and father, pushed against the back of an old comfy chair, my hands clutched. My husband—and, coincidentally, the sheriff of Summit County—sat on the ottoman before me, elbows resting on his knees, hands hanging limp between them.

"What are you saying, Vernon?" I asked him.

"I'm saying, Evie-girl, that it doesn't look good."

I swallowed hard then closed my eyes. When I opened them, I scanned the room around us, the muted shades of the walls, carpet, and furnishings against the vibrant colors outside the window: the newly turned leaves, the azure of the sky, the white fluffiness of the clouds. I blinked against an odd thought: would I soon not be witness to such beauty but instead be inside a six-by-eight-foot jail cell?

"Tell me again," Vernon said, his voice gentle, "what you and Doreen talked about when you went over there."

"I've already told you, Vernon. At least six times, I've told you."

"I know, honey. But tell me again. Maybe there's something you've left out. Something you aren't aware of."

I chewed on the inside of my mouth for a moment before taking another deep breath and exhaling. "Like I said before," I began through clenched teeth, "I got there a little after lunch—"

"And you went there because . . ."

"Because I wanted to talk to her about her drinking. I wanted her to think about getting some help."

I saw a pained expression cross his face then leave. "Okay. Go on."

"She didn't want me to come in. Inside the trailer, I mean."

"When you got there, did you see anything unusual?"

I paused, trying to remember exactly what I had seen, if anything. Then: "Nothing unusual." Another pause. "Oh . . . Doreen was watching television."

"How do you know? Could you see her through the window?"

"No. I could hear the voices. Probably a daytime soap from the sound of things."

Vernon patted my knee. "See, you're remembering things. Good." He removed his hand from my knee. "What do you mean, 'by the sound of things'?"

"You know. The way they talk in those things."

"No, I don't know, Evie. I've never in my life watched a soap opera."

"Well, then I don't know how to explain it."

"Try."

I opened my mouth to answer, but before I could speak another word, the doorbell rang. I started to rise, but Vernon held up a hand. "I'll get it," he said.

He stood and then walked out of the room. I remained where I sat, lips pressed together, a light quiver starting from deep inside. I looked down at my hands, then flexed them, stretching the fingers as far as they would go. They trembled, faintly at first, then more noticeably. I fisted them and then shoved them under my thighs.

154

Vernon returned then, followed by a tall young man with decidedly dark brows arching over light green eyes. He bore the scent of expensive cologne and he wore a suit, both sure indications of who he was. Who he had to be.

Vernon had told me the night before that an agent from the Colorado Bureau of Investigation had come into town to help with Doreen's homicide.

*Doreen's homicide . . .*

"Mrs. Vesey," the tall man said with a smile. "I'm CBI Special Agent Nate Sawyer. I understand your husband has been talking to you about what happened the day you saw the victim."

His words were almost too kind. I didn't like this. Not one bit.

"Yes," I said. There was, after all, no reason to deny it.

Nate turned his torso from left to right, then stopped as he glanced at the sofa on the other side of the room. "May I?" he asked.

Vernon jumped a bit. "Oh, sure, sure. Have a seat, Nate. Can I get you anything? Evie made a wonderful cinnamon-buttermilk coffee cake this morning. I can warm up a slice for you."

I glared at Vernon. How dare he offer this Judas a piece of my coffee cake?

Fortunately—for Vernon—Mr. Sawyer declined the offer. Vernon, who caught my glare and then blushed, shoved the ottoman with his foot, away from where I was sitting.

When both men had made themselves comfortable—Nate unbuttoning his jacket and bringing an ankle up to rest over the knee of the other leg—Vernon said, "Evangeline was just telling me that when she arrived at the trailer Doreen was watching a soap opera."

Nate looked from Vernon to me. "Which soap opera was that, Mrs. Vesey?"

"Which soap opera? I have no idea."

"Then how do you know it was a soap opera she was watching?"

I bristled. "Excuse me, but do I need an attorney?"

"You're welcome to call one if you think it necessary." He smiled.

155

"I'm not here to read you your rights, you know. I'm just asking for some information."

I looked at Vernon, who said, "My wife is not being formally charged with anything, then."

"No, sir. But, again, if she feels or you feel she *needs* an attorney . . ."

To which I said, "I do not *need* an attorney, young man, because I haven't done anything wrong. Now, to answer your question: I don't exactly know which soap opera she was watching. I said I heard the television through the door. The voices were muted and the tone was like what you hear when you watch a soap opera."

Nate nodded, cleared his throat, then pulled out a small notepad from inside his jacket. "Do you mind if I take some notes?"

"Not at all," Vernon answered for me.

I frowned at him.

"Mrs. Vesey, was there anything—anything at all—in those voices that might indicate what was said."

"I don't understand what difference that would make," I said.

Nate straightened his leg then pushed back against the sofa to readjust his position. "Well, what if you didn't hear the television? What if you heard voices? What if someone was on the other side of the door with the vic?"

"Can you not call her that?" I asked. "Her name was Doreen."

"All right, then."

"And quite frankly, I wasn't listening long enough to determine if there was anyone inside with Doreen or not."

"Were there any other cars parked at or near the trailer?"

"Not that I noticed."

"Okay." He made a few notes on the paper of the pad and then said, "Go ahead."

I paused to think some more. "Well, when she came to the door she didn't want to see me—"

"Why's that?" More note jotting.

I shrugged. "Well, you'd have to know the history."

"Go ahead," he said. The pen stopped scrolling across the paper.

"We have a history."

"I've explained that," Vernon interjected.

"But I went to talk to Doreen about her drinking. To beg her to get help."

"Isn't that a little unusual, Mrs. Vesey? I mean . . . what with your . . . history?"

Vernon cleared his throat. "Nate, you have to understand my wife. As a Christian she practices forgiveness. She prays. She asks God to love others—even those she has a history with—through her."

I looked from Vernon to Nate, whose brows had knit together. "I was right," the young agent said. "That is a little unusual."

I watched as he flipped the pages of his notepad backward, read a few lines, then flipped forward again.

"You know a Mr. Wade Gage?" he asked me.

"I do. And yes, I know he saw Doreen and me talking."

"According to him, you were fighting."

I gasped. "We most assuredly were not fighting," I insisted. "We might have been speaking directly with each other, but we were not fighting."

The dark brows rose as the green eyes moved to Vernon. "That's some temper your wife has, Sheriff."

"Evangeline," Vernon warned. "Calm down." Then he looked at Nate. "And let me make this clear: I'm not here in any legal capacity. I'm only here as Evangeline's husband. Refer to me from now on by my name, not my title."

"I'll make a note of that," he said.

At this I stood. "Vernon, I don't know how you can ask me to calm down." I pointed to Nate. "That man is here for one reason and one reason only. To arrest me! To arrest me for a crime I did not commit."

Vernon and Nate stood with me.

"Evie . . ."

"Mrs. Vesey, as I said earlier—"

I turned full on to the CBI agent. "Mr. Sawyer, let me make this clear to you. I never stepped inside that trailer. If anyone tells you I did, they are lying. Doreen came outside. We talked. She walked me to my car. We talked some more. She expressed sorrow at some of the decisions she's made in her life. She even told me she would think about getting help. Then she went back inside and I drove away. But I never once stepped inside that trailer. Not that afternoon, anyway. I've been inside it, of course, but not that day." I took a breath. "I'm not stupid, Mr. Sawyer. Not by a long shot. I've been around long enough to put two and two together and come up with four. Unless you can prove that I was inside that trailer, all you have is the testimony of a bunch of busybodies. Mr. Gage included."

Nate Sawyer didn't even blink. He just took a breath, blew it out, and smiled. Then, with a flip of the notepad, bringing the cover back over the pages, he said, "Like I said, Mr. Vesey, she's got some temper." Another smile. "And you are right, Mrs. Vesey. Right now, we can't put you inside the trailer. Mr. Gage says he saw the two of you outside, which is where you told me you were." He straightened his shoulders. "But here's the deal. Someone killed that woman. We have no report of serial killers in the area, we don't know of anyone else having an issue with the vic—ah, Ms. McGurk. And, we have a hysterical daughter screaming that she's pretty sure you did it."

I felt the blood rush from my head. "Donna?" I whispered. "Donna said that?"

Thankfully, he shook his head. "No, ma'am. Not your stepdaughter. The other one."

"Velvet," I spewed. "But what about all the men . . ."

Vernon placed his hands on my shoulders. "Careful, Evie. Don't say anything you might regret later."

I looked over my shoulder to the concerned face of my husband. Then I nodded. He was right, of course. The last thing I wanted to do right now was to bring up the unpleasantness of the past and hurt Donna with it. Besides, what I knew about Doreen's past was only what she'd told me.

I couldn't prove a thing.

———

A meeting of the catering club had been scheduled for the previous day, but what with Doreen's murder we'd postponed it until the following afternoon. Once Nate Sawyer had exited by the same door he'd entered—in other words, gotten out of my house—I began to ready myself for going to the boutique.

Vernon, of course, tried to stop me. "I'd stay in if I were you," he cautioned.

"Well, you are not me," I said. I stood in the master bath, staring into the mirror, brushing my hair in harsh strokes. "I'm not going to pretend I've done something wrong when I haven't." Then I slowly placed the brush on the vanity. "You do know that, don't you, Vernon?"

Vernon, God love him, managed to register both shock and anguish. "Evie-girl," he said, then opened his arms. I stepped into them, reaching my arms up under his and then clutched at his broad shoulders.

It was then that the tears came. Great sobs of tears formed out of fear and heartache. "Oh, Vernon," I sobbed. "As angry and as hurt as I've been with Doreen, I never wanted her dead. You know that, right?"

"Of course," he said, then shushed me.

"Vernon," I said when I'd finally caught my breath. "I haven't seen Donna since she took my statement . . ."

"Donna is exhausted. She was already working long hours."

"And now her mother is dead." The tears started up again.

Vernon, wisely, said nothing in return. He just patted my back. Patted and patted, allowing me to draw strength from him.

———

159

Donna didn't come to the meeting set for 3:00 at the boutique. Vonnie initially excused her, saying, "The poor dear was at my house yesterday and fell asleep before she could even eat the sunshine cake I'd baked for her."

"Sunshine cake," Lisa Leann quipped. "That's one I've never heard of."

Vonnie blushed like a schoolgirl caught in a lie, then said, "It was one Doreen used to make for her."

We were sitting in the front foyer of Lisa Leann's wedding boutique, which is not only where we gather for our meetings but also—in the cook's kitchen in the back—where we prepare many of our dishes for catered events.

"Doreen's mother used to bake them," I noted. "I remember my mother making them after her recipe." I looked over at Lizzie, who'd come from her work at the high school and was still wearing the teacher ID badge around her neck. "Remember, Liz? Remember eating them after school with a tall glass of milk back when it was the real McCoy and not that watered down stuff we've talked ourselves into drinking so we can stay healthy."

Lizzie was sitting near the window, a cup of vanilla bean coffee in hand, legs crossed daintily, one foot pumping as if to its own tune. "I remember it well," she said. Then she looked at Vonnie. "We girls used to gather over there, didn't we, Von? You and Evangeline and Doreen and me."

Lisa Leann, who was sitting near Lizzie, yawned. If I thought I looked haggard, I had nothing on her at this moment. I've never seen the woman but what she wasn't dressed to the nines. But today, and even though she wasn't dressed shabby by any stretch of the word, she just looked . . . worn out. "I'm sorry," she said, yawn over. "I'm just not getting a whole lot of sleep these nights."

"Why not?" Goldie, who sat next to me on the settee, asked. She took a hearty sip of the coffee Lisa Leann had served us earlier. "I know why I'm not sleeping, but what's got you up at night, Lisa Leann?"

Lisa Leann yawned again, I suppose in reaction to the question. Then I yawned, followed by Goldie. Vonnie and Lizzie both laughed, and we all followed suit. "Oh. My. Goodness," Lisa Leann said. Her eyes shimmered with tears brought about by the yawn. "I am *so* sorry." Then she swallowed before saying, "Mandy had to leave for Egypt, for those of you who don't know. Her husband has been in a serious accident while there, and our precious—albeit unsleeping—grandson has not wanted to settle down without his mama and daddy." She brought her hands to her face, pressed her fingertips against her cheekbones. "I'll tell you, ladies, it's been a long time since I pulled an all-nighter with a fussy baby."

Lizzie turned to look at Lisa Leann. "I wouldn't even want to think about that, Lisa Leann, but how's Mandy's husband?"

Lisa Leann nodded in appreciation. "Thank you for asking, Liz. Ray is holding his own. That much we know. Honestly, we don't know a lot, other than he fell and he's not looking too well. Mandy calls to update us, of course. But she knows very little herself."

"So no word as to when they'll be coming back?" I asked.

Lisa Leann answered only by shaking her head.

For a while we all just stared at each other, intermittently sipping our coffee, until I laughed lightly and said, "Well, aren't we a sorry lot, and us not even thinking to pray? Lizzie's got her mother's Alzheimer's to worry about, Lisa Leann's got a baby in the house, Goldie's in mourning." I turned to her. "You holding up all right?"

She nodded, not that I believed her.

"And I'm being investigated for murder." Then I looked at Vonnie. "Vonnie, what do you have?" I said, trying to lighten the mood before our meeting came to an official start.

"Me?" Vonnie looked startled. Then she shifted in her seat and said, "Well, actually, girls, I do have something we could pray about . . ." She stalled before elaborating. "It's Donna," she said finally. "I'm very—and I do mean very—worried about my girl."

# 20

## Chilling Spy

After the meeting at the boutique, I crossed the street and went into Higher Grounds, where I placed a takeout order for Waikiki meatballs, garden salad for two, and dinner rolls. I gave my order to Sally—longtime owner of the café—said I'd be back in a few minutes, and then left for the newspaper office a block away.

I stepped onto the sidewalk and turned my face toward the afternoon sun as it dipped ever closer to the peaks of the mountains surrounding Summit View. There wasn't a cloud in the sky. Not one. The backdrop of the scene before me was jewel-tone blue.

I took a step and shivered, then shoved my hands into the pockets of my lightweight all-weather coat. A few minutes later I stood in front of the *Gold Rush News*, where I pulled seventy-five cents from the change purse of my wallet. I slipped the coins into the newspaper stand outside the front door, listened for the release of the door, and then extracted a newspaper.

The *Gold Rush News* was a weekly paper that did all right for itself. It didn't hold to the national and international news like the

*Denver Post* did—unless, of course, it was relevant to the citizens of Summit View—but rather stayed true to what was important for the locals.

The front door of the building opened as the door of the stand clanked shut, startling me. "Oh!"

"Mrs. Prattle, how are you?"

"Why, Clay Whitefield. My goodness, how good to see you."

The young newspaper reporter gave me a brief hug. Clay was a contemporary of Donna's. At one time, he'd had quite the crush on her. That is until my son-in-law and his family came into town. Adam's sister Britney had caught Clay's attention—or maybe it was the other way around—and they were now engaged.

"It's good to see you too," he said.

"Just getting off?"

"I am," he said, checking his watch. "In fact, a little earlier than usual."

I tri-folded the newspaper and then crossed my arms for comfort's sake. "Tell me how you've been."

Clay, an unusual blend of Native American and Irish, blushed pink. "I've been good. I think Britney and I are ready to set a date."

"Really? When do you think?"

"Well, right now everything is all about the Founders Day festival, so we thought maybe three months after that."

"That's close," I said. "Will three months give you enough time to plan for the nuptials?"

Clay's *Gold Rush* jacket was draped over one arm. He slipped it off and then shoved his arms into the sleeves. "Small," he answered. "I told Britney we had to keep it small. I'm not a man for big weddings."

"And how does Britney feel about that?"

Another blush. "She feels the same."

"But it will be a church wedding," I said for clarification. "And you'll let us cater it . . ."

"Absolutely," he said with a smile. He took a deep breath and then exhaled. "How's Donna holding up?" He looked to his feet and then back up.

"In all honesty, I don't know for sure. We just had a meeting at the boutique. She wasn't there, of course, but Vonnie said she was having a pretty rough time with all this."

Clay looked over my shoulder to Main Street and the sidewalks and buildings on the other side, then returned his eyes to mine. "Working that crime scene was one of the hardest things I've ever done." He shook his head. "I've never actually *worked* the homicide of a loved one's family member."

I blinked. "Have you ever even worked a homicide?"

"Not in Summit View," he said. He looked past me again, briefly. "No, not in Summit View."

For a moment I thought our conversation had run its course. Then he said, "I understand the only suspect in the case is Evangeline."

I flinched. "Are you asking me as a reporter or as someone who is genuinely concerned?"

He laughed, keeping his eyes locked with mine. "Not as a reporter," he said. "But if it makes you feel any better, you can say, 'Off the record.'"

"All right, then," I said. "Off the record, I only know she's been questioned, but on the record I can tell you she didn't do it."

Again Clay looked past my shoulder. This time, I glanced behind me too, then back to him. "What do you keep looking at?"

"Not a what. A who."

"A who?" I started to look again, but Clay stopped me.

"No, don't look now."

I looked back to Clay, who was looking straight at me. Casually, he pulled his sunglasses out of his jacket pocket and slipped them on, pushing them firmly up the bridge of his nose with his index finger. I watched as his eyes glanced over my shoulder again, then he shook his head.

"He's walked away."

"Who has?" This time I turned to face the other side of the street. Now I stood shoulder to shoulder with the young reporter. "Who'd you see?"

"Some man. He was standing against the wall next to the Second Chance Consignment Shop. Looked pretty innocent until I noticed he was keeping his focus on you."

"On me?"

"I'm surprised you didn't feel a hole being bore right through you."

I shook my head. "What did he look like?"

"Not like anyone I know. Skinny. Wore his pants too big. If it weren't for the belt, they'd have fallen to his ankles."

I chuckled at the thought.

"Baseball cap. Pulled low enough I couldn't make out his face. But I know nearly everyone in town and can always make out a tourist. This man was neither citizen nor visitor."

I turned slightly to look at Clay. "Well, if he was neither one, what was he?"

"I don't know. But he sure was interested in you."

———

I walked back to the café, picked up my takeout order, and went back across the street to where my car was parked in front of the boutique. A few seconds later, my car was headed toward home, filled with the delicious aromas of food baked and prepared by Sally's number-one short-order cook, Larry.

What that young man lacked in social skills he more than made up for in his ability to maneuver himself around a kitchen.

Samuel was home when I arrived. Still in his suit and tie, so to speak, so I knew he'd not been home long. We greeted each other in the kitchen with a kiss, and then he said, "Not sure what smells better, you or the supper you're carrying in the bag."

"Ha." I handed him the takeout and then went to the kitchen table to drop my purse and remove my coat. That done, I pulled the paper from where I'd slipped it into the coat's pocket earlier, unfolded it, and placed it on the table. "We had a meeting today—the girls and I—concerning the Founders Day celebration."

"The bank is all atwitter about it too."

I looked at him with a smile. "Atwitter? What kind of thing is that for a grown man to say?"

He chuckled. "My secretary used it today, and I thought it was kind of funny. Thought I'd try it out on you."

I placed a hand on my hip and watched my husband as he removed two plates from the overhead cabinet and placed them on the counter. "And just how did she use it, pray tell?"

This time he shrugged before answering. "She said, 'My goodness, what with the murder and the Founders Day celebration, this bank is all atwitter.'"

I didn't know whether to laugh or cry. "What does the bank have to do with the murder?"

"Everyone—and I do mean *everyone*—is talking, Liz."

"About?"

"Evangeline, mostly. About the long-standing feud between her and Doreen. Of course there are a hundred and one different theories as to what happened at the trailer."

"Samuel, Evie did not kill Doreen. Surely you know that."

"Of course I know it." He heaped our dinner out of the takeout containers and onto the plates. "At least I don't think she would hurt Doreen on purpose."

"Samuel!"

Samuel jumped at my exclamation. "Don't get mad at me."

"I'm not mad. I'm stunned! You of all people should know that Evie couldn't do anything like this."

He looked at me hard. "That's why I said not on purpose. But things happen in the heat of passion . . . or when emotions run high. What if she accidently pushed her? You and I both know Evangeline Vesey can get pretty fired up sometimes."

That much was true. It hadn't been that long ago she and Donna had practically gone to fisticuffs in the middle of Main Street. Evie had told me all about it and, of course, I'd heard Donna's version of the story.

"One of the tellers," Samuel went on, "said she heard Evie and Velvet arguing on the street the other day, and another said she was in the grocery store when Evie practically bowled Doreen over with her shopping cart."

"That's not true. She did not bowl her over with a shopping cart." At least I didn't think she did. Not the way Evie had told Goldie and me at breakfast the other day.

I snapped my fingers. "Breakfast at Goldie's!" I said.

Samuel walked our plates over to the table at the same time as I walked to the cabinet to get tea glasses and then to the fridge to get our drinks. "What about breakfast at Goldie's?"

"When Evie and I had breakfast at Goldie's," I answered, "it was the day after Doreen was killed. Evie talked about having had a visit with Doreen, but there was not a tremble in her voice, no indication at all that anything had gone wrong. In fact, she said that Doreen wouldn't let her in the trailer."

I brought the tea and glasses to the table, poured one into the other, and then sat down.

Samuel joined me. "And that proves?"

"Samuel, the last thing Evie is, is a cold-blooded killer. If she'd hit Doreen or pushed her or whatever, and Doreen had fallen, she would have called 911. She'd never leave someone there to die. And *if* she did—which she wouldn't—but if she did, she'd certainly not be calm about it the following day."

"That much is true."

I waggled a finger at my husband. "I should call Vernon. Tell him this."

Samuel reached for my hand, held it, and brought it down to the table. "*After* we eat."

I smiled. "And after I read the paper." Then with a wink I added, "It's your turn to do the dishes, remember?"

———

While Samuel rinsed and stacked the dishes in the dishwasher, I stretched out on the sofa with the newspaper and a hot cup of mint tea. The front page was divided between the story surrounding the murder of Doreen and the upcoming Founders Day celebration. I ignored the first (vowing to call Vernon as soon as I'd finished reading) and concentrated on the second.

The Founders Day celebration was set for the third weekend in October. Friday night would feature a concert performed by our high school band and chorus. Working at the high school, I'd heard all about that. The school was, as Samuel's secretary would say, all atwitter with preparation. Saturday morning the city would block off Main Street at both ends and open it to pedestrian traffic only. Local businesses and individuals would pitch tent-booths to sell their goods. Anyone working in a booth was required to dress as if it were 150 years ago.

I smiled. *How fun!*

Pastor Kevin Moore, one article reported, would make an appearance at some point, dressed like the church's founder, Father John Dyer, snowshoes and all. I called out to Samuel and asked if he knew about that little element of the celebration.

He stuck his head out of the kitchen and said, "I do. He and I had a talk today about it as a matter of fact."

"Hurry up and finish in there so you can tell me about it," I said.

He nodded and then disappeared.

I went back to reading.

There would be fireworks on Saturday night as well as a catered— ta da!—sit-down dinner in Grace Church's fellowship hall. Tickets had to be purchased no later than the 6th of October so that the internationally famous Potluck Catering Club—ta da again!—would have a head count.

Dinner would be followed by fireworks over Lake Dillon.

I opened the paper to page 7, where images of old photographs from different eras were displayed. As I read the captions under each of them, Samuel walked in, plopped into his recliner, and said, "Your slave is finished with his chores, madam."

I dropped the paper and gave him my best "look."

"What?" he laughed.

"It's not like you had to scrub the pots and pans, Samuel Prattle." This time he gave me the "look."

"What?" I mimicked.

"It's not like you slaved over a hot stove."

"Touché, Mr. Prattle. Now tell me what Kevin said."

Samuel stretched. "Nothing, really. Only that he was going to be Father Dyer, that you girls were catering the meal, and that he hoped no one ventured around the church."

"What did he mean by that?" I folded the paper and placed it next to me on the sofa.

"Well, the sanctuary is going to be an absolute mess by that time—what with all the reconstruction going on—and, you know, this was Father Dyer's church. Folks are going to want to see what the sanctuary looks like. Especially with those stained-glass windows we have depicting Father Dyer."

"Hmmm . . . you're right there. What suggestions did you have for Pastor Kevin?"

Samuel crossed his ankles. "My thoughts were to have posters of the windows as displays in the fellowship hall and plaques with some of the history between them, you know, telling the story of Father Dyer, the church . . . that kind of thing."

I thought that through. "That's a good idea, Samuel. I'll share that with Lisa Leann. Maybe . . ."—I pondered before finishing—"maybe we can have some of the gold rush legends posted too. We've been talking about that lately, and I've heard that some of the history classes at the high school are researching them. Maybe we can get some of these stories from the kids."

Samuel pointed at me like I was a genius. "Good idea," he said.

I raised my brow and then winked. "You might even say that the school has been all atwitter with gold rush history and legend."

Samuel laid his head back and closed his eyes. "I'll never live that one down, will I?"

I stood to go to our bedroom, where I would call Vernon with what I remembered about the morning Evie and I had breakfast at Goldie's. Along the way I tweaked my husband's ear. "Not if I can help it," I said.

*Goldie*

# 21

## Tasting the Truth

I received a phone call from Vernon Vesey early Friday morning, asking if he could come by.

"I have some questions I'd like to ask you," he said.

I looked over at the clock. It was a few minutes after 9:00 and I was still shamelessly in bed. These days, I didn't sleep well at night, and often slept late into the morning. Had the phone not rung, I might still be in dreamland. "How about 10:00?" I asked.

"That's fine," he said.

I disconnected the call, groaned, and then sat up, pushing myself back against the pillows and the headboard of the bed. After a moment or two of deep breathing—a small effort to get my bearings together—I reached for my *Upper Room* daily devotional, which I kept on the bedside table.

The day's inspirational Scripture was from 1 Peter: "Cast all your anxiety on [God]," it read, "because he cares for you."

The prayer focus was for those in stressful situations.

I laughed, but not out of humor. It was like Evie had said

yesterday; we were quite an interesting lot, we Potluck girls. And it had felt good to pray together as we had. Still, I felt a heavy burden weighing on my shoulders. Today I would do something I'd never thought I'd have to do.

Today I would . . .

The phone rang again and I jumped.

"Hello?"

"Mom?"

"Olivia. What's wrong?"

"Nothing. I'm just calling to check on you."

Of course she was. How long, I wondered, would she feel the need to do this? I swung my legs over the side of the bed, slipped my feet into my bedroom slippers, and then trudged into the master bath. "To be honest with you, I'm just now getting up and I'm taking you into the bathroom with me."

"Good thing we're mother and daughter."

"Yes, it is," I said. Then: "Wouldn't you like it better if I called you back when I'm done? We can chat while I make a pot of coffee."

Olivia sighed. "Okay. Do that. Promise?"

"I promise, my child."

Minutes later, I called her back. I'd washed my face, brushed my teeth and hair, and had put on some clothes presentable for Vernon's visit. As I scooped my favorite coffee into the gold mesh coffeepot filter, I returned Olivia's call.

"So what are you doing today?" she asked once the preliminaries were over.

I started to tell her that Vernon was due over in a matter of twenty minutes but decided against it. She'd only tell me she was worried that he might want to get me involved somehow in the legal mess Evangeline was obviously in. She'd say that I had enough on my plate right now—what with Jack's death and all that went along with burying a spouse—and that I needed to stay focused on my own life. My own problems.

172

She had no idea . . .

So I decided against telling her the whole truth. I told a half-truth, instead. "I'm going to see Chris today," I said.

"What for? Do you need me to go with you?"

I pushed the start button on the coffeemaker and then went to the cabinet to get my favorite coffee cup, a black one that—when filled with any hot liquid—displayed the faces of my grandchildren. "Not unless you think it necessary to discuss my hours for the coming weeks."

"Oh, Mom!" she said. "Why do you feel you have to go back to work so soon?"

I closed the cabinet door. "Olivia, I can only hope that you don't have to experience this for yourself anytime soon, but one day you may find out that it is too easy to get mired down in grief. I'm ready to go back to work. Maybe not full-time, but I'm ready."

"It's not even been two weeks," she said through a sigh.

I knew how long it had been. I'd somehow managed to get through every painful minute of every single day.

My coffeepot sputtered. "Olivia, I appreciate you, my darling child. But you must stop babying me."

"I don't baby you . . ."

"Yes, you do. You either baby me or lecture me. I'm your mother, not your child."

"I know that, Mom, I just . . . I just worry. Dad always took care of certain things and . . ."

He certainly had done that. "I know, sweetheart. But the sooner I get on with my life, the better I'll be. He's not here but I am, and I want to keep on. Trust me. If I get overwhelmed, you'll be the first one I call."

There was a long pause before I heard her say, "Promise?"

"I called you back from earlier, didn't I? Just like I said I would?"

There was nothing she could say to that one. "Yeeeeees."

I poured a cup of coffee just as I saw Vernon's car rounding the corner from through the open kitchen window. "Honey, I'm going to drink my coffee now. Call me later?"

She said she would do better than that. She was coming by, she said, with a new potato recipe she'd made the night before. "It was delicious," she said, "so I saved some for you."

We said our good-byes. I pulled another cup from the cabinet for Vernon, just in time to hear the doorbell ring. A minute or so later and Vernon and I were sitting at my kitchen table, sipping on coffee and making pleasant conversation.

How was I holding up?

I was holding up fine. How about you?

He was holding up as best as could be expected considering that the mother of his only child was dead—murdered—and his wife was the only suspect.

That, he said, was why he wanted to come by and talk to me.

"I understand from Lizzie that she and Evie came by to see you one day last week."

"Yes, they did."

"Do you remember what day?"

I didn't have to think hard to give the answer. It was the same day I discovered that Jack had a son with Amy Morrow Jenkins. The day I'd known it for sure. "Wednesday," I answered.

"The day after . . ."

"After?"

Vernon shook his head. "Do you remember anything Evangeline might have said about my ex-wife?"

This time I did have to think. I'd been so wrapped up in my own grief and thoughts when Lizzie and Evie were here, I'd hardly paid attention to what they were saying. "Well . . ." I began, then took another sip of coffee to buy time. "Let me think . . ."

"Goldie, don't make anything up. I have to know exactly what was said."

I stood, walked over to the coffeepot, and poured myself another cup. "I remember," I said, turning back to Vernon, who had pushed back a little from the table. Try, hard as he might, to look at ease, he only looked tense. Worried. "I remember that she looked nice."

"In what way?"

"She was wearing pink. It looked nice. Her coloring was good."

"Anything else?"

"She said she went to see Doreen the day before." I returned to my seat at the table. "Just like that. Nothing major. Just that she went to talk to her about her drinking."

"So she told the two of you she'd done this."

"Yes."

Vernon slipped closer to the table again, close enough for me to think that I'd never realized just how blue his eyes were, how the crow's feet crinkled whether he was smiling or not. "How did she seem about the visit?"

"She seemed . . . she seemed compassionate toward Doreen. Worried about her drinking, but she certainly didn't seem like a woman who'd just killed somebody," I said. "Not even by accident."

Vernon looked at the half-empty cup before him. He cupped his hands around it, then looked back up at me. "Would you be willing to testify to that?"

"Absolutely."

Vernon took a last swallow of coffee, then stood. "I'd best get to the office. We have an agent from the Colorado Bureau of Investigation helping with this case and . . ." He sighed. "I'm worried that if he can place Evie in that trailer under any circumstance, we'll have a real problem on our hands."

I stood too. "Let me walk you to the door," I said.

Together we moved out of the kitchen and into the living room, toward the front door. As I opened it, Vernon said, "If you can think of anything else . . ."

"I'll call you," I said.

Vernon stepped back into the bright sunshine of the day. He

looked up. "Temperature is dropping," he said. "Won't be long before we'll be covered in snow."

I nodded. We'd already had a few flurries. "Won't be long."

He started toward his car. I watched him, my heart breaking for him. His shoulders were slumped, his walk heavy. "Vernon?" I called out.

He turned toward me. "Yeah?"

"Will it help if I tell you that she said she didn't get to go inside the trailer?"

"Did she say why not?"

"She said Doreen wouldn't let her."

Vernon nodded. "Thank you, Goldie."

"Sure thing."

————

I had an appointment with Chris Lowe at 1:00 that afternoon. I arrived a few minutes early.

Chris's office is above the Hallmark greeting card shop. You have to go through the shop, to a back door, and up a narrow flight of stairs to get to it. Today, I found Britney Peterson standing behind the cash register, back turned to the store, arranging a helium balloon display.

"Hello, Britney," I said as I passed toward the back of the store.

She turned. "Hello, Mrs. Dippel. How are you?"

By now she was resting her forearms against the counter, so I stopped to talk. "I'm okay," I said.

"When do you come back to work?"

"Soon," I answered. "I'll talk to Mr. Lowe about that in just a few minutes."

She nodded. "He just got back from lunch. He's with someone, though."

"Oh?" I looked down at my watch. Surely not a client. I'd made the appointment for 1:00—before the 2:00 onslaught of appointments—just so we'd have plenty of time to talk.

"But I don't think it was a client," she said, as though reading my thoughts.

I looked up. "Oh."

"A friend," she said.

"Oh," I said again, beginning to sound like a parrot. "So, Britney, have you and Clay set a date yet?"

She smiled broadly. "Not exactly, though we are actually pinning down some dates."

I returned the smile, remembering briefly what it felt like to be young, in love, and anxious for my wedding day. Remembering the day Jack and I had set our date. The bridal teas. The showers. The rehearsal dinner. And the feeling that the hour I'd be alone and intimate with Jack would never come.

I sighed. "What a precious time."

Understanding registered on her face. "I'm sorry, Mrs. Dippel. About Mr. Dippel."

"Thank you, Britney." I pointed to the back door. "I'll get going," I said. "Don't want to be late."

I took the stairs one at a time. I was in no hurry for what I was about to do . . . what I was truly about to do. When I reached the reception area of the office—my office—I found it empty. Chris's wife had been filling in for me while I was away, but she was nowhere to be found. Perhaps, I guessed, she was still at lunch.

From the back of the office I heard voices—two, both male. I knew instinctively that it was Chris and his . . . friend, as Britney had said. I wondered who it was and whether or not I should interrupt. I looked down at my watch. It was 1:00 on the button.

I coughed, hoping the noise would alert Chris that I had arrived. Sure enough, I heard his private office door open. He called out, "Goldie?"

"Yes," I answered.

"Come on back," he said.

I walked the length of the hall leading to his office. Chris stood in the open doorway with a sincere look on his face. When I reached him, he hugged me, whispered, "How are you?" to which I merely nodded.

It was *the* proverbial question. How was I? How do you think I am? My husband is dead. Jack's son—the one I didn't know he had—had made himself an odd part of my life. My daughter doesn't know . . .

"Goldie." My name was spoken from the other side of the door. I turned slightly and peered in.

Heaven help me. It was Van Lauer.

"Bet you didn't expect to see me here," he said. He smiled, handsome as ever.

I stayed close to Chris but shook my head. "No," I said. "But I saw that you had come by the funeral home."

"I'm sorry for your loss," he said.

I didn't know what to say. Had Jack not wooed me back into his arms, into our marriage, I might very well be married to this unimaginably good-looking man standing before me. No, there were no words to say.

I did what I'd learned lately to do best. Nod.

An awkward moment passed between us until he finally said, "Well. I suppose I'd best let the two of you talk." He shook Chris's hand, then as he passed me, reached out to lay his hand against my upper arm. He squeezed gently and I shuddered. "You're in my prayers," he said.

Again, I nodded.

And then he was gone.

———

Chris sat on the other side of his desk, staring at the paper I'd handed to him no more than fifteen seconds before. "Good heavens," he said. Then he looked up at me. "Are you sure this is legitimate?"

I couldn't help but chuckle. "A legitimate piece of paper declaring the birth of my husband's illegitimate son. Yes, I'm sure. It has the seal. It makes sense. Sadly."

"And you say Andrew has been coming to see you?"

"Just a couple of times. But he calls more often to see how I'm doing." I shook my head as I crossed my legs. "I know what he says. He says it is a part of his job. But I don't think so. He knows who Jack was to him. He knows and . . . I just don't know what he wants. Jack's will hasn't been probated yet, of course. I'm the only beneficiary, but I'm worried that Andrew might want to try to legally take something . . . something that would ultimately belong to Olivia."

Chris grimaced. "Do you want me to talk to him?"

"I honestly don't know, Chris. If I'm wrong—if he doesn't know the truth—then I've just informed him of his paternity. But if I'm right and I wait . . . it could hurt Olivia."

"Or you. By law, he could ask for a blood heir's portion."

"He'd have to prove it, though, right? I mean, really prove it?"

"That wouldn't be too difficult," Chris said, leaning back in his chair. "But it might end up being gruesome if he asks to exhume the body."

I covered my face with my hands. "Oh, Chris!"

"Then again, seeing as how Jack was at Morrow's, Andrew might have taken the samples he needed then." He grimaced. "Not so sure that's legal, but we aren't talking about that, are we?"

"No." I dropped my hands, horrified. "I don't know which is worse!"

Chris didn't answer at first, then said, "Tell me what you'd like me to do."

"What would you do, were you me?" I asked.

He looked down at the paper again. He picked it up, held it between his thumb and index finger, then dropped it on top of all the other papers and files scattered across his desk. "I don't know, Goldie. Give me a night to think on it, okay?"

I nodded as I pressed my lips together, fighting back tears. "There's one other thing," I said.

Chris leaned over, rested his arms on top of the pile of papers, then laced his fingers. "What's that?"

"I want to come back to work."

"When?"

"Monday."

# 22

## Hot Dog

"Now, Chucky, do you see all the trouble you caused?" I asked as I looked down at my naughty boy. He was busy watching the passing cars but turned and rolled his big brown eyes at me.

I glanced back at the street and slowed for a red light. "How many times have I told you, do not eat other people's food—*especially* cake reserved for Donna—*especially* after all she's done for you? Do you realize you'd still be a stray if it weren't for her?"

Chucky responded by licking his lips as if the memory of gobbling Donna's slice of sunshine cake still tasted sweet.

By the time Donna had fled my front porch and David and his—ahem—friend, had stepped into my home, Chucky was already covered in frosting and stained with blueberry-colored spots, as was my new carpet. David shook his head at the sight. "Chucky-boy, you're in big trouble, dog."

"Same as you, apparently," Bobbie had said, her arm hooked through the crook of David's as if she'd just won him as a prize.

Now, as I drove home with a freshly fluffed dog, I mentally

compared Bobbie to Donna. Bobbie was everything Donna was not. She was sophisticated, polished, and put together with the perfection of a store mannequin. She sat too straight, her hair was too perfect, and her smile too white. These were things I don't normally hold against a person, but I made an exception in this case because of my relationship with Donna. My Donna was a real what-you-see-is-what-you-get kind of girl. She was a natural, unenhanced beauty, though she tried to disguise her looks with too-short hair and a khaki green uniform and a badge. I didn't think she'd been too successful at keeping her beauty a secret, since all the single fellows in town had been smitten with her at one time or another. Not that she seemed to care.

How could this Bobbie hold a candle to my Donna?

"Be careful what you say about this woman," Fred had warned me after Bobbie and David had left to continue their journey to Aspen, another three hours away. "She could end up being our daughter-in-law, you know."

I'd gathered and stacked the leftover dessert plates and took them over to the sink. "I'll forget you said that and try to think positive," I'd said.

I was still trying to think positive now as I waited at the light. I ran my hand down the back of Chucky's head, wondering how my groomer had managed to transform the former mop with blueberry smudges into this angelic version of himself. "Are you sure you're the same dog I dropped off at Helen's?"

Chucky's tail thumped against the seat as if to say, "Yes, and I'm adorable."

I laughed, and when the light turned green I eased my foot from the brake to the gas pedal. I eyed the Gold Rush Grocery coming up on my left, wondering how long it might take to run in to get fresh blueberries and whipped topping plus a couple of things for dinner tonight. *Five minutes, tops*, I told myself. *Chucky will be okay here in the car for five minutes.*

I know you're not supposed to leave your dog in the car, but it was a wonderfully crisp autumn day, so what would be the harm? Besides, this was an emergency. David was coming over for supper, and I needed to pick up chicken breasts so I could make a batch of my pineapple ginger chicken. A good dinner was essential if my plan to get David to tell all would work. I had a few questions I wanted to ask him about Bobbie. For instance: *What are you thinking?*

I also needed to re-create the original cake I'd made for Donna. I felt like a traitor serving my surprise visitors the remainder of her cake, which had been stored safely in the fridge during the gobbling incident. But when Fred came home a few minutes after David arrived, it was he who opened the refrigerator door and proclaimed we would all sit down and have some of "Vonnie's nice cake."

I'd blinked back my tears, pasted on a wooden smile, and sliced Donna's cake, feeling as guilty as if I'd sliced her heart instead.

My plan was to whip up a new cake as soon as I got home, then drop it by Donna's house later this afternoon. I needed to see how she was doing and to find out what funeral arrangements were in the works for her mother. It was my hope, really, that the cake would serve as a reminder that her mom had really loved her. Lord knows she had precious few reminders of that little fact.

And yes, Doreen had loved her daughter. This I knew because I'd seen it in her eyes. The problem with Doreen was that she'd had the misguided belief that by leaving her child behind, she was doing Donna a favor. And after learning some of the details of Doreen's life after she left Summit View, Doreen may have served Donna well by leaving her out of her misadventures. But that logic did nothing to heal the sting of rejection Donna felt to this day.

I pulled into the grocery's lot and slipped my blue Taurus into an empty parking spot. I looked down at Chucky, who cocked one of his fluffy ears at me. "I'm only going to be gone a minute. Do you mind?" I'd asked him, cracking my window to ensure he got fresh air.

His trusting eyes sparkled.

"And when I come back, I'll bring you a treat."

Chucky wagged his tail, and I swung open my door and climbed out. I leaned down and scratched behind his ear. "Now be a good little dog, and no barking, okay?"

Chucky wagged his tail again and I shut the door, glancing at my watch as I hurried inside. I found my necessary ingredients, including a box of bone-shaped dog treats for Chucky, then rushed to Bella's checkout line.

Bella was a cashier who had worked at our market forever. She was probably in her late sixties, and her dyed black hair gave her face a pale, harsh look, as did the drawn-on brows that arched beneath her deepening wrinkles. We didn't know each other well, but we always exchanged pleasantries. I stood behind the patron in front of me and watched as Bella processed the customer's groceries. Bella reached for a can of frozen orange juice and swiped the bar code as the resulting beep served as an exclamation mark to her story already in progress. "It happened right here in my line," she said. *Beep!*

The woman, a Texas-tourist type, dressed in designer jeans and a high-fashioned tee, responded, "Really?"

"Sheriff's wife or no sheriff's wife, that Evangeline woman slapped Dee Dee then pushed her to the ground." *Beep!*

The woman gasped. "From what I've seen on TV, I thought Evangeline was one of those do-gooders. You know, a Christian and all."

Bella nodded. "Didn't see any proof of that, unless she said a blessing over the catfight. As soon as she knocked Dee Dee to the ground, she jumped right on top of her. Her stepdaughter, Donna, and I had to run over and pull her off the poor woman."

I cleared my throat. "That makes for an entertaining story, Bella," I said. "I know you're exaggerating because that's not how Evie tells it."

Bella, who was reaching for a head of lettuce, stared up at me.

"Oh, Vonnie, I didn't see you there. Of course you wouldn't believe the truth. You're one of her little followers." *Beep!*

"Excuse me?"

"Now don't get huffy, but we all saw how she was on TV. Even the folks at that *Showdown* TV thingy called her 'Evil Evie.' Now we know why."

I shook my head. "That was just a joke, a *bad* joke."

"Lots of truth tucked into some jokes you hear," Bella said as she shrugged and reached for a carton of eggs to scan. She turned back to her customer to finish where she left off. "It was quite the brawl. Gum and candy flew everywhere. Took me a while to clean it up." *Beep!*

"Now come on," I said. "Evangeline tripped over a fallen bottle of Cold Duck. She didn't pounce on Doreen. Why don't you tell that part of the story?"

Bella put both hands on her hips and cocked her head. "Oh? Were you here?"

"Well, no, but I can't believe—"

"Did you ask Donna?"

"Well, no, but—"

"It's the truth, Vonnie, a truth I'm willing to testify to in court."

My mouth fell open as the two women stared back at me, but before I could find my voice, my elderly neighbor, Abby Carlson, came bursting through the store's front door as fast as she could hobble. When she saw me, she practically shrieked, "Vonnie, did you know you left the door of your car open?"

"What!" *Chucky!*

I abandoned my cart and rushed to the parking lot, my heart hammering. Sure enough, the driver's side door of my car stood open, and my car sat empty. I looked around wildly, calling for my little friend. "Chucky! Here, boy!"

Other shoppers joined the hunt: looking under cars, down the alley, into nearby backyards, but after two hours, Chucky was nowhere to be found. And the thing was, that little dog was so attached to me that I knew if he could only hear my voice, he'd move heaven and earth to come to me. The only explanation was—he'd vanished.

Despite my tears, I'd somehow managed to retrieve my groceries, then drive home, all the while hoping my dog had somehow found his way back. He hadn't. Once in my kitchen, I put the whipped topping in the refrigerator, vowing I'd start the cake later, maybe after David left. I was too emotionally exhausted to do it now.

My head still spun over my dog's disappearance. *What could have happened? And who had opened my car door?*

I thought about some of my animal rights activist friends. Would someone, someone who didn't know me or my dog, assume the dog was being abused because I'd left him in the car? Had Chucky been dognapped in an effort to rescue him? Or, maybe this was just some prank pulled by a neighborhood kid who would show up at my front door any minute with my dog in hand ... or maybe, maybe it was possible that someone meant to steal or even harm my pet?

I shuddered at the thought before heading toward my coffeepot.

I opened the lid to my Folgers and breathed in the aroma of fresh ground coffee beans. As I scooped the grounds and dropped them in my coffeemaker, I continued to mull over Chucky's disappearance.

I created a plan of action: I'd make posters and put them around town. I'd use the picture Clay had taken the day Chucky had treed a cake-stealing bear in my own backyard.

I smiled at the memory of my brave little dog rescuing me and the members of my Potluck Club during our picnic.

I thought back to my plan. Now, if anyone saw the posters and knew of a family who had adopted a stray, then maybe I'd get him back ... and ...

A sudden memory of the open car door drew my thoughts back to the grocery store parking lot. The weird part was that no one had seen anyone around, other than a mom and her three kids entering the store and some guy buying a newspaper from a newspaper stand near the store's entrance. Neither report sounded suspicious. But one thing I knew, I had not left that car door open, and as Chucky was incapable of opening it himself, someone else had done so.

My phone rang, and I picked it up. Hearing Donna's voice was a welcome relief. "Vonnie, I hear you had some trouble at the market."

"Yes, Chucky disappeared from my car. I only left him a moment, and when I returned, the car was open and the dog was gone."

"That doesn't sound right."

"You didn't happen to hear if he was found, did you, dear?"

"I'm afraid not."

My tears started to flow again, and I must have sniffed because Donna said, "I'm so sorry, Vonnie. I know how you love that little guy. When I'm out on patrol tomorrow, I'll keep my eyes open. I bet he turns up."

I reached for a tissue and blotted my eyes. "Maybe, but his disappearance seems sort of purposeful, don't you think? How do these things turn out when they're on purpose?"

Donna was silent. "I wish I knew the answer to that and maybe we will soon. But try not to worry. Maybe a nice family found Chucky and they're spoiling him with affection right now. He could be home sooner than you think."

I poured myself a cup of coffee and sat down for a moment. "Do you really think so?"

"Why not believe that for now?" Donna said. "There's more than enough heartache going around these days, and we can't abandon hope altogether, right?"

I sighed. "But how are you doing, dear? I've been keeping you in my prayers."

"I appreciate that, Vonnie, I do. And, well, I'm really still a bit emotionally numb. It's going to take a while for me to process all that's happened."

"So, you *really* think Evie had something to do with your mother's death?"

"It's not like it's what I hope, but it's where the evidence continues to lead."

I took a sip of coffee and pondered that, then said, "As hot-tempered as Evie can be, if you look at her heart, I don't think you'll find a killer. I just don't believe she's capable."

"If this goes to trial, they'll probably have her on manslaughter. They'll say she got into another one of her arguments with my mother and shoves were exchanged, like what happened down at the grocery store. They'll say she didn't mean to push my mother down . . . that she didn't know Mom had hit her head . . ."

"But Donna, I can't believe Evie would willfully walk away from the scene of an accident without either a hint of remorse or a call for help. I don't think she's capable of that, do you?"

"It may not matter what I think, it may only matter what Nate Sawyer thinks."

"Who's that?"

"Dad called him in. He's from the Colorado Bureau of Investigation. I'm sure Nate will drop by to see you, to get a reading on your impression of Evie in the hours following Doreen's death."

I held my portable handset and rose and walked back to the coffeepot. "What does Mr. Sawyer think so far?"

"He's hard to read, but I think, like me, he suspects Evie."

I sucked in my breath. "Oh."

"I mean, who else *is* there to suspect?"

I topped off my cup then added another dollop of cream. "Have there been any other suspicious people or happenings in town, I mean, besides my losing Chucky?"

"Not that I've heard of, except for the usual: lost wallets, tipsy tourists. Oh, and a stolen bicycle."

"What does Clay have to say?"

"Don't know. Haven't caught up with him lately."

I took a quick sip from my mug. "So, to change the subject, when's Doreen's funeral?"

Donna paused and dropped her voice. "Not sure there's going to be one. Velvet is insisting Mom wouldn't want to be buried here. So I guess she's going to have her cremated as soon as the coroner releases the body. Velvet says she's going to scatter Doreen's ashes off the Grand Canyon or some such thing. Apparently I'm not invited."

"That doesn't mean you can't have your own memorial."

I could hear Donna sigh. "I'd like that," she said quietly. "I really would."

"Maybe Lisa Leann would help you with photos. I'll ask the girls to bring over any old pictures they have of your mother."

As we were saying our good-byes, Donna asked, "So, do you still have a slice of that sunshine cake waiting for me?"

"I'm making you a fresh one tonight, after David leaves."

"David's coming over?"

"Didn't he tell you?"

"No. I haven't talked to him, since . . ." We let the silence build until Donna said, "Hey, I gotta go. I'll call you later to see how that cake is coming along."

I hung up the phone and walked to my kitchen window, looking past its tumbling, stained-glass babies. I took another sip of my coffee as I studied a grove of golden aspens as they zigzagged up the side of the mountain. On a day like today, I was glad that I was surrounded by so much of God's beautiful creation. I whispered a prayer of gratitude. It was these little reminders of God's presence that kept me going. It gave me hope. And right now, hope was all I had.

# 23

## Poached

It had been six days since Henry and I had become full-time care-givers to our infant grandson, Kyle, and we were just starting to get the hang of things.

"It's all about schedules," I'd informed Henry as I sat on the couch, my arm resting on the Boppy as I fed Kyle his bedtime bottle of formula. Henry looked up from the book he was reading. "Could be. Things are settling down a bit."

"Except that he hasn't quite given up his 2:00 a.m. feeding," I teased. "Wanna do the honors tonight?"

"Sure."

I looked down at the precious face before me and watched as Kyle closed his eyelids. He was so sweet, so innocent, and so dependent on me, what with his mom halfway across the world and his dad still in an Egyptian hospital.

"Heard from Mandy today?" Henry asked from the recliner, peering over his bifocals.

"Not since she called yesterday."

Henry closed his book. "I wonder if I need to go over there and see what I can do to get those two home."

"I've wondered that too," I said.

I felt little Kyle relax into the crook of my arm, and I looked down at his sleeping face. Poor little fellow, he'd been tuckered out from our busy day, the first day I'd actually braved leaving the house with him, if only to stop by my wedding shop office for a couple of hours.

What an ordeal with the car seat and stroller, not to mention the trial of setting up Kyle's portable swing and playpen. How did new mothers today deal with all these baby gadgets? Though I had to admit, I'd been experimenting a bit with Kyle's high-tech equipment. Some of it, like the baby monitor with attached camera, was pretty cool.

But, by the time I'd gotten all of Kyle's gear in place and Kyle settled down at my wedding consultant shop that also served as the Potluck Catering Club headquarters, it was time to head for home and start the process of folding down and packing all of Kyle's baby gizmos—only to set them up again back at the house.

I rose from the couch, still cradling the baby, and walked to the guest bedroom where I positioned Kyle over my shoulder to give his back a gentle pat, pat, pat. When I heard his tiny but satisfying burp, I carefully placed him in his crib and covered him with his bright orange and blue Broncos baby blanket, a gift from his Grandpa Henry.

"Don't know how Ray's going to take that blanket and all, being that he's all about the Cowboys," I had teased when Henry had brought the blanket home from Walmart.

"Well, Kyle is under my roof now and we'll worry about that later," Henry joked. "At least, I hope so."

I turned down the light and tiptoed down the hall, retrieving my laptop from my home office. I returned to the living room and settled back on the couch as I accessed our wireless internet.

"I know Mandy hasn't been able to find out much about the

subway accident, so I've been doing a little Googling," I explained to my husband. I stood up and walked over to his recliner and handed my laptop to him. "What do you make of this?"

Henry read aloud, "Bomb in Cairo subway injured nineteen, including one American." He looked up, alarmed. "When did this happen?"

"The same day as Ray's accident."

"Mandy said he fell in the subway, do you think as a result of this blast?"

I bit my lip. "I dunno. Though whether he was caught in the blast or was shoved off the platform by a panicked crowd, I dunno."

Our eyes met and held. Henry glanced down then continued to read, "An al Qaida–linked group is believed to be responsible for the attack, said the Interior Ministry. The ministry said the suspects were part of a group called the North African Islamic Army. All suspects remain at large."

Henry pulled off his reading glasses. "Do you think Mandy knows about this?"

I nodded slowly. "Could be. It would be just like her to leave out a few of the worrisome details to protect us."

Henry stood, still holding the laptop. "Well, who's going to protect her? That's what I want to know."

I looked at my watch. "Let's see, it's 10:00 p.m. here, meaning it's 6:00 a.m. Cairo time. I'm guessing Mandy will call in soon with her daily report. Maybe we can find out more about what's going on."

Henry nodded and passed my laptop back to me. I carried it to the nearby kitchen table, where I called over my shoulder, "I'm going to design a poster for our upcoming Founders Day festivities."

"How are the plans for that little venture coming along?"

"Slow, but they're coming. With the catering group so scattered, I've only got Lizzie and Vonnie pitching in right now. In fact, Lizzie emailed me some great photos of Father Dyer and the church."

"You got those photos up for viewing?"

"I'm opening the jpegs now," I said as Henry leaned over my

shoulder, close enough that I caught a whiff of his Old Spice cologne. The picture that began to load on the screen was an old photograph of a clean-shaven, white-haired gentleman.

"Who's that?" Henry asked, leaning in for a better look.

"That, my dear, is Father John Dyer."

"He looks a lot like Ralph Waite, you know, the actor who played the dad on *The Waltons.*"

I nodded. "That he does."

Henry put his hand across my shoulder as he studied the photo. "Dyer was a Methodist circuit preacher, right? So, why did they call him 'Father'?"

"Because of his caring and his concern for the miners. Apparently, he knew every mining camp and miner in the region. He'd travel over mountains and through blizzards on homemade skis just to bring them the comfort of the Word."

I downloaded the next picture, which showed Grace Church in 1880. Surprisingly, it looked much the same as it did today. Well, except for our new buildings and the stained glass windows depicting Dyer and his skis.

"Look, there's a bell tower," Henry said, sitting down and pointing at the screen. "I wonder what happened to it."

"The miners blew it up when Father Dyer helped bring prohibition to town. It was never rebuilt."

Henry scratched at the stubble on his chin. "Is that so," he stated rather than asked. He stood and stretched the kinks out of his back with a contagion of pops. "Got anything to eat?"

I looked up and gave my husband a smile. "Try the almond bark in the pink tin in the refrigerator."

Soon, Henry was clanging open the tin just as my email account chimed. I switched windows to see who had contributed to my inbox.

CWhitefield@GRNews.com.

I clicked open the email, already knowing what Clay wanted. I read: "Need your latest Aunt Ellen column for next week's paper. Got it? Your Editor, Clay."

I loved writing my weekly relationship advice column for the local paper, unless my life blew apart, like it had this week. I typed back "Patience is a virtue," then hit send.

The phone rang almost immediately. I picked up on the first ring so as not to wake the baby.

Clay said, "A virtue? Not so much in the newspaper business."

"That was fast," I said. "And hello-how-are-you?"

"This isn't like you, Lisa Leann. You're always so punctual with your columns. Is everything all right?"

"You mean besides the fact that Goldie's husband just died and Evie's under suspicion of murder?"

"Well, there is *that.*"

"Then to answer your question, no. Besides all the other troubles, things are, well, ah, difficult here."

"You mean with Henry?"

"No, no. It's Ray."

Clay, always on the lookout for a good story, perked at that. "Didn't you say he went to Egypt on company business?"

"Yes, but he's still there. He was in an accident."

"Say, I'm in your neighborhood. Mind if I stop by?"

"You emailed me from my own neighborhood?"

"Sure, with my smart phone. Just dropped Britney off; I'm still in her driveway a few doors down."

"As long as you don't ring the doorbell. I just got Kyle to sleep."

"Baby?"

"My grandbaby, Kyle. We're watching him while Ray and Mandy are out of the country."

"I see. No doorbells then, got it. See you soon."

Moments later, there was a faint tap on the door. Henry, who was still holding the tin of candy, opened the door. "Hello, Clay." He held out the tin. "Want to try some of Lisa Leann's almond bark?"

"Britney has me watching my weight, but one little piece won't hurt, I guess," Clay said, reaching for a slab of almond-filled white chocolate. He bit into the delicacy. "Mmm. So, Henry, what's this about your son-in-law? Ray, is it?"

Henry finished chewing his candy and nodded, gesturing for Clay to join him on the couch while I waved from the nearby table. I'd switched out of the poster program and into my Aunt Ellen file, reading a few of the lovelorn emails I'd received of late.

Clay spied me working on my column and waved back. "Don't mind us, Lisa Leann. I'll just chat with Henry for a moment."

While Henry explained—off the record—the situation with Ray and the article we'd found on the Internet, Clay asked, "Mind if I take some notes? I'd like to check in with my sources at the paper, to see what I can find out for you."

"Go for it," I said, looking up from my work.

Fifteen minutes later, I'd written a snappy Aunt Ellen reply in answer to a query about the etiquette for dating more than one guy at a time. I attached the column to an email to Clay and hit send.

I closed my laptop and joined the boys on the sofa. "Clay, my column will be in your inbox before you get home."

Clay checked his phone. "Got it already."

He opened the attachment, scanned my column, and laughed. "Good one. Aunt Ellen does it again. Thanks, Lisa Leann."

I smiled, glad he enjoyed my work, but before I could get him to continue his congratulatory remarks, he asked, "So, Lisa Leann, what's your take on Doreen's murder?"

I glanced at Henry then back at Clay. "It's downright horrible."

"But you don't believe Evie did it, do you?"

I shook my head. "Well, no."

"Not even by accident?"

I leaned my head against the sofa and contemplated the idea for a second before looking back at Clay. "Nope, I just can't see it."

"Well, then, Lisa Leann, who *do* you suspect?"

Henry answered for me. "If Doreen was drinking like they say, she probably fell and hit her head all by herself."

Clay nodded thoughtfully. "I thought about that, but I was at the scene, you know, photographing it for the sheriff's department. And honestly, I think there was a struggle. A lamp was smashed on the floor, the curtains were ripped off the rod, and . . . well . . . even some of the pictures were knocked off the walls."

"I hadn't heard that," Henry said.

I crossed my legs. "Well, who besides Evie is being investigated?"

Clay's eye sparked. "No one. Which is why I'm here. I, too, think Evie is probably innocent. She doesn't strike me as the violent type, and what went down in that trailer was, well, violent. So, I'm trying to put together a list of other potential suspects."

I looked at my husband. "Well, it wasn't us. We were just getting in from DIA that night, with the baby."

Clay smiled. "Don't worry, you're not on my list."

"Then who is?" Henry asked.

Clay sighed. "It's really a process of elimination. The other two people closest to the scene of the crime were Wade and Velvet."

"You don't suspect them?" I asked.

"No, no. They've got good alibis."

I blew out a puff of air. "Good. Then that leaves . . ."

Clay shrugged. "A stranger, maybe? Have you heard anything about anyone new in town who could be trouble?"

"We do have a lot of construction workers in town, working on the church and at a few other properties in the area. Maybe it could have been someone like that? Dee Dee worked as a barmaid—maybe she met her killer at the bar."

Clay made a note. "Good thought. I'll go to the tavern and ask a few questions. Say, has anyone noticed strange happenings at the church during all your construction?"

I cleared my throat. "I'm on the building committee and there was some talk—talk about a missing shovel and a series of strange holes dug behind the sanctuary."

"A missing shovel is not so unusual at a construction site," Henry said. "But the holes? That is strange."

"What kind of holes?" Clay asked.

"There were about three of them, each about four feet deep. They showed up sometime last weekend."

Clay looked up from his writing. "Are they still there?"

"Oh no, we had them filled in. Didn't want anyone to fall in and hurt themselves, you know."

"Have you heard any reports about other strange occurrences in town?"

"You mean other than someone stealing Vonnie's dog at the Gold Rush Grocery parking lot?"

Clay wiggled his pen between his fingers and scowled. "Yeah, I heard about that. Do you really think he was stolen?"

Before I could answer, the phone rang. I sprang up. "I bet that's Mandy." Within seconds I held the receiver to my ear, breathless. "Hello?"

A female voice said, "This is dispatch calling to let you know the security alarm has been activated at your wedding shop."

"What!"

"We have someone at the scene, and they've found your back door standing wide open. Could you come down to see if there's anything missing?"

"Um, certainly."

When I shared the news, Henry and Clay stood. Henry said, "Lisa Leann, you stay here with Kyle, I'll go check on things."

Clay asked my husband, "Mind if I go with you?"

"Come on," Henry said, grabbing a light denim jacket out of the hall closet.

I walked to the front window and watched the headlights of Henry's truck and Clay's car disappear over the hill as they drove toward town. I felt fear tingle down my spine. *A break-in?*

The shop wasn't far from home, about five minutes, and Henry had promised to call me on his cell as soon as he could.

I walked back to the guest bedroom and looked down at the sleeping baby before carefully scooping him in my arms so as not to disturb him. He stirred but continued to sleep as I carried him back to the picture window that overlooked the road in front of our condo. The moonlight reflected on Gold Lake creating a shimmering moonbeam path. I looked down at baby Kyle, and though I was almost shaking with worry, the love I felt for him calmed my very soul.

A movement on the dark road caught my eye as a lone bicycle rider crested the hill. It was late for a ride, I decided as I watched as the rider approached our cluster of condos. Just as he neared my apartment, he stopped and slipped off his bike. Was he staring up at me?

The darkness wouldn't reveal his features so I quickly shut the drapes, then checked the door to make sure it was locked.

My heart had started a wild thumping, so when the phone rang I let out a cry of alarm that startled the baby into a fuss. "Shhh, shhh, shhh, little one," I said as I jostled him. I shifted the baby to one arm then grabbed the receiver. "Hello?"

"Mom, is that Kyle? Is he all right?"

Kyle settled down with my swaying. "He's fine, Mandy, just misses you, as we all do. How's Ray?"

"That's why I called. He's still in and out of consciousness. The police were here a few minutes ago. They want to take him down to the station for questioning."

"What? Are you kidding?"

"We're not in America, you know, they do things differently here. I finally convinced them to wait, at least for now."

I walked back to the front window and looked outside. The bike leaned against the condo gate, silhouetted against the moonlight. But the rider? He was nowhere to be seen. How odd. He wasn't on the property, was he? I looked down toward the bushes near my front steps. Was that movement?

I shut the curtain again as an uneasy feeling settled in the pit of my stomach, a feeling that pattered my heart to a faster beat. Could the break-in at the shop simply have been a ruse to get Henry and me out of the house?

I turned my attention back to Mandy as I half-whispered, "Oh, how frightening this must be for you."

I could hear muffled sobs from the other end of the line. "You have no idea."

I was now on full alert, trying to think what to do. I mean, I didn't want to end this call with Mandy; I had questions she'd yet to answer. But if there was a prowler outside, then I needed to call for help without alarming my daughter. Still holding the phone, I carefully put the baby on the couch, in his Boppy. Then I slipped to the front hall closet to retrieve my purse. I pulled out my cell phone, and, still holding the house phone to one ear, I managed to text Henry's cell phone. *Plz com bk. Prowler outside.*

Just as I hit send, I glanced at the front door. The doorknob slowly turned.

I must have gasped because Mandy said, "Mom, are you there? Is everything okay?"

"I gotta go, sweetheart. Someone's at the door. Call me back in an hour if you can," I whispered and clicked out of the call.

"Hello? Who's out there?" I called.

When no one answered I played a bluff and bellowed, "I'm from Texas and I know how to use this snubnose .38 I'm pointing right at you."

Seconds later, I heard the patter of feet running across the condo grounds. I walked to the window and pulled back a corner of the curtain. The bike was no longer leaning against the gate. It and its rider had vanished into the night.

# 24

## Scorched Heart

Last night I dreamed of my mother. The way she had been when I was a child. Her lovely voice sang each of the haunting verses of the Elton John song "Candle in the Wind" while glowing candles illuminated her beauty. As her song faded, a breeze blew through her hair and the candles flickered. She whispered, *You never knew me, you never knew me.*

Her beauty diminished into shadows as each candle gave way to the darkness. For an instant, her wrinkled face reappeared in a final flicker of light. Her eyes, grayed in death, opened and her pale lips quivered as she spoke, directly to me . . . *You never knew me.*

I awoke, my heart pounding, seconds before my alarm radio activated to Elton singing the same song. I sat up, then I pulled my knees to my chest in a hug that wrapped around my legs and allowed me to rub the goose bumps from my arms.

I got up and splashed my face with cold water before looking in the mirror, only to see how my mother looked some thirty years ago.

Blinking away the cobwebs, I readied myself for my Sunday day shift, glad I'd at least had Saturday off, and glad I'd actually taken the time to make my mother's chicken and rice casserole the night before. It was a recipe I'd found on one of the handwritten cards Vonnie had given me. In fact, I had enough of the dish left to eat it again for breakfast.

Once at work, I was more than a bit surprised by the report that Jerry had left for me. He'd had a busy night with the break-in at Lisa Leann's bridal shop as well as this business about a prowler at her house.

This news got me to thinking. With all these strange occurrences, what if Evie *was* telling the truth? What if someone else had been with my mother the night she died? But how would these events fit into the puzzle? Could the break-in and prowler be connected to my mother's death? I rubbed my forehead as I considered the possibility, or even the possibility of Vonnie's dog's disappearance playing a part in the crime. So help me if I didn't smile as I tried to imagine Chucky with a dangerous secret. I let my smile dissolve. None of this made sense. Unless, of course, my mother, Lisa Leann, or even Vonnie or her dog had something the killer wanted. But what?

I decided to start my morning patrol by swinging by the church. I drove slowly toward the parking lot, wishing I could be in worship today. But after the murder and all the things that went along with it, the department was more than a little short staffed. Besides, someone had to be on duty in case there were any more strange happenings. I hoped that by the time Nate Sawyer returned from his weekend off, I'd have some new leads we could discuss.

I noted that David's black Mazda sat next to Vonnie's Taurus. Well, at least he wasn't still in Aspen with his redheaded Barbie. I felt my brows pinch together. Just what was up with that? Not only did the man hide the fact that his friend was *female*, he'd failed to mention they'd once been engaged. Of course, as I was not returning his calls, I might never know what was going on with him.

I looked at my watch, realizing the morning service was already in progress. I decided to pull into the parking lot and walk around to look at the construction site. As I'd only just heard about the missing shovel and mysterious holes, I wanted to take a look to make sure there were no dead bodies buried out there.

I hopped out of my Bronco and walked around to where the new youth wing was going up. The construction site was the perfect picture of concrete and mud. I was glad to see that the foundation had already been poured and the steel structural framework, as well as the electrical wiring, was in place. It wouldn't be much longer before this framework had walls and a roof, which was a good thing, since it was almost snow season.

I decided to venture beyond the construction zone, to behind the church sanctuary. The good people inside wouldn't be able to see me from this angle, and I'd wanted to follow up on the report about the holes that had been dug back there. Sure enough, I saw the grassy area with three circles of packed, fresh dirt. *What in the world?*

I walked over and squatted down on one knee to get a better look, touching the earth before me. There were large boot prints around, probably belonging to the workmen who'd filled in the holes, but there were also a couple of bicycle tracks. No doubt belonging to some of the local kids who used this strip of land as a shortcut through the neighborhood.

"Donna!"

I was surprised to see David striding across the grass toward me. "I was in the foyer when you pulled in," he said when he'd closed the gap between us. David was dressed in high country church casual: khakis and a black golf shirt. His hands were in his pockets and the look on his face was mingled with both fear and hope. "What are you doing back here?"

I folded my arms. "Just snooping. Heard someone was digging around back here."

David's chuckle was low as I stood up. "Yeah, I heard something about that." He squinted at me. "So any theories?"

I nodded slowly and crossed my arms. "About the holes or my love life?"

David let a smile play on his lips. "I guess I'd be more interested in your love life."

"Well," I said, "I thought things were good, you know, with the guy I was dating. But . . ."

David braved another step closer. "But you're thinking he might really be a jerk? Right?"

I pressed my lips together and nodded. "Yeah."

"Well, what if he had a good explanation for the things he did? What if . . ." David pulled his hands out of his pockets and gestured with his palms up.

I held up a hand as if I was stopping traffic. "What kind of explanation could, let's say, a non-jerk have for failing to report he was spending time with an old flame?"

"You saw her, Donna. And you had to have noticed, she's artificial."

I crossed my arms. "What are you talking about? Her bustline or her veneers?"

"I'm talking about Bobbie Ann Jackson. Bobbie's real name is Roberta Anita Swartz, that is, until she changed it."

"You mean she remade herself, with a new name and a bit of plastic surgery?"

David narrowed his eyes. "Well, yeah, that and her shrink who's been busy reprogramming her head. You could say she's a whole new person. Not much like the woman I first met."

"Are you saying there's something wrong with trying to better yourself?"

"Well, no, if your goal is to be a better person. But it's like all of Bobbie's beauty treatments made her lose sight of her true self."

"Or else her true self was finally released."

203

David smiled and reached out as if he wanted to take my hand. "You're getting the picture."

I continued to hug my arms. "But she's out of your life, right? All I ever knew about your ex-fiancée was that she left you to get engaged to your best friend."

David shook his head and stepped nearer. "Well, they were engaged. But I guess they broke up."

I stepped back. "So she's on the prowl. Did the two of you hook up when you went to Aspen in the middle of the night? Alone? I mean, you could have invited your girlfriend along to chaperone."

David raised a brow at my question but never broke eye contact. "No, we did not hook up. The reason I didn't invite you is because I knew Bobbie would mistreat you. She's not always so nice."

I had to laugh at that one. As I walked past him, I turned around. "You don't think I can take care of myself?"

He turned to face me. "Of course I do, it's just that I didn't want to put you through that, especially after your mother was murdered. We haven't even had a chance to grieve together."

I turned and walked back to the parking lot as he followed me. "You're still a mystery to me, David. Sometimes I wonder if I even know you, not to mention your people."

David caught up with me at my Bronco. "Donna, you *do* know my people. Vonnie, Fred, and *you*, you're the only people I have."

I put my hand on the door handle of my truck and stared at David's reflection in my window. Without turning, I said, "I don't know if I'm buying that. You've lived your entire life without us. Without me."

"That life is in the past. I'm not living there, Donna. I'm trying to live with you."

I turned and swung open the door of my Bronco and climbed in as he said, "Wait, that didn't come out right. What I meant is—"

"Later," I said, shutting my door as I gave him a salute-like wave. I cracked my window. "I've got some things I have to check."

As I pulled out of the parking lot, my heart spun with questions about David, my mother's death, and the events of last night. I soon pulled my truck into Lisa Leann's driveway, walked up her front steps, and gave a little knock on the door. Lisa Leann never missed church, but under the circumstances, I suspected I'd find her home.

I wasn't surprised when she opened the door. "Donna, come in. Henry ran down to the church, but Kyle and I are here."

"How is the baby?" I asked.

Lisa Leann put her finger to her lips as she dropped her voice. "He's taking his morning nap." She gestured at the sofa for me to sit. "Have you had breakfast? Can I get you a cup of coffee?"

"I'm fine. Heard Ray is still in the hospital. When will he and Mandy come home?"

Lisa Leann shrugged. "We're not sure yet."

"I'm really sorry to hear that."

Lisa Leann approached me, then leaned down and gave me a hug. "Me too, and I'm very sorry about your mother."

When she pulled away, I stared down at my hands. "Yeah, it's tough. In fact, I'm wondering if I could ask you a couple of questions about my mom."

She sat next to me on the couch. "Don't know if I can help, but sure."

"Did you ever see her around town or ever really talk to her?"

"Not really." Lisa Leann slid one leg beneath her and turned to face me. "I saw her a time or two, like when she surprised you by singing at our Christmas tea, but I can't say that I ever had a real conversation with her."

I studied her for a moment. "I thought as much. But let me ask you this. Did the two of you have any friends in common?"

"Other than you and the potluckers? I don't think so."

"What about people here at the condo, would anyone here know both you and Doreen?"

Lisa Leann blinked. "I guess it's possible. I'm not privy to know who hangs out at the Gold Rush Tavern. But no one's ever mentioned her to me."

"Okay. Just exploring a theory."

"Wish I could be of more help."

I waved it off. "Back to business. I read the reports about the break-in at the shop. I understand Henry doesn't think anything was taken. But have you been down there and looked yourself?"

"Didn't need to." Lisa retrieved her laptop from her kitchen table. "Clay shot these photos for me and emailed them to me just this morning. Nothing's disturbed. See?"

I frowned and leaned in for a closer look as I flipped through the photos, one at a time, on the screen. "That's strange. Nothing looks out of place."

"No, except . . ."

"What?"

She pointed to a picture of a maroon-colored Persian carpet that was spread in front of the fireplace. "See, it's mussed. How could that have happened?"

"You don't think Clay or Henry or Jerry could have tripped over it?"

Lisa Leann walked over and looked at the baby monitor, which showed an image of her sleeping grandson, before turning back to me. "No, I don't think so. Henry said it was like that when they arrived."

I leaned back in my chair. "Well, you've had the baby over at the shop, right? Maybe it happened then?"

"The one time we went, Kyle and I hung out in my upstairs office."

"Ah. Okay. Well, I can't think of why any prowler would only move the edge of a carpet. Can you?"

"Not really." Lisa Leann stood, then fished a key out of her purse. "But would you mind dropping by to check it out?" She scribbled a code on a piece of paper. "Here's the alarm's key code. You've used it before, right?"

"I have. But before I go, tell me about the prowler you had here at the house."

"Soon as Henry and Clay left, some bicyclist, I couldn't make out who he was, parked his bike at the front gate, then walked over to my condo."

"Did he knock or call out to you?"

"No. He tried to open the door. I saw the doorknob turn."

"What did you do?"

"Thanked God I'd locked the door, then I scared him off with my comments about my gun."

That caught my attention. "You've got a gun here in the condo?"

"Well, darlin', I'm from Texas; what do *you* think? I didn't use it, I didn't even get it out, but the mention of it did the trick."

"I see. Do you mind if I go outside and look around?"

"Be my guest."

Moments later, I stood at the gate, looking up at Lisa Leann's condo while she stood at the second story window waving down at me. If that's where she was last night, when the cyclist came along, then there was no question that he saw her. And if the cyclist was the same person who broke into her wedding shop, then her husband would have passed him on the road. The cyclist very well could have known she was there alone.

I walked back toward the condo steps, watching the ground for anything of interest. I stepped over toward the shrubs near the first floor garage window. I tried it and found it locked shut. I kicked back at the flowers and shrubs. I stared down at a large boot print, which I photographed with the camera in my phone.

"What's this?" Could this print belong to the mysterious cyclist or perhaps someone in groundskeeping? But since when did the cyclists around here wear boots instead of bike cleats?

I started back toward my Bronco, but not before giving Lisa Leann a wave. I could see that she was now cradling her grandson in her arms. I held up the key and gestured that I was heading toward her shop. She nodded, then opened her front door. "Call me if you find anything," she called down.

"Will do."

Within minutes, I was at the backdoor of Lisa Leann's wedding boutique. I used the key, then stepped inside and quickly punched in the code on the alarm pad.

I shut the door and looked around. The old Victorian cottage was eerily quiet. "Hello?" I called into the silence.

I began by walking through Lisa Leann's state-of-the-art kitchen, then pushed through the double doors and into her front parlor. I looked at the oak floors, the mahogany woodwork, and the antique fireplace. This home was every bit as old as the church.

I walked toward the fireplace and stared down at the maroon rug, still mussed as Lisa Leann had said. I leaned down and straightened it out.

Odd that the carpet, a valuable piece, was only mussed and not stolen. I lifted the corner of the rug and pulled it back. The oak floorboards beneath it looked polished and sturdy. But the end of one of the boards was littered with soft scratches, like pry marks. I pulled on my latex gloves and touched the scratches with my fingers.

Then it hit me. Was the board loose? I pushed down on the board with three fingers and tried to wiggle it back and forth.

Yes, it had some play, but could I pull it out?

I went back into the kitchen and retrieved a hard plastic spatula, which I inserted between the boards before applying pressure like a lever. Slowly . . . carefully . . . the board lifted, and a small dark space appeared beneath the floor.

This was somebody's hiding place. I fished my flashlight off my belt, switched it on, and peered inside. Empty. Whoever had been here had to know just what they were looking for, but had they found it? Maybe not, especially if they'd bothered to drop by Lisa Leann's condo last night. What if the perp thought Lisa Leann had what they were looking for?

Whatever was hidden in this secret compartment could have easily been here since before the Lamberts bought this place, or even for the last one hundred plus years for that matter.

I'd have to go down to the county clerk tomorrow to check the history of who had owned this old house before the Lamberts. Maybe an owner's name or two would finally shed some light on what was really going on.

# 25

## Jail Dressing

On Tuesday, I was looking over my mother's old recipe for scalloped asparagus casserole when Vernon came home with the news.

"A grand jury is being presented with the evidence of the case, Evie. They're looking to arrest you."

He stood in the doorway of the kitchen, wearing his civvies and looking about as bedraggled as an old dog left out in the rain one too many nights.

I leaned against the kitchen countertop and sighed. "So that's why you took off so early this morning." I could barely hear my voice for the pounding of my heart in my ears.

He nodded, then pointed to the kitchen table and chairs, suggesting that we sit.

I didn't argue. I sat at one end of the table while he sat at another. Even if we stretched, we couldn't touch. Right now, I thought that was best. If his pinky so much as touched mine, I would dissolve into a torrent of tears and quivers.

"I got a call early this morning," he started. "From Nate Sawyer. You remember . . ."

How could I forget? "Yes." The room started spinning. I squeezed my eyes shut, then reopened them. "And?"

"He let me know that the evidence would be presented to the grand jury as soon as one could be assembled. Probably this afternoon at 2:00."

I looked at my watch. It was nearly 1:45. "Fifteen minutes." I swallowed hard. "Vernon," I said, looking up at my husband. "I did not kill Doreen."

"I know that."

"I never even went into her trailer."

"I know that too." He ran his thick fingers through the thinning silvery-gray hair at the crown of his head. "I told him what Lizzie and Goldie had said regarding your comments about Doreen the day following the murder. I told him that they said you gave no indication that you entered that trailer or that anything happened other than a discussion about Doreen's drinking."

"And? Didn't he believe it?" I placed my hand on the table and splayed my fingers before looking back at my husband. "What possible motive does he think I had?"

Vernon shook his head. "He's not telling me much," he said. "What with you being my wife . . ."

"What will they do, this grand jury?"

"The state is presenting the evidence. Donna is testifying, as are Nate and Jerry. Clay photographed the scene; he's been called. Velvet and Wade, of course. A few people from the grocery store and those who heard you and Velvet arguing."

I crooked my arm on the table and laid my head into it. "Oh, Vernon. I'm too old for this . . . this nonsense."

Vernon stood. I peered at him from the corner of my eye, watched him walk to the refrigerator, open it, and bring out a pitcher of iced tea. "Want something to drink?" he asked.

211

I sat up straight. "Yeah. Sure."

"You may think this is nonsense, Evie, but Nate Sawyer is dead serious." He placed the pitcher on the counter and then reached for a couple of glasses in the cabinet.

"But they have no evidence, Vernon. Not really."

"That's for the grand jury to decide."

"Aren't I going to be called to testify? Shouldn't I be?" I watched as tea sloshed from the pitcher to the glasses.

"Nate thinks he can get a warrant for your arrest whether you testify or not."

"A warrant for my . . ." I slammed my fist on the table. Vernon jumped, then calmly picked up the glasses and brought one to me.

"Prepare yourself, Evie-girl. I think they have enough evidence. I've seen grand juries bring charges with less. Besides, we don't know what evidence Nate has dug up."

My throat went dry. I tried to quench it with a swallow of tea, but it did little good. "Oh, God," I said, looking toward the ceiling and beyond that to heaven, "please don't let me be arrested. You know I didn't do this . . ." I looked down to the tea glass in my hand, then took another swallow. Then another followed by another until the glass was empty. Then I stood.

Vernon, who had returned to his seat at the other end of the table, asked, "Where are you going?"

I raised my chin. "I'm going to prepare my scalloped asparagus casserole," I said as though nothing was wrong. As though nothing in the world that might have an effect on me was going on. As though my own stepdaughter—whom I loved dearly—was not, at this very minute, giving some cockamamie testimony sure to have me arrested before the sun went down.

"Need any help?" Vernon asked.

"No," I answered. "I'm perfectly capable of cooking on my own."

---

I was arrested a few hours later.

When the knock came at the door, I was standing in front of our bedroom dresser, leaning over it and staring at my reflection in the mirror. I had taken a long, hot bath. I'd slathered myself in body lotion—Jergens, to be exact—and I'd slipped into a pair of black slacks, a white long-sleeved shirt, and a gray jacket. I accessorized with pink pearl earrings and a single-strand pink pearl necklace.

Lisa Leann says that pink brings out my natural beauty.

If I was going to be arrested, then by George I was going to look nice when they handcuffed me and marched me into the courthouse. No doubt with the press close at hand, ready to report that one of the stars of *The Great Party Showdown* was being arrested for the murder of her husband's ex-wife.

I heard the muffled voices of my husband and Nate Sawyer. I walked to the bedroom door, cracked it, and listened.

"I'll get her," Vernon was saying.

Then, to my horror, I heard Donna's voice. "Dad. Let me. Let me go talk to her first."

Vernon paused before saying, "All right, then."

I opened the door fully and then went back to the dresser, where my bamboo-handled purse sat waiting. I reached into it, pulled out a tube of lip gloss, and proceeded to smear the goo across my lips just as Donna entered the room.

"What are you doing?" she asked.

I continued with the application. "If I'm going to jail, then I'm at least going to look nice."

I heard the door click as Donna closed it behind her. "Listen, Evie. We need to talk."

I turned to her. She was dressed strangely similar to me. Black pants, white long-sleeved button-down shirt. The only difference was that she wore her black sheriff's jacket and no accessories. "I think we've said all there is to say," I replied.

Donna shook her head. "I don't think so." She jerked her head toward the front of the house. "You know we have a warrant, I suppose."

"I do."

"You know we went before the grand jury."

"Yes."

She crossed her arms. "Look, Evie. For what it's worth, there's something pretty weird going on around here . . . around town, I mean."

"Like?"

"Like holes being dug behind the church. The boutique being broken into. Lisa Leann's house nearly being invaded."

"Your father told me." I blinked a few times, then said, "You think all that is tied to Doreen somehow?" My voice was whisper soft, and I leaned against the dresser for support.

"I don't know what I think anymore. I tried to talk to Nate about it all this morning, but I think he's set on this arrest, and it really doesn't matter what I say or think. And to be honest, I no longer know what I think . . ."

Well, that was something, wasn't it? "But why?" I asked. "Why is he so interested in arresting me?"

"Because, Evangeline. You're the sheriff's wife. You're the one-time star of *The Great Party Showdown*. You're Evil-Evie."

I bristled at the words. "I most assuredly am not . . ." I waved my hands in the air as though erasing the words Donna had just said. "Donna—I. Did. Not. Kill. Doreen."

"Somebody did."

"Not me."

"Then who?"

"I don't know."

She sighed. "And you're all we've got."

"That *and* an arrest warrant."

"I'm afraid so." She paused. "I just wanted to tell you . . . before I walk you in there and . . . well, I just wanted to tell you that I have a few hunches. I don't know what they're going to lead to, but I promise you I'll do my best."

I walked over to my stepdaughter and cupped my hand on her shoulder. "I appreciate that, Donna. Knowing you thought . . . well, I just couldn't bear you thinking I'd done this."

We stared at each other for a good long time before she said, "Ready?"

"As I'll ever be."

———

I was given a cell of my own. I was led to a room where I was searched—and no, I don't want to talk about it—told to take off my clothes, put in an orange jumpsuit (orange!), and then told to put my nice suit into a small bag that was labeled with my name.

Evangeline Vesey: 20100003676.

I was being assigned to the B pod, according to the booking officer at the county jail. She said—oh-so-matter-of-factly—that I was practically going to be alone in there.

Not a lot of crime in Summit County, apparently.

I was taken to the single cot cell, given a pillow, a sheet, and a blanket, and told to get comfortable for the night. "Tomorrow you'll be arraigned," she said. Then she smiled at me. "I'm sure you'll be safe at home this time tomorrow."

I refused to sleep. I refused even to lie down. I made up my cot and then sat on it, sitting straight and tall for a good hour before I finally caved in and lay down. I crossed my feet at the ankles, laced my fingers together across my middle, and then stared up at the ceiling. I recited the Lord's Prayer, the 23rd Psalm, and any other Scripture verse I could bring to mind. I chided myself for not having memorized more.

I listened to the murmurings coming through walls from far away. I tried to make out the conversations but couldn't. Every so often I heard the opening and closing of a door, a desk drawer, and—at one point—soft snoring.

With a jerk, I realized it was my own.

At 7:00 I was brought breakfast. At 7:30 Vernon showed up. I've never been so happy to see anyone in my life. He held me for a moment then said, "You do all right in here?"

I nodded, but I didn't say anything.

"It was a long night without you," he whispered.

"For me too, without you, I mean."

He held me at arm's length. "You look like you didn't sleep a wink."

I felt myself blush. "Maybe for a few minutes."

Vernon looked down at his watch. "I've got Chris Lowe coming in a few minutes, Evie. He's bringing a guy named Van Lauer."

"Wasn't he . . ." I didn't finish my sentence.

"Wasn't he what?"

I shook my head. If I remembered correctly, Van Lauer was the attorney Goldie had been involved with—albeit briefly—back when she and Jack had separated. "Why is he bringing Van Lauer?"

"He told me that Van just happened to be in town, and he's a criminal attorney with more experience in this kind of thing. Chris thinks he'll do a good job for us. They were law school buddies."

I nodded.

"Just tell him everything you've told me. He'll do the rest."

"Okay."

Van and Chris arrived a short while later. We were taken to a small room with a metal table and four hard-as-brick chairs. Van pulled out a legal pad from his dark brown attaché case, then a pen from inside his suit coat pocket.

It looked expensive. Very expensive. I wondered how we were ever going to pay for this man's services. As I gave my version of the encounters I'd had with Doreen in the supermarket, Velvet on the street, and Doreen at her home, Van Lauer took detailed notes. Once I finished telling my side, he leaned back in his chair and said, "Okay. I don't think you're a flight risk. And you have no prior record. All they have is circumstantial, so I think we can have you released on your own recognizance."

"Thank God," Vernon said.

"Does that mean I can go home?" I asked.

Van Lauer—and goodness, but wasn't he a handsome man?—smiled. I watched the crow's feet gather around his eyes and then relax. "Yes, Mrs. Vesey. We'll have you home in no time."

———

The girls were sitting in the courtroom, waiting for me as I was ushered in.

So was the press.

I smiled at the first and sneered at the second.

By now I had redressed into the clothes I'd worn the day before. I'd combed my hair and even put on my lip gloss again. When I caught Lisa Leann's eye, she pointed to her own lips and then mouthed: "Looks good."

I couldn't help but smile. But only a little. After all, I had to convince this judge I was standing before that I was taking all this seriously—and I was—and that I was as innocent as I claimed to be.

The district attorney was asked by the bailiff to read the charges, and she did.

When the words "manslaughter in the first degree" were spoken out loud, I felt myself swoon. I had known this, of course. I'd heard these same words from the mouth of Nate Sawyer and had discussed them with Van Lauer and Chris Lowe.

"A person is guilty of first-degree manslaughter," Van Lauer had said, "when a person dies due to serious injury brought about by another person and the person committing the crime intended to do serious injury to that person."

Van said he expected that the district attorney would end up making us an offer to settle for manslaughter second degree, meaning that no malice had been intended.

"I never laid a hand on her," I said straightforward. "With malice or otherwise."

Then Van had only nodded. This time, he placed his arm around my shoulder and whispered, "You okay?"

I collected myself and stood straight once more.

"Mr. Lauer, how does your client plead?"

"Not guilty, your honor," he said. His voice sounded as strong and masculine as any I'd ever heard in my life.

The judge—a man in his early fifties, what with the salt and peppering of his hair and beard and with his reading glasses perched near the tip of his nose—turned back to the district attorney.

"We're requesting a million in bail, your honor."

Awe and shock rippled through the courtroom. The judge hammered his gavel. "Enough." Turning to Van, he asked, "Mr. Lauer?"

"Your honor, we request that Mrs. Vesey be released on her own recognizance. The evidence is circumstantial at best, she is a beloved member of this community, she's married to the sheriff and is the stepmother to the deputy sheriff. Her father was the former mayor and—"

The judge waved his hand around his head as though a bug had somehow gotten inside the courthouse and was buzzing around his ear. "I know who she is, Mr. Lauer. My wife and I watch television, and I've been a citizen of this county since the day I was born. Evangeline Benson Vesey is no stranger to me."

I looked at the judge and blinked . . . waiting. I could hear the held breath of every one of my friends and family members behind me. I could imagine the pencils of the reporters, poised over pads of paper, and their cameras ready to snap my photograph.

"Your honor," the district attorney began.

But the judge continued, "Enough, Ms. Bennett. I realize the seriousness of this crime, but I also know this woman doesn't have so much as a parking ticket. She's not going anywhere." Then he turned to me. "Mrs. Vesey, do you have a visa?"

I cleared my throat. "I do not."

"Well, then," he said. "I don't see you as being a flight risk nor do I think you are a danger to this community. I'm releasing you on your own recognizance, but I expect you to check in with the court at least once a week until trial, and I expect you not to leave the county."

I nodded. "I understand."

The judge looked over at the woman sitting to his left. "When do we set this for trial?" he asked.

After a moment or two of staring at a computer screen, she answered, "Week of January 7."

"Ladies and gentleman," the judge announced, "we're setting *voir dire* on January 7 at 8:30 a.m. Any questions?"

When no one answered, the gavel came down again, and with that I was dismissed to go home.

# 26

## Sweet Tea

Vernon had slipped me the key to the house, so the girls and I went over to the Veseys' immediately after court to prepare a luncheon for when he and Evie got back from the courthouse. They had to stay a while longer, of course, to finalize paperwork.

Well, I say "the girls." Donna wasn't there; she'd left the courthouse after the hearing and went back to working her shift.

"It's a shame Donna can't be here," Lisa Leann said as though reading my mind. "Did I tell y'all that she came by to see me the other day?" Lisa Leann placed a plate of Texas fried chicken on Evie's kitchen table. It was covered in aluminum foil and still I could smell its deliciousness from across the room where I stood at the stove dropping tea bags into a pot of boiling water.

"What'd she say?" Lizzie asked from the refrigerator. She was pulling a crisp tossed salad from the refrigerator, one she'd brought by before heading to the courthouse. "Anything in particular?"

Lisa Leann bobbed her head. "She said she's got a hunch about

220

something, though she didn't say what. She did go over to the boutique, though."

"How come?" I asked. I turned off the stove's burner, added two-thirds of a cup of sugar to the now-boiling tea, and then secured the lid onto the pot. I looked at the measuring cup in my hand and frowned. In my mother's day and in the earlier years of my marriage, more than a cup of sugar would have been added to the brew. But these days we were all trying to watch our sugar intake and stay healthy.

Fat lot of good it had done Jack.

"Why don't you try Splenda or something?" Vonnie asked from the other side of the room where she was warming potatoes in the microwave. "I just cannot believe all that sugar is healthy."

"No self-respecting Southern girl would dare put anything but sugar in her sweet tea," I said, adding an extra twang to my accent.

"No, ma'am," Lisa Leann seconded. "We Southerners know our way around a recipe for sweet tea, and it doesn't include anything artificial for sweetening."

I smiled at Lisa Leann. Bless her heart, she didn't realize that most Georgia-bred Southern girls don't consider Texas to be part of the South but rather the West, what with their ten-gallon hats for the men and pink cowboy boots for the ladies. "Back to Donna," I said. "Why'd she go to the boutique?"

Lisa Leann looked at me as though I'd just fallen out of a tree. "You know about the break-in."

I shrugged then reached for a gallon pitcher standing next to the stove. I took it over to the sink to rinse. "Of course I know about the break-in. I was just wondering if she had any leads."

"Well . . ." Lisa Leann lowered her voice. "I can tell you this much . . . nothing was taken from the boutique, but the carpet—you know the pretty Momeni at the fireplace?"

"The what?" Vonnie asked just as the microwave dinged, letting her know the potatoes were well heated.

Lisa Leann looked exasperated. "The Momeni . . . well, never mind. It's the maroon rug with the green leaves and the pretty flowers."

Yes, we knew the rug. I stopped rinsing the gallon pitcher and rested for a minute with my arms crossed, waiting for the tea to finish steeping in the pot.

"Anyway," Lisa Leann continued, "apparently someone had mussed it."

"Mussed it?" Lizzie chimed in. She'd already begun to set the table, and Lisa Leann joined in to help her. "Why would anyone go into the boutique and simply muss a rug?"

"I don't know. But she called me and asked if I knew who owned the house before Henry bought it for me so I could have my wedding boutique. I told her I didn't and she'd have to either ask Henry or go look it up. But Henry told her he bought it from the bank—from Samuel." She stopped in her table-setting tasks to look at Lizzie.

"Well, not from Samuel per se," Lizzie was quick to correct. "But from the bank, yes. But I can tell you who owned the house, and Vonnie will remember too. Old Mrs. Hirvela—"

Just then we heard the front door open. Evie called out, "I'm home!" as though she'd been gone a month of Sundays. We girls all stopped our lunch preparation tasks and hurried to the front of the house to greet her.

I have to admit, Evangeline looked like a caged bird set free. She was bustling about the living room, picking up the newspaper Vernon had apparently been reading earlier in the morning before he left for the courthouse.

"Oh, Vernon," she said. "Look at all this mess and us with company."

Company? We were hardly company. But then I looked toward the front parlor to see both Chris Lowe and Van Lauer stepping over the threshold of the front door and into the house. I felt heat rise in my cheeks, my natural instincts going to war with my love—my foolish, foolish love—for Jack.

I spun around before anyone might notice and returned to the kitchen, where I finished preparing the tea. And I listened as everyone clucked around Evangeline. Soon enough the whole lot of them had joined me. I stayed busy getting ice in the glasses, then pouring the tea and setting them at the top right of the plates.

"Please tell me," Van said from behind me, "that I'm looking at genuine sweet Southern iced tea."

I glanced up briefly and said, "Of course it is." Even to my ears it sounded as though I were scolding a boy rather than answering a man.

We had to set two extra places at the table because we'd not been told that Chris and Van were coming to the house. When they saw Vonnie make the correction they both apologized. But then Evangeline said, "After lunch we have to talk legal strategy." Then she pinked and said, "Not that I'm shooing you all away. I cannot tell you how much I appreciate all this."

As we took our places at the table I said, "That's okay, Evie. I'll be going up to the office after lunch anyway." I glanced at Chris. "I take it you've cleared your calendar for this afternoon, or do I need to do that?"

Chris shook his head. "Already taken care of, but thank you."

Lizzie added, "And I have to get back to the high school. The kids are working hard doing their research for the Founders Day concert next Friday night and I really need to be there to help."

"Oh!" Lisa Leann jumped in. "That brings up another point . . ."

But before she could finish, Vernon said, "Why don't I say the blessing so we can eat while we talk?" To which we all laughed, then sobered as Vernon prayed.

———

I was sitting at my desk by 2:00 that afternoon, listening to and noting the various phone calls that had come in that morning, mostly from reporters wanting to interview Evangeline, Chris, Van, or all three. I knew what Chris's response would be, but I placed the little pink message slips on his desk anyway.

Lisa Leann called at around 3:30 to say she was heading over to the church to store some things we'd need for the Founders Day dinner. "I've managed to find some old photographs of Father John Dyer that I've had blown up," she said. "And the card shop you're sitting on top of has ordered little plastic snowshoes that we're going to scatter all over the tables, so I was wondering if you could get them on your way out and drop them off at the church." It wasn't really a question of whether or not I could but if I would.

"Be happy to," I said. "It won't be until after 5:00 though."

"That's okay. I'll probably not get there until 4:00 or so because I need to stop at Walmart for some paper goods. Can you believe this thing is only a week and a half away?"

I looked at my desk calendar. Today was the 5th of October. Friday the 15th the celebration began. Ten days. Only ten days, and with so much going on I wondered how we were going to pull it off. "Good thing we had all that get-it-done-quick training from the TV show, huh?" I teased.

"You betcha it is," she answered with a laugh. "Okay, girl. I'm off . . ."

Van and Chris returned to the office no more than a minute after I hung up the phone. "Oh," I said, mostly because I was startled to see Van, though I don't know why. Seemed to me he just kept turning up every time I turned around. "Um, would you like some coffee?"

They both nodded and Chris said, "Thanks, Goldie, that would be nice. We'll be in my office talking. Can you just bring it in there?"

"I'd be happy to," I said, then stood and made my way to our little kitchen/break room where the coffeepot stood on its head in the drainer in the sink. As I set about to prepare the coffee I heard the door of the room next to the break room open and then close.

Someone—and it had to be Van—was using the restroom.

I knew it had to be Van because Chris would have used his

private bath. And then I wondered, as I measured out the coffee into the gold-wire filter, why Van hadn't just gone in there. I added the water to the back of the coffeemaker then pushed the start button.

"Hi." A voice behind me broke my concentration.

I turned. "Hello, Van." I swallowed hard. "I just started the coffee."

He leaned against the door's frame and crossed his arms. "So I see. Look, Goldie . . . I told Chris I needed to use the restroom, but really I wanted to talk to you. Privately."

I stood rigid. "So . . . talk." It wasn't like me to be unkind, really it wasn't. But this was too much and too soon after Jack's death. Goodness, he'd only been gone a few weeks. It was hardly appropriate for Van and me to discuss *anything* much less if it had to do with our one-time relationship.

Oh, why did he have to be so handsome?

"I just wanted to say," he began slowly, "that I don't want to make you uncomfortable, though clearly I am. I wanted to explain to you why I'm even here . . . why I came into town in the first place."

"Yes, why did you?" I crossed my arms.

He took in a deep breath and blew it out. "I was actually in Vail on vacation. I decided to take it a little earlier this year. Do some more golfing. No skiing this time."

I didn't respond. Mainly because I couldn't think of a single thing to say.

"And so," he continued, "when I heard about Jack's passing I asked Chris if I could attend the services with him and his family, and then I simply went back to Vail to . . . well, to enjoy the rest of my vacation. Then this thing happened . . ."

By "this thing" I assumed he meant Doreen's murder and Evie's arrest. "Just how long *is* your vacation?" I asked after mentally calculating the time line.

"It's over," he said. "But Chris said that Vernon was beside himself, and I knew that Evangeline was an old friend of yours . . . yours and Jack's."

"Yes, she was. Is! I mean, yes, she is."

He smiled, showing beautifully white, even teeth.

"Look, what I'm trying to say, and doing a bad job of it, is that I don't want you to feel uncomfortable. Yes, you and I . . . dated, if you want to call it that . . ."

"We were just friends, Jack."

He stared at me kind of funny.

"What?" I asked. "Why are you looking at me like that?"

"You just called me Jack."

"No, I didn't."

To which he chuckled. "Yes. Yes, you did. But I understand. And yes, we were just friends. Two friends who might have become more had Jack not been your husband and had I not been such a good guy." He raised his brow for effect.

And I smiled. "You *are* a good guy."

"Good. Then we both agree that we'll continue to be friends. You'll do your job for Chris and I'll do mine for Evangeline, and no more of this feeling strange around each other. Right?"

"Right."

And with that he winked, turned, and walked away . . . just as the coffeepot coughed and sighed, letting me know the brewing was done.

———

Before I left the office I received another call, this time from Andrew.

"Just calling to make sure you're doing okay," he said.

I hadn't heard from him in several days, and the call caught me as off guard as everything else had that day. "I'm fine," I said. "I went back to work yesterday . . . but I guess you know that."

"Actually, I do," he said. "I think it's a little soon, though. Are you sure you're up to it?"

Wasn't this just what I needed? Jack's daughter—*my* daughter— fussing over me all the time, and now Jack's son doing the same?

I closed my eyes. A dead husband in the grave and an old "friend" in and out of this office. Somewhere deep inside I wanted to just let out the most bloodcurdling scream ever let loose in the history of time. In fact, I thought, I just might go home and do that very thing later this evening.

No, I wouldn't, I told myself. I had too much pride for that. Besides, it would alert all the neighbors, and one of them might call Olivia, who would then pound on my door and demand to be let in. Or worse—she'd just use her key and let herself in!

My eyes popped open. "How'd you know I went back to work?" I asked.

I heard a low chuckle from the other end of the line. I couldn't help but think it sounded just like Jack's—just like his father's. "I was in the card shop today and Britney told me."

"What? Is my personal life suddenly subject for conversation?"

"No. I simply told her I'd seen your car parked around back, and she said you'd come back to work as of yesterday. We both think it's too soon, by the way."

I frowned. "You do, do you?"

"Yes. I would have just come up to talk with you but . . ."

He didn't finish. He didn't have to. I instinctively knew what the rest of his sentence would have been. *Should* have been. He didn't want Chris to wonder why an employee of the funeral home was checking up on the recently departed's widow.

And with that, my suspicions were confirmed: Andrew Morrow *knew* that Jack Dippel was his father.

And, if what I suspected was correct, he'd known it all along.

# 27

## Research Relish

I left Evie's and went straight to the high school. On the way I made two phone calls: the first to the center where my mother lives and the second to Samuel.

The center informed me that Mom was doing just fine, that she was comfortable, eating well, and I was to put my mind at ease. "Come by any time you'd like, Mrs. Prattle, but she's fine. She doesn't know when you come and when you don't, so don't make yourself feel guilty if you miss a day now and then."

Miss a day? Lately, it seemed, I'd missed a whole lot more than a day. But what with school, two jobs, worrying about Michelle wanting to get pregnant, taking care of Samuel, and now this mess with Evangeline, I hardly had time to take a bath much less make sure Mom had had hers.

My call to Samuel was quick and to the point. I'd already called him after court to let him know the results of the morning's hearing. Now I needed to tell him I would be late getting home from work. "Several of the kids are going to stay after school to work on the Founders Day research for the concert next Friday night," I said. "And, of course, I'll need to be here with them. There's a chicken tetrazzini in the freezer if you want to put that in the oven when you get home."

"Sounds good. Don't work too hard," he said.

We hung up after a couple of air kisses, about the same time as I drove my car into the faculty parking lot of the school where our flag continued to fly at half-mast in memory of Jack.

I sighed, then picked up my purse from the front passenger seat and reached to the backseat for the heavy sweater I kept there for days like today when I worked late and the temperature was sure to drop. Last I heard, it was supposed to get down to the low forties during the night. In a week or so—about the time for our Founders Day celebration weekend—we'd have nippy but sunshiny days in the mid-fifties and nights in the low twenties.

"Lord, just don't let it snow next weekend," I said, though the story of Father Dyer in his snowshoes would appear even more authentic if Pastor Kevin had to wear them to march along Main Street during the festivities.

My research team of high schoolers met me in the library after the final bell rang. There were four altogether—two girls and two boys—plus myself. They were all seniors who were studious. Good citizens. Polite to their teachers and truly interested in academics.

Daniel Sullivan and Carter Vandiver were the two young men who sauntered in first, their backpacks jostling between their shoulder blades until they got to the table I'd set up for our work. There, their shoulders shifted as they'd done thousands of times over the past twelve years, and the backpacks came tumbling down to the floor.

"Where are the girls?" I asked.

"They're coming," Daniel answered. Then he rolled his eyes and said, "They had to go to the little girls' room." He and Carter shared a laugh.

"Hey, Mrs. Prattle," Carter said as he pulled out a chair and sat in it. "Can I ask you a question?"

"Sure," I answered. I was carrying a stack of research books, which I placed on the table. "Fire away."

"Why do girls always have to go to the bathroom in packs? I mean, if I said to Daniel here, 'Hey, Dan . . . I've got to go to the little boys' room, wanna go with me?' he'd probably give me a beat down."

"No probably about it, dude," Daniel interjected. "I *would* give you a beat down."

"Well," I said, thankful at that moment I'd reared both boys *and* girls, "I really don't know the answer to that. Girls are just . . . chummy from the time they're old enough to know what friends are all about. We might fuss from time to time, but in general, what happens to one happens to the other. *And* when we go to the little girls' room, it's for more reasons than just . . . nature's call, if you will. We chat. We put on our makeup, if we wear any, and we ask each other if our outfits look good. Things like that."

I smiled at the perplexed look on the faces of the two young men. Carter finally shook his head and said, "Like I said, Daniel would give me a beat down."

"That's just one of the many, many differences in boys and girls." Then I grinned. "But aren't you glad for those differences?" Which, of course, brought a furious blush to the faces of the boys.

Just then, Barrie Owens—one of the prettiest girls ever to grace the halls of Summit View High—and her best friend Jocelyn Ritch came through the double doors of the library, whispering to each other at a rate only teenage girls can keep up with. For a moment I was hit with a sudden realization: these young people had their whole lives in front of them, and only the good Lord knew what the years ahead would hold. There had been a time, not too terribly long ago, that Evangeline Benson Vesey and I had walked through those very same doors. Evangeline, Vonnie, Doreen, and me. All friends at one time or another. All of us had gathered with some of the other girls in the bathroom to share high school gossip and to make sure our fashion was every bit as cool as we thought it was. Miniskirts and go-go boots.

And oh! The nights we held dances here at this school. Our dresses were fanciful. Lovely. Romantic. We felt like princesses because we looked like princesses. Some nights, it seemed, we spent as much time huddled in the ladies' room oohing and aah-ing over our dresses as we did sashaying them on the dance floor.

I blinked as Barrie said, "Mrs. Prattle? Are you okay?"

"What? Oh . . . yes. I was just thinking back. Sorry." I placed my hand on the stack of books. "Okay, ladies and gentlemen, here are four books to help get us started. I'm going to go to the stacks to get a few more. There's paper and pens in the middle of the table here. Let's see what we can come up with to entertain the masses during the concert next Friday night. I'm looking for myths and legends from around these parts that people might not know about . . . something to really *wow* them."

The four nodded, each appearing truly excited. They reached for the books, pens, and legal pads of paper while I returned to the stacks.

A few hours later we had woven some interesting tales—includ-ing a few haunted ones, which I said I would allow, even though I don't believe in ghosts.

Jocelyn was particularly excited over women's roles during the gold rush. "Women didn't work the gold mines," she said to us, her captive audience, "but many found ways to start businesses—legitimate businesses—during those days."

"Such as?" I asked.

"Such as setting up places for the miners to eat. Outdoor res-taurants made from picnic-styled tables and benches. Women cooked and cleaned and—oh, this one woman's journal talks about how she eventually made her husband a partner in her business."

We all laughed.

231

"Why don't we do a short play about it?" Daniel suggested. "We can show this man coming home late at night, mining dust all over his face and hands, and he stops. He sees his wife with all these other miners sitting around a table and he says, 'Woman, what in the world are all these men doing here?' and then she says, 'They're my customers!'"

Again, we laughed, this time at the tone of Daniel's voice, but then I said, "I think you have a good idea, there. Can you write it up tonight?"

"Sure," Daniel said, then made a note on his legal pad.

"Here's another one," Carter said. "And this one has to do with Father Dyer."

"Oh?" I said. "Tell us."

"It's the story of Father Dyer and a miner named Zeke Hannah. Crazy Old Zeke, he was called. Every Friday he'd go into the nearby town—it wasn't Summit View—and he'd go to the saloon." He cut his eyes toward Jocelyn. "Probably where the *women* were serving the liquor and charging for dances."

"Hey," Jocelyn said in jest. "A girl's gotta make a living."

"Yeah, yeah. Whatever. Anyway, this story talks about how he was always claiming to have found a mother lode of gold, but there was never any proof of it, so people just ignored him. Father Dyer, though, was always nice to him." Carter pointed down to the text in the book spread open before him. "This says that Zeke claimed to have hit gold, and he gave some of it to Father Dyer for safekeeping but that, when questioned, Father Dyer said that it wasn't gold he was given but a Bible. Zeke Hannah was never heard from again, and no matter how hard this group of bad boys tried to find the satchel Father Dyer had been given, they never could find it."

"So?" I asked. "What do you think? Was it a Bible or was it gold?"

"I say it was gold," Daniel interjected.

"Me too," they each agreed.

"Who wants to write this story for us? Make it a sort of *Twilight Zone* feel where one of you walks out and recites the legend," I asked.

"Here's something else," Carter said, still reading in the book. "Legend has it that if you stand in a certain place at night you can see the old lantern of Zeke waving back and forth in the hills."

"Wooooooo," Daniel teased. "He's still looking for the gooooooooold."

"Cut it out, nut case," Carter said.

"I wonder . . ." Barrie began.

"Wonder what, Barrie?" I asked.

"Well, remember when we were kids? We'd all go out and look for the lode of gold that was supposedly lost? Or the treasure chests of gold from the stagecoach robberies?"

They all said they remembered.

"Even I remember that," I said. "Those legends have been around since the late 1800s and—believe it or not—I wasn't even born then."

The foursome giggled. Barrie continued, "I was just wondering if the lode Crazy Old Zeke found was one of the same ones that we read about in school when we were kids. The one that was lost or stolen? What if Zeke saw a robbery in progress and then was able to get part of the gold?"

"Why wouldn't it be feasible that he was just a part of the robbery?" I asked.

"Because Father Dyer took the gold and didn't turn him or the gold in. Father Dyer would have never taken stolen gold."

"That's true," I said. "At least from what we know of the man."

"Unless he didn't know it was stolen," Daniel said.

"That could be true too," Carter said.

"Well," I said, "let's put our heads together and see if we can read enough of the myths and legends from that time period, lay out the evidence, and see what we come up with."

"Let's do it." Daniel nearly jumped in his seat as he spoke.

———

"So . . ." I said to Samuel later as we got ready for bed, "here's what we came up with: there was a stagecoach robbery not too far from here about the same time as the legend of Zeke Hannah and Father Dyer takes place. Father Dyer, according to the records, was in a small mining town—no longer in existence—about twenty miles from here when the robbery took place. The robbery was about ten miles north of that settlement. And, according to the records, his next stop was south to Summit View, where the foundation of Grace Church had already been laid and some of the original walls had been erected."

"Okay," Samuel said, listening intently as he turned down the covers of our bed. "And?"

"And, what we think happened is this: Father Dyer didn't know the gold was stolen, of course, because the robbery occurred north of where he was. Not to mention, he was headed south. So, he took the gold for Old Zeke and ended up storing it around here somewhere."

"Where do you suppose it was hidden?" Samuel asked. There was mirth in his eyes, and I could tell he wasn't buying a word of our theory.

"Carter thinks it was hidden in the church, Mr. Smarty. Maybe even in the foundation."

With that, Samuel blanched. "Now, look here, Liz. Don't start spreading *that* rumor. You do, and everybody and his brother will want us to start digging up the foundation of the church, and the good Lord knows we've got enough problems with the restoration and addition right now."

"But the play . . . the program!" I plopped down on my side of the bed. "It's going to be such an important part of the evening."

"I'm not kidding, Lizzie. Tell it any way you want to tell it, but leave Grace Church out of it."

I frowned, then sighed. "I'll tell the kids," I said. "We won't mention the theory of the gold being buried somewhere on church property."

Samuel gave a nod of his head. "Good. Because, in reality, Liz, you don't know that it is. Old Father Dyer might have just used up that gold to do the good Lord's work. After all, like you said, he didn't know it was stolen."

I lay back on my pillow and pulled the covers up to my chin. "We don't *think* he knew."

"And don't go ruining the good name of Father Dyer, either. Everything we know about the man is good and decent."

I rolled onto my side and faced my husband. "I agree, Sam. I do. So if he didn't know the gold was stolen and the gold *was* stolen, and he thought it belonged to a man no one ever heard from again so he couldn't have given it back . . . *where* do you suppose it is?"

Samuel turned his head to look at me. "I have no idea. Go to sleep, Lizzie. Maybe you'll dream of finding a map."

I returned to my back. "Or maybe there's a legend we just don't know about yet."

"Lizzie. I'm tired, sweetheart."

"That gold is around here somewhere, Samuel. Maybe I just got caught up in the legends and myths some teenagers were weaving from books. Or maybe, just maybe, we've stumbled on a secret that's been well-kept over the years."

"Well, let's just hope the five of you are the only ones who know about it." He reached over and turned off his bedside lamp. "Because the last thing this town needs is more excitement than we already have. Now, I love you and good night."

# 28

## Fishy Business

The worst thing about the evening of my boutique's break-in and our near home invasion, already three days ago, was the fact I'd hung up on Mandy.

That wouldn't have been so bad except that was the last communiqué we'd received from our daughter. Henry was beside himself with worry; worry that grew after we'd rented then watched the movie *Rendition*, the story of a man who is falsely accused then tortured in an Egyptian jail. Was that why the authorities wanted to question Ray at the police station, so they could accuse him and imprison him for a crime he hadn't committed?

Our calls to the Cairo hospital had garnered no information other than a young male receptionist's insistence, in broken English, that "Sorry, only member of family can speak for him." Whatever that meant.

But besides Ray's condition, the question was: where was Mandy? Why couldn't we reach her at the hospital or her hotel, or even through her cell phone, which had been set up for worldwide calling? Why hadn't we been able to reach anyone from the company Ray was working for?

Even Clay hadn't been able to find out anything. "It looks to me," he'd said in a phone call late last night, "like one of you is going to have to fly to Cairo to get to the bottom of this."

"I'll go," Henry had said as he'd dined on a midnight bowl of my crabby corn chowder. He'd held his spoon aloft then added, "Lisa Leann, you'll need to stay here with Kyle. I'll fly over and make sure Ray and Mandy are okay. I'll get the State Department involved if I have to. But because of that prowler the other night, maybe you and Kyle could stay with one of your Potluck friends while I'm gone. Do you think?"

"But what if Mandy should call here?" I asked.

"Simple," Henry explained. "We have call forwarding—just forward our phone to your cell."

———

It was Vonnie I'd thought of first, probably because, with her vast baby doll collection, she seemed like the one who would most welcome having a real-life baby move in with her. She hadn't hesitated about my self-invitation when I'd phoned the next morning. In fact, I could almost picture her jumping in glee. "Lisa Leann, nothing would make me happier."

So before I'd left to drop Henry off at DIA, he'd spent the morning helping me move Kyle's crib and baby backpack, as well as a few of my suitcases over to Vonnie's guest bedroom, which had been readied for our arrival.

As Vonnie held the baby and Henry and Fred set up the crib, I arranged a few of his disposable diapers in the basket storage unit of his changing table. As Kyle cooed, Vonnie said, "Lisa Leann, I'm so pleased you thought of coming to stay here. It's been a bit lonely without my dear little Chucky."

I looked up and into my friend's sad, blue eyes. "Any idea as to what could have happened to him?"

Vonnie, dressed in her favorite gray sweatpants and rosy sweatshirt, kissed the top of Kyle's head as he nestled deeper into her arms while she rocked him in my rocking chair, a chair that had been carried inside only moments before. "I wish I did, but with my car window cracked open the way it was, I guess someone was able to unlock the door and make off with my little pup."

"Still," I said. "With all the creepy things going on around town, I just can't help but wonder if somehow these things aren't connected."

"If you figure it out," Vonnie said, "be sure and let Evie know. She could sure use a 'get out of a criminal trial free' card about now."

A few minutes later, when Henry and I got ready to head to the airport, Vonnie had insisted on taking charge of Kyle, looking as happy as I'd ever seen her. "Now, don't you worry. Though I've never raised any little ones of my own, I'm an old hat at caring for the babies in the church nursery. He'll be fine with me for a few hours. Plus, Fred's here; we'll be safe till you get back."

---

Still, I'd dreaded getting in the car with Henry, because I didn't want to be reminded of my past sins with his favorite country music. But this time, instead of punching "play" so his CD player could blast Shania Twain's "Whose Bed Have Your Boots Been Under," he tuned in to the Christian radio station, where Natalie Grant belted out her "Perfect People" song, a song acknowledging that perfect people don't really exist. *That much is true*, I thought as I listened.

We sat quietly as that and other songs poured from the radio, one following the other. As we neared the airport turnoff, Henry spoke. "Lisa Leann, I think I owe you an apology."

Startled, I looked up at my husband, who hid his expression behind his dark sunglasses. "What do you mean, Henry?"

"Before Mandy and Kyle came, you should know that I'd planned to leave you."

238

My eyes stung, and I looked toward my husband of almost thirty years. "Is that still your plan?"

He shook his head. "No. What you did was wrong, your affair with Clark, I mean."

I closed my eyes and took a deep breath. "I don't know if I can bear rehashing my misconduct again, Henry. It happened two years ago, and you know how sorry I am. I don't know what more—"

His voice stayed steady. "What I want to say to you isn't about that."

I watched as he followed the curve of the Peña Boulevard exit off I-70. "Then what is it?"

His voice sounded tired, as if he was giving up a restricted confidence. "I've allowed myself to live in a secret state of anger."

I cut my eyes toward him. "Maybe it hasn't been as secret as you think."

Henry nodded, grasping the steering wheel as he merged onto the boulevard. "I figured as much. But that's what I wanted, to hurt you as much as you hurt me."

"I can't tell you how sorry I am."

Henry's head turned toward me before he turned back to the traffic that was building around us. "I know. But I'm the one who allowed anger to fester."

"So what's changed?"

"Everything. With all that's happened, then the thought of losing you and the baby the other night, plus what's going on with Ray and Mandy, I've reconsidered both my behavior and decision to leave."

I turned to my husband, a man who never admitted when he was wrong. I felt nothing but absolute shock. "You have?"

He continued. "Deep down I know the truth. You cheated on me because I wasn't enough."

I shook my head. "Henry, don't say that."

"It's true. In most all our years in Texas, the years the kids were still at home, I was absent from your life with my work and such.

239

But seeing you with our grandson, it's made me remember what we once were."

I nodded and dropped my voice to an almost-whisper. "We were in love."

"Now I'm thinking I want that again, to be in love with you, if that's okay."

"You don't think it's too late for us?"

Henry shook his head. "It's only too late if I can't find a way to forgive you."

I pushed my sunglasses off my nose and onto the top of my head and studied my husband. "Can you? Can you forgive me, I mean?"

Henry pulled into the far left lane, toward the airport's west departure sign before taking the turnoff. "I'm only human, but . . . I've been thinking."

"And?"

"I'm not a strong enough man to forgive you. So I decided to ask God to give me the strength, his strength—to forgive you through me."

We pulled up to the curb in the drop-off zone, and Henry and I both got out of the car. We met at the trunk, where he retrieved his suitcase. I tentatively ventured, "Is your prayer working?"

"Let me put it to you like this," Henry said as he placed his suitcase down next to him. He stepped toward me, wrapping me in his arms, and drew me into a kiss so tingling that my knees grew weak and my toes curled inside my pink sneakers. I think we would have stayed in that embrace for eternity if one of the policemen managing the traffic and pedestrians hadn't tapped Henry's shoulder. "Break it up, you two," he said with a wink. "You're holding up traffic."

Henry unlocked his lips from mine then handed me the keys to the car before turning to walk toward the glass airport doors. He stopped to wave at me one last time, then he was gone.

I got back into the car and looked up to see the policeman signaling me to enter the flow of traffic. I obliged despite the tears streaming down my face. *Henry still loves me. He's chosen to forgive me.* Despite all the trouble we were dealing with, I knew I'd just witnessed a miracle.

"Thank you, Lord," I whispered. As I drove back to the high country I continued to praise God and to pray for my family's safe return.

———

Though I'd been gone from Summit View for about four hours, the late afternoon sun still shone brightly on the glowing aspens that brushed the mountain slopes with gold. But before I turned toward Vonnie's house, I decided to swing into the alley behind my boutique so I could run in to my office and download some emailed invoices since Vonnie's home was internet free.

I pulled into my parking spot then hopped out to unlock the back door before keying in the code and switching off the alarm.

Despite the break-in, the place looked the way I'd left it the last time I'd been inside, the day I'd brought the baby over. I walked through the kitchen and into the living room, where I gazed at the rug in front of the fireplace. I stepped toward it, then kneeled down, turning the edge of the carpet back. Sure enough, I saw the scratches I'd been told about on one of the wooden planks. Moments later, I was able to lift the plank and peer down into a small cavity, a perfect hiding place for some past resident of this old home. *But who?* All I knew was it had been bank-owned before Henry had made a deposit on the place.

I carefully replaced the plank and smoothed down the carpet before standing. My eyes slowly scanned the room in the afternoon light. Who knew how many hiding places an old home like this could have? Henry and I hadn't found anything out of the ordinary when we'd remodeled the kitchen last year, but what if this house contained other unexplored secrets that might still be undisturbed?

I followed the spiral staircase up to my office, walked over to my desk, and booted up the computer. While it booted, I let my eyes trace the floral wallpaper, the upstairs fireplace, the floor, and even the ceiling for clues of other hiding places. Nothing looked amiss, though there was no way to see if anything could be hiding inside my walls, besides maybe a mouse or two.

After logging into my email account and printing the invoices, I gathered up my purse and went downstairs.

But instead of heading toward the back door, I turned down the hall toward the cellar door. It creaked open to a set of wooden steps that disappeared into the darkness below. I pulled out my cell phone and turned it on so that its light would illuminate my journey downward.

When I reached the bottom, the light of the phone glowed a soft blue into the darkness. The cellar had quite a few boxes stacked around the room, creating odd silhouettes against the dark walls, the perfect hiding place for a felon, I decided. I walked to the string hanging from the middle of the ceiling and pulled it, watching the shadows give way to the yellow glow of the overhead bulb. Besides the boxes that Henry and I had placed down here ourselves, the room was devoid of any mysterious crates or bundles. I walked around the cellar's perimeter, looking at the concrete floor. If something was buried down here, I wouldn't know how to detect it, not beneath the concrete, which had probably been poured in the seventies or so.

My walk took me behind the old wooden staircase and the crawl space beneath it. It appeared empty, though I decided to give it a closer inspection. I turned on my cell phone's light again and leaned into the dark space. Everything looked normal. That is, except for the wider base on the bottom step. I knelt down and studied it. *Is that a loose board?* Brushing aside the cobwebs, I tugged at the board, and it pulled open, revealing another cavity. I bent down, shining the light of my phone into its darkness. *Ho! What is this?* I gingerly tugged on a corner of a crackled piece of leather. It slid toward me and into the dim light until I could see that I had found a leather pouch, a bit heavy and tied with an ancient string.

But before I could open it, the back door, not far above my head, suddenly swooshed open. "Hello?" a male voice I didn't recognize called.

I froze. Hadn't I locked the door and reset the alarm? Apparently not. I quickly walked to the center of the basement and pulled the string to extinguish the light before rushing back to the cubbyhole beneath the stairs. All the while, the footsteps continued to echo overhead. The footsteps stopped at the top of the stairs above me. "Anyone down there?" the voice called through the open door and into the darkness.

I held my breath, wondering if the beat of my heart was loud enough for the intruder to hear. I heard a footfall on the landing above me, then another, as a man descended the stairs. A voice I didn't recognize said, "Lisa Leann? Are you down here? It's Nate Sawyer from the Colorado Bureau of Investigation. I saw your car outside, and you didn't answer my knock. Is everything okay?"

Knees trembling, I crawled out of my hiding place. "I'm here," I simply said. "I was just moving a few boxes around."

"In the dark?" Nate finished his descent.

"No, you scared me; I turned off the light."

Nate arrived at the bottom step just as I found the string and pulled it. "There," I said as the room flooded with yellow illumination.

"Sorry, ma'am, I was just checking on you. Your back door was cracked open and there was a bike leaning against the steps. Seemed suspicious after the trouble you had the other night."

Shock smacked me hard. "My back door was open?" But before Nate could answer, the cellar door above us slammed shut and loud footsteps reverberated toward the back door.

Nate looked alarmed. "Is someone here with you?"

When I shook my head no, Nate's hand automatically went for

his holster before he turned and ran back up the stairs. After finding the door locked, Nate battered it open with his shoulder. "You
stay here," he called from the top of the staircase before running
out the back door.

I felt my heart pound. Someone had been in the house while I'd
been down in the cellar. If Nate hadn't happened along . . . I shuddered and hurried back to where I'd left the pouch, then stuffed it
into my purse just as Nate returned to the top of the cellar steps
a few minutes later.

"It's safe to come up now," he said. "Whoever was inside is long
gone."

"Did you get a chance to see who it was?" I asked as I ascended
the stairs. Nate stood in the shattered door frame. "Unfortunately,
I didn't see anyone. Though the bike's gone."

When I reached the top landing, Nate escorted me to the living
room, where we sat down in front of the fireplace. "So, why were
you in the neighborhood anyway?" I asked.

"I dropped by to see you," he said. "I was just wondering if you had
any theories about why your friend Evie would kill Ms. McGurk."

"Gracious," I said, standing with a start. "Evie didn't kill anybody."

Nate stood too. "How can you be so sure?"

"For starters, shouldn't you be trying to track down that prowler?
I mean, for all you know, he may be Dee Dee's killer."

"Any ideas on who your prowler could be? You may be the lady
with the clues for all I know."

"I don't know anything, but if this mystery guy reveals his identity
to me, I'll let you know."

"How do you know it's a *he*?" Nate asked.

"Well, that sure wasn't Evie up there."

"What makes you so sure?"

"You'd never catch her on a bike, for one thing, and for another,
she wouldn't have locked us in the cellar."

Nate smirked. "If you say so."

I picked up my purse and swung it over my shoulder as Nate said, "That looks pretty heavy. What do you carry in that thing, rocks?"

I smiled sweetly, though I was irritated with the man. So irritated I decided not to show Nate my find, but to talk to Donna instead. "Just a few office supplies," I said. "Now if you don't mind, I have a baby to attend to."

# 29

## Bubbling Memories

Fred was playing with Kyle and I was pulling my deep-dish pizza out of the oven when Lisa Leann burst through the front door, looking as if she'd seen a ghost.

"Everything all right, dear?"

"There was a prowler at the shop."

"Not again," I said, putting the pizza pan on my ceramic doll trivet and turning to face her. "Was anything missing?"

"That detective Nate showed up and scared him off."

"Did Nate at least see him?" Fred asked, bouncing Kyle on his knee.

"I'm afraid not," Lisa Leann answered.

"Well, at least no one got hurt," Fred said, turning his attention back to the baby.

Lisa Leann nodded, so I asked, "Did you get Henry situated at the airport?"

She took a deep breath and gave me a twitchy smile. "I did. He called while I was still driving home, just before his plane took off for New York." Lisa Leann set her large pink and black quilted purse on the kitchen desk and looked at her watch. "He should be landing at JFK soon, in fact. He won't be in Cairo until sometime tomorrow."

When she heard Kyle chuckle, she turned and spied Fred playing peekaboo with her grandson. Fred had perched the baby in his recliner while he knelt beside it, hiding his face behind a pillow, then popping out. "Boo!"

Lisa Leann walked toward the pair, grinning. "You two look like you're having way too much fun."

"Dinner's ready," I called from the kitchen. "Go wash up and meet me at the table."

Lisa Leann didn't say much at dinner, chewing slowing and staring at Kyle, who was rocking merrily away in his nearby baby swing. I didn't push her to confide her thoughts as I knew she must be frightfully worried about her family. So I wasn't too surprised when Lisa Leann pushed back her plate with half a slice of my pizza still intact. "Sorry, Vonnie, your pizza is good, but I'm just too nervous to eat much. Let me help you clean up."

"Don't worry about these dishes, dear. Fred will help me."

Lisa Leann stood. "Then I think Kyle and I will get ready to retire for the evening."

I watched her walk over to the baby and reset his swing to continue rocking. I said, "Are you sure? It's only 7:00 p.m."

Lisa Leann strolled to the kitchen counter and began to prepare a bottle for Kyle; she glanced over her shoulder for a second. "When I was back at my office, I grabbed some invoices and such." She opened the can of formula and reached for the scoop. "So, I think I'll feed Kyle and get him situated, then get a little work done in our room, if you don't mind."

"All right," I said as I pushed my chair back and reached for a couple of dirty plates.

Lisa Leann turned around to face me as she leaned against the sink while she twisted a nipple top onto a bottle. She turned to open the microwave. "Oh, and I'm calling a Potluck planning meeting for tomorrow night, as we've got a crowd to feed for the Founders Day festival the weekend after this one. I'm going to announce the menu and pass out the prep assignments to our team."

I gathered the dirty silverware and stacked them on top of the plates. "Do you want the girls to meet here, instead of at your shop?"

"Let me think for a minute," Lisa Leann said. I continued picking up as Lisa Leann tested the formula before walking back to the baby. She lifted him from his swing as he reached his chubby hands toward his bottle. "There you go," Lisa Leann cooed as Kyle pulled the bottle to his lips with a contented sigh. She looked up at me as I carried the last of the dirty dishes to the sink. "Yes, we'll meet here. Do you think we could serve the girls maybe a salad buffet at about 6:00 p.m.?"

"Sounds good," I said as I scooped up the leftover pizza slice from my baking dish and wrapped it in cellophane. I placed the slice in the refrigerator. "I was planning to run to the grocery tonight to pick up a couple of things. I'll grab a couple of heads of lettuce and a tomato or two while I'm there."

Lisa Leann smiled as she retrieved her purse from the desk and then carried the baby to her bedroom. She paused at her door. "What would I do without friends like you?"

———

Twenty minutes later, I pulled into the grocery store parking lot then climbed out of my car and stepped into the October chill, glad I'd brought my favorite blue sweater. I looked through the parking lot's umbrella of light that showered from the streetlight above. I squinted past it, as if I could possibly see my lost dog out in the darkness that surrounded me. I walked past the cars and to the sidewalk that led to the grocery store. Instead of walking toward the path of light that spilled from the store's open door, I stopped, turned, and took a couple of steps into the night.

"Chucky, here boy!" I called. Somewhere I could hear the bark of a dog. The sound felt like a sign that I was to continue to walk down the dark sidewalk, past gloomy shops and residential homes with their windows illuminated from the inside by flickering television sets. "Chucky!" I called.

I walked a block, circled it, then walked another. "Here, Chucky!" I searched for my friend for about an hour as I hugged myself against the night air while brushing tears off my cold cheeks. Finally I stopped and stared at the fluorescent sign of the Gold Rush Tavern, now just across the street from where I stood.

I couldn't help but give a little sniff, not only for my lost dog but for my lost friend Doreen. To think that only a week earlier she'd been inside those walls, alive. I shuddered. What had happened to her? Had she met someone at the bar who had gone to her trailer and demanded her very life? I stepped off the curb just as a pickup truck lumbered past me with a loud blast of its horn. I jumped back, surprised at myself for being so caught up in my thoughts that I'd forgotten to check for traffic. I stopped, looked both ways, then ran across the street and up the steps to the tavern door.

I didn't know what I expected to find inside. Maybe I just wanted to breathe the same air that Doreen had breathed, to see where she'd worked, and to find out what her last days had been like. Never mind that I'd never been inside an establishment of this sort before. The good Lord knows I don't even drink.

When I burst through the door, the air was stuffy and filled with a sort of yellow haze as patrons leaned over tall glasses of beer, talking in low voices. I was surprised at how many people were inside. Maybe the patrons were all within walking distance, or had traveled here packed in the few cars that sat outside in the lot, or had ridden bikes like the one leaning against the building. I was suddenly aware I was the only customer who appeared to be alone.

The bartender, an older gent, looked up from wiping down a glass. "Can I help you?"

I glanced around. "No, I . . ."

He stared down at me as if sizing me up. "Are you looking for someone?"

"An old friend once worked here," I said.

He motioned for me to sit at the bar. "I'm new here, so I'm not sure I would have known him. What's his name?"

I looked into the man's dark eyes. They might have been blue, but in this light, they appeared almost black. The man was about my age, tall, with graying hair parted in an attempt to hide his balding head. He should have given up the practice of combing his last few strands of hair over his bald pate as more skin than hair shone in the dim light.

"Her, she was a her. Doreen McGurk, though folks around here called her Dee Dee."

The man's eyes lit with recognition. "Yes, ma'am. There was a Dee Dee that used to work this very shift, till her untimely murder a week or so ago. Heard an old friend done it." He eyed me suspiciously. "That wouldn't be you, would it? You being an old friend and all?"

I made eye contact with the man as I shook my head. "Heavens, no. It certainly wasn't me. I've not even been accused."

The man let out a breath. "Well, that's good. What can I get you?"

"Do you have iced tea?"

"We've got a special blend from Long Island. Would that be all right?"

I nodded, still looking around, now at the mirror behind the man, where I noticed I could observe the bar's patrons, including a couple of seedy men who seemed to be watching me. "That would be fine," I said all matter of fact.

The bartender busied himself with my order. "How long have you worked here?" I asked to the back of his black tee shirt.

He answered without turning around. "Just since Dee Dee's death. I'm just filling in till they find someone else, since I've got a day job too."

The bartender brought me my tea and set it before me as he said, "I don't believe I caught your name, Mrs. . . ."

"Westbrook. Vonnie Westbrook. And your name?"

His dark eyes glittered, and he stuck out his hand for a shake. "They call me Hoss."

"You mean like Dan Blocker's character on *Bonanza*?"

Hoss nodded. "Long story, but the name's related to my bronco-busting days."

I took a sip of my drink and sputtered. "Whatever did you put in this tea?"

He laughed good-naturedly. "This drink's got a little vodka, gin, and bit of tequila, but no tea."

I waved my hand over it and blotted my lips with my napkin. "Goodness! Take it away."

Hoss looked a bit bashful. "Sorry for the mistake, ma'am. I didn't realize you were a genuine teetotaler. You don't meet many of those in here," he said as he whisked away the drink.

"How about a Diet Coke instead?" I asked.

"That we have plenty of. Want me to put a little gin in it?" he asked, teasing me.

"No, thank you."

When Hoss brought my new drink, I took a sip and smiled. "Much better."

"I aim to please," he said, slapping a dishcloth over his shoulder.

The man's deep, honeyed voice made me feel comfortable, so I braved, "Do you mind if I ask a question?"

"Be my guest."

"What do the people here at the bar think happened to Doreen? I mean, are they buying the story that the sheriff's wife killed her?"

"Most do. But I've heard a few rumors."

I put my elbows onto the counter so I could lean in. "Like what?"

"Like, she may have been killed over lost gold. Have you heard anything about that, Mrs. Westbrook?"

251

"No. Though I don't see how Doreen's death and our many lost gold legends would coincide with one another. What exactly did you hear?"

Hoss shrugged. "Just that she'd come into some gold. Do you think that could be true?"

"I strongly doubt it." I stirred my Diet Coke with my straw as the ice clinked against the glass. "Did you hear about any particular gold legend? We have a few, you know."

"Well, I heard there was a stagecoach robbery somewhere north of here, in a place called Central City. Heard the robber, a fellow named Zeke, buried a chest of gold out by the church in the middle of the night."

"You mean Grace Church?" I laughed out loud. "I hardly believe that. God would have surely led the good members of the church to find a chest of gold by now. Besides, think of all the good a chest of gold would do toward the Lord's work, especially accounting for inflation and all."

Hoss's eyes sparked again. "Yeah, that *is* something to consider."

I laughed. "I doubt very much that Zeke could have hidden a chest that hasn't been found, not with all the tourists and treasure seekers scouring every nook and cranny of this county."

Hoss nodded. "I see your point. But can you imagine the value of such a chest of gold? If it weighed more than sixty pounds, it could be worth up to a million dollars or more."

"Well, if *I* find the treasure," I said with a grin, "I'll be sure to let you know. How's that?"

Hoss winked at me as the door behind me opened. "Deal," he said.

I rotated my bar stool just enough to see who'd walked in. "Velvet," I said. "Come over here and let me buy you a Coke."

Velvet stopped in front of me, a kind of wild look on her face. "Mrs. Westbrook, what in the world would make you come in here?"

I patted the seat behind me. "Dear, I'm remembering your mother. Care to join me?"

Velvet, who was dressed in a black tube top and a rabbit fur coat tossed over her shoulders, took a step toward me. "What would you know about my mother?" she asked, with a lilt of menace in her voice.

"Only that when she was about your age, we were dear friends." I looked down at the rings of water my glass had made on the bar's oak top and blotted them with my napkin before looking back at Velvet. "I've missed her."

The hardness behind Velvet's eyes seemed to crumble. "You and my mother were friends?"

She sat down beside me, and I signaled for Hoss to bring Velvet a Diet Coke, like mine. "We were, dear." I reached over and patted her hand. "I can't tell you how sorry I am about what happened."

"That old bat Evie killed her," Velvet said, almost through her teeth as Hoss plopped her Diet Coke in front of her.

"Do you really think so?" I asked.

Her eyes narrowed into tiny slits. "I do."

I pressed on while Hoss waited on another customer at the other end of the now-crowded bar. "But do you recollect if anyone else threatened your mom or made her feel unsafe, besides Evie?"

"You mean like one of her ex-husbands? Most of them were nothing but mean."

"Oh dear," I said. "Sounds like your mother had a pretty rough time of it."

"You could say that, but she's a survivor." Her eyes drooped. "I mean *was*."

"Have any of her exes ever come out this way lately, to Summit View?"

Hoss reappeared. "Need any peanuts, ladies?"

"No, thanks," Velvet said before answering my question. "Not that I know of."

Hoss went to fill another order, and Velvet's face softened in a way that reminded me of Donna when she was a girl. She said, "Can you tell me what my mom was like, when you knew her?"

I finished the last of my Diet Coke and signaled Hoss to hit me with another. While he used a hose to spray it into my glass, I turned back to Velvet. "I'd be delighted."

I described to her a younger Doreen and told stories about how we'd grown up together. Somehow in all the telling, I lost all track of the time. It wasn't until Clay charged through the bar door that I realized it was getting late. "Mrs. Westbrook, *there* you are."

"Why, Clay, I didn't know you frequented this establishment."

Clay blushed. "I'm not here looking for a drink, I'm looking for you."

"Whatever for?"

"Well, when you didn't come back home from the grocery store, Fred drove over there only to find your car—with you missing. He and Donna are out looking for you now."

"Oh dear," I said, glancing at my watch. It was almost 10:00. "I didn't realize the time."

"When you didn't answer your phone, Donna called me and asked if I had seen you about town."

"My phone!" I opened my purse and pulled it out. "Oh dear. I forgot to turn it on," I admitted.

Clay grinned. "I can see that. Do you mind if I escort you back to your car?"

"Let me pay my tab first," I said, looking around for Hoss. When he didn't appear, Velvet said, "Hoss is probably on break, but don't you worry about the tab. Tonight was special, and the Diet Cokes are on me."

"Dear, are you sure?"

Velvet grinned, reminding me even more of Donna. "Absolutely."

Velvet said her good-byes, and Clay and I hurried to his jeep before driving the few blocks to the grocery store. He asked, "Do you mind telling me why you left your car in the grocery lot?"

"I couldn't resist the temptation to hunt for Chucky."

Clay's eyebrows arched. "In the dark?"

"It's the thought that little Chucky might be out there and that I might find him that caused me to throw caution to the wind, I guess."

Clay looked amused. "So, did you think he might be in the tavern?"

I felt warmth kiss my cheeks. "No, ah, I just wanted to be where Doreen was the last day of her life. She was my friend once, you know."

"I see."

When Clay pulled next to my car, I climbed out of the jeep as Clay leaned toward me. "Mrs. Westbrook, there's been a lot of strange occurrences around town these last few days, and, well, I wouldn't really recommend that you wander off searching for your dog after dark. I'd hate for anything to happen to you too."

"Thanks for your concern, Clay." I practically giggled. "But who would want to hurt *me*?"

"Just promise me you'll be careful, okay?"

I walked over to my car as Clay called out, "I'll call Fred, David, and Donna and let them know I found you."

"Sure, and thanks." I fired up my engine and turned on my lights, the signal Clay was waiting for as he pulled his jeep onto the street. But before I could follow him, I noticed an envelope tucked under one of my wiper blades. I watched Clay's lights disappear as I turned off the ignition and stepped back into the night. I picked up the envelope and opened it and pulled out a piece of typed white paper, which I read under the streetlight.

MEET ME BEHIND THE CHURCH SUNDAY
NIGHT AT MIDNIGHT ALONE—
THAT IS, IF YOU WANT TO SEE YOUR DOG
AGAIN.

# 30

## Gnawing Doubt

I was glad Vonnie was safe at home this morning. She'd given us quite the scare when she'd disappeared from the grocery store parking lot. I still hadn't heard where Clay had found her.

I stood at my kitchen counter, looking out my window in the direction of Mount Paul. From the way the sun lit the pines gilded in frost, it looked like this would be a perfect October morning, despite my personal storms.

I turned to look at the pumpkin that adorned my counter and gave it a pat. Ms. Betty's class had given it to me yesterday, my gift for dropping by for career day with Pete, Wade's 12-year-old nephew. I still cherished my friendship with the boy after all we'd been through last spring. So, it was good to see him and his family back in town and reunited, save for his dad. I have to say I missed the late-night chili invitations he and his uncle Wade would call in whenever I worked the late shift.

I gave the pumpkin another pat. It would be perfect to cook in my crock-pot today. That seemed like a good idea with the emergency meeting of the Potluck Catering Club tonight at Vonnie's. I smiled as I thought of surprising the girls with my mother's steaming pumpkin soup. I pulled out my mother's recipe card from the wooden recipe box I'd bought at Walmart and studied it for a moment to make sure I had all the ingredients. When I saw that I did, I picked up the smooth, orange pumpkin and rinsed it in the sink before placing it on my old wooden cutting board. I selected my largest butcher knife, cut the gourd in half, and scooped out the seeds. I chopped its pale orange flesh, skin still attached, into large chunks before adding it to my crock-pot. I added the rest of the ingredients before setting the pot to high. Then I made a mental note to stop at the store to pick up a loaf of garlic bread and a carton of sour cream before I came home from work.

Now that my morning routine had been interrupted by a pumpkin, I scurried to get ready for work. I was just climbing into my Bronco when my cell phone chimed with a text. It was David: *Bak on days. Meet me at cafe 4 lunch @ 12.*

I couldn't help but smile. It was about time he got off the night shift and joined me for some daylight time. Though I hadn't totally released him from my grudge over Bobbie Ann, I'd missed our phone calls as well as our midnight lunches behind the bank. I texted back: *C u there.*

The morning flew by as I continued to follow up on leads concerning my mother's murder, knocking on doors at her trailer park, talking to whatever resident I found home. But every conversation fell short. One elderly woman in a faded cotton housedress put it this way: "I didn't have on my hearing aids that afternoon, so maybe that's why I didn't hear anything till Velvet got home. My, what a ruckus *that* was."

After finishing my survey, I headed back to the office to meet with Nate. Once in the building, I strolled down the hall and tapped on his open door.

He looked up, glad to see me. "Donna. I was hoping you'd drop by."

I slouched down in the wooden chair across from his gray metal desk. He pushed aside his open briefcase with its piles of papers stacked neatly inside. I said, "Regarding my mother's case, I feel we've missed something."

Nate smirked. "Now I've done my best to prove Evangeline's innocence being that she's a member of your family and all. But if she looks guilty, that may be more her fault than mine."

I stretched my feet in front of me and crossed my ankles just under the desk. "But what if she's not guilty?"

Nate chuckled. "Look, I know this must be painful for you, but we've got her. There's just too much evidence putting her at the scene *with* a motive."

"I'm curious, what motive are you referring to, exactly?"

"Well, it's no secret that she hated that Doreen had been married to your father."

I shook my head. "So? That doesn't mean she killed my mother."

Nate looked sympathetic. "Cases like this are hard. I'd say Evangeline's gotten to you, hasn't she?"

"No. It's not that, it's just that I have a hunch that there's a piece missing."

Nate shrugged and looked at his watch, then gave me a bright smile. "Unless you can bring me another theory, say, over lunch, then I think my work here is done."

"No can do on lunch."

Nate looked disappointed. "Going out with one of your TV boyfriends?"

I sat up straight. "What's that supposed to mean?"

"Nothing, just still playing detective, though I don't see what either of those two guys have over me."

I laughed. "Over you? Well, Nate, for one thing, you just arrested my mother-in-law for murder. I'm afraid I'll have to take that into consideration regarding any plans for *our* future."

Nate gave me a grin. "Then prove me wrong so I can show you a better side of me."

I rolled my eyes and glanced at my watch. I stood with my jacket. "We'll have to hold off on lunch, but I'll call you if I dig up anything."

Nate grinned. "I hope to hear from you, I honestly do . . ."

Five minutes later I walked into the Higher Grounds Café and looked around for David. When I saw he hadn't yet arrived, I found a corner table and sat down near where Clay had spread out his laptop and a pad of notes. He looked up and gave me a bit of a wave.

"So, where did you find Vonnie last night?" I asked.

He arched his furry brows. "Didn't she tell you?"

"No."

"She was at the tavern."

I couldn't help but laugh. "That's crazy talk."

"I'm serious. I found her having a little powwow with your sister."

"Velvet? I bet that was interesting. Did she tell you what they talked about?"

"Your mother, I presume."

I checked my watch again as Sally handed me a menu. "Dining alone today?" she asked.

"I'm waiting for someone."

I took a drink of the ice water Sally poured into my glass. David was late. I picked up my cell phone to check if I had missed a message. When I saw that I hadn't, I looked up to see Wade making a beeline for me. "Do you mind if I sit down?" he asked.

"Well, I'm waiting—"

"Just for a minute? It's about that day your mother died."

I pointed to the chair, and he sat. "What about it?" I asked.

"I don't think Evie went into Dee Dee's trailer. Evie was leaving while your mother stood on her porch."

"Did you see Evangeline leave?"

"No, I was distracted by the phone when Evie was talking to Doreen."

"Then you're another person who was at the scene without an alibi. I wonder why Nate doesn't suspect you?"

"Well, Louie, the manager of the Hotel Summit View, you know him, he was with me before and after I ran over to my trailer. I was only gone for a few minutes and there's a telephone log of me on the phone with Louie that whole time I was gone. So, Louie would have heard me if I'd been involved in any kind of commotion." He paused, looking to see if I believed him. I did. He continued, "Plus there's the fact I've got no motive."

I studied Wade's intense blue eyes. "Do you remember anything else from that afternoon? A detail you maybe didn't mention to Nate?"

"That's what I wanted to tell you: there was this cyclist."

"Someone on a bike?"

"Yeah, I didn't tell Nate this, but I left my tool belt in my trailer, and after I'd driven about five minutes, I realized my mistake. I turned around and went back to the park. That's when a man on a bike came shooting down the sidewalk, cutting in front of me."

"Why didn't you tell Nate?"

"The cyclist seemed unimportant at first, and well, I didn't want to be on his list of suspects as I may have been in the area when Dee Dee died."

"Did you recognize the guy?"

"Can't say that I did, but there was something about him that struck me as strange. The dude was wearing street clothes—jeans, a black tee, and tennis shoes, instead of the usual high country biker's gear—spandex and cleats."

"Was he wearing a helmet?"

"Nope."

I nodded. "That is a bit strange, at least for up here in the high country."

"Yeah, most of the cyclists wear black shorts and bike jerseys."

"Did you get a good look at the guy?"

"I didn't see his face, but he was wearing a black baseball cap with a yellow logo of some kind."

"Did you see which way he went?"

"He just turned west and up the sidewalk. I didn't see where he went after that."

By now I had my clipboard out and was taking notes. I looked up. "So I have to ask. Do you think Evie killed my mother?"

"No. Of course not."

As I wrote down a few more notes, Wade stared. "Is it true that you and David broke up when he spent the night with his old girlfriend?"

I looked up abruptly. "What?"

"I mean, 'cause if you did break up, I'd love to take you out again."

"I'm going to ignore your question to say this: you and your mother make a fine couple, and three's a crowd."

Wade looked genuinely hurt. "Donna, that's not fair. My mother does not factor into who I date."

"Really? Then when we *were* dating, why didn't you take me over to her house and let her know I was your girlfriend?"

"Well, I didn't want to put you through that."

I slammed the notebook on my clipboard shut. "Since when do men around here think I'm too fragile to take care of myself?"

"I never said—"

"I won't play second fiddle to your mother, especially if you won't defend me to her."

Wade suddenly gave me a lopsided grin. "So, in other words, you *are* available."

I took another sip of ice water. "I never said that."

Wade grabbed my hand. "So, if I were to stand up to my mom, then you and I could get back together? Is that what I'm hearing?"

Before I could respond, the café door burst open and David rushed into the room. He froze when he saw me holding hands with Wade. I retrieved my hand and stood as David walked toward us.

"Sorry I'm late, Donna. Is everything okay here?"

"Wade and I were just talking about my mother's murder," I said.

261

David shot a look at Clay, realizing he'd been near enough to hear my and Wade's conversation. "Is that so?" David said, seemingly to Clay as much as to me.

"Hello, David," Clay said.

I punched David in the arm with my balled fist so he would face me. "Don't you believe me?"

As if in response to my question, David's pager beeped. He checked it and said, "Big accident out on the freeway. Multiple injuries." With that he turned and disappeared out the door.

My beeper was next to respond. I called over to Sally, who was watching from behind the cash register, "I'll come back later for lunch."

As I grabbed my jacket, Wade said, "What about us?"

"What us?" I growled. "Like I said, you already have the woman of your dreams—your *mother*." I followed David out the door and into the afternoon sun, my Bronco keeping pace with his ambulance all the way to the accident scene.

———

The three-car pileup kept David and me so busy that we barely spoke as we worked the accident scene. While he ran the crash victims to the hospital, I directed traffic and tow trucks. But even despite all the trauma of the afternoon, I'd managed to make it to the store and then home to blend my pumpkin soup into a warm, creamy treat for the girls.

I arrived with my crock-pot just in time to place it in the buffet. "Donna," Evie said as she lifted the lid, "this looks wonderful. Is it pumpkin?"

"It is. It's my mother's recipe," I said quietly. Evie looked up at me with a start. To my surprise she replaced the lid then wrapped me in her arms. "Oh Donna, I'm so, so sorry you lost Doreen." When she pulled away, I could see tears in her eyes as she held me with a hand on each shoulder. Her chin tilted down as she made eye contact. "But you know—you have to know it wasn't me. Right, Donna?"

I sighed. "If I could prove that, Evangeline, it would make things around here a lot simpler."

Vonnie, who was placing a pitcher of Goldie's sweet tea onto the table, said, "You can say that again."

Soon the potluckers and I had filled our bowls with soup and covered our plates with salad. Lisa Leann, who was holding her grandson on her lap, said, "Do you mind if I say grace?" We all mumbled agreements as we bowed our heads. Lisa Leann prayed, "Lord, we got a heap of trouble on our hands: a lost mother, a lost husband, a missing daughter, my son-in-law in the hospital, and Evie facing charges for a crime she didn't commit. Plus a cherished pet's simply vanished."

There was a murmur of "Yes, Lord" from the women around me.

"So, Lord, since we don't know what to pray, we ask for miracles. We agree together that it's your turn, Lord."

"Amen," we said, practically in unison.

As we dined, we quizzed each other about the various dilemmas we were facing.

"Have you heard from Henry?" Lizzie asked Lisa Leann, who was spooning my warm soup between her lips.

Lisa Leann, still holding Kyle in one arm as she bounced him with her thigh, managed a peek at her watch. "Not yet. Though I'm expecting his call any minute."

Vonnie finished a long sip of sweet tea. "What about Mandy? Have you heard anything from her?"

Lisa Leann responded by shaking her head then braving a smile at the baby. "We'll hear from Mommy soon, won't we?" she said in baby talk.

Goldie, who was holding a piece of my still warm garlic bread, asked, "Any word about Chucky, Vonnie?"

When Vonnie didn't answer, I looked up from my soup, alarmed. "Is something wrong?"

She shook her head. "No, no. I haven't heard anything."

I narrowed my eyes, my suspicions alerted. *Is Vonnie keeping a secret from me?*

Vonnie changed the subject. "Any more clues regarding your mother, Donna?"

"Not much to speak of, but I'm hoping for a break in the case."

Evie replied under her breath, "You're not the only one."

With that, Lisa Leann stood and handed Vonnie the baby. "Would you mind?" She turned to face us. "I think I may have something of interest that might even relate to the case." She stood and walked back to her room, retrieving a large pink purse. She cleared a spot at the table and set the purse down. She opened it and pulled out an antique leather satchel.

"After I dropped Henry off at the airport yesterday, I swung by my boutique. While I was there, I looked around for hidden cubbyholes inside the house."

"Looks like you found one," Lizzie said.

"I did, down in the basement beneath the bottom landing." She untied a fragile string that held the satchel closed.

"For goodness sakes, what is it?" Vonnie asked as she suddenly stood with Kyle on one hip.

"Patience, everyone," Lisa Leann said as she pulled out an old revolver. Goldie screamed, and I jumped to my feet.

I ran around the table, reaching for the gun. "What do you have there, Lisa Leann?"

"Don't worry. It's an old Colt, gold rush era. It's not loaded and the firing pen is frozen shut. I checked." She handed me the gun while I inspected it. She said, "But there's more."

She pulled out both a yellowed envelope and a tiny brown leather pouch with a drawstring. She held up the pouch. "For the record, this is a couple of thousand dollars' worth of gold dust, as valued on today's market."

We all gasped as one while Lisa Leann continued. "There's a note." She placed the smaller pouch on the table, and Goldie picked it up, carefully opening the pouch to peek inside. She pulled out tiny gold nuggets the size of sand and held them up between two fingers. "That's gold, all right," she said with the first grin I'd seen on her face since Jack's death.

Lizzie was on her feet walking toward Lisa Leann. "Is there a name on that envelope?"

Lisa Leann nodded and read it aloud: "To Father John Dyer."

I'd already opened the Colt and was checking the cylinders when I gasped. "The minister who founded our church? What does the letter say?"

Lisa Leann carefully unfolded the aged paper and began to read: *Padray, u mite not here frum me no more but no the + is my trezur. Zeke Hannah*

Lizzie reached for the letter. "Do you mind if I have a look?"

Lisa Leann nodded as Evie chimed in, "Old Zeke. My daddy used to tell me stories about him. And, you know, if I'm not mistaken, the Hannahs in town are his relations." Her eyes sparkled. "And wasn't old Mrs. Hirvela, the one who used to own Lisa Leann's Victorian, a Hannah before she married?"

Lizzie nodded. "That's right, and to maybe shed some more light on this, I just read that Zeke was married to one of the Martin girls when he disappeared. According to the records I uncovered, his wife's parents built a home on Main Street."

"My wedding boutique," Lisa Leann stated, guessing the truth.

Lizzie nodded, looking rather proud of herself. "You got it. Old Mrs. Hirvela is a relative of Zeke's, a great-great-niece or even a descendant, I'd bet."

Evie said, "Isn't Mrs. Hirvela living still—in that nursing home with your mom, Lizzie?"

Lizzie snapped her fingers. "That's right! In fact, I saw her not too long ago. She's still sharp as a tack." Lizzie paused, then added, "Though she couldn't have possibly been alive when this letter was written, being that she's only in her nineties." She held the letter up to the light and squinted at it. "This letter has to be over 130 years old."

Lisa Leann's phone rang. She grabbed for it. "Hello, Henry?" We all held our breaths until she said, "How's Ray?" She nodded. "Have you found Mandy?"

We waited until Lisa Leann gasped. "Oh, Henry, no, *no!*"

"Oh dear, what's happened now?" Vonnie cried.

# 31

## Condensed Meeting

As soon as Lisa Leann disconnected her phone call with Henry, she gave us the frightening news: Mandy seemed to have vanished in Egypt. Between gulps of hysteria, she told us only bits and pieces of information, then promptly passed out cold on the living room floor.

Vonnie, still holding Kyle, sprang into action. "I'll get her a wet washcloth," she said, then started for the hallway.

Lizzie grabbed one of Lisa Leann's hands and began to pat it. "Lisa Leann, do you hear me?" As Lisa Leann's eyes blinked, Lizzie looked up and added, "We need to organize a prayer vigil. This is huge."

"I'll call Pastor Kevin," I said, then dug around in my purse for my cell phone and stepped into the kitchen for privacy.

Pastor Kevin answered about the same time as Evangeline stepped up behind me. "Did you get him?" she asked.

I nodded and held up my index finger. "Pastor Kevin, this is Goldie," I said.

"Goldie! I understand from Lisa Leann that a meeting is in full force. Do you have a question for me?"

"Uh—no. We have—"

"What's he saying?" Evangeline asked.

I turned to face her. "Wait a second, Evie." I gathered my bearings. "Pastor Kevin, Lisa Leann just got news from Henry—who's in Egypt, if you didn't know that already—that Mandy is missing over there."

"Whoa. Hold on. I knew Henry had left to go . . . what do you mean, exactly, that she's missing?"

"To be honest, that's all we know."

Evie put her hands on her hips. "Tell him Ray is in the hospital."

"He knows that, Evie."

Pastor Kevin interrupted. "Yes, I know that. Okay, Goldie. I'm going to call Esther Hopkins. She'll get prayers started for Mandy. And for Ray." For as long as I could remember, Esther Hopkins had been in charge of the church's prayer chain.

"Is he calling Esther?" Evie asked as I disconnected the call.

I sighed. "Yes! My goodness, you are being a pest."

She looked hurt, and I instantly regretted my words.

"I'm just trying to help," she said.

I patted her arm. "I know you are." I looked toward Vonnie's living room. "Let's get back in there and see what's going on, shall we?"

Evangeline was the first to announce that "we'd" called Pastor Kevin and that Esther Hopkins was organizing the prayer chain, which was nothing but speculation. Or, faith in action. By this time, Donna had taken Lisa Leann and Kyle back to her house to pick up some papers on Mandy, and Lizzie was collecting plates and discarded napkins.

"I told Lisa Leann she could leave Kyle here," Vonnie said. "But she wouldn't hear of it."

I nodded. "I imagine not," I said. "Well, I suppose we'll have to have the organizational meeting another time."

Vonnie's phone rang, and she answered it, carried on a quiet conversation for a minute or two, then hung up the phone. "That was Dora Watkins," she said. "She's the person who calls me on the prayer chain."

"Who do you call?" I asked.

"Me," Lizzie supplied as she walked past me and toward the kitchen door. Then she stopped and looked at Evie. "And I call Evangeline."

"Who calls me," I said. My call was to Sarah Brim, a woman who played the organ for the church. "I'll call Sarah as soon as I get in the car."

Forty minutes later we had Vonnie's house back in order, dishes put away, and leftovers covered and either in the refrigerator or in our hands. We said our good-byes and headed for our individual cars.

As soon as I settled into mine—and before I turned on the car—I placed three calls. The first was to Sarah, who wasn't home, so I left a message on her answering machine. The second was to Olivia, who was bathing the baby.

"I'd like to come by this evening," I said to her. "I'd like to talk to you about something."

"It sounds serious," she said with a forced lilt to her voice.

"It is. But I'd rather come when the kids have been put to bed. Tony should be there too."

There was a long pause before she said, "Okay. Sure. I'm getting the kids ready for bed now. So . . . in about an hour?"

"Make it two."

"Mom, it's 7:30 now."

"I know, Olivia. I've been able to tell time since I was a child." I felt my shoulders drop. I hadn't meant to snap. "I'm sorry, honey. I have one other thing I need to do before I get there."

"Well, okay, then. We'll be waiting up for you. But, Mom. Don't keep me waiting too long, okay?"

269

Honestly, sometimes I wondered who the mother was and who the child was within our relationship.

After I hung up with Olivia, I called Andrew Morrow's cell phone number, the one he'd given me if I "ever needed anything."

"Can you meet me at the house?" I asked him.

"Sure, in say . . . about an hour?"

"Can you make it a half hour?"

"I guess I can. I was just walking in the door of my apartment. I'll grab a quick bite and be right there."

"I appreciate it." With those words I started the car.

"Is there anything wrong?"

"No," I said. "But you said if I ever needed anything . . ."

"Yeah. Sure." He sounded genuinely interested in whatever help he could be. Now, I thought, if I could just figure out exactly what I was going to do next.

———

I'd only been home a few minutes when the front doorbell rang. I opened the door to see Andrew standing on my front porch, sporting a suit and looking remarkably like Jack. For a split second I wondered how it could have been that I'd never noticed—that no one had noticed before.

I forced a smile. "My goodness, that was fast."

He stepped into the living room as I stepped back to allow him entrance. "I was worried something was wrong. I figured I could eat dinner later."

"Do you want me to fix you something?" I said. "I've got some ham, some leftover green field peas . . ."

He chuckled. "You always seem to be offering me ham."

"Well, it's delicious. And this time it's my own. I made a wonderful raisin sauce."

"Maybe later." He took a deep breath then blew it out the way men do. "I was thinking on the way over . . ." He paused and pointed to the sofa. "Can we sit down?"

I felt myself blush. Offering to seat your guest was the job of the hostess, and here he was taking over as if he owned the house. "I'm sorry. Yes."

I went immediately to the sofa. Andrew sat in Jack's favorite recliner. He unbuttoned his suit coat as he did, then flexed his broad shoulders and allowed his elbows to rest on his knees. "I was thinking on the way over here . . ." he began again, then hung his head. He looked like one of those bobbing head dogs my father used to have sitting on the front dashboard of our old family Buick. Only Andrew appeared that his spring had sprung.

"You said that."

He looked up sharply. Even from my place on the sofa I saw his Adam's apple slip up and down behind the tanned skin of his throat. "You know, don't you?" he asked.

I was momentarily caught off guard. Then I said, "I'm supposed to be asking you that question."

He buried his face in his hands and then used them as though they were a washcloth and his forehead needed to be scrubbed. "Oh, man . . ." Then he stopped and looked at me again. "I never wanted this . . . for you to find out . . . I was hoping . . ."

"What were you hoping?"

"That somehow I could get close enough to you to get to Jack's papers . . . to make sure he hadn't done anything stupid like leave any damaging evidence behind. Anything that might make you think . . ."

The room around me grew thick with emotion. I felt myself split in two somehow: there was the emotional Goldie, who knew beyond the shadow of a doubt that she was sitting across the room from her dead husband's illegitimate adult son, and the detached Goldie, who was only viewing the scene as though watching it unfold on a movie screen. "Think what?" I finally mustered.

"Think bad of . . ."

He didn't finish, so I finished for him. "Your father?"

His eyes closed. He squeezed them, then relaxed, then reopened them. "Yes."

And then I laughed. "Oh, Andrew," I said, dabbing at my eyes with my fingertips. "I've lived three decades knowing the worst about my husband." Then I sobered. "And the best. Finding out about you is more or less the icing on the cake. Or, maybe the straw that breaks the camel's back, if you can stand two clichés at once."

"I don't think I follow you."

I stood and started out of the room. With a crook of my finger I said, "Follow me."

He did, straight to my bedroom and the jewelry armoire, where no less than two dozen pieces of stunning jewelry shimmered on top of velvet-lined drawers. I picked up the pieces, one at a time, and told him the story behind each one. "Your grandfather—Jack's father—was a womanizer," I began. "Jack's mother told me about him the first year Jack and I were married. When each affair ended, he gave her a beautiful piece of jewelry to make up for it." I rolled my eyes. "As though it could."

"Are these hers?" Andrew asked. With a thick finger he touched a topaz brooch.

"No," I said. "These are mine."

I watched as recognition fell across his face. "Jack?"

"Your mother wasn't the first. She wasn't the last." When I saw the hurt on his face, I placed a hand on his arm. "I'm not saying that to hurt you. I just want you to know that you have no worries when it comes to protecting me."

He blushed then.

I shut the individual drawers and said, "I called you here to ask you what you wanted from me. I guess now I know."

He crossed his arms across his thick chest. "If you mean do I want money or anything like that? No. To be honest with you, Jack set up a small fund for me years ago. It wasn't a lot, but when

I got old enough I invested it wisely. I've got a good job and I'm doing all right."

I had to take a moment to process what he was saying to me before I replied, "Have you always known?"

"Not always, no. My mother told me when I was in high school. I came home one day and asked her if my biological father had relatives around here because every time I looked at Coach Dippel I couldn't help but think I kinda looked like him."

"You look very much like the Jack I knew many years ago." I spoke softly.

His arms uncrossed and his hands went to his hips. "My mother told me that Jack was my father . . . that they'd had a fling that hadn't meant anything really, except for the fact that it had given me to her and for that she would be forever grateful." He blushed appropriately again. "I'm not trying to defend my mother here, you understand, but she's not a horrible person. I want you to know that."

I could only nod.

"Anyway, she said that he'd given her a lump sum of money to help raise me. It wasn't much, on his salary, but it helped. Of course when she married Dad . . . and she had her own job, so . . ."

This raised another question, one I couldn't help but ask. "Did Jack know that you knew?"

He was still for a moment before answering. "He never knew that I knew he was my father, no. Mom told him that she would tell the same story to everyone, including me. That my biological father had died in a car accident." He grimaced. "So, no. He didn't know. Or, if he did, he never let on to me."

"My gosh." If Jack had known he would have brought Andrew into our family; that much I knew for sure.

We stood silent until Andrew said, "Well, then. I guess my work here is done. I'll leave you alone from now on. Oh, and you don't have to worry about anyone knowing. About me, I mean. My mother taught me well to keep private things private."

I linked my arm into his and guided him back out of the bed-room and toward the hallway door. "Actually, I'm leaving in a few minutes to go see Olivia," I said. "To tell her."

He stopped short. "Why? Not on my account, I hope."

"No. Mostly for her own good. Olivia needs a lesson in just how strong her mother really is. *And* she needs to come off her high horse a little. Realize the world doesn't always come out in black and white. There are not always right or wrong answers. Sometimes we have to take life as it comes and make decisions based on the moment." I tossed my hair a little. "And hope for the best in the end."

We started back down the hall again. "What do you think she'll say to all this?"

"Oh, her first reaction will be to defend her father. Then she'll want to make sure you're not going to try to take advantage of me." We reached the living room again. "But in the end, she'll want to know more about the brother she never knew she had. And, I imagine, she'll want you to know your father from her point of view. Bottom line is, she'll live."

A hint of pink rushed across his high cheekbones. "I admit I always wanted to get to know her better."

"Well," I said, "I think after tonight, you'll have your chance."

# 32

## Dishing Drama

First thing Friday morning, I sent a message via my assistant to the homeroom teachers of Barrie, Jocelyn, Daniel, and Carter, asking that they be excused for a brief meeting with me in the media center. Within a matter of minutes, four excited-looking teenagers burst through the door of my private office amid a flurry of "What's going on?" and "Hey, Mrs. Prattle, what's up?"

I had brought four chairs into my office and placed them so that they faced my desk, where I was now sitting. "Everyone sit," I said. When they had, I pulled open a side drawer of my desk, removed my purse, and then slipped a piece of paper from between its satiny lining. "This is to be kept in complete confidence," I said.

"Sure," Barrie said.

"Does this have to do with what we were looking into the other night? The hidden gold?" Carter asked.

I gave the students a weak smile, not wanting to give too much away. "It may." I placed the paper on the desk before me, then leaned over, resting my forearms on either side. "I don't want you to get too excited. But I seriously think we might have something here."

I unfolded the paper before I went on.

"Yesterday the Potluck Catering Club had a meeting to talk about the Founders Day celebration and what we need to do to get ready. Before we could get into that, Lisa Leann—Mrs. Lambert—pulled out an old leather pouch she found hidden in the boutique." I paused, wondering if I should tell them about the gold and the gun, then decided against it. "There were several items inside the pouch, all from over a hundred years ago. Well over a hundred years ago. Gold rush days." I raised my brow for effect, which worked because the four students sitting before me were barely able to keep to their seats. "Mrs. Lambert had handed it to me when a phone call came in, she had to leave, and—shortly after that—I realized I was still holding the note. At first I was just going to return it, but the more I thought about it, the more I decided we've come this far in our investigation, why not go all the way?"

"Well, it would help if we knew what it said," Daniel remarked.

I turned the note around, and the four leaned over.

"What in the world?" Jocelyn said. "What's that first word?"

"I'm going to see if you can figure this out," I answered. "Come on, now. You are all honor roll students."

"Padre," Carter said. "Like, 'father' in Spanish."

"So, this was written to Zeke Hannah's father?" Barrie asked him.

"I guess," he answered with a shrug.

"Zeke Hannah . . . wasn't that the Crazy Old Zeke we were talking about the other day?" Jocelyn asked. "Didn't you read about it, Carter?"

"Good, Jocelyn," I said. "What do you remember about him?"

"He was a miner."

"Okay, what else?"

"He went to dances on Friday nights," Daniel supplied. "And he was always claiming to have found a mother lode."

"But no gold was ever found," Barrie said. "Most people just thought he was crazy." She paused. "Oh, except Father Dyer."

"Padre!" Carter said with a jump.

"Hey, man, you think the note is to Father Dyer?" Daniel asked him.

"Sure. Why not?"

Four expectant sets of eyes looked to me for affirmation.

"That's exactly what I think. Now, let's look at the rest of the note. Barrie, what would you say it says?"

Barrie read the note silently then answered out loud, "You might not here . . . no, hear . . . from me no more but know the plus is my treasure." She gave a funny look then added, "Zeke Hannah."

"What does that mean, Mrs. Prattle?" Jocelyn asked. "The plus is my treasure?"

I rested my elbow on the top of my desk, then my chin in the palm of my hand. "Well, I have to say that part had me pretty stumped too. Until I realized"—I pointed to the plus sign—"that the plus is a cross."

"Ohhhhh," they all said.

Then they were silent until Daniel said, "But what does that mean? The cross is my treasure?"

I frowned. "That's the part we have to figure out."

The four blinked at me, wordless.

Just then the first period class bell rang. It was time for them to go.

———

I called Donna's cell phone number as soon as the students had left my office. "Hey, Liz," she said in answer.

"Donna," I said. "What's the latest on Lisa Leann?"

"Nothing that I know of," she said. "I took her back to her house so she could get some paperwork on Mandy . . . you know, birth certificate, social security card copy, and the latest photographs. Then I took her back to Vonnie's."

"Have you called and talked to either one of them?"

"No, not yet. I was just sort of waking up, to be honest with you. I'm pulling a night shift tonight."

"Oh, I'm sorry, Donna. I hope I didn't wake you."

"You didn't. I was just lying here reading a little before I got up. No biggie."

I thought for a moment before continuing. "Donna, what were the final plans for your mother?"

"Velvet has taken complete charge of everything and left me out entirely. Mom was cremated. She has the ashes. Says she'll scatter them anywhere but here, but that she wants to wait until after Evie's trial."

I sighed. "Oh my goodness. I'm so sorry, Donna."

"It's okay. At least I got to know Mom a little bit before she . . . you know . . . died."

"But Donna, you really don't think Evangeline did this, do you? I mean, Evie can be a bit to take at times, but she is not a murderer. Even an accidental one."

"I agree. And I'm doing everything I know to do to try to put another theory on the table."

"Well, if anyone can figure this out, you can."

"Thanks, Liz. Listen, if you hear anything more about Mandy or Lisa Leann, let me know, okay?"

"I will. You do the same."

We disconnected our call. I sat back in my chair and allowed myself time to think about how Lisa Leann must be feeling. I wondered if I should call her, then decided to wait and just drive to Vonnie's after work. I figured that any time the phone rang would be difficult for her, especially when the person she wanted to hear from wasn't on the other side.

I then thought about my own daughters, especially Michelle. Since the day we'd seen Vernon and Donna at Higher Grounds— the day Doreen's body had been discovered—she and I had not spoken again about her concerns over starting a family. This was really important to her, I thought, and I'd basically cast it aside. Then I thought of my own mother struggling to keep up with the moments of the day and the memories of the years. I wondered how much time I had left before she simply didn't know me at all.

I pulled my cell phone from my purse and called Michelle at her office in Breckenridge, using the TDD operator to tell Michelle that I loved her and wanted her and Adam to come over for dinner the following night. "I thought I'd have everyone come," I said. "The whole family or as much as we can get together. Go ahead," I said, using the code that allowed the deaf listener to know it was okay to speak.

"Adam told me he's had a yen for your black bottom pie," she said, using the TDD operator as her voice. "If you promise you'll make it, I can assure you we'll be there." She giggled, then said, "Go ahead."

"You've got yourself a deal," I replied. "One more thing. If you can, visit your grandmother this weekend. Go ahead."

"Will do, Mom. Go ahead."

"See you tomorrow at 6:00?" I asked. "Go ahead."

"Okay, 6:00 it is."

———

On the way to Vonnie's I stopped by the church when I saw Pastor Kevin's car in his parking place. I hoped he had some good news concerning Mandy Lambert Donahue. I pulled my car into a space nearby then grabbed my sweater, shoving my arms into the sleeves. When I got out of the car and locked it, I looked around at the work being done. The workers were still hard at it. Most of those outside were wearing long-sleeved flannel shirts and jeans, and a few had baseball caps on their heads.

I refocused my attention and went in the side door nearest Pastor Kevin's office. His secretary was already gone for the day, but I found the door to his private study open. He sat at his desk, feet propped atop it and crossed at the ankles. He was reading a book and seemed to be completely engrossed in it, though I didn't know how with all the hammering and buzzing going on around the building.

I tapped lightly on the door. He jumped a little, then swung around to face me. "Lizzie," he said, "come on in."

I took a few steps into the outer office. "I was just wondering if you'd heard anything else from the Lambert home."

"I have, actually," he said. "I talked with Lisa Leann about an hour ago. I'm surprised you haven't."

"I've been at work and I figured it would be best to go by there rather than call. When I saw your car I thought I'd stop here first."

"Well, the good news is that Henry has seen Ray, and he's holding his own. The bad news is that no one has seen or heard anything from Mandy."

I sighed. "I don't know how Lisa Leann is going to get through this."

"'I can do all things through Christ who strengthens me,'" Pastor Kevin quoted from God's Word.

"Well," I said, "you know what I mean."

"I do, and I'm calling Esther to start an update"—he looked at his watch—"in about ten minutes. She had a dentist appointment and called me earlier to tell me if there was any news not to call until after she got home."

"Go back to your reading," I said. "Though quite frankly I don't know how you work in all this noise."

"Coming from someone who works in a high school all day, I'd say that's pretty funny."

I laughed lightly, then turned toward the door. "You've got a point. Everything coming along okay here?"

"Right on target," he said, walking beside me and out into the hallway. "I'll just be glad when the sanctuary is back to normal and we can resume services in there. You've never seen such a mess in your life."

"I remember when we renovated our kitchen. Four months of absolute torture."

"If we have to endure four months of this, I really will go insane."

I smiled up at him in wonder. His countenance was always peaceful, no matter what the circumstance. A year ago, when his wife passed away unexpectedly, his face expressed anguish. But, in the oddest way, a remnant of peace remained around the edges. "Well, you're a strong man," I said.

We reached the outer door, and he pushed it open for me. I stepped out to see one of the workers across the parking lot as he hopped onto the seat of a bike pointed toward the street. As he pedaled away I said, "Must be quitting time." The door swung shut behind us.

"More or less. That's Hoss. He's leaving this job for his other job."

"Oh?"

"He took Doreen's old job at the tavern."

"Oh."

Kevin shoved his hands into the pockets of his chinos. "I've spent some time talking to him. Interesting fellow. He's got a real knack for construction, knows a lot about the old churches around here. A lot about their history."

"Really?"

"I found him in the sanctuary one day when no one else was there. Said he was just killing time during his lunch break. That's when he started telling me some of the architectural facts about the church I thought I'd share next Friday night at the dinner. Really interesting facts about the stained glass windows. The old flooring. Were you aware—"

Before he could finish, my cell phone rang from inside my purse. "I'm sorry," I said. I fished it out, saw it was from Summit Center, and said, "This is about my mother. It's their daily update. I'm sorry."

Kevin touched my shoulder briefly. "No worries. I'll leave you to your call, then."

"Hello?" I answered, then turned toward where my pastor had been standing to apologize again. But he had already gone back inside the church.

*Vonnie*

# 33

## Deep-Fried Danger

It was Sunday night and I'd been lying in bed with Fred; his soft snores tried to lure me to sleep. But despite the temptation to roll onto my side and snooze with my husband, worry held my eyes wide open. I glanced at the glowing green digits of the bedside clock. It was already 11:20 p.m. and I once again began to rehearse my plan to sneak out to a midnight meeting with Chucky's captor. I'd gone to bed wearing my black sweats for pajamas; all I'd have to do was step into my tennis shoes, grab my purse and jacket I'd stashed by the door, and slip into the night, then drive to the church, where I hoped I'd find my lost Chucky waiting for me.

When the clock's digits read 11:30, I knew it was time to go. I slowly sat up, moved back the covers, and stepped barefoot onto the cushy carpet. I reached down and picked up my tennis shoes stuffed with clean socks and quietly pushed open my bedroom door. Once safely on the other side of the door, I bent down to slip my feet into my socks and tie my shoes before tiptoeing to the front door. I opened it to let in the night.

"Where are you going?" a voice from the dark living room asked.

I turned to see Lisa Leann sitting in my recliner, illuminated by the soft light of her cell phone.

I clutched my chest. "Oh! I didn't see you there."

"Sorry. Are you going somewhere?"

I shook my head so fast I could feel my jowls wiggle. "No, no, just checking the weather. Thought I heard some thunder." I peered out, as if to prove my story, and then shut the door. I turned around awkwardly and stared back at Lisa Leann who appeared as though she'd been crying. I stepped toward her. "Have you heard from Henry? Is Mandy okay?"

Lisa Leann stood and walked toward me. "I just hung up from talking to him. Henry thinks he has a lead in finding Mandy."

I turned and walked toward the kitchen as Lisa Leann followed me, trying not to glance at the clock above the refrigerator. "That's wonderful," I said as I opened the refrigerator. I pulled out what was left of my chocolate coconut meringue pie and held it toward Lisa Leann. "Care for a midnight snack as you tell me all about it?"

Lisa Leann shook her head no, and I slid the pie back into the refrigerator, untouched. I didn't really have time to eat pie anyway.

"Well," she said as she sat down at the table, "there's been a report that a redheaded woman—a possible mugging victim—is at a women's ward in a hospital across town from where Ray is a patient."

I joined my friend at the table. "Is there any word on the woman's condition?"

Lisa Leann looked glum. "Not really. In fact, Henry's not sure if he can learn anything or not."

"Why not?"

"The hospital ward in question is under quarantine."

"For heaven's sake, why?"

The baby cried out and Lisa Leann stood. "Swine flu, if you can believe it."

"Oh no!" I said, rising with her.

"I'd better attend to Kyle," she said, disappearing down the dark hallway. She paused at the door to her bedroom. "Maybe Henry will know something soon."

I was relieved when she shut her bedroom door. I stole a peek at the kitchen clock. It was a quarter till midnight. Without further ado, I headed toward the door, grabbed my purse and my jacket, and slipped into the night.

I glided down the front steps, glad I'd parked my car on the curb instead of in the attached garage. That way I wouldn't wake the house by powering open the door or turning on the ignition.

I knew my family and Donna would never approve of what I was up to. They'd flat-out forbid it. I myself had second thoughts about following through with this meeting, especially with what had happened to Doreen. I mean, what if this dognapper was somehow connected to her death? It was only the remembrance of Chucky's innocent brown eyes that gave me the courage to go on.

As I drove through the dark streets, fear pattered my heart as I wondered what this dognapper could possibly want from me. Revenge? Information?

It was more likely he wanted some of the cash I'd won on *The Great Party Showdown* reality show earlier this year. That's why I'd stuffed a couple of thousand in twenties in the bottom of my bag. "Insurance money" was what I was thinking.

I didn't have much time to ponder the answers to these questions because I soon pulled into the church parking lot at five minutes to midnight.

I turned off the engine and killed the lights and tugged my arms into my jacket. I opened my heavy, beige leather purse, which was big enough to serve as a small duffle bag, and pulled out a large flashlight. Before I opened the door, I sat quietly and bowed my head. "Dear Lord, please go out into the dark with me. Keep me safe, and most of all protect my little dog, Chucky. Bring him back home to me, in the powerful name of Jesus."

I pushed open the door and stepped into the parking lot. As I did, a cold breeze blew straight down the neck of my jacket, setting me into shivers. The overhead parking lot lights were turned off automatically at this hour, so I switched on my flashlight and began to shine it around the area. As far as I could tell, I was alone.

The dark shadows behind the church began to beckon me. I stepped toward them, as a tiny schoolgirl voice called from my senior-adult body. "Chucky?"

Silence.

The mountains that surrounded our valley shrouded all hope of illumination from the black sky, so I followed the beam of my flashlight that split the darkness at my feet. I called again. This time my voice was stronger, but with a wobble. "Chucky?"

The silence pulled me forward on my path of yellow light.

Just as I started to round the corner of the building, a truck roared into the parking lot. I turned to see glaring lights pointed in my direction. A door flew open, followed by a clamor of feet as Donna called, "Vonnie Westbrook, just what do you think you're doing out here?"

*Donna*

# 34

## Chewing Over a Clue

I felt sorry for Vonnie, I really did, and I could understand why she took the chance she had even though she had done so at great risk. I tried to explain that the next morning when I dropped by her house.

As she sat at the kitchen table with Lisa Leann, I held out a large white evidence bag. "Take a look," I said.

I opened the mouth of the bag, and she looked down at a roll of duct tape and wad of skinny rope.

"What's all this?" Vonnie asked, her eyes still puffy from her night of sobbing over Chucky.

"I found these behind the church this morning. I'm thinking they were meant for you. They were next to a shovel and a hole, which may have been planned as your shallow grave once you gave him whatever it was that he wanted."

Vonnie gasped.

I turned and looked at Lisa Leann, who was holding baby Kyle. She stood and peered in the bag too before looking back at Vonnie.

"Oh, Vonnie, you would have been killed. What if I hadn't called Donna?"

I turned to my dear friend. "Vonnie, you have to call me if you get any more of these notes. Promise me."

Vonnie nodded. Then asked, "But did you see any sign of Chucky?"

I shook my head. "I doubt he was even there."

She hung her head, and I said, "Okay, then. I'm on duty today so I'll check in later, all right?"

Vonnie nodded glumly, and Lisa Leann stood and walked me to the door. Lisa Leann looked over her shoulder at Vonnie then back at me. "I'll take care of her," she said. "Don't you worry now."

"I appreciate that. And call me if she does anything else suspicious."

"I will," Lisa Leann said as I skipped down the steps to my Bronco. Lisa Leann called after me, "Oh, and you'll pick up the carrots and pineapple for the gelatin salad?"

"Sure thing. I'll deliver it to the boutique and put it in the fridge for tomorrow's work day."

A few minutes later, I headed toward the nursing home to talk to the only person in town who was still on my list to interview.

I walked into the Summit Center to be greeted by a row of elderly women and a couple of men sitting in wheelchairs, lined from the front door to the nurse's station. Some of the aged residents stared absently, lost in a world of their own, while others smiled and lifted a brown-speckled hand as they nodded a greeting. "Mornin', Deputy."

It was the woman on the end who caught my eye, a frail woman with soft white curls and ancient eyes that still sparkled. As I approached, her gnarled hand reached for mine as she exclaimed, "Well, if it isn't Deputy Donna. I'm so glad you dropped by to see me."

A nurse wearing a dark rose uniform stood from behind the desk. "May I help you?"

"Actually," I said, looking down on Mrs. Hirvela, "I've come to chat with an old friend."

Mrs. Hirvela gave a playful laugh as I pushed her chair toward the parlor. "I'm not that old, Donna. I'll only be ninety-four at Christmas, and a lot of folks around here are a lot older than *that*." I positioned her to face me while I sat down on the hearth. Mrs. Hirvela said, "So what brings you in to visit your mother's sixth-grade teacher?"

I took her hand. "You taught my mother? I didn't know that."

"Oh my, your mother was a live wire, you know." She giggled. "For instance, there was the time I caught her kissing that little boy behind the school building. Vernon, was it?"

I nodded. "My dad."

"He became our sheriff, didn't he? But whatever happened to your mother?"

I blushed again and shook my head. "She recently passed away."

Mrs. Hirvela patted my arm. "So sorry to hear that. I was really very fond of her."

I blinked and cleared my throat. "Actually, I came because I wanted to ask you something about your old house."

She frowned. "Is it all right? It didn't burn down, did it?"

"It's fine and beautiful as ever. It's a wedding boutique these days, and the woman who owns it lavishes it with love."

Mrs. Hirvela smiled. "That's good to know."

"That old house has a lot of secrets, doesn't it?"

"Oh my, yes, it's one of the original houses in Summit View, built in 1880 by my great-grandfather—he was a merchant, you know—came to town to keep an eye on his son-in-law, a gold miner who lived about twenty miles from here."

"Who was your great-grandfather's son-in-law?"

"My great-uncle Zeke. He was always claiming to have found the mother lode, and maybe he did. Tom's Baby, that thirteen-pound gold nugget, was found not that far from here, you know."

"Is that what you think? Old Zeke found the mother lode?"

Mrs. Hirvela shook her head. "From the way I heard it, one day, Uncle Zeke came home with Mildred, his pregnant wife, packed his bags, and left Mildred behind. He never returned. It all seemed suspicious to the family, especially with that stagecoach robbery over in Central City. Those suspicions weren't eased when my great-grandmother happened to look in one of Uncle Zeke's favorite hiding places, a loose floorboard in front of the fireplace."

I leaned closer. "What did she find?"

"A gun, a letter, and some things my great-grandfather put in a safe place. But there was also what looked to be a treasure map—a crude hand drawing of our town. But the interesting thing was there was a big X where the church is. Old Zeke had been helping Father Dyer build it, you know."

"Was there anything else on the map?"

"Some cryptic words, pirate-like talk, you know, like 'X marks the spot.'"

I felt my eyebrows leap at that. "Does anyone beside you know about this map?"

Old Mrs. Hirvela smiled wistfully. "Not many of us left. But I do have this one nephew. Sings like an angel, you know, but I'm sorry to say that's where the resemblance ends. He's been in a lot of trouble with the law—in and out of jail more than a few times. He's been to see me of late. In fact, he was here earlier this morning."

I felt my pulse begin to race. "Who is your nephew, Mrs. Hirvela?"

The old woman looked stunned. "I should think you would know him, Donna. He was the choir director down at the church, you know. Horace Shelly. And . . ." She put her hand to her mouth, then spoke quietly. "Why, that's right! He was once married to your mother."

My jaw dropped. "Horace Shelly is in town?"

"Yes, dear, said he came for the Founders Day celebration. He's been here a few weeks, I'd say."

"What does he look like?"

"Don't you remember him?"

"I think I was four when I saw him last."

Mrs. Hirvela thoughtfully touched her chin. "That would be about right. That's when he took off with your mother. Well, he's changed a bit in these past thirty or so years. He's still as strong as an ox, though he has a few wrinkles, you know. He's balding, though he still has a bit of gray hair." Mrs. Hirvela laughed. "In fact, now that I think of it, I'm not sure his own mother would recognize him, may her soul rest in peace."

"You wouldn't happen to have a photograph, would you?"

"I'm afraid not."

I smiled, trying to keep the conversation pleasant. "Do you know where he's staying?"

"Believe he's camped near here somewhere. He and his little dog, Lucky, is it?"

"Camped where?"

"Wish I could tell you. But if I see him again, I'll ask him for you."

"That would be great, only don't tell him I was here, okay?"

"Is anything wrong?"

"I hope not," I said. "Though, I'd love a chance to talk to him."

"I hope you get your wish, then," Mrs. Hirvela said as I stood.

I leaned down and gave her a hug. "You and me both."

# 35

## Half-Baked Romance

Of all things, on Friday afternoon the high school was hit with a power outage. At the last minute, the girls and I—along with the band mothers—worked a quick change in the venue from the school to the church for the night's event. As I hurried around the church kitchen I stopped to look at the baby monitor I'd set up between the church nursery and the kitchen. On the screen I could see Kyle sleeping in one of the cribs while Vonnie's husband Fred sat in the rocking chair and peeled apples for our apple and cheese crisp we were serving for the concert.

It was hard to believe it was already Friday. The week had flown by and was made all the better by Henry finding Mandy, who was in quarantine in the hospital across town from Ray.

Lizzie asked, "So what's the latest news on your kids?"

"Ray is doing great, aside from his broken legs, and Henry thinks he'll be good enough to travel in the next couple of days."

"And Mandy?"

"She apparently fell and hit her head during a mugging. She was unconscious for a day, and the Egyptian authorities didn't know who to contact since she was without her identification. All I can say is it was a good thing Henry showed up."

"Is she out of the hospital yet?"

"No, her ward was in quarantine because one of the other patients had some kind of flu. Though we're hoping the quarantine will be lifted soon."

"But how's she doing otherwise?"

"Well, Henry's spoken to her by phone, and he's convinced she's fine."

"That's such a relief," Lizzie said.

The team and I, minus Donna, who was working today, chopped and baked with a few of the band mothers while the high school band and choir set up in our church fellowship hall. I kept an eye on them through the window over the counter that opened from the kitchen and into the fellowship hall.

We were just pulling out the last couple of pans of apple and cheese crisp from the oven when the evening crowd began to arrive, and along with it, Donna, still in her deputy's uniform.

I gave her one of our pink aprons to put on before she got busy making gallons of industrial-strength tea, which we would serve after the concert. While we worked, a couple of people stopped to talk to us through the window, though we weren't yet serving food. A young man named Andrew dropped by to say hello to Goldie. He somehow seemed familiar to me, though I couldn't put my finger on why.

A few minutes later I looked up to see Nate, the detective who'd rescued me from my would-be-intruder down at the shop. He stood facing the window with a lovely young lady by his side.

"Hello, Nate," I said. "Who's your friend?"

The girl, a beauty with long blonde hair, held out her left hand. "We're engaged," she said as if that answered my question.

Nate looked sheepish. "I just popped the question last night."

"And I said yes," the girl said with a giggle.

I noticed that Donna had stopped her tea-makings. "Congratulations," she called from over my shoulder.

"Thanks," Nate said, then turned to the girl. "Kate, would you mind grabbing a couple of seats for us? I have a bit of unfinished business about a case I'm working on."

Kate giggled again. "See you in a minute," she said as she disappeared into the crowd.

Once she left, Donna stepped next to me to face him. "So, here you have a girlfriend while you got me believing you were waiting for me," she teased.

"You can't blame a guy for some harmless flirting."

"Sure I can," Donna shot back, her hands on her hips.

Nate grinned. "No harm done, but if you recall, you implied you wouldn't date anyone who believed your stepmother was guilty."

Donna laughed. "Your loss, because I just had a breakthrough in the case. Of course, you'd know that if you'd finished going through the paperwork I put on your desk."

Evie, who had been in the back pantry, suddenly joined us. "Breakthrough in the case?"

"Can't talk about it, Evie," Donna said. "Not now, and certainly not with you."

Evangeline quickly disappeared as Nate said, "Well, good luck to you then. Call me and fill me in later. Okay?"

"Sure thing," Donna said.

I raised my brows then turned to look at Donna. "So, you and Nate?"

She shook her head. "No, no. That was just silly talk."

I pointed to Wade, who was entering the fellowship hall with his mother. "Then are you still in love with Wade?"

Donna narrowed her eyes. "Well . . . I don't . . ."

"Well, why don't you take a break and go say hello," I said, still trying to keep my promise to Wade to help him connect with my friend.

Donna sighed. "He's with his *mother.*"

I put a stack of paper plates on the counter. "What difference does that make?"

"I'll show you," Donna said as she pulled off her apron and walked out through the kitchen door and into the crowd. I followed at a safe distance to observe.

Donna strolled over to the row where Wade and his mother were just finding their seats. "Mrs. Gage, Wade," Donna said. "Hello."

Mrs. Gage looked up at Donna and narrowed her eyes. "Can't sit here, there's no room."

Donna pointed to the empty seat next to Wade. "I think that's for Wade to decide. Right, Wade?"

Wade turned to his mother's scowl. "Don't you think Donna could . . . ?"

"No. Why would she want to bother us; there are plenty of other places for her to sit."

Donna simply smiled as if the exchange was not meant to hurt her feelings. "Well, it's up to you, Wade. Shall I join you?"

Mrs. Gage answered for him. "I should say not!"

"Is that right, Wade?" Donna asked, slowly but deliberately.

Wade shrugged. "Now may not be a good time," he said. "Let's talk later, okay?"

Donna nodded. "Not a problem." She turned abruptly and headed back to the kitchen while I hurried to catch up with her. I grabbed her by the elbow and pulled her into the kitchen pantry where there was some privacy. I stared into Donna's red face.

"Do you see what my problem was?" she asked me, arms crossed. "I couldn't compete against his dogged loyalty to his mom."

"'Honor your mother and father,'" I quoted from the Ten Commandments, since I was still rooting for Wade.

"Okay, but where does that leave 'Therefore a man shall leave his father and his mother, and cleave unto his wife?'"

She had me there.

She continued, "Do you know that in all the time we dated, Wade's never once, *once*, stood up to his mom on my behalf? I suppose if we were married I'd have to grin and bear it. But we're not married and . . . we'll *never* be married. It's over."

"Then why did you try to sit with him?"

Donna laughed. "Because I was showing *you* his heart. There was no chance Wade would go against his mother. I was beyond safe."

"Then why are you so ticked off?"

Donna's cheeks pinked again. "Sorry, that woman still gets my dander up," she admitted. "But as far as Wade goes, I've been over him for some time."

"Then where does that leave you with your love life? With David? I mean, you two have been dating all summer, haven't you?"

Donna sighed and dropped her hands by her side. "Well, yes. And I really care about David, I do." Her eyes glistened. "But I can't help but wonder if he's really the man I thought he was."

"I see," I said. "What does Vonnie have to say about it?"

"She's too close to the situation. I can't talk to her."

"Maybe the person you really need to talk to is David."

"You're right. And to his credit, he's tried. But every time we try to be alone, we get interrupted with things like my mother's murder, or work even. I haven't even had time to sleep, much less talk to him." She swatted a tear. "That man has really stolen my heart, and now it looks like it was all for nothing."

Lizzie came and tapped on the pantry door. She looked nice in one of her black velour outfits, even if she was wearing a pink apron over it. "It's starting, you two. Come out and see the skit my kids are doing to kick things off."

Donna and I slipped from the pantry and through the kitchen door to join Lizzie and the team, who stood watching from behind the now-filled hall. I could see David leaning on the opposite wall. He must have come in on break from his shift tonight.

From the stage, one of Lizzie's high school students was dressed like a gold miner from the gold rush days. He was a tall, thin young man doing a little monologue about what it was like to be a failed gold miner then a stagecoach robber named Old Zeke. All the while, he was dragging a chest across the stage, pretending it was extraordinarily heavy. Another student actor, this one with powdered-gray hair and carrying a couple of cross-country skis and a Bible, stopped him. "Hi, Zeke. What you got there in that chest?"

"Why, Father John Dyer, this is my treasure," the kid playing Zeke replied.

"Old Zeke, don't you know the Good Book says, 'Do not store up for yourselves treasures on earth, where moth and rust destroy, and where thieves break in and steal. But store up for yourselves treasures in heaven, where moth and rust do not destroy, and where thieves do not break in and steal. For where your treasure is, there your heart will be also.'"

"Is that so?" Old Zeke said. "Then Father Dyer, where's your treasure?"

"Zeke, my treasure is in the cross."

"Then that's where I'm going to put my treasure too," Old Zeke said, dragging the chest off the stage.

Donna gasped.

I turned to her. "What is it?"

She shook her head, looking dumbfounded. "I think I just had another break in the case."

"Tell me!"

She shook her head again. "Not yet," she said. "But be patient, I may be able to solve this thing yet."

# 36

## Case Crackers

The Potluck Team worked late into the night, cleaning up after the dessert for the concert then getting things ready for tomorrow's Founders Day dinner. So it was no surprise when the girls and I missed Saturday's parade down Main Street. I, for one, hated to miss seeing our pastor ride on a float dressed as Father Dyer. So I was glad when he appeared at the church to give the public a tour of the sanctuary.

I slipped out of the kitchen to join in the tour, hoping I might get a glimpse of Horace Shelly in case he was in the crowd. I was on the lookout for a man in his late fifties, with a bit of gray hair on a balding head. And as most of the balding gentlemen in town wore baseball caps, I'd have to keep a sharp lookout for all things suspicious.

I followed the group as they entered the foyer with Pastor Kevin dressed in full character, his hair sprayed gray with hair paint.

"Good afternoon, ladies and gents. I'm Father John Dyer. I came to Colorado from Minnesota in 1861 to see Pikes Peak. I stayed to preach to miners and settlers. For twenty-nine years I traveled from camp to camp on 'snowshoes' I crafted from Norwegian pines. The miners knew I cared about them, because I attended the sick and preached against gambling, drinking, and prostitution. So with all this caring, why would the miners blow up the church's bell tower just because I helped establish prohibition in these parts?"

Everyone laughed, and Pastor Kevin went on to show the sanctuary: the hand-hewed pine floors, the stone wall behind the choir loft with its big wooden cross set into the stones themselves.

I kept an eye on the crowd, but no one acted suspicious or made a comment that seemed out of place, so when the tour was over I headed back to help the girls. When I got to the kitchen, Vonnie called me into the pantry. She pulled a couple of letters from her pocket. "Donna, I have something for you."

"What's this?"

"First, this note was on my car last night, here in the church parking lot."

I snatched it from her hand and read the typewritten words:

> Meet me behind the church, during the dinner tomorrow night. Come alone if you want your dog back.

"Does anyone else know about this?" I asked.

"Only Lisa Leann. She was going to come tell you if I didn't show you first."

"I see. What's this other letter?"

Vonnie held it out to me. "It's to you from Bobbie Ann Jackson. It came to my house, I presume because she didn't have your address."

I glanced at the LA postmark as I opened the letter. It was written in neat script:

> Dear Donna,
> I can't believe I'm telling you this, and if I hadn't met

somebody new, well, the man I work for, actually, I wouldn't say anything. David chewed me out for the way I treated you. I came all the way from LA to win David back. But after the first five minutes of riding in his car, I could see he was in love with you. You were all he talked about; how beautiful you are, how genuine, how he knew he loved you the moment he saw you, how he was waiting for you to realize you were in love with him. I was angry.

When we got to Aspen, I did my best to lure David to my hotel room. But instead of letting me seduce him, the man tried to share his faith with me! That was the wake-up call I needed to see he'd changed into someone I didn't want to spend my life with. Still, I care enough about the man to want him to be happy. So here's my good deed, more to him than to you. David was loyal to you, just as he was loyal in his care for his Hollywood mom, Harmony, when she was dying of that terrible cancer.

Since that reality show, David's turned down television appearances and fame, just to ride in an ambulance and to be with you.

I hope you know how lucky you are.

Bobbie Ann Jackson

I looked up at Vonnie through a sudden mist and folded the letter, tucking it into my jeans. "How long have you had this?"

She looked worried. "It came in the mail today. Is everything all right?"

I felt a silly grin spread across my face. "You could say that."

"Well, after the way that woman treated you, I just didn't want . . ."

"It's okay, Vonnie. You did the right thing in giving this to me. Have you seen David?"

"He's running an errand right now."

"Do you know when he'll be back?"

She shook her head as Lisa Leann walked into the pantry. "There you two are. We got the last of the stuffed chicken breasts in the oven back at the shop. Fred's watching over things there so I thought I'd come over and see how things were going." Lisa Leann stared at Vonnie. "Plus, I wanted to be sure you showed Donna that note. You did, right?"

Vonnie nodded as Goldie, then Lizzie, who held baby Kyle, joined us in the pantry. "Isn't this cozy," Lizzie teased before smiling down at the sleeping baby in her arms.

I teased back. "Glad I called this meeting. But the truth is, I need your help."

Evie poked her head in. "Room for one more?"

I nodded. "Ladies, I know who killed my mother."

"Who?" they asked in unison, causing baby Kyle to almost shudder himself awake. I lowered my voice. "Horace Shelly."

"Horace?" Evie's eyes about popped. "You mean the choir director that ran off with your mother?"

"Yes. And as I've discovered, he's in town. At least according to his aunt. Could it be that one or two of you has seen him—a balding man with gray hair?"

Vonnie looked puzzled. "Horace . . . I wonder. Maybe Horace is the Hoss who works at the Gold Rush Tavern. He took over Doreen's job when she died."

"Did he look familiar to you?" I asked.

"He's not the young man I remember, but come to think of it, I thought that honeyed voice of his sounded familiar."

Lizzie's eyes lit up. "The Gold Rush Tavern? Pastor Kevin says that one of the construction workers here at the church moonlights there in the evenings."

I turned to Vonnie. "I think Horace took Chucky, and I believe he's the one who tried to lure you behind the church in the middle of the night."

300

"What?" Goldie almost cried. "Vonnie! You didn't fall for that, did you?"

Vonnie nodded but said, "Donna stopped me." She paused. "You know, Velvet said her mother's exes were mean, but she also said none of them were in town. So how do you explain that when she'd seen Hoss around?"

"She might not even know him," Lizzie said. "After all, Velvet hadn't been born yet when Doreen was married to Horace."

"But," Evie interjected, "why would Horace be after Doreen, or Lisa Leann, Vonnie, or even Chucky, for that matter?"

"I have a theory about that too. Horace's great-great-uncle was Old Zeke."

"From the skit?" Goldie asked.

"Yeah, only the real one. I believe he thinks Old Zeke buried the gold at the church. He believes that some of us have information— maybe the letter Lisa Leann found at the shop—that will lead him to the gold. I believe he thinks we have the clue he's been seeking."

"You mean," Goldie asked, wide-eyed, "the legend is true?"

"Maybe. But for now, I have a plan. Lisa Leann, do you have your baby monitor here?"

She nodded.

"Okay, good. Would you mind showing me how it works?"

———

Later that evening, the food was prepared and the trap set. We'd set up the baby remote control monitor for lowlight, making sure it was full of batteries and switched to on when we hid it in a nearby tree. Then, once we'd served the meal, Lisa Leann slipped into the nursery, set her video camera on a desk tripod, pointed it at the monitor, and hit record, filming whatever the baby monitor displayed.

One by one, we all broke away from our duties and joined Lisa Leann and Vonnie. Evie lead the prayer: "Lord, please protect our friend. Please let this night lead us all to truth."

"Amen," Lizzie said, swaying with the baby still in her arms.

I turned to Vonnie. "You don't have to go through with this, you know."

"This is for Doreen, Evie, and even Chucky," she said before she walked into the night armed only with her flashlight and her purse, which she'd showed us was full of cash.

"In case I need it as a bargaining chip," she said.

We held our breath as Vonnie rounded the corner to the back of the building and called into the darkness. "Anyone out there?"

We heard a voice answer back. "I'm glad you could make it; did you bring any of your little friends this time?"

I could see Vonnie step into position. "No, it's just me. Do you have my dog?"

A man stepped out from behind the woods at the edge of the church property and into full view of the monitor's camera. He didn't look anything like the man I'd always imagined Horace Shelly to be. This man was old. Used up. An aura of evil hovered around him.

*So this is the man? This is the man my mother left Dad and me for?*

"First," Horace said to Vonnie, jarring me back to the present, "you've got something I want."

"Money?"

"I heard that Lisa Leann found a satchel filled with things Zeke left at my aunt's old house and I figure you'll tell me all about it, that is if you want your dog back."

"How did you hear about the satchel?"

"It's funny, that pastor of yours never seems to notice when a workman's hanging around when he's on his office phone. I overheard that Lambert woman tell him everything."

Vonnie pursed her lips together. "Then, is that why you killed Doreen? You thought she might hold the key to finding Zeke's riches?"

"I don't know what you're talking about."

"Don't you? For goodness sake, tell me what happened."

"Nothing happened."

"Are you sure? Because I'm terribly worried about Evie."

"You mean because she got arrested?" He laughed then spat in the dirt.

Vonnie put her hands on her wide hips. "This has been a terrible ordeal for her. It looks like she's going to trial."

"So? With all her fancy lawyers she'll get off. And by then I'll be long gone."

Vonnie pleaded in that soft, little girl voice of hers. "Hoss, tell me what really happened to Doreen, won't you?"

He shook his head. "She got what she deserved."

"You killed her then?"

"We had words. It got physical."

"You pushed her?" Vonnie asked.

"She fell."

"Because you pushed her?"

"It wasn't my fault that I'd come to the wrong conclusion about her, okay? She told me she'd hit pay dirt at the gold rush. How was I to know she was only talking about a promotion at her stupid job?"

"So you're saying you pushed her?" Vonnie asked again.

"Well, yeah. I thought maybe you ladies had let her into your confidence since you all used to be friends. I'd seen you all on TV, talking about the gold legends and all. Then when I heard about Founders Day celebration, I figured you women might dig around the church and make a move on what was rightfully mine. I had to try to make her tell me the truth."

I held my hand up. "Stay here, everyone," I said to the girls as they clustered around the monitor. "The man's already given me what I need for a conviction."

Evie said, "Then I'm off the hook?"

I looked over my shoulder as I headed out of the nursery. "You are."

With my hand on my holster, I ran to the front door of the church, then silently made my way around the building, not realizing the girls had followed me like a line of silent ducklings.

I pointed my gun with both hands. "Freeze!" I called out to Horace, who had grabbed Vonnie by the arm.

When he saw me, he let go of Vonnie and ran to his bike, which was stashed behind a nearby bush.

"Stop or I'll shoot," I called as he positioned himself on the bike seat and started to crank the pedals. I didn't get a chance to fire my gun. Without warning, Vonnie conked Horace with her oversized purse, and he fell from his bike. "You killed my friend Doreen," she cried as she struck him again.

Evangeline joined the fray. She too hit him with *her* purse. "And you tried to hurt Vonnie."

Goldie and Lisa Leann joined the brawl. "Shame on you!" Lisa Leann cried, striking him with her red Brighton purse. "You scared the liver out of me, twice!"

Vonnie struck him again. "You took my dog and put my life in danger because of a stupid treasure hunt!" Horace stumbled and fell on one knee on the grass while the girls, minus Lizzie, continued to pummel him. Horace managed to stand and stumbled toward his bike. He teetered as he tried to stick his feet on the pedals. But before he could accomplish the task, Lisa Leann grabbed the handlebars with a jerk, sending him tumbling back to the ground.

"How dare you try to hurt my friends!" she cried as her purse came down on him once again.

Poor Horace could only cover his head while I holstered my gun. "Ladies, ladies, settle down!" I said as I knelt down to handcuff the man. I pulled him into a standing position. "Pal, you're coming with me."

As I walked Horace to my Bronco, people started to pour out of the church. I opened the back door of my truck and locked Horace inside. Then turned to walk around to the driver's door. But before

I could climb inside my cab, David's ambulance, sirens blazing, turned into the church parking lot.

David braked to a stop in front of Lisa Leann. He hopped out of the truck and ran to open the back doors. "Come with me," he told her.

"What's happening?" Lisa Leann cried as Clay ran toward her with his camera ready.

David grinned. "There's someone here—fresh from DIA. And don't worry, this is one ambulance bill I'm covering myself."

Lisa Leann screamed as Clay's camera flashed and Henry peered out of the truck. "Surprise!" he shouted before he turned to help their daughter down. Mandy, who was looking pretty well, actually, opened her arms and ran to her mother and laughed. "We made it, Mama. We made it home."

"Where's Ray?" Lisa Leann demanded.

"I'm here," a voice called from the back of the truck. I looked to see. Sure enough, there sat Ray, both legs in casts but sitting comfortably in the back of the ambulance.

"Where's my baby?" Mandy asked, looking around the crowd. Lizzie ran to her with little Kyle in her arms. The baby squealed in delight as his mother wrapped him in a hug and Clay's camera flashed again.

"However did you pull this off?" Lisa Leann asked David after a few minutes of celebrating with her family.

"With a little help from Fred and Henry," he said with a grin.

The church folks had crowded around, laughing, hugging, and praising God that the lost had been found. But no one enjoyed the moment more than Lisa Leann. She laughed till she cried, then she laughed again. "Thank you, God," she called as she waved at the heavens. "Thank you!"

And all the while Horace sat in the back of my Bronco, seething, looking like the lost son of Grace Church he was, God help him.

---

Later, once Horace had been processed down at the jail and Lisa Leann's video, complete with the purse attack, had been admitted into evidence, David and I drove over to Horace's campsite and retrieved Vonnie's dog from a rope tied to a tree. Chucky was a bit muddy and hungry but otherwise okay. We rushed him to Vonnie's, where we watched as her furry pet, mud and all, leapt into her arms, then covered her cheeks with kisses.

While Vonnie hugged and petted her baby, David and I walked out to the porch and sat on the front steps beneath the night's bright stars. He reached for my hand, and I leaned my head on his shoulder.

"Remember that day last year when you asked me to marry you?" I asked, looking up at him.

David nodded. "You just about broke my heart when you ran out of the restaurant."

"I wasn't ready then," I said.

"But now?"

"If you really want to know the answer to that, you should ask me again."

Our foreheads touched as David grabbed both my hands. Then he went down on one knee as his brown eyes softened with love. "Donna Vesey," he whispered, "my heart belongs to you. Would you marry me?"

I nodded. "Yes. Yes, I will."

He wrapped me in his arms as our lips met. When we finally pulled away, I said, "I hate to change the subject. But I know where Old Zeke hid the gold."

David kissed me again. "No kidding? Where?"

I kissed him back then pulled away, laughing. "He hollowed out the cross at the front of the church before setting the whole thing into the stone wall."

David laughed. "Are you going to tell anyone?"

I shook my head. "No. Let's leave it as it is. For as Old Zeke himself said—"

David laughed and said it with me: "The cross is my treasure."

He kissed me again.

Why, look at us—we'd found pure gold.

## Corned Beef and Cabbage

|              |                                            |
|-------------:|--------------------------------------------|
| 4 cups       | cabbage, shredded                          |
| ¼ teaspoon   | salt                                       |
| dash         | of pepper                                  |
| ½ teaspoon   | caraway seeds (optional)                   |
| 1 can        | cream of celery soup                       |
| 1 can        | corned beef                                |
| 1 package    | cornbread mix                              |
|              | necessary eggs and milk (according to the mix) |

Preheat oven to 375 degrees. Place shredded cabbage in 2½ quart baking dish and sprinkle with salt and pepper and caraway seeds. Spread celery soup over cabbage. Crumble corned beef and scatter over top of soup. Prepare cornbread mix according to the package directions and spread over top of corned beef. Bake for 25–30 minutes.

Serves 3–4.

**Lizzie's Cook's Notes**

*This is the perfect dish for those days when your schedule is more consuming than you have time for. My family enjoys a nice tossed salad served with it, or in summer months, a sweet congealed salad.*

# Chicken Potpie

|  |  |
|---|---|
| 2 | regular-sized piecrusts* |
| 3 | large chicken breasts, cooked and diced to bite-sized portions |
| 1-2 cups | fresh vegetables, cooked (broccoli, shredded carrots, peas, mushrooms, etc.) |
| 1 can | cream of chicken soup |
| 6 tablespoons | chicken broth |
|  | salt and pepper, to taste |

Bake one piecrust according to directions. Cool. Combine chicken, vegetables, soup, broth, and seasonings. Place in baked piecrust. Place second piecrust on top of mixture, crimp edges, make slits on top of crust.

Bake in a preheated 370-degree oven until crust is brown.

Serves 6.

**Goldie's Cook's Notes**

*What I often do is place the chicken and veggies in a crock-pot on low all day. Then, when I get home from work, all I have to do is bake the crust (or I can do that before I leave so that it has the day to cool), take the chicken and veggies from the crock-pot to the crust, and finish baking the pie.*

_____

_____

_____

_____

_____

_____

*Be sure to buy piecrusts that come rolled up, not already in pie plates.*

# Smothered Pork Chops

|  |  |
|---|---|
| 4 | pork chops |
| 1 envelope | Lipton onion and mushroom soup mix |
|  | salt and pepper, to taste |
| ½–1 cup | water |

Fry pork chops (breaded or unbreaded) in just enough olive oil to cover the bottom of a frying pan. Blend soup mix, salt and pepper, and water, then pour over chops. Cover and simmer for 15–20 minutes.

Serves 4.

### Evangeline's Cook's Notes

*The amount of water may vary according to your desires. Personally, I find that half a cup to a cup works just perfectly for me. Vernon likes this served with mashed potatoes, green peas, and dinner rolls.*

# Hot Fudge Pie

1 (1 pound)
  package  brownie mix
  9–inch  pie shell, unbaked
  ¼ cup  chocolate syrup
  ¼ cup  chopped nuts (pecans or walnuts)
        whipped cream or ice cream

Prepare brownie mix as directed on package then pour the mixture into the pie shell. Pour chocolate syrup over top and sprinkle with nuts (optional). Bake in 350-degree oven for 40–45 minutes. Serve warm, topped with whipped cream or ice cream.

### Lisa Leann's Cook's Notes

*This recipe always makes me lonesome for the Texas Hill Country, especially at bluebonnet time.*

# Cold Pasta Chicken Salad

| | |
|---|---|
| 8 ounces | vermicelli pasta noodles |
| 1 cup | French dressing |
| 10 | fresh mushrooms, sliced |
| 1 cup | fresh broccoli florets, blanched |
| 10 | sliced cherry tomatoes |
| ¼ cup | ripe olives, sliced |
| 1 can | artichoke hearts, sliced |
| 2 cups | chicken, cooked and cubed |
| 1½ teaspoons | dried basil |
| ⅓ cup | pine nuts, toasted |

Cook pasta, drain it, and place in mixing bowl. Toss with ⅓ cup of salad dressing and toss well. Chill 3 hours then mix in mushrooms, broccoli, tomatoes, olives, artichokes, and remaining dressing. Stir in chicken, basil, and nuts and store in refrigerator.

Serves 6–8.

## Donna's Cook's Notes

*I love pasta dishes, especially for lunch, and this one stirs up pretty fast, especially when I use canned chicken.*

# Pecan Cobbler

**Crust**

½ cup  butter, melted
1 cup  self–rising flour
1 cup  sugar
1 cup  milk

**Filling**

⅓ cup  butter, melted
3  eggs, slightly beaten
⅔ cup  sugar
1 cup  dark Karo syrup
1 cup  pecans, chopped

For crust, pour melted butter in a 9-by-13 casserole dish. Mix flour, sugar, and milk in a separate bowl, then pour mixture over butter. For the filling, without stirring, layer the butter, beaten eggs, sugar, syrup, and pecans over crust mixture. Bake at 350 degrees for 35–40 minutes or until done. Serve with whipped cream, dessert topping, or vanilla ice cream.

Serves 6–8.

**Vonnie's Cook's Notes**

*One mention of this treat, and friends and family come running. I'll have to make it again, and soon.*

_____

_____

_____

_____

_____

# Incredible Peach Cobbler

| | |
|---|---|
| 1 stick | butter (do not use margarine) |
| | fresh peaches, cut up |
| 1 cup | self–rising flour |
| 1 cup | sugar |

Set butter out to room temperature. Butter should not be left out any longer than 30 minutes. Cut up fresh peaches (enough to fill about ½ to ¾ of a 6-by-9½-by-2 Pyrex pan). Place peaches in pan. Then, using a fork, crumble butter, then stir in flour and sugar. Blend until all three are nice and crumbly. Sprinkle on top of fruit.

Place in oven. Bake at 425 for 15 minutes then turn oven back to 350 for half an hour.

### Lizzie's Cook's Notes

*Other fruit options: fresh pears (cooked) or blueberries. If you use blueberries, you will have to add water about ⅔ the way up the fruit once you have it in the pan.*

# Peanut Brittle

2 cups sugar
1 cup clear corn syrup
½ cup water
½ stick butter, softened
3 cups peanuts
1 teaspoon baking soda

Blend sugar, syrup, water, and butter. Using a candy thermometer, cook on stovetop to 230 degrees. Add peanuts, stir constantly, and cook to 305 degrees. Remove from heat. Add baking soda and stir quickly until mixture foams. Quickly pour onto large greased baking sheet. Spread thinly over entire surface of pan. Cool until hard. Break into small pieces.

**Evangeline's Cook's Notes**

*This is one time you don't want to substitute margarine for the butter.*

# Cashew Chicken Wraps

### Dressing

| | |
|---|---|
| ½ cup | mayo |
| 6 tablespoons | honey mustard |
| 1 tablespoon | red wine vinegar |
| ½ teaspoon | salt |
| dash | pepper |

### Meat Mixture

| | |
|---|---|
| 3 cups | chicken, cooked |
| 2 cups | celery, chopped |
| ½ cup | cashews, chopped |
| ¼ cup | onion, chopped |
| 6 | flour tortillas, 10-inch |
| ½ cup | cheddar cheese, shredded |

In a large bowl, create the dressing by stirring together mayo, mustard, vinegar, salt, and pepper. Next, add the chicken, celery, cashews, and onion to the dressing. Stir well. Scoop ½ to 1 cup of chicken mixture into the center of each tortilla then sprinkle with shredded cheese. Fold like envelope and roll up.

### Lisa Leann's Cook's Notes

*These little wraps are perfect when you have to eat on the go. I like to make them for car trips. I put them in the cooler and eat them cold, though they are delightful warm from the microwave as well. Just heat each for about 30 seconds for best results.*

# Baked Corn

| | |
|---|---|
| 1 (1 pound) can | cream–style corn |
| 1 cup | milk |
| 1 | egg, well beaten |
| ¾ teaspoon | salt |
| ¾ teaspoon | pepper |
| 1 cup | cracker crumbs (Ritz, Saltines) |
| ½ cup | buttered cracker crumbs |

Preheat oven to 350. Heat corn and milk. Gradually stir in egg. Add seasonings and cracker crumbs. Place in a greased 1½ quart baking dish. Sprinkle buttered crumbs over top. Bake for one hour.

Serves 4–6.

### Goldie's Cook's Notes

*Buttered crackers can be butter-flavored, Ritz-type crackers. I prefer to use Ritz crackers all the way through the recipe.*

# Apple Salad

|           |                              |
|-----------|------------------------------|
| ⅓ cup     | flour                        |
| ¾ cup     | sugar                        |
| 1 large can | crushed pineapple          |
| ½ stick   | margarine                    |
| 4         | large apples peeled and diced |
|           | Cool Whip                    |
| ½ cup     | pecans, chopped              |
| ½ cup     | cherries                     |

Combine flour and sugar; add crushed pineapple with juice. Cook on medium heat until thick. Add margarine. Let cool. Fold in apples. Put into 3 quart Pyrex dish and spread with Cool Whip. Sprinkle with chopped pecans and cherries.

## Evangeline's Cook's Notes

*Personally, I like the little maraschino cherries, drained, but fresh cherries are good too.*

# Onion and Cheese Meatloaf

| | |
|---|---|
| 1⅓ cups | French's French Fried Onions |
| 1½ pounds | ground beef |
| 1 (10 ounce) can | condensed tomato soup |
| 2 tablespoons | Worcestershire sauce |
| 1 | egg |
| ⅓ cup | cheddar cheese, shredded |

In bowl, crumble ⅔ cup of fried onions then add meat, ⅓ cup of soup, Worcestershire sauce, egg, and cheese. Knead ingredients into meat then shape into a loaf (approximately 8-by-4 inches). Place meatloaf in shallow baking pan then bake for an hour at 350 degrees.

Drain meatloaf then spoon remaining soup over top. Sprinkle with remaining fried onions. Bake another 5 minutes or until onions are crunchy.

**Vonnie's Cook's Notes**

*I've made a lot of meatloaf in my life, but this one is my favorite.*

# Gold Rush Brownies

| | |
|---|---|
| 2 packages | graham crackers, from box of three |
| 2 cans | Eagle Brand milk |
| 1 package | chocolate chips |
| 1 cup | pecans, chopped |

Set oven for 350 degrees. Put crackers into a Ziploc bag and crush into crumbs with a rolling pin. Mix crumbs with Eagle Brand milk, chocolate chips, and pecans.

Spray a 9-by-13 pan with cooking spray and sprinkle with flour. Press brownie mixture into pan and bake for 30 minutes or until top is golden.

## Donna's Cook's Notes

*I'll never forget all my cooking lessons at Vonnie's. Thank goodness she was there for me. I think about her every time I make these treats.*

# Scrambled Egg Gourmet

|           |                          |
|----------:|--------------------------|
| 6         | eggs                     |
| ¼ cup     | sour cream               |
|           | salt and pepper, to taste |
| 1 tablespoon | onion, minced (optional) |
| 2 tablespoons | butter                |
| 4 slices  | bacon, cooked            |

Beat eggs and sour cream together; season with salt and pepper. Melt butter in a skillet (if onions are used, sauté in butter). Pour egg mixture into skillet; scramble egg mixture, tossing lightly in hot butter until done. Crumble bacon and sprinkle over eggs.

Serves 3–4.

## Lizzie's Cook's Notes

*Sometimes I prepare this on Saturday evenings to have for breakfast before church on Sunday morning. A perfect way to start the Lord's Day!*

## Prissy Pecans

|              |                         |
|-------------:|-------------------------|
| 2 teaspoons  | powdered instant coffee |
| ¼ cup        | sugar                   |
| ¼ teaspoon   | ground cinnamon         |
| 2 tablespoons| water                   |
| dash         | salt                    |
| 2 cups       | pecan halves            |

Combine all ingredients in saucepan. Bring to a boil over medium heat and boil 3 minutes. Stir constantly. Spread on waxed paper and separate pecan halves as they cool. Pecans will be sugar coated, not sticky.

**Goldie's Cook's Notes**

*These make a wonderful teacher's gift, for Christmas or the last day of school. They're also a nice gift for family and friends. Perfect for "noshing." Simply place them in a Mason jar, seal, cover the lid with a pretty piece of material, then tie off with a bow. Fun for the children too!*

#  Smash Cake

|            |                           |
|-----------:|---------------------------|
| 1 cup      | canola oil                |
| 1 box      | brown sugar (2 cups, packed) |
| 3          | eggs                      |
| 1 teaspoon | vanilla                   |
| 1¼ cups    | self–rising flour         |
| ½ cup      | pecans, chopped           |

Preheat oven to 325 degrees. In mixing bowl, add oil and brown sugar and beat until well mixed. Add 1 egg at a time, beating well. Stir in vanilla. Add self-rising flour until blended. Stir in chopped pecans. Spread dough into well-greased and floured 9-by-13 pan. Bake 20–25 minutes. About 15 minutes into baking, open the oven and shake the cake so that it will fall. Put the cake back into the oven and continue baking. When the cake is done, take the cake out of the oven and shake pan so cake falls. Then with the bottom of a glass or ceramic mug, gently smash cake. This will give the cake the consistency of a brownie/pie.

### Lisa Leann's Cook's Notes

*You wouldn't think that shaking a cake-like brownie into a denser version of itself would be so delicious or such a hit with the crowd. When I take this to parties, I've seen grown men fight over the last piece. Try making it yourself and watch it disappear.*

_____

_____

_____

_____

_____

_____

# Sunshine Cake

|              |                                      |
|-------------:|--------------------------------------|
| 1 package    | moist yellow cake mix                |
| 4            | eggs, slightly beaten                |
| ½ cup        | vegetable oil                        |
| 1 (11 ounce) can | mandarin oranges with half the juice |

Preheat oven to 325 degrees. In large bowl, lightly beat (with spoon or whisk) cake mix, eggs, oil, and oranges with juice into a batter. Pour the batter into either one or two greased and floured 9-by-13 pans. Bake about 20 minutes for two layers, or about 35 minutes for one layer. Cool on wire rack.

Note: you can use two 9-by-13 pans so you will have two thin layers with frosting in the middle; or, if you use one pan, you can cut cooled cake in half if you want frosting in the middle.

### Frosting:

|                    |                                  |
|-------------------:|----------------------------------|
| 1 (12–16 ounce)    | frozen whipped topping, thawed   |
| 1 (3.4 ounce)      | package instant vanilla pudding  |
| 1 (15 oz)          | can crushed and drained pineapple |
| 1 cup              | fresh blueberries (optional)     |

Mix together whipped topping, pudding, and crushed pineapple. Place in refrigerator to set. Frost when cake has thoroughly cooled. Garnish with blueberries, if desired.

### Donna's Cook's Notes

*This recipe of my mother's is one of my favorites.*

# Fred's Barbecue Chicken

**BBQ Sauce**

|  |  |
|---|---|
| ½ cup | ketchup |
| 1 tablespoon | prepared mustard |
| 1 tablespoon | molasses |
| 1 tablespoon | Worcestershire sauce |
| 2 cloves | garlic, minced |

**Chicken**

|  |  |
|---|---|
|  | skinless chicken parts |
|  | covered grill |
|  | foil |
| 2 cups | water |

Stir together ingredients for sauce in a large bowl. While grill is heating to medium-high, shape foil into a pan-like shape and place on the grill. Pour 2 cups of water into foil "pan." Add chicken parts to water and close lid.

After 20 minutes, baste with BBQ sauce. Repeat basting procedure every 5 to 10 minutes, closing lid between bastings. Chicken will be done in about 50 minutes of cooking time.

**Vonnie's Cook's Notes**

*Fred finally figured out a way to keep his barbecue chicken from burning. This is a moist, delicious way to go to the grill.*

# Cinnamon-Buttermilk Coffee Cake

|        |                          |
|--------|--------------------------|
| 2 cups | all-purpose flour        |
| 2 cups | firmly packed brown sugar |
| ½ cup  | butter, softened         |
| ⅓ cup  | all-purpose flour        |
| 1      | egg                      |
| 1 cup  | buttermilk               |
| 1 teaspoon | baking soda          |
| 1 teaspoon | ground cinnamon      |
| ½ cup  | chopped nuts             |

Preheat oven to 325 degrees. Combine 2 cups flour and sugar in a large mixing bowl. Cut in butter until mixture resembles coarse meal. Set aside ⅔ cup crumb mixture. Combine remaining crumb mixture and ⅓ cup flour. Add egg, buttermilk, baking soda, and cinnamon; stir until mixture is moistened.

Pour batter into a greased 9-inch square pan. Combine reserved crumb mixture with nuts; sprinkle over batter. Bake for 1 hour or until done. Cut into squares.

Serves 9.

### Evangeline's Cook's Notes

*This makes a quick and easy breakfast sweet dish. Unless, of course, you expect to serve the state law enforcement while they question you as though you are a suspect in a murder case. Ahem.*

_____

_____

_____

_____

# Waikiki Meatballs

| | |
|---|---|
| 1½ pounds | ground beef |
| ⅔ cup | cracker crumbs |
| ⅓ cup | minced onion |
| 1 | egg |
| 1½ teaspoons | salt |
| ¼ teaspoon | ginger |
| ¼ cup | milk |
| 1 tablespoon | shortening |
| 2 tablespoons | cornstarch |
| ½ cup | brown sugar, packed |
| 1 (13½ ounce) can | pineapple tidbits, drained (reserve syrup) |
| ⅓ cup | vinegar |
| 1 tablespoon | soy sauce |
| ⅓ cup | green pepper, chopped |

Mix thoroughly beef, crumbs, onion, egg, salt, ginger, and milk. Shape mixture by rounded tablespoonfuls into balls. Melt shortening in large skillet; brown and cook meatballs. Remove meatballs from skillet. In a mixing bowl, mix cornstarch and sugar. Stir in reserved pineapple syrup, vinegar, and soy sauce until smooth. Pour into skillet; cook over medium heat, stirring constantly, until mixture thickens and boils. Boil and stir 1 minute. Add meatballs, pineapple tidbits, and green pepper; heat through.

Serves 6.

**Lizzie's Cook's Notes**

*Great for a meal or a party!*

_____

_____

_____

# Potatoes Gourmet

| | |
|---|---|
| 6 | medium potatoes |
| ¼ cup | melted butter or margarine |
| 2 cups (8 ounces) | shredded cheddar cheese |
| 1 (8 ounce) carton | sour cream |
| 3 | green onions, chopped |
| 1 teaspoon | salt |
| ¼ teaspoon | pepper |
| 2 tablespoons | butter or margarine |

Peel potatoes and then cut into medium-sized cubes. Boil potatoes in salted water until tender. Combine ¼ cup melted butter and cheese in a heavy saucepan; cook over low heat, stirring constantly, until cheese is partially melted. Combine potatoes, cheese mixture, sour cream, onion, salt, and pepper; stir well. Spoon potato mixture into a greased 2-quart shallow casserole dish and dot with 2 tablespoons butter. Cover and bake at 350 for 25 minutes or until done.

Serves 6–8.

### Goldie's Cook's Notes

*Olivia was right. This is delicious!*

_____

_____

_____

_____

_____

_____

# Pineapple Ginger Chicken

| | |
|---|---|
| 1 (14 ounce) can | pineapple chunks |
| | leftover pineapple juice, from can |
| 3-5 | whole or split chicken breasts |
| ½ teaspoon | salt |
| 1 teaspoon | pepper |
| 1 teaspoon | dried rosemary, crushed |
| 10-12 | green onions |
| 2 teaspoons | candied ginger, finely chopped |

Pour juice from can of pineapple chunks into bowl, then set aside. Next, rub chicken with salt, pepper, and rosemary before placing it in a shallow pan for baking. Chop green onions and sprinkle over chicken. Add candied ginger to pineapple juice then pour over the chicken and onions. Bake, uncovered, at 375 degrees until the chicken is done, about 45–55 minutes. Periodically baste the chicken with juices from the pan. Ten minutes before the chicken is done, spoon pineapple chunks over chicken then continue baking.

Serves 4–6.

**Vonnie's Cook's Notes**

*This really is a tasty dish. Whenever I make it, I always wonder why I don't make it more often.*

Almond Bark

1 teaspoon   butter
1 cup   whole blanched almonds
1 pound   white chocolate

Spray a 9-inch glass pie plate with cooking spray, then add butter and almonds to plate. In microwave, cook almonds and butter at maximum power for 2 minutes. Stir then cook another 2 minutes. Stir again. If the almonds are not yet toasted, cook another ½ to 1 minute before stirring a final time. Set the almonds aside. Use the microwave to melt chocolate in microwavable bowl at maximum power for 2½ to 3 minutes, or until softened. Stir almonds into bowl and pour mixture onto a wax-paper-lined baking sheet. With spatula, spread soft mixture across wax paper until desired thickness. Refrigerate. When bark is set, break it into serving-size pieces.

Yield: 1½ pounds.

### Lisa Leann's Cook's Notes

*Nothing could be more decadent yet easy to create than this little treat.*

# Doreen's Easy Chicken and Rice Casserole

1 (10 ounce) package  saffron yellow rice (Vigo)
1 (10 ounce) can  premium chicken in water
1 can  cream of chicken or cream of mushroom soup
½ cup  milk
French-fried onions
cheese
paprika

Cook rice as directed on package, except only simmer for 15 minutes instead of the 20–25 minutes called for on package.

While rice is cooking, drain water from canned chicken. In separate bowl, combine chicken with soup. Add cooked rice to soup and chicken mixture then stir in approximately ½ cup of milk, to create the consistency you desire.

Cook uncovered in ungreased casserole dish at 350 degrees for 15 minutes. Top with fried onions and cheese and bake another 5 minutes. Sprinkle with paprika.

Serves 4–6.

**Donna's Cook's Notes**

*Though I don't remember for sure, I know my mother served this dish to me as a child. It's funny how important these recipes are to me now.*

_____

_____

_____

_____

# Scalloped Asparagus Casserole

1 medium can  asparagus
1 cup  medium sharp cheddar cheese, grated
2 cups  white sauce (see recipe below)
4  boiled eggs
paprika

Fill greased 2½-quart baking dish with alternate layers of asparagus, cheese, white sauce, and sliced eggs. Sprinkle with paprika. Bake in 400 degree oven for a half hour.

Serves 4–6.

### White Sauce

3 tablespoons  butter
½ teaspoon  salt
3½ tablespoons  flour
1½ cups  milk, scalded

Combine butter, salt, and flour. Add milk slowly, stirring constantly. Cook over low heat until thick and smooth.

### Evangeline's Cook's Notes

*To scald milk, start by pouring milk into a heavy-bottomed pan. Place on low heat. Stir occasionally until milk is just hot with steam and little bubbles appear around the edges. Do not boil. Remove from the heat. This simple method "scalds" your milk.*

# Chicken Tetrazzini

|              |                         |
|-------------:|-------------------------|
| 1 (4½ pound) | roasting chicken, cut up |
| 3 cups       | hot water               |
| 4 teaspoons  | salt                    |
| 1 teaspoon   | onion salt              |
| ½ teaspoon   | celery salt             |
| ½ pound      | thin spaghetti noodles  |
| 6 tablespoons | butter                 |
| ½ pound      | sliced mushrooms        |
| 1 tablespoon | lemon juice             |
| 2 tablespoons | flour                  |
| ¼ teaspoon   | paprika                 |
| ¼ teaspoon   | pepper                  |
| ⅛ teaspoon   | nutmeg                  |
| 1 cup        | heavy cream             |
| ⅔ cup        | grated Parmesan cheese  |

A day before, in a deep kettle, place chicken, water, 2 teaspoons salt, onion salt, and celery salt. Simmer chicken, covered, until tender. When cool enough to handle, remove meat from bones in big pieces. Refrigerate at once. Reserve 2½ cups broth. To the rest of the kettle, add:

|               |       |
|--------------:|-------|
| 3 quarts      | water |
| 2 tablespoons | salt  |

When this boils, slowly add spaghetti noodles and cook 6 minutes. Drain and place noodles in a 9-by-13 baking dish. Meanwhile, in a skillet, heat 3 tablespoons butter, add mushrooms, and sprinkle them with lemon juice and ½ teaspoon salt. Sauté until soft but not brown; toss them and the butter with spaghetti noodles; refrigerate all, covered. In saucepan, melt 3 tablespoons butter, remove from heat, and stir in flour, paprika, remaining

1½ teaspoons salt, pepper, and nutmeg. Slowly stir in 2½ cups reserved broth. Cook sauce, stirring, until thickened; add cream, then pour over chicken; refrigerate. Next day, 1 hour before serving, preheat oven to 400 degrees. With fork, stir up chicken and sauce, then pour as much of sauce as possible over noodles while tossing. Place rest of chicken mixture over noodles, sprinkle all with Parmesan cheese and paprika. Bake 25 minutes.

Serves 8.

### Lizzie's Cook's Notes

*Do not use angel hair pasta as it is too thin. Use thin spaghetti noodles.*

# Southern Sweet Iced Tea

|            |                              |
|-----------:|------------------------------|
| 3–4 cups   | cold or tepid water          |
| ¼ teaspoon | baking soda (or a "pinch")   |
| 4          | family–sized tea bags        |
| 1 to 1⅓ cups | sugar                      |

Bring 3–4 cups of water to a boil in a pot on the stove. Add a pinch of baking soda to the water and then 4 family-sized tea bags. Remove from heat, add sugar, and cover. Allow to sit for at least 10–15 minutes. Pour into gallon pitcher. Then fill with cold water, stir, and refrigerate if there's time. Otherwise, serve over ice in large tea glasses. Enjoy!

**Goldie's Cook's Notes**

*The soda takes out the bitterness and darkens the tea but won't change the taste a bit.*

# Crabby Corn Chowder

| | |
|---|---|
| 1 | large onion, diced |
| 1 | large potato, diced |
| 1 | bay leaf |
| ½ teaspoon | dried marjoram |
| ⅛ teaspoon | cayenne |
| 1 (15 ounce) can | fat-free chicken broth |
| 1 (17 ounce) can | cream-style corn |
| 1 (8 ounce) can | corn, drained |
| 1½ cups | milk |
| ¼ teaspoon | black pepper |
| 1 (7 ounce) jar | roasted red peppers, drained and diced |
| ½–1 pound | crab or artificial crab meat from deli, chopped |

Spray cooking spray into a large saucepan then sauté onions well before sautéing the potato, bay leaf, marjoram, and cayenne. Stir in chicken broth, then heat on high till boiling. Reduce heat to medium low and cook 8–10 minutes or until potato is softened. Stir in both kinds of corn, milk, and black pepper. Turn burner to medium high and heat but do not boil. Add red peppers and crab. Heat until steaming hot for another 2–4 minutes.

Serves 6–8.

### Lisa Leann's Cook's Notes

*This chowder is a warm and tasty bowl of comfort if I ever saw one. Some days need more comfort than others.*

# Quick Potluck Pizza

| | |
|---|---|
| 1½ pounds | ground beef |
| ½ cup | onions, chopped |
| 1 (15 ounce) can | pizza sauce |
| 2 tablespoons | grated parmesan cheese |
| 2 (12 ounce) cans | refrigerated biscuits |
| 1 (3.5 ounce) package | pepperoni, sliced thin |
| ½ cup | green pepper (optional) |
| ½ cup | black olives (optional) |
| ½ cup | mushroom slices or 8-ounce jar of sliced mushrooms (optional) |
| 1½ cups | shredded sharp or cheddar cheese |

On stove top, sauté ground beef and onions, drain grease. Stir in pizza sauce and parmesan cheese and simmer while you make the crust.

Pop open cans of refrigerated biscuits and place the biscuits in a 9-by-13 pan before pressing dough together and up sides of pan to form the crust. Pour in sauce mixture and top with pepperoni, green peppers, black olives, mushrooms, and cheese. Bake at 350 degrees for 25–30 minutes or until crust is done and cheese is melted.

Serves 4–8.

### Vonnie's Cook's Notes

*Don't tell Fred or Lisa Leann how easy this dish is to prepare.*

_____

_____

_____

_____

# Easy Crock-pot Pumpkin Soup

|   |   |
|---|---|
| 1 | medium pumpkin |
| 4–5 | sweet potatoes |
| ½ | large onion, diced |
| 2 | chicken bouillon cubes |
| 1 cup | water |
| 2 tablespoons | brown sugar |
| 1 tablespoon | Italian seasoning (like McCormick or Tone's) |
| 1 teaspoon | garlic powder or 2 large garlic cloves, crushed |
|   | cheese |
|   | sour cream |

Wash and chop pumpkin. Remove seeds but not skin, as skin will soften during cooking. Chop potatoes and onion and place into crock-pot along with the pumpkin, chicken bouillon, water, sugar, seasoning, and garlic. Turn crock-pot to high and cook for about 5 hours or until potatoes are soft.

Blend soup in blender or with hand blender until smooth then top each serving with a pinch of cheese and a dollop of sour cream.

Serves 6–8.

## Donna's Cook's Notes

*I like to make this soup now in the fall and remember my mother. It freezes well too.*

# Raisin Sauce for Ham

|   |   |
|---|---|
| 2 tablespoons | brown sugar |
| ½ teaspoon | grated orange rind |
| 1 teaspoon | dry mustard |
| 1½ tablespoons | cornstarch |
| 1 cup | orange juice |
| ⅓ cup | seedless raisins |
| 1 tablespoon | ham drippings or butter |
| ½ cup | ginger ale |

In a small saucepan, combine brown sugar, orange rind, mustard, and cornstarch. Stir in orange juice. Bring to a boil, lower heat, and continue to simmer until mixture thickens (5–10 minutes). Add raisins and butter or drippings from ham; cook another 3–4 minutes. Stir in ginger ale.

Spoon over rolled slices of baked or pan-fried ham.

**Goldie's Cook's Notes**

*Makes about 1½ cups sauce. When we have a lot of folks for dinner and the ham is large, I double this recipe.*

# Black Bottom Pie

| | |
|---|---|
| 1½ cups | fine gingersnaps crumbs |
| ⅓ cup | melted butter |
| 2 cups | milk |
| 1 envelope | unflavored gelatin |
| ¼ cup | cold water |
| 4 | medium eggs, separated |
| 1 cup | granulated sugar |
| ¼ teaspoon | salt |
| 4 teaspoons | cornstarch |
| 2 squares | unsweetened chocolate |
| 2 teaspoons | vanilla |
| 1 cup | heavy cream |
| 2 tablespoons | confectioner's sugar |

Mix crumbs and butter; pat evenly in deep 9-inch pie pan. Bake 10 minutes at 350 degrees. Scald milk and add gelatin soaked in cold water. Beat egg yolks with ½ cup sugar, salt, and cornstarch. Add milk slowly, beating constantly. Cook over boiling water in a double boiler, stirring occasionally until custard coats spoon. Remove from heat.

To 1 cup of custard, add 1½ squares chocolate that has been melted. Add 1 teaspoon vanilla. Beat with rotary beater, cool to room temperature. Pour chocolate mixture into baked pie shell. Chill until firm. Beat egg whites until stiff; gradually beat in remaining ½ cup of sugar. Fold into remaining cool custard with remaining 1 teaspoon of vanilla. Pour custard over chocolate mixture in pie shell. Chill until firm. Whip cream until stiff; fold in confectioner's sugar. Spread over pie and sprinkle with remaining ½ square of chocolate which has been finely grated. Chill before serving.

## Lizzie's Cook's Notes

*You can delete the heavy cream and confectioner's sugar and replace with a prepared whipped topping, including "lite" brands.*

# Chocolate Coconut Pie

|            |                             |
|-----------|-----------------------------|
| 1 teaspoon | flour                      |
| 1 | frozen pie shell, defrosted        |
| 2 squares | semisweet chocolate         |
| ½ cup | butter                          |
| 1 cup | sugar                           |
| ¼ cup | light corn syrup                |
| ⅛ teaspoon | salt                       |
| 3 | eggs                                |
| ½ teaspoon | vanilla extract            |
| ⅓ cup | flaked sweetened coconut        |

Sprinkle flour over surface of defrosted pie shell.

Melt chocolate and butter in a medium saucepan on low heat. Remove pan from heat and add sugar, corn syrup, and salt. Stir mixture well. After mixture has cooled slightly, add eggs, vanilla, and coconut and stir well. Pour mixture into pie shell and bake at 350 degrees for 35 minutes or until filling has set. Be careful not to overbake.

Serves up to 8.

**Vonnie's Cook's Notes**

*When the going gets difficult I rely on a couple of things: prayer and my mother's chocolate coconut pie recipe. It makes for a powerful combination to brighten my world.*

_____

_____

_____

_____

_____

# Golden Carrot and Pineapple Salad

| | |
|---|---|
| 1 (3 ounce) package | orange gelatin (Jell-O) |
| 1 (8 ounce) can | crushed pineapple (do not drain) |
| ½ cup | water |
| ½ cup | celery, diced |
| ⅓ cup | nuts, chopped |
| ½ cup | carrots, shredded |
| 1 cup | miniature marshmallows |
| ½ cup | golden raisins |
| ½ cup | whipped topping, thawed |
| ½ cup | light mayonnaise |

In large bowl, add gelatin mix. In separate saucepan, heat pineapple with juice and water until boiling. Pour boiling pineapple mixture over gelatin in bowl and stir until gelatin is dissolved. Chill until very thick but not set. Mix in celery, nuts, carrots, marshmallows, raisins, whipped topping, and mayo. Pour mixture into 9-by-13 inch pan. Chill until firm.

## Donna's Cook's Notes

*Lisa Leann says you can also pour this into a large Jell-O mold (that holds 4 cups). But as we're cooking for a crowd, we made three triple batches and let it set in the refrigerator overnight so we could cut and serve it on a lettuce leaf. It made a colorful side dish for our Founders Day dinner.*

# Apple and Cheese Crisp

| | |
|---|---|
| 21 large (or 42 medium) | apples, cored, peeled, and sliced |
| 2 cups | water |
| ¼ cup | lemon juice, plus 2 tablespoons |
| 8 cups | all-purpose flour |
| 8 cups | sugar |
| 2 tablespoons | cinnamon |
| 1 tablespoon | salt |
| 4 cups | butter or margarine |
| 8 cups | shredded cheddar cheese |
| | vanilla ice cream (optional) |
| 4 | greased 9-by-13 baking pans |

Spread apples into 4 pans. In large bowl, combine water and lemon juice and sprinkle over apples. In mixing bowl with mixer, combine flour, sugar, cinnamon, and salt. Add small amounts of butter at a time until crumbly. Turn mixer off and stir in cheese. Spread flour and cheese mixture over apples. Bake at 350 for 30–35 minutes, or until apples are tender and topping is crisp. Serve with ice cream.

Serves 100.

## Lisa Leann's Cook's Notes

*We had to make five batches of this dessert to feed the crowd at the Founders Day concert. But it went over very well, especially when we topped each serving with a scoop of premium vanilla ice cream.*

# Stuffed Chicken Breasts for a Crowd

| | |
|---:|---|
| 7½ pounds | butter |
| 60 | chopped onions |
| 23 pounds | frozen spinach, thawed and drained |
| 60 pounds | ricotta cheese |
| 60 | eggs, slightly beaten |
| 15 cups | chopped fresh parsley or 5 cups of dried parsley |
| 2 cups | dried oregano |
| ⅔ cup | nutmeg |
| | salt and pepper, to taste |
| 500 halves | of chicken breasts, skin on, boned |

Melt butter and sauté onions until caramelized. In large industrial bowls, evenly divide ingredients and stir onions and butter into spinach, cheese, eggs, parsley, oregano, and nutmeg. Season with salt and pepper.

On butcher board, place each breast half skin-side-up and trim excess fat. Loosen skin from one side, making a pocket. Stuff approximately ⅓ cup of mix under skin. Tuck skin and meat under breast, forming a rounded dome. Put chicken breast on greased baking dish to either bake or freeze.

Preheat ovens to 350 degrees. Bake thawed breasts for 30–35 minutes until golden brown.

Serves 250–500, depending on portion.

## Donna's Cook's Notes

*Lisa Leann says this is the perfect chicken for serving large crowds. Maybe someday, I'll figure out how to cut the recipe down so I can make a couple just for me and you-know-who, now that we've set our wedding date. I mean, we've waited long enough, don't you think?*

# Acknowledgments

In the course of a novel, there are many to thank and acknowledge. In the course of *six*, there are many, many.

Always and forever, thank you to our Lord and Savior, Jesus Christ. Without you, there would be no us.

Thank you to the Revell editors who have shaped our work and made it sizzle: Jeanette Thomason (who was the first to see merit in the idea), Dr. Vicki Crumpton, and Kristin Kornoelje. And, of course, to Dwight Baker, president of Baker Publishing Group, who believed in "the potluck girls." Without your support, this project would only be half-baked.

Thank you to our friends and family members who took the time to read our work as we wrote, and to the awesome girls of AWSA (Advanced Writers and Speakers Association) who prayed for us. You are the *bouquet garni*!

We'd also like to give a special thank-you to Sarah Cruz, who guided us through New York City while we researched *A Taste of Fame*. You are the cherry on the jubilee!

To our husbands and families . . . you know how much we *knead* you! How much we love you! Thank you for the sacrifices you made while we wrote.

Linda sends a special thanks to her wonderful agent, Janet Grant, as well as her friend Deborah Dunn, author of *Stupid About Men*. Deborah, thanks for helping me sort out a certain character's romantic dilemmas with your expert insights.

Eva Marie says "ditto" to her agent for this project, Deidre Knight.

And finally, to women everywhere, *savor friendship*! It is one of the finer spices of life.

**Linda Evans Shepherd** is the author of over thirty books, including *When You Don't Know What to Pray: How to Talk to God about Anything* and *When You Can't Find God: How to Ignite the Power of His Presence*, and the co-author of the popular series the Potluck Club and the Potluck Catering Club. Linda is an international speaker and media personality and is the creator of RightToTheHeart.tv and appears as a frequent host of Daystar's *Denver Celebration*.

She's the leader of the Advanced Writers and Speakers Association and president of the nonprofit ministry Right to the Heart, which has seen over 300,000 people come to faith. She's married and has two children. To learn more about Linda, her speaking, and her ministries, see VisitLinda.com.

**Eva Marie Everson** is the author of over twenty-five titles and is the Southern Fiction author for Revell. These titles include *Things Left Unspoken* and *This Fine Life*. She is the co-author of the multiple-award-winning *Reflections of God's Holy Land: A Personal Journey Through Israel* (with Miriam Feinberg Vamosh) and, of course, the Potluck Club and the Potluck Catering Club series with Linda Evans Shepherd.

Eva Marie taught Old Testament theology for six years at Life Training Center and continues to teach in a home group setting. She speaks to women's groups and at churches across the nation and internationally. In 2009 she joined forces with Israel Ministry of Tourism to help organize and lead a group of journalists on a unique travel experience through the Holy Land. She is a mentor with Christian Writers Guild and the first president of Word Weavers, a successful writers critique group that began in Orlando and has since gone national.

Eva Marie lives with her husband, Dennis, and their fourth (and final) child, Jordynn. Eva Marie and Dennis are parents to three incredible adult children and the grandparents of the five best grandkids in the world.

To learn more about the Potluck books and the authors, go to www.PotluckClub.com.

# Don't miss the first two books!

## The Potluck Catering Club series